PRAISE FOR *SAVAGE ROAD*

"Hayley Chill is relentlessly smart and brave in this twisty, electrifying thriller."

—Karin Slaughter, #1 internationally bestselling author

"Hauty has done it again. *Savage Road* is a rocker of a novel. Whip-smart and propulsive, it dives into geopolitical cyber warfare with twists and turns you won't see coming. A must-read."

—Connor Sullivan, author of *Sleeping Bear*

"Hayley Chill: a protagonist with so much bite, readers had best wear a flak jacket. . . . *Savage Road* is a brilliantly plotted thriller with plenty of edge-of-the-seat moments, twists, and turns to satisfy the most ardent of fans."

—*Mystery and Suspense* magazine

"Wildly entertaining."

—*Booklist*

"A riveting read."

—*Fresh Fiction*

"It is a high hurdle for an author of a highly successful first novel to come back strong with a second. But Chris Hauty has certainly done that. In fact, as much as I admired *Deep State*, I like *Savage Road* even more."

—*Deadly Pleasures Mystery Magazine*

"There are thrillers, and there are THRILLERS, and Chris Hauty's scintillating *Savage Road* falls squarely in the latter category."

—*The Providence Journal*

PRAISE FOR *DEEP STATE*

and engrossing with an atypical protagonist, it keeps you guessing until the final pages are turned. Chris Hauty has just placed a marker in the world of political thrillers."

—Matthew Betley, acclaimed author of *Rules of War*

"Engrossing . . . Kick-ass."

—*Publishers Weekly*

"Screenwriter Chris Hauty's talents are on full display in his terrific debut, *Deep State*, a crackling and perfectly timed political thriller. . . . All the ingredients of a Brad Meltzer or David Baldacci–like sizzler of a story."

—*The Providence Journal*

"*Deep State* is a compelling page-turner with an unpredictable last-minute twist that will knock you off your feet."

—*Library Journal*

"With his super-charged plot and a perfectly timed, mind-bending twist, Chris Hauty becomes the latest writer to take the thriller world by storm. . . . *Deep State* will compete for best debut novel of 2020 and have readers dying for the anticipated follow-up."

—*The Real Book Spy*

"*Deep State* lets readers think they know what's going on, right up until a jaw-dropping finale. . . . [A] magnificently crafted thriller."

—*Shelf Awareness*

Also by Chris Hauty
Deep State

SAVAGE ROAD

A THRILLER

★ ★ ★ ★ ★ ★ ★ ★

CHRIS HAUTY

POCKET BOOKS

New York   London   Toronto   Sydney   New Delhi

Pocket Books
An Imprint of Simon & Schuster, Inc.
1230 Avenue of the Americas
New York, NY 10020

This book is a work of fiction. Any references to historical events,
real people, or real places are used fictitiously. Other names,
characters, places, and events are products of the author's
imagination, and any resemblance to actual events or places or
persons, living or dead, is entirely coincidental.

First Pocket Books paperback edition October 2021

POCKET and colophon are registered trademarks of Simon &
Schuster, Inc.

For information about special discounts for bulk purchases,
please contact Simon & Schuster Special Sales at
1-866-506-1949 or business@simonandschuster.com.

The Simon & Schuster Speakers Bureau can bring authors to
your live event. For more information or to book an event, contact
the Simon & Schuster Speakers Bureau at 1-866-248-3049 or
visit our website at www.simonspeakers.com.

Interior design by Erika R. Genova

Manufactured in the United States of America

10 9 8 7 6 5 4 3 2 1

ISBN 978-1-9821-2662-9
ISBN 978-1-9821-2663-6 (ebook)

For Pat and GT

Truth will ultimately prevail where pains is taken to bring it to light.

— GEORGE WASHINGTON, LETTER TO
CHARLES M. THRUSTON

PROLOGUE

★ ★ ★ ★

ayley Chill exits the Oval Office through a door that opens onto the Rose Garden and must pause to admire the absurd perfection of the balmy weather outside. The bright sunshine and brilliant green of the executive mansion's grounds are a stark contrast to the bedlam inside the West Wing on this dreadful day. The twenty-seven-year-old White House staffer—flaxen hair and powder blue eyes notwithstanding—is unnoticed by Secret Service and FBI agents driven into a frenzy by the unfolding crisis. *Wait until the full story comes out,* Hayley muses as she walks up West Executive Drive. *America won't know what hit her.* But the pandemonium has provided Hayley with a welcome diversion. Weighing on her mind as she leaves the White House complex, most likely for the last time, is the awareness she will be on a list of those held accountable. This failure of national proportions will demand a host of sacrificial lambs.

Hayley catches up with three housekeepers—two Filipinas and a Latina—as they exit the security gate at

Seventeenth Street, on the west side of the Eisenhower Executive Office Building. The residence staff members were the first to be released by the Secret Service.

"I'm looking for Alberto Barrios, one of the president's valets. Have you seen him today?"

The Latina housekeeper nods and points across Seventeenth, indicating a man on foot, just turning the corner at G Street and heading west.

"Alberto," the housekeeper says.

By the time she has jogged across the bustling avenue and rounded the corner at G Street, Hayley sees Barrios has already advanced halfway up the block. The Cuban, tall and broad shouldered, walks with a brisk pace. Hayley increases her gait to narrow the distance between them. She hasn't a coherent plan or strategy. Barrios must be apprehended, at the very least. Stopping him before he flees the country is all that matters.

What is the extent of the man's training? Is he armed? Where does he intend to rendezvous with his compatriots? These questions stay unanswered as Hayley follows Barrios up the mostly quiet side street. The skills she developed in the US Army, as one of the first female graduates to earn the blue cord, kick into gear. Intercepting the Cuban well before he makes contact with his associates is an absolute imperative. By any means necessary, she must detain him long enough for the police to arrive. Careful to maintain a discreet distance from her target, Hayley retrieves her phone and dials 911.

"Nine one one, what's your emergency?"

Hayley covers her mouth as she speaks into the phone. "A man and a woman are fighting on the sidewalk. Twenty-one hundred block of G Street."

"Ma'am, do they have any weapons?" the operator asks.

"The man has a gun." She sees Barrios crossing the street in the middle of the block. Has he detected her pursuit? Into the phone, she says, "Please send the police. Quickly!"

Hayley disconnects the call before the operator can request she stay on the line. Pausing on her side of the street, she observes her target entering the GW Delicatessen. His turn toward the store is abrupt. Not natural in the least. To prolong the hope that Barrios is unaware of her presence would be a dangerous indulgence in wishful thinking. The real chase has begun.

As Hayley crosses the street, she considers the possibility that the deli has a rear exit, one that will provide the Cuban an escape. She could continue to the end of the block with a plan of intercepting him on Twenty-Second Street. But Barrios could be watching from inside and exit through the front door once she's around the corner. Hayley calculates that her best chance for success is to follow him inside.

She imagines how the next few minutes will unfold. Violence will come. Blood will be spilled. Hayley has been here before. The experience has always been the same. There is a flattening of sound. Colors become oversaturated. Time is elongated, certain to be followed by a sudden lurching of events into hyper speed. Instinct is a pivotal factor in these situations. Training. Muscle memory takes over, as well as the brute willpower to prevail and survive. She pauses at the threshold of the convenience store, to breathe and modulate heart rate. Her eyes take in everything. Ears detect every sound, however minuscule.

Now, Hayley tells herself. *This.*

Pushing the glass door open, she enters the cramped delicatessen. Occupying a narrow storefront, the owners have maximized the limited space with high shelving that runs the length of the interior. A female cashier restocks the shelves directly behind a checkout counter, to the left of the entry door. The Cuban operative is nowhere in sight. As Hayley makes her way toward the back of the store, she notes the absence of surveillance cameras. Did Barrios, familiar with the store, select this location for that reason? Hayley feels the hairs on her forearms go up.

The deli counter at the rear of the store is deserted. Looking past the refrigerated case displaying an assort- ment of meats, cheeses, and salads, Hayley clocks the rear emergency exit door she intuited would be there. Weighing the likelihood that Barrios has fled, Hayley considers her next move. A restroom to the right of the rear exit offers another possibility. Checking the door, she finds it unlocked.

Every instinct sounds an alarm. Hayley puts herself in Barrios's shoes. *He thinks he can take me.* She pauses to look over her shoulder, to the deli counter behind her. A magnetic strip over the prep counter is easily within access, offering an array of long knives. She quickly discards the thought. Instead, Hayley retrieves her set of keys, positioning three of them between her index and middle fingers.

She pushes open the door.

The dingy restroom isn't much larger than a broom closet, fitted only with a filthy washbasin. Her prey is not in sight. A door leading into what must be the toilet is to Hayley's left. She sets her feet far apart for a stable foundation and pushes the inner door open, revealing Barrios crouched on the toilet seat.

The Cuban agent seizes Hayley by the left arm and hauls her toward him. Simultaneously, he steps off his perch and thrusts a knife at her with his other hand. Hayley deflects his knife thrust with her left arm and punches with her right fist, driving the spiked keys into the soft tissue of Barrios's face. She strikes him this way repeatedly in swift succession, gouging the Cuban's cheeks and right eye. He wobbles under her furious assault, regains traction, and comes at her again with his fist closed around the knife handle. Striking out blindly, Barrios connects with a blow to her right temple. Hayley's knees buckle. As she starts falling, he kicks her hard in the shin with a steel-tipped boot. Pain rockets up her spine and seems to explode from the top of Hayley's head. Constricted by the narrow confines, Barrios awkwardly flips the knife forward and stabs at his adversary. She ducks, avoiding the blade by inches. The knife's tip pierces the cheap, hollow-core door behind her. The big Cuban expends a few precious seconds to extract the knife, providing Hayley the opportunity to regroup.

In that cramped space, the two operatives—one male in his forties and the other female, twenty-seven—trade desperate blows. Their fight is ferocious but not long in duration. Barrios cannot exploit his larger physical size. Can't extend the full reach of his punches. Hayley brings force to bear with the understanding that she made the correct decision in rejecting the choice of a long knife from behind the deli counter. Her spiked fist is equally devastating and much more maneuverable. Her agility overwhelms the Cuban. Hayley inflicts far more damage on him than she receives.

Barrios isn't the first opponent to underestimate her. Being sold short has been an undercurrent in Hayley's life. Her gender, family background, and West Virginia accent have all played into her status as an underdog and not one she encourages. But she won't hesitate to exploit that poor judgment. *They just think they're going to win.* Barrios laid his trap, miscalculating the advantages of Hayley's smaller size in the cramped toilet. The error is a catastrophic one. He failed to foresee the sheer ferocity with which his pursuer would wage close-quarters combat. Who would? Her destructive force is freakish and, in that way, completely unpredictable.

As she slams her spiked fist repeatedly into his face, Hayley recognizes one unavoidable fact: the Cuban will not be taken alive. Barrios will fight as long as he is physically able. The longer their brawl continues, the greater his odds of success. Though Hayley has gained the upper hand, the ultimate result of their fight is not predetermined. She could die here, in this fetid toilet.

She drives her elbow into the man's head. The blow causes him to drop his knife. Hayley retrieves the knife from the floor and, holding it close to her body, buries it in Barrios's chest as she stands up straight with knees locked. The Cuban struggles for a few moments, as she drives the blade deeper into his thoracic cavity, and then goes limp. He falls backward, sitting comically on the closed toilet seat. The blare of a siren signals the approach of the police, summoned by Hayley's call to 911.

Winded and delicately spritzed with her adversary's blood, she withdraws her phone from a pocket. After snapping a photo of the dead man on the toilet, she quickly exits the bathroom. Standing again at the rear of the long, narrow storefront, Hayley can hear the cashier ringing up a sale and chatting with an unseen customer.

The past days have posed a dilemma, with rapidly unfolding events forcing her to choose between the worse of twin evils. Duty bound and genetically unable to shirk her responsibilities, she has thrown herself against the country's inexorable creep toward the precipice. There is no time to lose. With Alberto Barrios's death, she has given the United States a slim chance to avert a domestic catastrophe. Turning right, Hayley Chill, a covert agent for the "deeper state," exits the delicatessen through the rear door.

1

★ ★ ★ ★

THE LIVES WE SAVE

TEN DAYS EARLIER

Wednesday, 8:25 a.m., Kyle Rodgers, a bespectacled black man of expanding girth, is waiting for Hayley when she walks through the office door. His coveted position as president whisperer and sounding board landed Rodgers with premium real estate on the West Wing's main floor. Richard Monroe's chaotic first year as president culminated with an attempt on his life. The wholesale purge that followed those tumultuous events spared the genial and eminently capable senior advisor. Among several outstanding attributes, Rodgers is notable in Washington for having gained his influential position without having made bones of anybody.

He is as good a boss as one can expect in the White

House's pressure-cooker environment. For that indisputable fact, Hayley Chill esteems and admires Kyle Rodgers. The feelings are mutual. His office is the best run in the building, and he has his young chief of staff from West Virginia to thank for it. The secret machinations of Hayley's superiors in the deeper state—a clandestine association of former presidents and Supreme Court justices, retired directors from the intelligence community, and other discharged heavyweights of the government establishment that calls itself "Publius"—placed her in the West Wing twenty months ago as an intern. But it has been by the sheer dint of her extraordinary skills that Hayley is where she is today: fifty feet down the carpeted corridor from the Oval Office.

"Thank God you're here," Rodgers says without looking at her. "Today is going to be insane." He mixes sugar-free Red Bull with coffee at his desk, his go-to breakfast.

Hayley's meteoric rise from humble intern to the chief of staff for one of the president's key advisors generated widespread acrimony among the other West Wing staffers. The army veteran—possessing only an associate's degree from a two-year community college and an accent particular to people from the Appalachians—is widely considered by her peers to be undeserving of her fantastic success. Hayley Chill has dealt with this poisonous envy all her life and unfailingly turns it to her advantage. But the exertions of holding down two high-pressure jobs—as White House staffer *and* covert agent—has taken its toll. Twenty-hour workdays are the norm.

Wearing a Jones of New York knee-length, dark blue skirt, a tie-front silk blouse, and sensible shoes, she drops her knock-off tote on the couch. "What's up?"

Rodgers scans his computer screen for Monroe's daily schedule, a detailed, minute-by-minute rundown available only to West Wing staffers. "Okay. First off, we—"

"—need to get the president up to speed on the *LA Times*, *Washington Post*, and *New York Times* hack." Hayley read reports on her way into work. Coordinated cyber-attacks hit computer servers at printing plants across the country. The nation's major newspapers managed to get the day's editions out, but only after significant delays.

"Yeah, I heard about that," Rodgers says absently, taking a sip of his energy drink concoction. Glancing toward his young chief of staff for the first time since she'd arrived, he notes Hayley's slightly haggard countenance. "What happened to you?"

She got only a few hours of sleep the night before. Hayley spent most of her Tuesday at the Library of Congress; the president's speechwriters required material for Monroe's address to workers at an auto plant in Ohio on Wednesday, and the job was tasked to Kyle Rodgers's wunderkind. A two-hour workout—six sets of a circuit of exercises that included timed pull-ups, crunches, and push-ups, followed by a twelve-mile run—followed a nine-hour stint at the library. After a quick dinner, Hayley put in several hours compiling a detailed weekly report on the president's activities for her superiors in the deeper state. Naturally, she squeezed in another workout this morning before leaving for the White House.

She disregards her boss's question. "Has there been any attribution yet?"

"Who do you think?"

"We can't always blame Russia, sir. Other players out there have the same capabilities. North Korea, for instance. Tehran."

Rodgers shrugs and turns his attention back to his computer, reading through an email to the president's chief of staff and vice president one last time before sending. He had joined Monroe's presidential campaign just before the start of the primary swing, proving indispensable in tailoring the candidate's message for early contests in Iowa and New Hampshire. A veteran of numerous national and state-level campaigns, Kyle Rodgers possesses the highly desirable ability to distill a politician's incoherent and insecure ramblings into network-ready sound bites. Married to his college sweetheart and distracted dad of four-year-old twin girls, he is a pessimistic optimist. Rodgers recognizes humanity is on a collision course with its stunning idiocy. Simultaneously, he believes in the restorative powers of a competent executive branch. Bolstered by that conviction, Rodgers sets himself apart from 98 percent of the other political wonks in town mired by their jaded nihilism.

Hayley persists. "Communications working on a statement?"

"The president will continue treating these low-level, nuisance attacks on private sector institutions as a non-government matter," Rodgers says by rote. He checks his watch. "I'm heading up to the residence to talk to the big guy." He hurriedly loads files and briefing books into a large leather satchel. "Don't forget. The Rose Garden thing has been moved to nine forty-five."

"Shutting down the printing operations of the three national daily newspapers seems something more than a nuisance, sir." Hayley adds, with greater emphasis, "You might even call it a direct attack on the First Amendment by one of the nation's historic enemies."

Her boss doesn't seem overly concerned. "Well, if Moscow really wants our attention, they'll just have to turn off the lights at the Pentagon."

"Y'all know they can do that, don't you?" Hayley shouts after her boss as he heads out the door with his satchel. Of course, Kyle Rodgers is well aware of the capabilities of Moscow's cyber army. They match those of the United States. Soldiers at Cyber Command could turn the lights off in the entire country of Russia with a few clicks on a computer keyboard. But having that power is a far different matter from exercising it. The consensus in Washington is a cyber Mexican standoff will continue for the foreseeable future.

With a cascade of pressing concerns requiring President Richard Monroe's attention, Rodgers offers only a raised middle finger as he heads up the corridor. He thinks the world of his chief of staff but finds her to be galling as hell at times, too.

WEDNESDAY, 10:10 A.M. President Monroe strides down the West Colonnade accompanied by a navy chief in full dress uniform. The president's affinity for the Rose Garden is easy to understand. The outdoor location has been an effective tool for White House communications for decades, used as a backdrop for welcoming other world leaders, staging official ceremonies, signing significant pieces of legislation, and holding non-campaign campaign events. More so than his predecessors, Richard Monroe has deployed the French-style garden adjacent to the Oval Office as his preferred venue for presidential stagecraft. With chiseled features and a hawklike profile that wouldn't be out of place on Mount Rushmore, his looks are perfect for the iconic setting.

The president steps down from the colonnade, turns to face the one-hundred-plus invited guests—members of his cabinet, assorted dignitaries, military brass in dress uniforms—and blasts them with his trademark grin. A career soldier before winning his first and only political campaign for president of the United States, Richard Monroe led a tank charge across the sands of Kuwait in Operation Desert Storm. Later, as a major general and commander of the First Armored Division, he drove the tyrant Saddam Hussein from Fortress Baghdad in Operation Iraqi Freedom. His obvious strengths, commanding presence, and unassailable integrity have been the perfect tonic for a nation torn by division and political polarization.

Everyone stands with the president's arrival, the electricity in the Rose Garden supercharged by his charismatic presence. Monroe smiles good-naturedly. This morning's event is one of the "good" ones, a time of celebration. After a wet and cold spring, the weather in the nation's capital has finally turned. Bright, warm sunshine bathes the proceedings in magnificence. The president is relaxed, and his casual attitude goes a long way to putting all in attendance—especially the US Navy warrant officer who accompanied him from the Oval Office and now stands at attention beside him— at ease. Monroe gestures with both hands. "Thank you, everyone. Please, sit."

All those assembled before the podium take their seats, while aides and staff members to either side of the garden remain standing.

"Thank you again, everyone, for coming out for today's event. It gives me enormous pleasure to be here today to honor one of America's finest and a true hero, US Navy chief Edward Ramos. The Medal of Honor is the highest award our great nation bestows on an individual serving in the Armed Services of the United States. Chief Ramos receives this award, the Medal of Honor, for conspicuous gallantry at the risk of his life above and beyond the call of duty as a Hostage Rescue Force Team Member in Afghanistan in support of Operation Enduring Freedom on November 9, 2012."

Generous applause washes over the president and his invited honoree. Hayley watches from the sidelines, standing next to Kyle Rodgers. She listens to the president's speech and reflects on her extraordinary journey from an impoverished childhood in West Virginia to the White House Rose Garden. The deeper state plucked her from the army's infantry ranks, trained her in covert operations, and infiltrated her into the West Wing as an intern. Hayley fully appreciates the enormity of her responsibilities.

After Monroe finishes his speech and has draped the medal around the war hero's neck, the assembled crowd remains seated while the president and Ramos turn and retreat to the West Colonnade. A trio of Secret Service agents follows at a discreet distance. Kyle Rodgers and Hayley Chill, having ducked out from the ceremony moments from its conclusion, wait near the French doors leading into the Oval Office as the president approaches with his honored guest.

Monroe exchanges small talk with Chief Ramos as they stop in front of the West Wing staffers. "Well, the weather couldn't have been better for the occasion."

The war hero is understandably stiff in the presence of his commander in chief. "Yes, Mr. President. Thank you."

"So very grateful for your service, Chief." Monroe gestures toward his top advisor. "Mr. Rodgers will show you the way out of here. Kyle?"

Hayley looks to the ground to avoid Rodgers's startled expression. He's not used to being dismissed in favor of his much more junior chief of staff.

"Yes, sir. Of course," says Rodgers. He indicates the way back up the West Colonnade. "Chief, after you."

CWO4 Edward J. Ramos and Kyle Rodgers walk off, leaving the president alone with Hayley outside the French doors that lead into the Oval Office. They remain there, rooted in place, avoiding whatever prying eyes or electronic ears might be lurking on the other side of those doors.

"What do you want?" Monroe's voice is flat and hostile. That he hates the young woman with the powder blue eyes is abruptly clear. His transformation from charismatic chief executive to an angry old man is instantaneous.

Hayley absorbs the president's aggressive malice with cool aplomb, glancing over her shoulder to ensure the president's protection detail, posted at different points on the colonnade, is out of earshot.

Turning back to Monroe, she says, "You read my message earlier. Otherwise, you wouldn't have saddled Kyle Rodgers with the task of the lowliest aide."

"I'll flag the dead drop when I go upstairs again before lunch . . . *okay*?" The man's bitterness doesn't befit his station. Hayley ignores it.

"Ask them if they know anything about the cyber-attack on the newspapers' servers last night."

Monroe smolders. He cannot bear taking orders from the twenty-seven-year-old female. By all appearances, he has no choice but to do so.

"Mr. President?" Hayley prods him, desiring only one thing: his unquestioned compliance.

"I'll ask them, goddammit." His voice is a low growl of frustrated rage.

"Good. That's why you're here, sir, remember? Instead of a federal prison."

Monroe's lip curls as if he's on the verge of a bestial snarl. But he remains silent.

"Хорошо. До скорого." Hayley's Russian is flawless, spoken only with the slightest American accent. *Good. Until later, then.*

The president of the United States looks over his shoulder, confirming their privacy. He grudgingly says, "Всего." *Later.*

Monroe turns and reenters the Oval Office, where a scrum of subservient aides meets him. Hayley Chill remains just outside the door, watching him. Inside that hallowed space, Richard Monroe is the leader of the free world, the face of the greatest democracy that humanity has ever achieved. But Hayley—and only Hayley, in these precincts—knows better. Since before her arrival at the White House as a covert agent of the deeper state she has known the truth. Richard Monroe is a Russian mole, covertly entering the US with his parents as a one-year-old and since then under orders of the Main Directorate of the Russian General Chief of Staff. Moscow's corruption of America's highest office represents the most successful operation in history until Hayley Chill flipped Richard Monroe and, as his handler, uses him to undermine Russia.

Message delivered, and anxious to get to other pressing tasks, she turns away from the door and nearly collides with a female Secret Service agent. Hayley experiences a sharp, stabbing fear. How long had the agent been standing so close behind her and the president? How much did she hear?

The expression on the woman's face is stern, even for a Secret Service agent. Her eyes are accusatory.

Stepping aside, Hayley begins improvising a response to a possible inquisition. Why is she speaking Russian with the US president?

The agent peers through the glass door, into the Oval Office, and then looks to Hayley again. Her expression softens, culminating in a friendly smile.

"It never gets old, does it?" she asks.

Hayley effortlessly masks her relief, returning the other woman's smile. "No, ma'am, it never does."

———————————

KYLE RODGERS HAD correctly predicted the day would be a difficult one. But that's a safe bet on almost any day in the Monroe White House. The president was elected on the promise of being a disrupter. The voters who turned out for Richard Monroe, of course, didn't know just how much of a destructive force his Russian handlers intend for him to be. Blunting that attack on US institutions is only one of Hayley's responsibilities. Another is turning the Russian mole Richard Monroe back on Moscow in the form of a disinformation campaign. In both cases, Hayley relied on her supervising agent with Publius, Andrew Wilde, for direction. He contacted her before five that morning with new orders regarding the night's cyberattacks on the nation's major newspapers. Even for someone as cold and relentlessly officious as Wilde, so devoid of human emotion, his manner seemed brusque. Has she done something to displease her superiors in the deeper state? Paranoia is a career hazard in both of her worlds, public and covert. One fact for certain is that the low-grade insanity of running Kyle Rodgers's office seems like a vacation in comparison to her clandestine duties for Andrew Wilde and the deeper state.

Leaving the White House complex after ten that night, she Ubers to the Darlington House, a restaurant in Dupont Circle on Twentieth Street. For forty years, the Darlington was one of Washington's legendary bars. Musical artists, including the Ramones, Bonnie Raitt, and Bruce Springsteen, wailed, thrashed, and bounced across its ancient floorboards. In 2007, new owners gave all three levels of the building a makeover. They made only a faint effort to preserve the venue's original ambiance, with electric guitars bracketed to exposed brick walls. Open mic night once a week fails to capture the magic of a bygone era.

The guy behind the bar greets her with a friendly wave.

"Repo?"

She nods and pulls up a stool at the all-but-deserted bar.

Billy Esposito has long nurtured a thing for Hayley Chill, one that the White House staffer has deftly sidetracked. Her work for the deeper state precludes a normal life, but this simply perpetuates a long pattern of Hayley's being stubbornly single. Physical entanglements have been easy and, no doubt, she has been willing to go there in more convenient times of her life. Some of those casual affairs ended badly. Others were complete debacles. Hayley long ago made peace with the realization that she might not fulfill a man's vision of a female partner. If hindsight is twenty-twenty, then her ability to predict the inevitable failure of a possible romantic entanglement is positively uncanny. Love is for civilians. She's got a job to do.

Grabbing a bottle of tequila from the shelf behind him, Billy pours her a double.

"An hour ago, this place was packed. Think it was something I said?" He grins, hoping for a kind smile or full-fledged interaction.

"Not you, Billy. Them."

The bartender takes her polite response as an invitation to hike one foot up on the cooler behind the bar and settle in for a more extended conversation. Hayley feels her phone vibrate. Checking it, she finds a message from her drinks date canceling five minutes after their meeting time. Hayley would throttle her phone if it did any good.

"I tell you about the gig I've got next weekend? We're playing—"

She raises a hand. "You mind, Billy? Need a little downtime."

He drops his foot down and backs away with both hands raised, grinning sheepishly. "Like I said. Radio-active."

Billy retreats to the far end of the bar, leaving Hayley to her concerns about the president's hostility.

Will Monroe have increasing difficulty concealing his potentially dangerous emotional outbursts? Hayley can hardly blame him. He's in a terrible situation despite being "the most powerful man on Earth." Richard Monroe is beholden to rival espionage entities simultaneously. Even Hayley has no idea what the endgame is here. These uncertainties do nothing to mollify Hayley's perennial feelings of isolation and exposure.

"Hey, there." The voice is a male. Mid- to late twenties, she surmises, keeping her gaze fixed on the Strat on the opposite wall. Friendly and assured.

"Bad timing, friend," Hayley says, without looking in that direction. "I mean, bad in a tragic, gothic kind of way."

"Guess I'm the run-toward-danger type of guy," the male voice says, not too close to her ear to be weird but not exactly fleeing for the hills, either.

Hayley slowly turns to look at him. He has an open expression and hazel eyes under an unruly mop of auburn hair. The stubble on his face suggests either a careless man or one too busy to bother shaving. The DC Fire Department T-shirt he wears isn't clean, either. An off-duty fireman is an easy guess. The "run-toward-danger" comment, then, was tongue in cheek. Funny, even. He seems harmless enough. But, as she stated, tonight is not a good night.

"Honestly, you have a better chance driving over to Arlington National Cemetery and romancing Jacqueline Kennedy Onassis," Hayley says, despite feeling that particular feeling.

The fireman puts up both hands in mock surrender and moves so that one empty bar stool is between him and Hayley.

The bartender approaches. "Usual, Sam?"

Sam McGovern nods.

Hayley silently curses herself. If she didn't want human interaction, why come to a bar?

"Put it on my tab, Billy," she says. Or maybe it's just because he is so good-looking.

Both Billy and Sam are surprised by the gesture. Without further comment, the bartender draws a tall, chilled mug of Bass Ale for the firefighter, who casts a questioning look in Hayley's direction.

She fixes her gaze on the Strat but feels his eyes on her. "For the lives you saved today," says Hayley.

Billy places the beer in front of Sam, who lifts it high.

Sam says, "To the lives we save."

The bartender retrieves his bottomless mug of heavily iced diet root beer from next to the cash register and clinks it with Sam's.

_____

MORE THAN TWO hours later, Hayley stands on the sidewalk with Sam McGovern outside Darlington House. Despite the late hour, a warm breeze wafts over them. The grin on the firefighter's face is playfully inebriated, a testament to several pints he raised to defuse a stressful day. But it's not just the alcohol. Sam vibes on Hayley in a way that he hasn't felt in a long time. The opportunity presents itself. Their initial banter, easy and jocular, begat actual conversation, words that fit together like one thousand puzzle pieces to form a picture of something real.

Hayley gives him a quizzical look. "What the hell are you thinking?"

He only laughs, at himself, in response.

"I'm not going home with you," she says.

"I don't remember inviting you."

"That smile was invitation enough." Her resolve is especially admirable given the amount of tequila consumed and regrettable history of casual intimacies.

"What's *yours* saying?" Sam asks, appreciating her beaming face.

Hayley realizes how rare it is for her to smile and says nothing.

"I want to see you again."

"I'm a busy girl."

"That's not a valid excuse."

"How do I get in touch with you? Dial 911?"

He laughs. "Sure. Ask for Sam."

She turns and takes a few steps toward the Prius that has just stopped at the curb, her Uber.

"I had fun," Hayley says over her shoulder, her right hand reaching for the door handle. "Thanks for cheering me up."

She climbs into the back of the Prius and pulls the door closed, leaving Sam feeling weirdly bereft. As the vehicle pulls away, however, the rear window rolls down and Hayley's face appears.

"Hayley Chill. I work at the White House. Last I checked, we're listed."

ARRIVING AT HER apartment on P Street near Logan Circle well after midnight, slightly buzzed from the tequila she consumed, Hayley discovers the door ajar. Sobering instantly, she pushes it open and sees the place is ransacked. She remains on her guard; whoever wrecked the apartment might still be inside. Keeping her back to the wall, Hayley moves quickly to the kitchen area and retrieves the biggest blade in the knife block. Checking each room and closet with the butcher's knife in hand, the White House staffer establishes she is alone in the apartment.

She picks up one of her dining chairs lying on its side and sets it upright. After retrieving her laptop from her bag, Hayley accesses the server that stores images from the surveillance cameras she placed inside the apartment for precisely this occasion. She has zero concerns that the break-in has compromised her identity as a covert agent for the deeper state. Hayley carries on her person at all times the KryptAll phone issued to her by Andrew Wilde. No other physical evidence exists tying her to Publius. But was the break-in an ordinary case of robbery, or was it counterespionage?

Locating the minicam's footage online is a trivial matter. Motion-activated, the camera's recording is time-stamped a few minutes past three that afternoon when Hayley would have been at the White House. With the camera focused on the main living area of the apartment, the single intruder enters the frame from the left.

The individual is slim and average height, wearing loose-fitting dark clothing and a balaclava mask that obscures the entire head and face. Gender is impossible to establish. Stopping, the individual scans the entire living room for several seconds. After that lengthy pause, he or she approaches the camera with a purposeful stride. Hayley can now see the expandable steel baton in the individual's right hand. The intruder draws nearer to the surveillance camera and swings the baton violently forward as the footage abruptly ends.

Hayley looks up from the computer and glances toward the shelf on the opposite wall, where she wedged the matchbox-size minicam between a stack of books. She reverses the recording playback and then freezes frame on the intruder approaching the camera. There is much to suggest the break-in was something more than simple robbery. The tactical balaclava and telescoping steel baton are not the typical kit of the average meth addict, but these objects aren't absolute proof of a professional operative. Nor is the fact that the front door showed no sign of forced entry. What troubles Hayley most is how the intruder methodically scanned the room and so readily spotted the recording device, as if they knew to look for it.

The break-in indicates the possibility of a severe security breach. Suspicion of her being something *more* than a White House staffer is the only reason to target Hayley. Before doing anything else, including putting her place back together, the deeper state operative knows what she must do. Reaching for her KryptAll phone, she prepares in her head how best to communicate the news to Andrew Wilde.

THURSDAY, 5:15 A.M. When she sets out for her run the next morning, the season's first hint of predawn humidity reminds her of Fort Hood, in Killeen, Texas. Hayley enlisted in the US Army straight out of high school, reveling in the regimentation and directedness of military life. At that time, a career with the army seemed more rewarding than anything available to her back home in Lincoln County, West Virginia. In a single meeting at a Red Lobster fifty miles south of the base, Hayley's journey shifted, taking a turn that she could never have predicted. Having appeared in her life only the day before, like the professional spook that he was, Andrew Wilde offered the opportunity for patriotic service that far surpassed her role as a corporal in the US Army.

Since she was a child, Hayley's almost daily runs have been an integral part of her exercise regimen. She eschews high-tech training attire, favoring her old army PT gear instead. Her gait is effortless. Automatic. With physical conditioning at peak levels, breaking a sweat requires a high-energy output. Hayley quickly overtakes a 63 Metrobus devoid of passengers lumbering south on Thirteenth Street. After fifteen minutes at a fast pace, sweat drenches her shirtfront. She eases up with that intensity, feet thinking for her as she turns east on K Street. The capital's streets are gloriously traffic-free.

Within a few minutes of easy jogging and cooling down, Hayley arrives at Franklin Square.

Last renovated in the administration of Franklin Roosevelt and eerily suggestive of that era's Great Depression, the park seems inhabited by ghosts of unemployed tramps and phantom breadlines. Fifteen minutes until sunrise and not another living soul is in evidence. Hayley enjoys the strangeness of the place, especially at this time of day. She customarily pauses on the west side of the park to stretch, near the commanding statue of John Barry, an officer of the Continental Navy and one of three contenders for "Father of the American Navy."

Andrew Wilde is waiting for her on a bench near the Barry statue.

He says, "Too predictable. Too routine."

Hayley does nothing to disagree with Wilde's assessment. She finds herself marveling at Wilde's deep tan. When they first met, the spy explained his skin tone was a result of a vacation home in Puerto Rico. Hayley assumes this is only one more cover story. The man's inherent gravitas convinced Hayley of the significance of his recruitment pitch. As it turned out, that first impression was fully warranted. She has gotten enough gravitas in her association with the deeper state to last a lifetime.

"What's up?" she asks, guarded. Andrew Wilde had only popped up like this once before when he first appeared at one of her amateur bouts at Fort Hood. Following her recruitment, their communications have been limited to encrypted messages, calls, and emails over the KryptAll phone.

Wilde shrugs. "Checking up, face-to-face. What with the break-in and all." He says the second sentence archly and with a tinge of mockery.

"Are we okay here?" Her voice becomes sharper. "*Am I okay?*"

"What on earth do you mean?"

"Have I done something to displease you or whoever it is that's above you?"

"You're insecure. Why?"

Hayley scoffs. "What's going on? Please, sir. You owe me that much."

"We all appreciate the challenges inherent in your mission, Hayley. It would be impossible for me to over-state the pressures you're under."

"... me. You don't have to worry about me." She feels the heat of anger, her affliction, go up a few degrees. *What does he actually want?*

"Tell me more about this break-in. Could it have been a disgruntled lover?"

"If you know enough to find me here at thirteen minutes before six, you know 'man trouble' isn't exactly in the cards."

"Then . . . what?"

Hayley stares off.

Wilde doesn't wait for her answer. "We've analyzed the images you forwarded last night. There is little question the individual is trained and professionally equipped."

She cannot argue with that assessment. "Nothing was found. I'm good."

"Why would you be targeted? A low-level staffer for an advisor to the president wouldn't typically fall in the sphere of interest by foreign intelligence services."

"But that's a possibility, sir. Or, I'm simply the victim of a very meticulous junkie."

Wilde stares at Hayley with a placid expression, his tan face infuriating in its impeccable smoothness. "Would you like to be replaced?"

The question is a thunderbolt, out of the blue and shocking.

"What? No!" Her mind races. Her worries that she has done something to displease Wilde were well placed. But why? She has filed her reports in a timely fashion and maintained perfect mission integrity. Hayley can't think of one misstep or careless incident.

His gaze holds hers. With a long history in intelligence work and overseas covert operations, Wilde possesses a better understanding of human psychology than many trained mental health professionals. He has Hayley Chill's number. She will do whatever it takes to succeed at an assigned task.

"If you've been compromised in any way, you're done."

Hayley controls her emotions. Life as an army boxer taught her many lessons. A rudimentary one is the art of the counterpunch. "If I'm compromised, someone in the organization screwed up. Not me. Maybe if you figured out who broke, the threat could be neutralized."

"We're working on it." He doesn't seem all that concerned, however. "This cyber business. Monroe is contacting his Russian handler?"

"Yes, sir. We should hear something in the next day or two."

"Good." Wilde stands. "We're done here."

Without further ceremony, he turns and strolls quickly away, heading toward I Street along the southern reaches of the park. The first pedestrians are entering the park a few hundred feet away.

Hayley watches her deeper state supervisor go, attempting to decipher the true meaning behind his final words. *We're done here.* As with everything in this clandestine world of subterfuge and deceit, the surface of things is all for show. The real truth lies beneath that veneer. *Trust no one.* That was the first lesson she learned in this town, spoken to her by a mentor, the president's assassinated chief of staff. They remain words to live by.

———————

THURSDAY, 10:50 A.M. Four people await the president's arrival in the Oval Office. Sitting in awkward silence on the couch and chairs at the opposite end of the room from the *Resolute* desk is Vice President Vincent Landers, National Security Agency director General Carlos Hernandez, and secretary of Homeland Security Clare Ryan. Standing nearby is senior advisor, Kyle Rodgers, with an attentive Hayley Chill at his side. She possesses the necessary security clearance in case someone needs a fresh cup of coffee, the identity of Russia's State Duma chairman (Vyacheslav Viktorovich Volodin), or the technical name of the synthetic chemical compound more commonly known as the nerve agent VX (O-ethyl S-2-diisopropylaminoethyl methylphosphonothioate). Hayley impresses many of her colleagues in the White House with her astounding wealth of knowledge. Only her boss, Kyle Rodgers, knows her gift of eidetic memory is behind her erudition.

The attack on the nation's newspapers required the president's attention. With Hayley's pressure on Kyle Rodgers the day before, time was made in Monroe's schedule for a sit-down with the government officials most responsible for cyber preparedness. But the meeting's participants have been waiting for some time, Monroe's problems keeping to a meticulously crafted daily schedule legendary. Hernandez impatiently checks his wristwatch. Clare Ryan clears her throat. Rodgers is about to stand to check on the president when the door leading to a private study adjoining the Oval Office swings open. Richard Monroe enters the room like a summer storm. Everyone stands.

"Sorry for the delay, folks." Monroe drops into an upholstered chair before the dark fireplace. The others take their seats as well, greeting the president respectfully. Hayley remains to the side of the room. The president knows she's there but refuses to look in her direction.

"So, this cyber business. Who wants to start?" the president asks.

Clare Ryan, in her forties and possessing an efficient

intensity that commands attention, beats the NSA director to the punch. "Mr. President, as you know, DHS hasn't
the mandate to provide network protection for the private
sector. As much as we'd like defending the American people from these attacks—whether on the major newspapers
or Iran's Operation Ababil against the US banking system
a few years back—our directives are clear. Government
networks are the responsibility of Homeland Security. And
we're confident with those protections we have in place."

Monroe looks to Hernandez, a lean man in his fifties
with a prominent forehead and iron-gray hair. He wears
his US Army uniform with enormous pride. "Cyber
Command is responsible for defending military networks, Mr. President, while the NSA is by its mandate
an offensive component," he says.

"The private sector is expected to fend for itself?"
asks Monroe.

"Yes, sir. Entirely," Clare Ryan says.

"Is that something that should change?" asks Vincent Landers. As vice president, he is upset about the
uselessness of his position. Only one of the manifestations of that frustration is Lander's habit of forcing his
way into a conversation with leading questions.

Hernandez says, "Not a problem if you've got ten
years and about that many trillion dollars to spare."

Monroe frowns, unhappy with his vice president's
interruption. "We have neither."

"Sir, as long as we can do to them what they can do
to us, we're in a stalemate not unlike the nuclear standoff of the last *six decades*," Hernandez says.

The president reacts to Hernandez's hectoring with an exasperated sigh. "What about rogue or terrorist actors? Radical Islamists claimed credit for this latest thing. What'd they call themselves? 'Cyber Jihad'?"

Hernandez adopts a more respectful tone. "Mr. President, analysis and accurate attribution is in the early stages. We were able to trace the malware, in this case, a logic bomb, back to servers in Estonia."

"Logic bomb? What the hell is that?" asks Landers.

Clare Ryan elbows her way back into the briefing. "Mr. Vice President, a logic bomb is a small bit of code inserted into a computer system that will set off a malicious function when specified conditions are met. In this case, servers at the targeted newspapers were wiped out simultaneously, the conditions being the time and date. North Korea, China, and Iran have used these same hijacked servers in the past."

Hernandez shoots an angry look at his Department of Homeland Security counterpart. Their shared animosity is well-known in Washington.

"For the sake of getting our hands around a coherent policy, let's agree it's impossible to know who's hitting us," Kyle Rodgers says.

"Well, *that* makes my job so much easier," says Monroe, adding sarcastically, "If we can't possibly know who's attacking us, we can counterattack anyone we please."

"Mr. President, we've had time to study the malware used in the attack on the newspapers. It bears signatures of code we've associated in past attacks with the GRU's

Unit 26165," Hernandez says, referencing a cyber-specific division of Russia's military intelligence agency. Under the direct command of the Minister of Defense, the Main Directorate of the General Staff of the Armed Forces of the Russian Federation runs a more orthodox hacking operation than the FSB, which outsources missions to independent hackers and criminal groups.

Clare Ryan scoffs. "Big surprise."

The general presses his case with Monroe. "Sir, I propose we respond with an action that degrades comparable assets in Moscow."

"Comparable assets?"

"Computer servers at the GRU or any of the FSB's hacking centers in Saint Petersburg."

Monroe dismisses the suggestion with a wave of his right hand. Everyone in the room is aware that Hernandez's only son had been a passenger on Malaysia Airlines Flight 17, shot down by a Buk surface-to-air missile launched from pro-Russian separatist-controlled territory in Ukraine on July 17, 2014. GRU Unit 26165 was accused of hacking the international investigations into the incident. The general's antipathy for Russia ought to have disqualified him for the jobs he currently holds as director of both the NSA and US Cyber Command. Powerful allies in Congress, however, helped secure his position. His expertise in signals intelligence is second to none, and he is an adept administrator. Nevertheless, the president was advised by Kyle Rodgers to keep a tight leash on the general. Hernandez has been looking for any excuse to punch Moscow's lights out since his first days running the show at Fort Meade.

Clare Ryan seizes the opportunity to gain an advantage over her rival. "An alternative, Mr. President, might be emergency legislation that provides the funding for DHS to ramp up the defense of the nation's most vital and vulnerable civilian targets. What's of critical need, sir, is a federal initiative to protect our electrical grid, utilities, and financial networks."

Her suggestion prompts another glare from the NSA director. The kind of money she is talking about would finance an extra battle group or stealth fighter battalion. No one in Washington with any power would let a rival incur that kind of windfall, not without a fight.

Before Hernandez can deploy his counterargument, Monroe shifts uneasily in his chair. Kyle Rodgers takes the president's restlessness as his cue to wrap up the meeting. "We'll table this until the folks over at Savage Road develop confirmable attribution," he says, referring to the physical address of Fort Meade, headquarters for both the NSA and Cyber Command.

A visibly relieved Monroe stands. "Who knows? This attack could be a one-off. We might never hear from Cyber Jihad again." He looks to Rodgers, signaling for him to clear the room, and makes a beeline for the door leading to his private study.

The meeting's participants head toward the exit to the Outer Oval Office. Kyle Rodgers follows General Hernandez and Vice President Landers out the door, the men engaged in a private conversation that seems intentional in its exclusion of Clare Ryan.

The DHS secretary pauses to buttonhole Hayley, who remained respectfully behind while the principals cleared the room. "Ms. Chill? You have a second?"

"How can I be of assistance, Madam Secretary?" Hayley has met Clare Ryan a dozen times in the past year. She always found the older woman to be unusually inclusive and cordial, despite the difference in their government pay grades. West Wing scuttlebutt had it that the DHS secretary's marriage was a rocky one. Hayley is sympathetic to the cabinet secretary's plight as the only female in Monroe's cabinet.

"Is it my imagination, or are these meetings in the Oval becoming shorter and shorter? This is the presidency by haiku."

"A lot on his plate, ma'am," Hayley says, carefully neutral.

"We both know of General Hernandez's penchant for blaming the Kremlin for everything but bad weather. I hope I can count on your wise counsel in a policy discussion that is certain to get rough."

"Madame Secretary—"

"Please, call me Clare."

That sort of casual familiarity with a cabinet secretary isn't in Hayley's DNA. "Ma'am, I'm only a staffer working for—"

The secretary for Homeland Security interrupts her a second time. "Your special standing with the president couldn't even be classified as an open secret. Nor could your keen insight and true, patriotic commitment to our nation."

Singling her out in this way makes Hayley uncomfortable. Her role as an agent for the deeper state requires she seek neither attention nor commendation.

"Words like 'patriot' are too often co-opted by politicians and ideologues, ma'am."

"'Freedom' is another."

"Yes, ma'am."

"What does compel you to be here, Hayley? It can't be the money."

"A devotion to country, ma'am, and its Constitution. There's never been a better articulation of democratic goals."

The West Wing aide's sterling sincerity is humbling. Clare Ryan can't help but admire Hayley. "I don't think I have to convince you of the threat cyberattack poses for the United States. We need your help." Clare emphasizes her last sentence with a squeeze of Hayley's forearm.

"Of course, ma'am."

The cabinet secretary smiles inscrutably and continues out the door, disappearing into the reception area. For a moment, Hayley Chill is left alone in the office where so much history has been made. The Secret Service agent was exactly right the day before. No matter how many times Hayley has ventured into this hallowed room, the Oval Office never ceases to instill awe in the young woman from West Virginia.

The vibration of her phone snaps Hayley out of her reverie. As she retrieves the device from a jacket pocket, her face reflects surprise. She can't recall the last time her younger sister, Tammy, called.

———————————

SHE REQUESTS TIME off from both of her bosses, public and covert, to attend Jessica Cole's funeral in Charleston. Kyle Rodgers tells Hayley to take as much time as she needs. Andrew Wilde is a more stringent taskmaster. He grants her only two days, barely enough time given the almost seven-hour drive. Hayley has not seen Jessica, her best friend growing up, since returning home for her mother's funeral years earlier. They spoke a few times on the phone—desultory conversations that left Hayley somewhat depressed—but their shared, scarred history bound them in ways that can't be said of many childhood friendships. Now Hayley is going back home for Jessica's funeral, a disorienting event but not wholly unexpected.

Jessica never left Green Shoals, marrying a boy from their high school and becoming pregnant almost immediately. Two more babies followed, a burden too great for the young marriage to bear. Jessica's husband lit out for California and a less demanding future. Like many in her situation, the young, single mother developed a dependence on opiates that left her incapable of performing parental duties. The children were raised by their grandmother as Jessica's illness devolved into a harrowing heroin addiction. Her repeated overdoses were unremarkable except for the last one that claimed her life. A motorist found Jessica's rail-thin corpse in the bathroom of a gas station.

Only seven other mourners attend the funeral service

and interment. Drug addiction has so thoroughly ravaged the community that scenes like Jessica's burial are
sadly commonplace. Standing at the gravesite and staring intently at the coffin poised for burial, Hayley feels
unconnected to the event. Rain threatens, a prospect
that matches the ritual's mood. In these circumstances
and others, Hayley's primary emotion is a pronounced
lack of emotion. How strange, too, that she can't recognize any of the faces encircling this black hole in the
ground. Bearing witness to the ceremony's dreary conclusion, Hayley reflects on her long absence from home and
childhood friends, and is ashamedly grateful for it. Had
she remained in West Virginia, would she have raced her
friend to an even earlier grave?

She strolls through the pointless garden of gravestones,
returning to her car in the cemetery parking lot. Hayley
prefers remembering Jessica for the giddy, scrappy girl of
her school years. For that reason, she avoids the requisite
conversations with the bedraggled funeral-goers that would
only corrupt those memories. Her youngest sister, Tammy,
lives in Chapmanville. Hayley points the car for the drive
south. In passing the speck of a town that was once her
home, Hayley once again feels nothing. She barely glances
at the bland structures that jut from the green landscape.
Green Shoals represents a prior life that has no connection to the one she lives now. This whole trip, it occurs to
her, is a continued exploration of emotional detachment.
She came because that's what people do. They attend the
funeral of their best childhood friend. But there's no guarantee you feel anything in the process, right?

Tammy answers the door, her girth enlarged with pregnancy in its eighth month. She is the only one of Hayley's five siblings to have stayed local. Nineteen years old, Tammy married her high school boyfriend the day of their graduation. With a calm smile and freckled cheeks framed by long, straight red hair parted down the middle, she looks every bit the high school homecoming queen she once was. Hayley adores her little sister in a way possible only with siblings separated in age by nearly seven years. That adulation is mutual. Tammy never tires of telling friends her big sister works in the White House, rubbing elbows with the president and inhabiting a city that is a veritable Shangri-La in comparison to Chapmanville. The sisters hug with genuine affection. Hayley is relieved to feel a stirring within her heart. Finally! She feels something genuine. In an instant, she knows that thing is love.

Tammy's husband, Jeff, is at work at a Walmart in Logan, giving the sisters plenty of time to visit. Hayley tells Tammy about her job as Kyle Rodgers's chief of staff, about the travesty of her romantic life, and, surprisingly, even about meeting Sam McGovern. Having talked plenty enough about herself, only something a favorite sister could draw out of her, Hayley goes silent and listens. Tammy opens up and relays the details of a small life by comparison but, in most ways, good. Jeff is proving to be a better husband than one might have considered possible of someone so young and inexperienced. The expectant parents are thrilled about the prospect of starting a family. They've enthusiastically outfitted their small rental home with items from Walmart for the baby's arrival. Sitting in a chair in the kitchen—the cherry tree outside the window having bloomed a month earlier but offering the ghost of a sweet scent even still—Hayley is flooded with emotion. These robust feelings are a welcome change to the existential void she'd experienced at Jessica's gravesite. A valiant sun has broken up the storm clouds' monopoly of the sky. Hayley decides her younger sister is an angel on earth.

Toward evening, Tammy retrieves a big cardboard box stuffed haphazardly with family photos. They are artifacts from a pre-smartphone era, and the two sisters delight in picking through the pile of random snapshots. So many photos of the six kids! The old photos incite more chatter between the sisters about their other siblings. Robert, second to the oldest, is stationed at Fort Benning, having washed out of Ranger School. Next is Harper, sickly like their mother was, who lives in Richmond and works at a Waffle House there. Sadie, a year younger, is shacked up with a biker dude in Florida. William, the youngest, hasn't been heard from by anyone in more than a year. The unspoken truth is that, of the six siblings, Tammy and Hayley seem to be doing the best.

Near the bottom of the pile, Hayley unearths a photo of four Marines grouped in front of a shrapnel-pocked armored personnel carrier. The man at the far right she recognizes as her father, glaring sternly at the camera in a clear effort to look sufficiently badass. Hayley holds the borderless photograph with reverence as if it were a religious icon.

"Wow," she says.

"Look at Daddy. Such a stud."

"This could've been taken in Fallujah."

"Is that where . . . is that the place where he was killed?" Tammy asks. His death in combat occurred when she was barely walking.

"Yeah. He'd been home just four months before. We had a party for him, down at the community center."

"That must've been really something," Tammy says, wistful.

Hayley continues to gaze at the picture, looking for answers. "I wonder who these other guys are."

Four Marines. High and tight haircuts. Tall, lean, and muscled. Two white. One black. One brown. The men represent the great melting pot that is the US military. Except for any differences in skin color, they are interchangeable. They are men at war. Brothers. One of them was their father.

"I wish I'd had a chance to really know him."

"He was a good man, Tammy." Hayley doesn't know what else to say, wishing she could give her sister more. "He was a really good man."

It's getting late. Hayley has to get on the road for the long drive back to Washington. She places the photograph to the side.

"Mind if I borrow this?" she asks, gesturing.

"Of course! Take it! Jeez, you have as much a right to it as I do. Take as many as you like."

Hayley shakes her head. "I just want this one."

WELL PAST TWO a.m., after she returned to her apartment on P Street, a last name scrawled on the back of the photo and sleuthing on the Internet has led Hayley to determine the identity of at least one of the other Marines. Charles Hicks has retired from active duty in favor of a desk job at the Pentagon. He is the other white guy in the photo and resembles Tommy Chill enough to be his brother. They stand next to one another, arms thrown over each other's shoulders. Without access to classified military databases, Hayley has never been able to gather details of her father's death. Despite repeated requests, the military refused to divulge more information other than the barest essential facts. Thomas Chill was killed in action during the later stages of the Second Battle of Fallujah. The old snapshot has had the profound effect of igniting within Hayley a desire to know more. Answers are within reach, as close as across the Potomac River. Sitting behind a desk in the Pentagon.

Hayley shuts down her computer and stands up from her seat in the apartment's living room. She has restored order to the space since the break-in, replacing those few items that she couldn't fix. Her place is a refuge again, familiar and organized. This new determination to learn more about her father's death is a good thing, Hayley decides. Not knowing the whole truth for so long is a source of constant anxiety. She wonders if the damage done, like her belongings in the busted-up apartment, can ever be repaired.

2

★ ★ ★ ★

THE BLUE LINE

***M**onday, 7:56 a.m.* Two days after returning from Jessica's funeral in Charleston, Hayley catches a southbound train on the Washington Metro Blue Line. She arrives at the Pentagon subway station nine minutes later. Charlie Hicks had expressed surprise to receive an email from the daughter of an Iraq War buddy and, with some hesitancy, agreed to her request for a face-to-face meeting. Passing through a secured-access facility on the ground level, Hayley is soon in search of Hicks's office in a building that is almost seven million square feet in size and the work site of more than twenty-three thousand civilian and military personnel. The pervasive orderliness and gleaming surfaces are a contrast to the West Wing's cluttered, chockablock work space. Exuding competence and devotional caretaking by its occupants, the Pentagon is the US military's mountaintop. Here warriors hold council.

As much as she was reluctant to do so, Hayley requested more time off. Public and covert supervisors granted her leave—a few hours of the morning at most—but more grudgingly this second time around. Andrew Wilde's text was terse in the extreme. *No more.* Her typical discipline and focus notwithstanding, Hayley feels compelled to take this small amount of time to search for answers regarding her father's death in Iraq. As she prowls the gargantuan military headquarters in search of Charlie Hicks's office, Hayley is confident the truth can be found somewhere within its walls.

SLID DOWN LOW in a chair by the door of a Starbucks on E Street in Foggy Bottom, he wears a Manchester United soccer jersey, black tracksuit pants, and snapback ball cap from the Iron Pony Tap Room. Outside the window to his right, morning in the nation's capital unfolds with the promise of a gorgeous spring day. It's perfect riding weather, but duties prohibit rolling his motorcycle out of the garage. Rafi Zamani considers ordering another tea, delaying a return to his dark apartment on F Street. With straight black hair, full eyebrows, a fine nose, and dazzling white teeth, he appears younger than his twenty-nine years. Effectively masking the clatter of the coffee shop with wireless Jabra earbuds, he thumb-scrolls the screen on his Pixel 3 XL, checking out custom motorcycles on Instagram. Rafi owns a Ducati Monster, but he pines for a

BMW R nineT because that was Tom Cruise's ride in the latest *Mission Impossible* movie.

His French bulldog, Yazat, strains on his leash lashed to the chair leg, toward a crouching coed from Georgetown—long blond hair, dimpled smile—who offers a friendly hand. She says something to Rafi, but he makes no effort to hear her. So fucking annoying. Can't she see he's busy? For maybe the hundredth time, he opens the Signal app to see if the message he has been waiting for has come from the Boss.

Sure enough, it's there. A two-word message.

Do it.

Finally! He'll make a quick dash back to the apartment and tap a few keys on his laptop. The rest of the day will be his to fill as he pleases. Maybe ride up to Bob's Motorcycles in Jessup and road test that BMW. Why the fuck not?

He slips the phone into his pants pocket, unlashes Yazat from the chair leg, and stands. The blond chick is saying something to him, about the dog no doubt. Rafi taps one of the earbuds, pausing playback.

"So cute!" the coed says in regard to Yazat.

Like, he hasn't heard that before?

Rafi says, "Thanks."

"Just. So. Cute."

He checks her out from head to toe. What he could do with her, Rafi muses. Man, how incredible would that be?

"What's his name?" she asks.

They never want to know what *his* name is.

"Yazat," he says without expression, staring at her with hollow eyes.

Same old story. Why believe it would be any different this time? He's a handsome guy, with an insanely adorable dog. Good-looking women are friendly to him . . . initially. But within moments of meeting—and the inevitable awkward conversation that always follows—that look came over their faces. Disinterest. Rafi has learned from experience that attractive females won't give him five minutes of their precious time, let alone any sex. Fuck 'em. He taps the earbud again. Music resumes playback. This dumb blonde won't let up, though, cooing over the dog like she's never seen one before. Stupid fucking bitches. He's outta here.

———————————

MONDAY, 8:48 A.M. She finds Charlie Hicks's small, windowless office, 2B513, on the second floor, B ring. Rapping gently on the open door, Hayley strolls into the cramped office—repository to stacks of stuffed file folders, binders, and loose papers—and finds it empty. Hicks isn't in. She steps back into the gleaming hallway and looks in both directions for her father's war buddy. There's no sign of him. Hayley reenters the office and stands just inside the doorway, contemplating her next move.

Her vetting of Charlie Hicks revealed that he had been a Marine scout sniper with seventy-eight confirmed kills in three tours of duty, bouncing between Iraq and Afghanistan. Never married, Hicks seemed to have little life outside the military. Taking a desk job at the Pentagon

pushing paper following his discharge several years earlier seemed the logical solution for a man with few other
interests. Hayley knows a small army of keyboard punch-
ers is required to spend $680 billion a year. The resultant
mountain of paperwork has given Charlie Hicks a job for
life. But why stand her up? Hayley checks her phone for
the email confirming their meeting time.

The office phone on Hicks's desk jangles. After three
rings, Hayley goes to the desk.

"Charlie Hicks's office," Hayley says into the phone.

"Oh my gosh. Hayley Chill? Is that you?" The voice
of a middle-aged male possesses the same sort of twang
of the Southeast shared by so many of the US military's
members. It is the accent that Hayley will ease back
into after a few too many shots of tequila. From Hicks,
though, there is a brittle edge. Fear creeps in from the
corners of his voice.

"Yes, sir. This is Hayley. Am I speaking with Charlie
Hicks?"

"Yes, Hayley. I'm sorry. Something called me away
from my office. And I . . . I didn't have your cell phone
number on me. Truly, I couldn't avoid this. I'm really
very sorry."

"Are you in the building, sir? I can come—"

"No, Hayley. I'm sorry. I can't even talk long here on
the phone. Maybe if we reschedule another time? I'm
really sorry about this mix-up. I was really looking forward
to meeting Tommy's daughter, all grown up. And working
at the White House! My gosh, that's really something!"

How else is it possible to make the dead tangible

again but through their offspring? Cognizant of the fact she is her father's surrogate, Hayley allows for Hicks's emotionalism.

"I can wait a bit, if—"

"Gosh darn it. I'm going to be hung up here, on another floor. Just a ton of paperwork, as you can see. Now you know where old Marines go to die!" he says, too brightly.

"Not all of them," Hayley says with flat intonation. She doesn't care if he suffers from survivor's remorse. Fuck that. What about *her* survivor's remorse?

The silence over the phone line is abruptly mournful. She has struck a nerve.

"Your father was a good man. Saved plenty of lives over there. Tough-ass Marine."

"Thank you, sir . . ."

"Please, everyone calls me Charlie."

There isn't a chance of that. "I hoped you might help me out with something, sir."

"Oh, man, I only have a few more seconds here. So sorry, really."

She retrieves the snapshot and studies it. "The photo I emailed you, sir. Where was this taken? Do you recall?"

His voice regains some strength. "Sure, I do! Camp Fallujah. The Eighty-Second Airborne took it from the Mujahadeen-e-Khalq in 2003 and the First Marine Expeditionary came in a year later, in 2004."

"Okay . . ." She doesn't need a history lesson.

"Gosh, Hayley, I'm sorry but I really gotta be going . . ."

"Can you identify the other two men?"

"Of course, I can. Ernesto Miranda, my sniper team partner, is one. And Eugene Davis. He was in Tommy's company and probably your dad's best buddy. Good Marine."

Hayley jots down the names in a small notebook. Over the phone, Hicks continues talking, unprompted and somewhat nervously. His agitation seems beyond his control. As he talks, Hayley considers a strong possibility the combat veteran suffers from post-traumatic stress.

"Ernesto and me were assigned to Tommy and Eugene's unit, Alpha Company, First Battalion, Seventh Marine Regiment. We were pretty popular, to tell you the truth. Everybody likes a sniper team on overwatch, know what I mean? We saw some shit in Anbar, excuse my French."

"I was in the army, sir," Hayley says, dismissing Hicks's flimsy attempt at decorum.

"You never thought about joining the corps?"

"I wanted to serve in combat arms, and the Marines seemed a less likely opportunity for that."

"No longer the case!" Hicks says with pride.

"Do you know where I can find Mr. Davis or Mr. Miranda now, sir?"

"Both in Arlington, I'm sad to say. Gene was killed in action less than a month after Tommy. Ernesto, car crash about two years back, in Oklahoma City."

Hayley nods, taking a beat before asking her next question. "Can you tell me about the day my father died?"

"The day he died?" His voice sounds distant, as if he'd lowered the phone away from his mouth.

"Yes, sir."

"What do the brass hats have to say about all of that?"

"I'm curious what you have to say, sir. And I'm having trouble hearing you now. Can you—?"

Hicks's voice is louder and more emphatic. "Did you read the battle report? Did they give the family that much?"

Hayley files away Hicks's use of "the" rather than "your."

"Yes. I've read the report. Years ago, when I was at Fort Hood. There wasn't much to it. Second Battle for Fallujah. The date. Contractor Bridge. KIA. That was about it."

"That's all, huh?"

She can feel the rush of blood under her skin. A quickness of breath. The anger. There has always been that. And Hicks's brittle evasiveness is doing nothing to mollify it.

"You were there, sir. You must know something more than what's in the official battle report."

"Hayley, I really wish I could help. But I *wasn't* there. Ernesto and me were tasked to a different unit that day. We were all on the same operation, infiltrating the city, sector by sector, gunning after fleeing enemy forces. By mid-November, it was mostly a mopping up exercise. Almost every day we would stumble on pockets of resistance. It was a hot mess, ya know? Lotta confusion. After ten days straight of fighting, we were all bone tired. Tommy's unit was sweeping a block just to the west of our unit. I heard the explosions. We all did. By the time we got over there, well . . ."

"Yes?" Hayley asks impatiently, pressing.

"A lotta guys . . . lost a lotta good guys." The inelastic tone of his voice suggests Hicks is struggling for composure.

"Yes, sir. Including my father."

"I don't even know who else was with Tommy when . . . when all of that happened. Like I said, after ten days of hard fighting, things had kinda busted down. You could be a hundred yards away from a unit, might as well have been on another planet. That place, I tell you, that place was just hell on earth."

Hayley didn't need Hicks to tell her how bad it was there. As an eight-year-old, she learned firsthand the destructive power of war. Unable to accept the truth of his death, she broke into the funeral home where Tommy Chill's casket had been deposited the day before. Prying open his government-issued coffin, the child bore witness to her father's obliterated remains. Was it IED or RPG? Was her father's unit under attack or on the offensive? Had other Marines in his unit been killed at the same time? Who was with her dad when he died, someone who might provide firsthand knowledge of the incident? She has so many questions that demand answers. Despite the years that have passed since her father's death in Iraq, Hayley becomes enraged all over again. How many more times will she experience this explosive dread?

"But other men in my dad's unit survived. They walked out of there. Didn't *they* report anything about what happened?"

Over the phone line, she hears the former Marine mumble to himself, his words garbled and indistinct. How could she have pressed him like this? The man is a ruin, obviously having ducked meeting her in person because of his debilitation. Their phone conversation has revealed the former sniper's cluttered, little office in the Pentagon is more a spider hole than cushy retirement gig.

"I'm sorry, sir."

Hicks emits only a strained grunt before the phone line goes dead.

God, what have I done? she wonders with burning regret.

———————————

MONDAY, 10:07 A.M. She catches the Blue Line heading north, which travels under the Potomac and into the federal district. Hayley estimates she'll be at her desk in the West Wing by ten-thirty a.m. As the train leaves the subterranean Pentagon station, she decides it's time to get back to work in more ways than one. This renewed obsession with her father's death in Iraq is a vicious spiral that leads only downward. Let the dead stay dead. And leave Charlie Hicks in peace. Further inquiry would be both futile *and* sadistic. She has enough on her plate already.

Checking her KryptAll phone before the train heads into the tunnel that goes under the river, Hayley sees she has received a message from Andrew Wilde.

No further information regarding your intruder.

So analysis by Publius of the surveillance footage of her apartment break-in proved futile. Hayley isn't surprised. From the outset, Andrew Wilde was dismissive of her concerns. Is his indifference evidence of the imminent termination of her work for the deeper state? Or was the incident nothing more than a random robbery? To the best of her knowledge, the intruder took only a jar of quarters she kept on the dresser. For someone like Hayley, the uncertainty is maddening. Without one shred of actionable intelligence, there is nothing to be done.

Her only recourse is to continue operating with her customary caution. She will exercise extreme vigilance for any sign of surveillance or investigation by a bad actor. Nevertheless, Hayley must recognize her position with Publius feels increasingly tenuous. The more she thinks on it—her train reaching its mandated top speed of 59 mph—the less sure Hayley feels about *anything*.

She clocks that funny itch on the back of her neck. A sense of foreboding. Seconds later, a terrifying, metal-on-metal screech fills the train car's interior. Because of that premonition and her excellent reflexes, Hayley can brace herself with both hands against the seat back in front of her a fraction of a second before the entire train bucks violently and lurches to the right. Most passengers are ejected from their seats as the lights flicker off. The nightmarish roller-coaster ride continues for ten agonizing seconds longer, the racket deafening, when the thrusting and violent thuds finally cease. Abrupt silence follows. In those earliest moments, there is only disorientation and disbelief.

The wails and moaning that rise from the inky gloom are evidence there have been many injuries. Unable to see in the darkness, Hayley runs both hands over her body and finds no injuries. Searching her bag in the dark, she ascertains the KryptAll phone is safely stowed and then retrieves her regular work iPhone. Utilizing the flashlight feature, Hayley observes the scene around her. The train car seems intact, contrary to her earliest fears, but its passengers—she estimates there are approximately twenty in total—lie scattered throughout the length of the carriage.

Hayley stands and moves forward, illuminating her way in the darkness with her phone. Doing a quick triage on the passengers she encounters, Hayley determines a woman—in her sixties, dress blood soaked—has sustained the most severe injuries. Suspecting the victim's femoral artery might be bleeding out, Hayley stops there to lend first aid.

Another man about her age sits on the floor next to the older woman, nursing what looks like a broken left hand.

"Is your other hand okay?" Hayley asks the young man. He nods, his stunned expression pale in the dim light of her smartphone.

"Hold my phone. I've got to stop her bleeding," the deeper state operative says, gesturing toward the woman. Her voice—calm and knowing—demands obedience. The young man takes the phone and directs the flashlight downward.

Hayley pushes the woman's skirt up to her hip, exposing a gaping wound that pulsates dark blood with every beat of her heart. Checking the gash for any foreign objects, she has difficulty seeing in the unsteady light.

"Hold still!" she says to her helper. Off his embarrassed expression, Hayley softens her tone. "She'll lose forty percent of her blood in less than three minutes."

"Should we make a tourniquet or something?"

Hayley has finished her inspection of the wound and is confident there are no foreign objects embedded there. She starts removing her sweater.

"Unless you happen to have a commercial tourniquet on you, direct pressure is more effective . . . especially with the femoral artery."

With her upper body weight, Hayley presses her rolled-up sweater on the gash. The semiconscious woman moans but doesn't appear to be in shock.

"My hand is pretty fucked-up," the young man says, apropos to nothing.

Hayley ignores him, focusing her attention on the older woman again. Satisfied the leg is well supported, she leans with most of her weight on the wound. Minutes tick past. The young man looks on, thoroughly chastised. His grip on the phone is steady. Hayley's calm competence makes a strong impression on him. Tomorrow he will enroll in a free class at the local Red Cross, where he will acquire certification in first aid and CPR. That experience will compel him to return to college, which he never completed, and pursue premed coursework. Five years after the subway accident, he will enter medical school and ultimately acquire his degree, with a specialty in emergency medicine. Throughout a thirty-eight-year career, Hayley's dragooned helper on the Metro car will save countless lives. He will retire eventually and live a quiet life in Bethesda, Maryland, in the company of kids and grandkids, forgetting entirely the example of the competent, young woman who inspired him to alter his life's path.

The woman's blood loss appears to have been slowed by Hayley's efforts. "I think she's going to be okay," she says to no one in particular.

Shouts drift into the car from outside, accompanied by flashlights that play across the shattered windows and subway tunnel walls. Having approached via the subway tunnel leading from the Rosslyn station, first responders flood onto the scene within ten minutes of the derailment. Firefighters relieve Hayley.

"You saved her life," a firefighter says to the White House staffer as she steps back to give the emergency workers room to do their job. Hayley doesn't respond, following other firefighters who lead ambulatory passengers off the train and back up the tunnel illuminated by dozens of helmet-mounted flashlights. Glancing over her shoulder, she sees where the train's first three cars have jumped the track. Hayley considers herself fortunate to be walking away from the accident without a scratch.

She treks back to the Rosslyn station through a mostly dark subway tunnel. Thirty minutes later, Hayley finally emerges into daylight again as she climbs the last steps up to the sidewalk along Fort Myer Drive. Bright, spring sunshine casts the scene of pandemonium in a garish light. Emergency personnel give aid to the injured. A growing crowd of gawkers, drawn by media reports, clogs the sidewalks. Police and emergency vehicle sirens wail in every direction. Hayley's path forward is blocked by the mob of onlookers. Impatient to get back to work, she forces her way through the crowd to the open street, where she hails a passing cab.

MONDAY, 1:03 P.M. When Hayley walks into the office, Kyle Rodgers looks up from work on his desk with an alarmed expression.

"My God, Hayley, are you okay? Shouldn't you be at the hospital?" He stands and goes to her.

"I'm fine, sir. Really."

Rodgers points at the blood on her forearms. "You're bleeding!"

"Not mine. I was lucky."

She allows him to guide her to a chair.

"You should take the day off."

Hayley shakes her head, adamant. "I've wasted enough time, sir. Is anybody saying what caused the crash?"

"Metro's system network went down. The entire Blue Line was affected. Cyber Jihad claimed responsibility ten minutes after the derailment."

"Sir?" Hayley hadn't even considered the possibility of sabotage.

"Fort Meade is all over it."

"General Hernandez thinks Cyber Jihad is a Russian cover."

"I was at the meeting. Remember?"

She nods, preoccupied. What she really wants to do is question the president whether or not he'd made contact with his GRU handler. Cyber sabotage of Washington's Metro Blue Line required much more sophisticated skills and premeditation than the hack of the nation's newspapers. Hayley guesses only a handful of players possess the know-how to hit, with precision, a single line of the district's mass transit system. With nothing more than a layman's awareness of signals intelligence, she feels ill-equipped to deal with the looming specter of a first cyber war between superpowers.

MONDAY, 2:15 P.M. Riding in the back of his chauffeured SUV, General Hernandez scans a report compiled by Unit F6. It's the one department in the entire agency he trusts to get attribution right. Alfred Updike, nominated for a slew of prestigious prizes in computer science and winner of the Turing Award, runs the unit. The team he has assembled is equally superb. Their preliminary analysis of the incident suggests the malware inserted in the Metro's computer network originated from the same server in Estonia that had been used in the newspaper hack. Fucking Russians. Hitting the *New York Times* so that a single day's edition couldn't make its press run is one thing. But derailing a train in the nation's capital is a goddamn act of war!

As if that indignation isn't enough, now he has to trot over to DHS headquarters to brief that know-nothing cabinet secretary. Plucked from Congress after a long stint manufacturing aircraft and missile systems, what does Clare Ryan know about cyber security? Hernandez, a combat veteran and holding master's degrees from Defense Intelligence College and USC, resents answering to the refugee from Boeing's executive offices. Less than one hour after the attack on the Metro, Monroe signed an executive order that expanded DHS mandate, merging it with Cyber Command's spectrum of operations. Hernandez suspects Kyle Rodgers had something to do with the surprise move by the president, a ham-handed attempt to muzzle him. Fat chance of that happening.

Almost impossible to believe, Clare Ryan keeps him waiting in the reception area for fifteen minutes past their start time. A television mounted on the wall is tuned to CNN, with the volume turned down. Hernandez watches news coverage of the train derailment. The cyberattack on the newspapers, ironically, generated practically zero press whatsoever. Who cares about newspapers? Today's media coverage is a different animal entirely. Though there were no fatalities, more than sixty passengers were taken to area hospitals for treatment, and a dozen of them are reported to be in critical condition. Fanned by the cable news hysteria machine, Cyber Jihad's claim of responsibility stokes fears of Islamic fanatics attacking the nation's transportation, financial, and utility networks with more and deadlier cyber weapons. In the aftermath of the Metro attack, public hysteria has gone from zero to sixty in a single news cycle. Some pundits—irresponsible nitwits who have no real skin in the game—go so far as to call the derailment of the Blue Line train a precursor to the next 9/11. In Hernandez's opinion, the Metro attack is a harbinger of far graver dangers than what happened in New York.

Clare's assistant replaces her desk phone handset in its cradle. "The secretary is ready for you now, General."

Hernandez, wearing his army service uniform, stands and strides through the open door. Secretary Ryan is indeed waiting for him. Alert and relaxed, she stands up from behind an emphatically clean desktop and comes around to shake hands with the director of both the NSA and US Cyber Command.

"General Hernandez, thank you for coming over to my neck of the woods. Please, take a seat."

He follows her into the expansive office. "What can I do for you, Madam Secretary?"

The general's bearing isn't friendly. They are rivals for everything there is to contest in Washington: money, power, and influence. Both recognize that one of them will ultimately prevail over the other. Monroe's executive order has had the effect of throwing two pit bulls in the same ring, with a raw steak between them. There are no draws in this fight. One winner and one loser. Time will tell.

Clare suppresses a scoffing laugh. Hernandez's casually insincere question hardly befits a day of America suffering its worst cyberattack. "General, we're going to be asked by the president for our recommendation. It's our responsibility to prepare a measured and thoroughly vetted report, especially considering some of the irresponsible news coverage of the attack. For the sake of the country, it's time we shelve any animosity between us. A united front is highly preferable."

The general is unmoved by Clare's appeal for cooperation. "My advice to the president will be the same as before. We must respond to the Russian action with a cyberattack of proportionate scope. Anything less than an aggressive and dynamic response will be viewed by our adversary as an indisputable sign of weakness, and accurately so."

"You've confirmed attribution, with a high level of confidence?" Clare asks with bald skepticism.

"No, not full attribution. But you can be confident I have my best people on it, Madam Secretary."

"By best, I assume you mean Alfred Updike?"

"F6 has been on this since before the attack on the newspapers."

"Good. I would love to see the report."

Hernandez visibly stiffens. "The data is still pretty raw."

"President Monroe's executive order mandates our cooperation, General."

Hernandez looks like he's just taken a spoonful of lukewarm castor oil. "You're not getting your paws on F6. Updike is mine!"

Clare is unfazed by the director's outburst. "I could be persuaded to ease off. The Department of Homeland Security has mathematicians on staff as gifted as anyone over at Savage Road. But I need to know that we're all on the same team."

Hernandez has managed to compose himself. Losing his temper will help nothing. "What do you want, Madam Secretary?"

Clare smiles lightly. Male blowhards like Hernandez have been a fixture in a professional life that included Boeing and the House of Representatives. "If we're going to advise the president to start a cyber war, attribution can be nothing short of gold plated, General."

As he suspected, the executive order was Kyle Rodgers's attempt to silence him. That's tough. Hernandez has no intention of playing nice if it means ignoring his patriotic obligation to punish the Russian bear. "You're free to tell POTUS whatever you please."

Clare frowns, her voice flattened by sarcasm. "How kind of you. I'll try remembering your generosity when Russia responds to the NSA's provocation by moving troops into Ukraine."

Hernandez shrugs. "Moscow does as Moscow wants." He turns for the door.

"Can my people see the report? What F6 has come up with by way of analytics?" she asks to his back.

Hernandez barely pauses on his way out. "Keep checking your inbox, Madam Secretary."

———————

HAYLEY DOESN'T LEAVE the White House complex until ten that night. The fresh air and balmy temperature—

a harbinger of muggy days to come—is a relief after being cooped up in the West Wing. Following the Metro attack, simmering concerns about the nation's cyber security have exploded into a real crisis. Monroe rises to the occasion, of course, presenting just the right measure of calm leadership and firm resolve. He "plays" president well, which might explain why Moscow covertly drafted him as a candidate for the nation's highest office. For the time being, at least, the Metro attack has had the positive effect of silencing Monroe's critics. Among administration staffers, hopes for a second term have been reignited.

Hayley knows better. Over the past twenty months, she has witnessed the president's terrible mood swings and depression. Even without the psychological training received at the deeper state's training site in Oregon, she understands that Richard Monroe desperately craves escape from his impossible predicament.

She takes her time on the walk home. It had been an emotionally draining day, beginning with the unsettling visit to the Pentagon to see Charlie Hicks and only getting worse with the Metro derailment. Only now does she recall the voice mail on her office phone from Sam McGovern. He called the White House in the late afternoon, following up on their chance meeting at Darlington House. But his voice message barely registered in a day of seemingly unending chaos. Hayley's mind works in such a peculiar way, her encyclopedic memory like an overstuffed closet. Essential items can become lost in the clutter. In her roundabout way, she only now recalls this effort Sam made to connect with her. Brooding on it, Hayley realizes his call was easily the best thing that happened in an otherwise dreadful day. As she strolls north, Hayley reaches for her phone and dials the number he left in his voice mail.

Sam answers on the second ring.

"How's it going?" he asks brightly.

"I was on that train, slugger."

"What? Are you okay?" Sam's alarm seems authentic.

His concern moves her, an emotion she pushes down. "I'm fine, really. My paramedical training came in handy."

"Gosh, I wish I could've been there to help. Our unit was working a building fire on Twenty-Fifth Street."

"Honorable mention for being the first person in a long time to say 'gosh.'" She thinks about it for a second. "Maybe ever."

Sam is undoubtedly secure enough to laugh at himself. "I didn't even realize I said it."

"That's okay. I like it."

In his embarrassment, the fireman changes the subject. "Cyber Jihad, huh?"

"If that's what the TV says."

"Are you sure you're okay? Can I see you? Buy you a drink?"

"I'm whipped. Rain check?"

"Sure. Call me when you're ready. I don't want to be a pest."

"You're not a pest." After a pause, she says, "I'm glad you called."

Sam's inordinately pleased she has said these words. "And I'm glad you weren't hurt."

They continue talking for a few minutes, relieved that the hard part of just *making* the first phone call was over. Hayley tells him about the crash and suspicions of a Russian-sponsored cyberattack. He asks questions and never once acts like he knows more than she does. It feels easy, the banter between them. After they make their goodbyes, Hayley is surprised to be standing across the street from her apartment building. Without realizing it, their conversation has carried her the whole walk home. Recognition of her nearly immediate connection with the fireman troubles Hayley. Does she have the time and energy for something resembling a real relationship? For most of her adult life, the deeper state operative has adopted more of a "gun-and-run" romantic strategy. A prospective partner who seems, superficially, at least, to be a normal, well-adjusted man slightly unnerves her. As she crosses the street, approaching the entrance to her building, Hayley decides she won't call him for at least a week. Better to allow the urgency of this thing between them, whatever it might be, to flatten out and test its durability. If she still has the itch to see Sam McGovern again after a cooling-off period, then maybe there's something to it.

As Hayley punches the entry code to unlock the door to the building, she hears movement in the darkness to her right and instinctively braces for an attack.

"You look like shit," a female voice says, without menace.

A young woman, wearing ripped jeans, a James Perse T-shirt, and a Chanel bouclé jacket, steps out from the shadows. Hayley hasn't seen April Wu in more than two years, not since leaving the Publius training camp in central Oregon. They had a rocky start there, to the extent that Hayley broke April's finger in a "test your mettle" fight over cafeteria seating. That hostile rivalry quickly evolved into a friendly one. Of the several dozen agent candidates vying for the assignment of the organization's first operation, the deeper state would select only one. Mission details were unknown at that time. Hayley would eventually learn the truth, of course, but their superiors never informed the other agent candidates of Richard Monroe's identity as a Russian mole.

Hayley is pleasantly surprised to see her rival from training camp. But she remains guarded, nonetheless. Her orders are clear. The exact nature of her operation at the White House must be withheld from April. Publius wants its agents compartmentalized when it comes to privileged information.

"Maybe I don't feel like spending half of my annual income on clothes. What the hell are you doing here, April?"

April laughs, incredulous. *"Half?"* She gestures toward the door. "You mind?"

Hayley privately chides herself. Whatever her deeper state colleague has to say requires privacy. They head inside her building.

"You've been in DC all this time? Why didn't you contact me? Are you active duty?" Hayley's questions come rapid-fire. She wants to point out that she thought they were friends and that the army lieutenant's negligence to visit has hurt her feelings, but she refrains from saying the words.

April isn't the least bit contrite. "I didn't know you were here, either. That is, not until I saw your name splayed all over the news after that business at Camp David," she says, referring to the assassination attempt early in the president's second year in office. "I don't think they wanted us just hanging out."

Hayley nods, in control of her emotions. Some unidentifiable thing about April seems off. What is it? Until she knows the reason for this surprise visit, the less said the better.

"Was that your mission? To protect the president from the . . . *Shady Side cabal*?" April asks, mockingly waggling all ten fingers.

"You know I can't talk about the specifics of my assignment."

"Well, it's kind of obvious, isn't it?" It still irks her that their superiors selected Hayley for Publius's first mission. *She* could be going to work at the West Wing every day. *She* could have saved the president's life.

Hayley asks, "What about you? Are you still in?"

"With Publius? Of course. Not long after you left training camp, they sent us all back into the world. Sleeper agents, I guess you could call us. I went back to where they first found me."

"Cyber Command?"

April nods. "I like the work. Most of the people there are humongous math nerds, but I can deal with that."

"Being kind of a nerd yourself."

"There are worse things," April says, finishing her beer. Like Hayley, April hasn't managed to forge much in the way of stable relationships as an adult. Despite relaxing into spontaneous chatter, there is a sense of buying time.

They talk. All the while, Hayley studies April's every move. What is it about the other woman that nags at her? Hayley has relied on a preternatural instinct for deception all of her life. And those alarm bells clang loudly inside her head.

April stands up from the kitchen table to grab a couple more beers. "You want another, right?"

"Sure." Hayley watches April go to the refrigerator. As casually as possible, she says, "Weird thing is, I've been getting this vibe from Andrew Wilde."

"Really?" April starts to return to the table with two fresh bottles.

"And whoever he answers to."

The army lieutenant nods, seemingly intrigued, and starts to sit down again.

"You mind grabbing me the charger? My phone's almost zeroed out."

"Sure." April turns and retreats into the kitchen. She stops in front of the middle drawer, pulls it open, and retrieves the charger.

Returning to the table, she freezes, a stricken look on her face. "Shit."

Within only a few seconds, April finds herself on the floor, flat on her stomach and right arm wrenched behind her.

Straddling the other woman's back, Hayley leans down close to April's ear. "It's almost as if they don't trust me."

Clenching her teeth against the quickly intensifying pain radiating from her right shoulder, April says, "I guess they don't."

"So it *was* you."

"Ripping this Chanel jacket won't necessarily facilitate my cooperation."

"But it might."

"Get off me for Christ's sake. I was only following orders."

Hayley releases her submission hold and stands up. April also gets to her feet, albeit more slowly.

April sits. She takes a few extra seconds to crack open one beer and then the other, needing the extra moment to compose herself. "The charger fetch was just for confirmation. What gave it away?"

"The things a black balaclava can't hide." She points at April's face. "Your eyes." Then traces her finger down the length of the army lieutenant's body. "The way you carry yourself."

April shrugs but betrays a measure of defeat. "Like I said, I was only following orders."

Hayley sits. "The standard defense of concentration camp guards, not good friends."

"Good? Really?"

Hayley accepts the bottle from April and takes a quick drink. "You didn't find anything, did you?"

"I also didn't break anything . . . of real value."

"You owe me about fifteen bucks. My laundry money."

"Fourteen-fifty, to be exact."

"They tell you why?"

"My instructions were to look for anything weird. Anything out of place." She shrugs. "Consider it due diligence."

Hayley ruminates on it for a moment. "These fucking guys."

"They really don't trust us, Hayley."

"Why should I even trust you?"

"Don't. It's your choice."

"Due diligence for what?"

April grins, all of a sudden having a good time. "For joining my team."

"Excuse me?"

"Cyber Jihad. Publius wants to know who's behind the cyberattacks and doesn't trust the administration or IC to provide accurate attribution," says April, referring to the intelligence community.

Hayley is still trying to wrap her mind around her recruitment by April Wu. "But you're stationed at Cyber Command, a computer science major from West Point. I'm stuck in an office at the White House and can't program a microwave oven. How am I supposed to help you?"

"I don't know, Hayley. Maybe you can tell me," April

says pointedly. The army lieutenant tilts the Pabst Blue Ribbon beer, drains the bottle, and then slams it down again, releasing a loud belch.

"God," Hayley says, waving a hand in the space between them.

April stands and heads for the door visible through the kitchen doorway.

Hayley jumps to her feet and follows April into the kitchen area. As much as she needs her friend's expertise to cope with the threat posed by Cyber Jihad, it irks her the way Andrew Wilde has engineered their partnership. "Next time you need to search my place, maybe just ask."

"What fun would that be?"

The door is shut with an exclamation mark.

Hayley spins on the balls of her feet and marches back into the kitchen, where she left the KryptAll phone in her bag.

She trashes my place, THEN you ask me to back her up?

After Hayley has sent the message, she stares at the phone's screen and waits for a response from Andrew Wilde. It comes within seconds.

I don't know whether to be impressed by your skills or disappointed in hers.

Hayley taps out her response. *What the hell is going on?*

For a long moment, there is no reply from her superior. Then, the phone vibrates with the entirety of Wilde's message back. *Help her but your mission is the priority.*

Hayley rears her arm back to throw the device against the wall and barely refrains from doing so. Raised in poverty, she appreciates the value of things.

———————————

TUESDAY, 5:50 A.M. She meets Clare Ryan at Lincoln's Waffle Shop on Tenth Street. A spring shower releases a near torrent on the street outside, but inside the tidy restaurant, it's dry and wholly welcoming. To say the place is no-frills is an understatement. Lunch is available for less than five bucks if you don't mind settling for a not-bad hot dog. The Homeland Security secretary has ordered one of Lincoln's signature waffles. Hayley makes do with coffee, dry wheat toast, and a hard-boiled egg.

"How the hell do you get through a morning on that?" Clare asks, gesturing toward her companion's Spartan breakfast.

"I had a big dinner last night."

"No, you didn't." Given the unfolding crisis, Clare knows no one in the West Wing had the time to eat a damn thing yesterday.

"Light eating, light on my toes, ma'am."

Clare unabashedly digs into her waffle. "What would I know about that?"

Though the cabinet secretary is ten pounds over what would be considered an ideal weight for a woman of her age and body frame, Clare Ryan couldn't care less. Her well-tailored wool crepe suit, nude kid leather pump, and shoulder strap Tanner Krolle purse are a testament of a woman of a certain means, taste, and achievement. Her self-esteem is secure.

"I'm not going to have any luck getting you to call me Clare, am I?" she asks, happily chewing her first big bite of fried, doughy goodness.

"Not likely, ma'am."

Clare shrugs. "So I had a fascinating meeting with the NSA director yesterday afternoon, who was nice enough to swing by my office. I don't think anyone has talked to me like that since the third grade."

"General Hernandez can be abrupt."

The cabinet secretary lets loose a sharp laugh. "Abrupt? I love it! I can see how you've gotten as far as quickly as you have."

Clare Ryan was born in 1975 and raised in Santa Cruz, California. Both of her parents were professors at the university and encouraged curiosity, intellectual rigor, and athletics in their only child. An accomplished surfer by the age of eight, Clare spent countless hours in the lineups at Pleasure Point and Steamer Lane. Having a high school boyfriend who worked weekends and summers at Santa Cruz's boardwalk had its perks. Fifteen-year-old Clare attained local fame by setting an unofficial record for the most continuous rides in a single, twelve-hour day of operation (144) on the Giant Dipper roller coaster. Besides these achievements, Clare was an excellent student with a host of community-minded extracurricular activities. Acceptance by every college submitted an application wasn't a surprise, nor was her selection as valedictorian at Brown University four years later.

As she embarked on her business career, few obstacles remained in her path for very long. Following a two-year stint at Goldman Sachs, Clare obtained an MBA from Harvard and then resumed her meteoric rise. Recruited by the Boeing Corporation not long after the transfer of its headquarters from Seattle to Chicago in 2001, Clare gravitated toward the company's defense-oriented division for no other reason than missiles offered the quickest advancement. With typical competence and focus, she was a driving force behind Boeing's development and manufacture of the SLAM-ER (Standoff Land Attack Missile-Expanded Response) precision-guided, air-launched cruise missile weapon system, an early utilization of terminal phase target acquisition via an onboard computer (DSMAC). Clare's superiors in the company were not the only folks to take note of her outstanding achievement in the deployment of these tactical weapons.

The War Resistance League, headquartered in London, boasted a global membership of fewer than one hundred people. What the outlaw organization lacked in numbers was more than made up for by the outlandishness of their criminal actions. Mail bombs, sabotage, and kidnappings were all tools employed by WRL in pursuit of its political goals. Fighting fire with fire was the organization's governing philosophy. A profile of Clare in *Forbes* magazine, trumpeting her work in the international sale of the Harpoon weapons system, propelled her to the top of the activists' target list. Snatched from the parking garage of her condo, Clare was held captive by domestic terrorists—four men and three women—for fifty-one days in a rented farmhouse in the Upper Peninsula of Michigan. Miles from the closest neighbor and ineptly heated, the ramshackle structure was Clare's prison until Boeing paid a ransom of $500,000 and took out a full-page advertisement in the *New York Times* apologizing for the suffering around the world caused by weapons the company had manufactured.

Within a week of Clare Ryan's release, the FBI captured all seven of the plot's active perpetrators and arrested a dozen of their supporters. The experience was life altering for the conspiracy's sole victim. Clare quit Boeing, got her law degree from the University of Chicago Law School, and ran for political office, winning a seat to represent Illinois's Fourth Congressional District. With an indomitable resolve forged in the crucible of her kidnapping ordeal, Clare dedicated herself to mastering issues of domestic safety. In her third term, she secured the coveted chairmanship of the House Committee on Homeland Security. After Richard Monroe's election, Representative Ryan was the logical choice for heading up DHS. It seemed a long and twisty journey—from surfing the break at Pleasure Point to cabinet secretary—but also a perfectly logical one. The woman with iron determination running the show at the Department of Homeland Security is the same who secured the record for most consecutive rides on the Santa Cruz boardwalk roller coaster. Clare Ryan knows what she wants and, more crucially, how to get it.

Marriage came later in her life. Not until her first

reelection to Congress did Clare truly appreciate the
advantage of having a husband. Otto, a successful
Georgetown heart surgeon, brought her companionship,
an end to the rumors that she was gay, and, at the age of
forty-three, a son. With both of them being extremely
busy people, their time together has been limited since
their earliest days of matrimony. Like many romantic
unions of the high-powered, the whiff of a corporate
merger permeates the relationship. And after nine years
of business, the marriage appears bankrupt. Otto has
betrayed a singular lack of imagination by selecting his
yoga instructor as a girlfriend. Clare, with nobler aspirations as mother-protector of the nation, buries herself
in work at DHS. Otto Jr. has become a bit lost in the
shuffle. A team of well-paid helpmeets is available for
around-the-clock support.

At Lincoln's, the cabinet secretary mops up the
remaining globules of maple syrup from her plate with
the last bite of waffle and pops it into her mouth. The
chatter between Clare and Hayley is staccato, a con-
versational volley that reveals a potential for kinship
between the two women. Though they come from
wildly different socioeconomic backgrounds, the DHS
kingpin and low-level West Wing staffer share a dis-
ciplined temperament and dedication to the country.
The older woman sees her best qualities in Hayley. If
Clare weren't pressed for time—a meeting with officials
from the Centers for Disease Control and Prevention
is scheduled at 8:15 a.m.—she would probably order
another waffle. She feels positive about this little alli-

ance with Hayley Chill, one that she congratulates herself on having the cleverness to nurture.

"In the aftermath of COVID, the CDC and FEMA
have required rebuilding from the ground up. Same as
what happened to the intelligence community after
9/11, the reorientation of huge swaths of the federal
bureaucracy has been a monumental undertaking. All
hands on deck. The president has asked me to help out
in any way I can."

"Yes, ma'am."

Clare gestures impatiently. "Old news. We have
more immediate issues to discuss."

"Madam Secretary?"

"General Hernandez. You understand the precarious-
ness of the situation, don't you, Hayley? Left unchecked,
the NSA is going to talk the president into jumping off a
cliff . . . and take the whole country with him."

Hayley understands what the cabinet secretary
wants from her. She also knows privileged information
isn't something you just give away. Her silence speaks
volumes.

Clare says, "Of course, I won't easily forget your
assistance."

"Assistance."

"A fly on the wall. Chatter in the West Wing that
you think might be of interest to me. Any influence
you might wield in the pursuit of national security and
safety."

"This conversation is making me uncomfortable,
Madam Secretary."

"I'm not asking you to betray anyone. I need allies, Hayley."

"Sounds like you need a spy, ma'am."

"As I said, your service won't be forgotten."

Hayley knows she is supposed to name her price—everyone in Washington has one. But she remains silent.

Clare smiles knowingly. "You're *too* good."

Hayley shakes her head. She hasn't asked for anything in return because she doesn't know yet what she needs. "As I said before, ma'am, nothing is more important to me than service to country."

"Great! Then we're in agreement."

Hayley can't help but smile, marveling at the older woman's persistence. "I've agreed to what exactly?"

"To keep an eye on things. Be vigilant against any plan of action that deviates from the measured approach of prior administrations. And if you can, report back to me."

Hayley shrugs. "I'm only a small cog in a very big machine, ma'am."

Clare understands why the younger woman must play it coy and is willing to play that game. "You have a special relationship with the president, Hayley, a commodity of incalculable worth in this town. It's a great comfort to know I can count on you." Checking her lipstick in a Givenchy compact, the cabinet secretary says, "Together, we can keep our country safe." Standing up, she places a twenty-dollar bill on the tabletop and gestures to the younger woman.

"Come on. I'll drop you."

TUESDAY, 8:05 A.M. April Wu knows she could kick the guy's ass with one arm tied behind her back. Hell, wrap both her hands, and she'd still triangle choke the little freak in three seconds flat. But even April has to admit the dude one table over in the cafeteria of the Big Four—as its brainy occupants call the NSA's main building—possesses some historical justification in ostentatiously talking shit about soldiers like herself. His disdain is evidence of an entrenched and divisive dynamic on the campus at Fort Meade, an installation shared by the civilian National Security Agency and the more recently created, military-run US Cyber Command. Most civilians employed by the NSA possess advanced degrees from fancy universities and, by those lofty educational heights, look down their noses at the enlisted cyber warriors. The ridicule isn't the first (or last) time civilians deem a US soldier as something less than a professional. The bias could trace its origin back to the complacency of 1950s America when pursuit of the dollar replaced the honor of military duty as a national priority. At Fort Meade, the forced cohabitation between military and civilian agencies is like a blended family: part sitcom and always awkward.

The NSA, with offensive strategic ambitions, has its illustrious past, as well as seemingly limitless funding. In that long shadow, Cyber Command, created in 2009, has been hell-bent on being perceived as something other than the National Security Agency's idiot (and mostly useless) younger brother. Theirs was a sibling rivalry that shared not only a campus but also, in General Carlos Hernandez, leadership as well. To the surprise of many, USCYBERCOM has been flirting with a dramatic, come-from-behind parity in the last few years. With more significant influxes of funding and personnel, the military command became completely independent of its big brother in 2018 and increasingly positions itself as an offensive force. But the civilian NSA employees seem unwilling to let go of long-held prejudices. Physical altercations are not unknown, most often occurring in the Big Four cafeteria where both sides frequently mingle.

Her nemesis this morning is an improbably named Antonio Ferrari, a math wiz on loan from an assistant professorship at Rensselaer Polytechnic Institute. April has swapped her torn denim and Chanel jacket for her army combat uniform in an operational camouflage pattern. She has been sharing a few minutes of coffee time with some of her fellow soldiers before heading downstairs to the unit's basement offices. Ferrari gets April's attention by loudly complaining about the agency's perfectly good code getting "urinated" on by the "grunts" in Cyber Command. Who the hell says "urinated" anyway? They exchange more harsh words. Soon enough, the West Point grad is out of her chair and charging toward the civilian math nerd. Aware of the consequences of a physical assault charge, April's fellow soldiers spring from their chairs and stop her.

The Rensselaer prof, attached to the NSA's Information Systems Security Directorate Group 6 and backed up by his agency colleagues, feels secure enough to remain seated.

"Don't you have any *villes* to torch, G.I. Jane?" Ferrari asks April, arms casually crossing his chest.

April badly wants to pound the guy, but her fellow soldiers push her back toward her chair. "It's not worth it, Lieutenant. Let it go," one of them says.

She allows herself to be guided away from what would surely be a one-sided fight. Her tormentor laughs, enjoying her frustration.

"That's good. Hate me," he says, chuckling. It just so happens that all of Ferrari's colleagues at his table from Group 6 are male. Buttressed by these disproportionate numbers, April's nemesis feels he has yet another line of attack on her character. "Bros before hoes, right?"

All personnel in the vicinity of the two tables freezes. The soldiers surrounding April stop and turn to face Ferrari, with faces of stone. Two of April Wu's fellow soldiers are female. In unison, they move aside so that the first lieutenant has a clear path toward her nemesis. Ferrari loses his smug expression, replaced by something that looks like real fear.

"Now wait a minute," he says as April draws within arm's reach.

April is gunslinger cool. "I'm not going to hit you."

Ferrari is relieved. "You're not?"

She shakes her head. "The truth is, I wanted to ask you out."

The NSA systems engineer, despite his brilliance, is

utterly confounded by April's behavior. His arrogance prevents him from maintaining a healthy skepticism. Ferrari wants to believe this attractive female in an army combat uniform is sexually attracted to him.

"You do?"

"Yeah. I'd like to invite you to the award ceremony at the European Conference on Object Oriented Programming in September. I'm being given the Dahl-Nygaard Prize for the young researcher who has demonstrated great potential in software engineering. If you happen to find yourself in Barcelona."

April turns and heads toward the cafeteria exit, trailed by the other soldiers from her unit. Ferrari hasn't quite figured out just how badly she's burned him.

"Is Dahl-Nygaard even a thing?" he asks one of his tablemates.

The career NSA staffer throws a balled-up napkin that hits Ferrari in the head. "Yes, you idiot. It's a *very* big thing."

Antonio Ferrari frowns, his humiliation sinking in. That shame will grow, with increasing weight, until it bogs down his soul. It will reside there for the remainder of the day and the following week, too. The gnawing mortification will fail to ebb even six months later after the professor receives commendations from the Group 6 leader and returns to Rensselaer. That disgrace will infuse every aspect of his hard-won tenured professorship. No matter how many papers he publishes in prestigious periodicals or lofty mathematics awards he receives, Ferrari cannot completely ice the blister inflicted on him by the army lieutenant in the cafeteria of the Big Four that fateful morning. Over years of failed relationships that never quite warrant an attempt at matrimony and a cheating scandal that will scuttle his position at Rensselaer, Ferrari will repeatedly return to that brief confrontation with April Wu. He will search in vain for the forgotten detail that might alter his memory of it and thereby alleviate his suffering. In the year before his premature death from colon cancer at the age of fifty-four, Antonio Ferrari finally acknowledges his full culpability in the cafeteria incident. How soothing it is to admit, yes, he truly was an awful prick that day. And, in this moment of startling recognition, the disgraced professor finds some solace.

MINUTES AFTER TANGLING with Ferrari, April and her fellow cyber warriors sit down at forty-two-inch-wide curved monitors in their basement, blast-hardened office suite. A Category 5 hurricane could sweep across the state, but down in Cyber Command's lairs, no one would be the wiser. With the colonel in charge of the unit out of the country, April is the ranking officer. Enlisted personnel rotating through USCYBERCOM from other service branches fill out the roster, integrated under the shared mission to coordinate cyberspace planning and operations in defense of the nation's interests. The current project of April's unit—reverse engineering framework process with Ghidra software for the Pentagon's supply chain risk-management needs—isn't exactly on the front lines of any cyber war, declared or not.

"Anybody else curious about who's responsible for derailing the Metro Blue Line train yesterday under the Potomac?"

All of April's fellow cyber warriors are eager for a meatier assignment and furious that an enemy has so viciously attacked the US. Fingers flying across their respective keyboards, they intend to find the individuals responsible.

TUESDAY, 9:11 A.M. The National Press Building at 529 Fourteenth Street is home to the TASS Russian News Agency's Washington bureau. Aleksandr Belyavskiy arrives there for work every weekday morning at eight thirty. His cover—working journalist who reports on the US political developments for news consumers back in Russia—is obvious to even the rankest beginners in the CIA's counterespionage units. In his forties, with a broad face and penchant for the nondescript style offered by L.L.Bean, Belyavskiy hardly fits the stereotype of a chain-smoking, hard-drinking Russian journalist. His comprehension of English is rudimentary. The qualities he possesses that secured him this highly desirable posting were neither his distinguished military record nor his keen patriotism, but rather his birthplace of Mirnyy. Just northeast of Moscow, the village was also where Richard Monroe's grandparents lived. The rural locality continues to hold an extreme sentimental pull for the US president. Their shared geographical history made Belyavskiy the ideal candidate to become Monroe's GRU handler after the Russian mole's election to that highest American political office.

Though they have yet to meet face-to-face, Belyavskiy is in frequent contact with the president. A staff member inside the White House residence, whose identity is unknown to both Belyavskiy and Monroe, serves as their intermediary. If Monroe wishes to communicate with Belyavskiy, he signals the intermediary by shifting two volumes on a bookshelf in his White House bedroom. He leaves a note in one of them, volume three of the Sangamon edition of Carl Sandburg's biography of Abraham Lincoln. Monroe can expect a reply left between the pages of the same volume within forty-eight hours, signaled by the book's return to its original placement. When Belyavskiy needs to communicate to Monroe, he uses a dead drop near the TASS offices. A small maintenance box at the southwest corner of Franklin Square is the designated site.

He has dutifully reported on Monroe's psychological deportment over the last year. Unlike his jocular messages with the president, Belyavskiy's dispatches to his superiors in Moscow are officious and free of editorializing. The information the Russians have obtained from their asset in the Oval Office—from extensive alterations in US foreign policy to top secret planning for new weapon systems—has been deemed of immense value. But the fear in Moscow, of course, is that American intelligence services have discovered Richard Monroe's true identity. That they have flipped their prized mole. Consequently, the US president is under unusually intense scrutiny by

Russian intelligence. Every minute detail of Belyavskiy's interaction with his asset is analyzed. The Directorate thoroughly screens anyone who comes in contact with Richard Monroe for having possible clandestine affiliation with the CIA or FBI.

The longer Monroe remains in the White House, the more Moscow's insecurity grows. Such is the cost of the operation's astonishing success. Belyavskiy's direct superior, Konstantin Tabakov, a GRU officer stationed at the Russian Embassy on Wisconsin Avenue, has been demanding meetings and detailed interaction reports with increasing frequency. These clandestine get-togethers have taken place at shopping malls, the zoo, and even a bowling alley in Columbia Heights. Such subterfuge is a waste of time and effort in Belyavskiy's opinion. He has absolutely no doubt the American intelligence agencies are aware of his every move and Tabakov's movements as well.

Belyavskiy exits the National Press Building and turns right on Fourteenth Street. Holding an umbrella as a shelter against the showers that have fallen intermittently throughout the morning, he relishes this bit of inoffensive weather. Spring in Washington is an all-too-brief interlude between a cold, gray winter and the long, muggy summer that will follow. Atypically, the Russian spy looks forward to his assignation with his superior. Of the seemingly countless museums and memorials he has eagerly sought out during his stay in Washington, Belyavskiy has never visited the National Museum of Women in the Arts. He is keen to sample its offerings.

With bushy eyebrows and a stocky build, wearing a
suit bought off the rack at GUM, Konstantin Tabakov
looks out of place in the gallery filled with artistic efforts
of Frida Kahlo, Lee Krasner, and Faith Ringgold. A former officer in the special forces–oriented Spetsnaz GRU
and since reassigned to lighter duty at Russia's embassy
in Washington, Tabakov is a dour man in his late fifties with an uncanny resemblance to Leonid Brezhnev.
Belyavskiy approaches his superior, who is busily scru-
tinizing Leonora Carrington's surreal *Samhain Skin*, a
narrative painting depicting mysterious people and spirits participating in bizarre rituals. The two GRU agents
have the room to themselves and converse easily in their
native Russian.

*"The obscenities of the West never cease to astonish
me,"* Tabakov says to his underling, gesturing with disgust at the painting. He retrieves a sunflower seed from
a bag in his jacket pocket and plops it in his mouth,
spitting the shell out moments later onto the carpeted
gallery floor.

Belyavskiy pauses to study the work, tilting his head
to one side in the semblance of a connoisseur. He says,
"Celtic borrowings, I believe."

Tabakov is surprised by the junior officer's display
of culturalism and intellect. *"How in the world would
anyone know?"*

Eager not to offend his powerful superior, who could
have him posted to Outer Mongolia with a single phone
call, Belyavskiy improvises. He proffers a museum
pamphlet.

"Research, sir! Never fail to research!"

Mollified, the senior GRU officer turns his back on the aberrant artwork. *"Why am I here, in this repulsive place? Is it Polkan?"*

Headquarters had assigned the president a code name, one going back decades and starting with Monroe's entering the US Army. Polkan is a character from Russian folklore, a half human, half horse that possesses great strength and speed. The code name seemed apt for Russia's most successful mole ever.

"Polkan made contact, an urgent request regarding the cyberattacks on the subway system and American newspapers."

"What of them?" Tabakov asks gruffly.

"Sir, he wants to know if this was an operation originating with Spetssvyaz," he says, referring to the Russian Special Communications and Information Service. The agency is responsible for only a small percentage of that country's signals intelligence. Even as the statement escapes his mouth, Belyavskiy knows how stupid he must sound. He is aware Spetssvyaz is an entity responsible for the collection and analysis of foreign communications, not inserting malware in enemy computer networks. But Belyavskiy must report Polkan's messages, word for word. For all the glamour of the spy business and relative luxuriousness of his current posting, he misses the old days in the army. Are fresh orange juice and American baseball worth the uncertainties of being a spy behind enemy lines? Belyavskiy misses his wife, Katrina, as well. Twice-weekly trips to

a Thai massage parlor in Hyattsville aren't a satisfying substitute.

"Spetssvyaz? This is what Polkan asked? About Spetssvyaz?" Tabakov's reaction is so extravagant that spittle shoots from his mouth and splatters on the Carrington painting. Only Belyavskiy seems to notice the artwork's defacement. He refrains from mentioning it. Senior officers from the Spetsnaz GRU aren't renowned for their appreciation of the absurd.

"Yes, sir. He specifically said Spetssvyaz."

Tabakov broods for a moment, turning away from the other man as if he didn't even exist. *"Mention this to no one. Understand? No one!"* He flips another sunflower seed into his mouth.

"Sir?"

The senior GRU officer pauses to spit out the seed husks and says in a tone of voice reminiscent of an impatient grade school teacher, *"Polkan knows Spetssvyaz is a defensive unit, you fool. He could have chosen from a dozen different units, official or unsanctioned, that perform this sort of work. Instead, he chooses the only one that wouldn't do this sort of work, not in a million years! This could be a signal that Polkan's under suspicion . . . or worse! His communications with us might be compromised!"*

Belyavskiy is slightly taken aback by his superior's hysteria, just more paranoia revolving around their golden goose in the Oval Office. *"But how shall I respond, sir? Was it our boys who did it? Or the FSB? The derailment of the American train seemed just the perfect degree of harassment. They don't dare retaliate!"* No sooner than he finishes speaking these words, Belyav-skiy feels his face reddening. He's done it now.

Tabakov gawks at Belyavskiy as if the junior man has lost his mind. *"Who knows who did it? I don't concern myself with such things and nor should you!"* These last words escape the GRU officer's mouth as a hiss, between clenched teeth. He turns to leave and then stops, facing his underling again. *"Not a word to anyone until I've made my report to Moscow, Belyavskiy. Not one word!"*

The senior GRU officer stomps off, leaving the partially masticated seed husks scattered on the gallery floor. He can't get out of the museum fast enough. Women artists? Ridiculous!

Belyavskiy waits until his superior has disappeared through the gallery's entryway and then turns to face the Carrington painting again. Long an avid aficionado of the mystical and folktales, he finds the images mesmerizing. Composing a response to Russia's mole inside the White House can wait five minutes.

3

★ ★ ★ ★

THE WEASEL

*T*uesday, 9:25 *a.m.* Kyle Rodgers brings Hayley with him into the Oval Office to take notes. The president's first order of business is a call with the secretary for Homeland Security, who had requested a sit-down meeting. Monday's attack on the DC Metro train has moved the issue of cyberterrorism front and center. As a White House operator connects the ever-determined Clare Ryan with Richard Monroe, Hayley reflects on her breakfast with the cabinet secretary two hours earlier. Clare was entirely respectful, her appeal for "collaboration" refreshingly pragmatic. Hayley appreciates straight talk, a rarity in Washington, and admires the older woman's apparent dedication to the country. In the few seconds before Clare Ryan's voice comes over the phone console's speakerphone, Hayley decides she will cooperate with the cabinet secretary.

"Mr. President, thank you for taking my call."

"Of course, Clare. Any success with attribution for this Metro business?"

Hayley studies the president closely. He seems off, lacking his usual calm and forceful demeanor. It was Richard Monroe's charismatic persona—war hero and effective communicator—that had stunned the nation and won an electoral victory more than two years before. Moscow could not have anticipated a more convincing deep-cover agent. But she can see the events of the last few days have taken their toll on the president. He seems haggard and on edge.

"No, sir. Attribution will take time . . . potentially much more time. Which is why I want to emphasize caution. Immediate retaliation of any kind ought to be out of the question."

"Yes, yes. I haven't forgotten your position, Clare. But I can't be seen doing *nothing*."

"I understand, sir."

Monroe slides a look toward Kyle Rodgers. Into the phone, he says, "Folks over here worried a presidential address might elevate the stature of the attack. Make these sonsabitches bigger than they really are."

"I would concur with that advice, Mr. President," Clare says.

"Perhaps you can get out front of it. Put a face on our absolute resolve. Hold a press conference, okay? Dampen the speculation. Diminish fears of further attacks."

"Yes, sir. Of course, I'll make arrangements the

second we get off the phone. I can speak from over
here. Limited questions from the press. That sort of
thing."

"Yes, that's good. Thank you, Clare."

"What's truly needed, Mr. President, is a broader
mandate for the DHS, above and beyond your executive
order. Civilian targets are woefully defenseless. Working
with Congress, we—"

Monroe cuts her off. "Long term, Clare. After the
dust settles."

"Sir—"

"Thank you, Clare. I'll be watching later today. I'm
sure you'll be just great!"

Kyle Rodgers disconnects the call for Monroe.

The president says, "That woman is going to make a
helluva president someday."

"General Hernandez is next, sir."

"These two should just get a room."

Rodgers laughs mildly at Monroe's joke. Hayley,
sitting in a chair to the side with notepad open on her
knee, remains expressionless.

"Don't write that down," he needlessly instructs
Hayley.

"No, Mr. President."

"Shall I connect the general, sir?" Rodgers asks.

"Yes. Let's keep going, Kyle."

Rodgers presses the necessary buttons.

"Mr. President! Thank you for giving me a few minutes, sir!" The NSA director's voice booms from the
console speaker, fortified by the conviction that he

is making history. Cyber Jihad is *his* Cuban Missile Crisis.

"What do you have for me, Carlos?"

"We were able to locate the exploit in the transit system's computers used by the attackers."

The president nods, peering into space with great intensity. "I see."

"Sir, the actual coding of the malware isn't terribly sophisticated. Any computer science major could write the lines of software. What takes advanced skill and understanding is knowing how and where to place it in the Metro's network. The hack represents a textbook 'gray-zone aggression,' precisely targeted, with the clear intent of taking down the Blue Line. Few global actors have that capability, all of them nation states. This is no jihadist or lone wolf behind these attacks. The operation has the Kremlin written all over it."

"Gray zone?"

"Sir, gray-zone conflict is state-sponsored activities that are coercive and aggressive, but deliberately designed to remain below the threshold of conventional military conflict and open war. A gray-zone operation is an ambiguous and usually incremental aggression."

"Okay," says Monroe with something well short of presidential authority. Hernandez's eagerness to pin the cyberattacks on Moscow seems to rattle Monroe. He sits upright in his chair again and props his head up with one hand while scratching his scalp with the other.

"What's your confidence level on these findings, Carlos?"

"Moderate, sir."

Monroe exchanges a look with Kyle Rodgers.

Hernandez takes the silence over the phone line as an indication of the president's skepticism. "We started with a set of plausible actors, sir, based on the nature of the attack, the target, and the incident context. In our analysis, we're careful to avoid cognitive bias, using analysis of competing hypotheses and other proven analytic systems. By evaluating multiple competing hypotheses based on the observed and uncovered data, Mr. President, we narrow down our list of potential actors. Sir, I expect to assign the highest level of confidence to our analysis within a matter of days, if not hours."

As the NSA director drones on about the basis for his determination, Hayley continues to observe Monroe, seeing in him an uptick of nervous anxiety. She hides her concern, wearing a mask of professional attentiveness.

Hernandez's voice becomes more strident. "Mr. President, the Russians are testing us. That's the goal of any gray-zone aggression. We absolutely need to respond, within the same strategic sphere. But doing so requires executive action. Our hands are tied without your direct command."

Monroe reacts to the NSA director's hectoring by slapping his right palm down on the desk.

"Thank you for reminding me I'm the one in charge, goddammit!"

"Sir—"

"Do your job, Carlos, and I'll do mine!" the president

shouts into the speakerphone before disconnecting the call with an emphatic stab of his finger.

Kyle Rodgers, mindful of Monroe's volatile mood swings, keeps his voice extra calm and nonjudgmental. "I'll circle back with him, Mr. President."

Monroe's outburst concerns his most trusted advisor. POTUS needs to keep his shit together; they are only at the beginning of a growing national crisis and the president's schedule is absolutely jammed today. Rodgers can't help but recall the chaos, indecision, and lack of action that greeted the recent catastrophic pandemic.

"Fort Meade is a strange place, sir. Folks over there, they're just different."

The president looks down at his desktop, as if unable to meet his advisor's eyes. "I need a few minutes before my next thing."

Hayley and her boss withdraw from the room without another word, exchanging a glance on their way out.

They stop in the corridor outside the Oval Office.

"Thoughts?" Kyle Rodgers asks Hayley, clearly referring to the president's emotional state. "You're the one with the 'special relationship' with him."

Ignoring her boss's pointed gibe, Hayley says, "The president is good, sir. Rock-solid."

Kyle Rodgers nods curtly. He wants to believe her assessment is accurate. They head off in opposite directions.

———————————

TUESDAY, 10:40 A.M. Rafi Zamani takes Yazat outside after a long, lazy morning just kicking back and watching television, mostly Premier League football. Morning showers have given way to a sky lightly populated with benign, white clouds. As a rabid supporter of Manchester United, Rafi dons a Paul Pogba jersey, one of three he owns. This kit is his oldest and most favorite, seemingly bringing good fortune to his team whenever he wears it on game day. Yazat craps within ten seconds of stepping out the door, but Rafi decides a walk might be nice, so continues without bothering to pick up after his dog. It's going to be another beautiful spring day, with temperatures in the high sixties. Perfect riding weather, Rafi muses. Even Yazat—usually dragging his ass around the block as if to the slaughterhouse—seems to have a little jaunt to his step.

Rafi continues to feel the buoyant afterglow left by the train derailment, instigated by a few keystrokes on his laptop. Watching all those jerks coming out of the tunnel was an absolute kick. He should've stayed the hell away from anything that even *smelled* like the Metro Blue Line but, fuck it, how often can a hacker put eyes on the fruits of his labor? The Metro malware executed flawlessly. The damage was limited to the Blue Line's grids, leaving the rest of the servers untouched. Flawless. *As-salamu alaykum*, motherfuckers. Cyber Jihad strikes again! The next exploit he has lined up is dope, too. With any luck, the Boss will contact him soon with the go-ahead.

Rafi is annoyed that Yazat is stopping at every park-

ing meter, signpost, and fire hydrant to piss. He gives
the French bulldog a pull as two dudes about his age
approach from the opposite direction. Once he gets
Yazat moving again, Rafi turns and only then sees the
young men, stopped and standing in his path. One
of them—the shorter guy dressed in baggy jeans and
Adidas T-shirt—says something. But Rafi, Iron Pony
snapback pulled down tight on his head, is streaming
Martin Garrix over his earbuds and can't hear a goddamn thing. He reluctantly presses the side of his right
earbud, silencing the music.

"—that some kinda bulldog, man?" the shorter guy
finishes asking.

"French." Rafi doesn't speak with any kind of accent.
But dressed in that trippy, red soccer jersey, with black
hair, feminine eyebrows, and a dark complexion, he
looks to the two dudes from Edgewood like just another
freak from God knows where in the world. Pakistan?
India? What difference does it fucking make anyway?

"Gimme your dog, man." The shorter guy says this,
but it's the taller one who bends down to snatch Yazat.

Rafi steps between the muggers and his dog. "Not a
fucking chance."

The taller guy stands up straight again and pulls an
ancient-looking Röhm RG-14 .22 revolver—a gun made
infamous by John Hinckley in his assassination attempt
on Ronald Reagan—from under his waistband. He has
brought the gun only halfway up toward Rafi's face
when he experiences the bizarre sensation of a four-inch
blade plunged into the center of his throat. Rafi yanks

his right hand back from the taller guy's neck, withdrawing the knife with a twisting motion. Blood geysers from the wound. The gunman drops to his knees and keels forward comically flat on his face, extremely dead.

The gunman's friend turns to run in the direction they came but is caught by his shirt by Rafi and hauled backward. Rafi, right-handed, sets the edge of his knife's blade on the right side of the dude's throat, just above the collarbone and *pushes* a deep, oblique, long incised injury across the front of the neck. He makes a shallow cut at the beginning that tapers off at the opposite side, leaving a tail abrasion. With this unorthodox technique, Rafi has ensured forensic investigators will file their reports with the grim conviction that the perpetrator is left-handed. Obfuscation is the name of the game, yo.

Holding the dead man upright, Rafi releases his grip on the back of the guy's shirt and allows him to fall to the sidewalk. Yazat, that little putz, is lapping up the first guy's blood, forcing his owner to give his leash a firm yank. With possible witnesses in mind, Rafi looks around his environs and sees no one. He bends down and picks up his dog—the better to make a fast getaway—and notices a speck of blood on the sleeve of his lucky football jersey. From the second kill, he speculates. Determined to keep his Pogba kit pristine, Rafi heads for a corner 7-Eleven across the street and up the block.

He pushes the door open and enters the convenience store, still carrying Yazat under his arm. No one is inside other than the clerk behind the cash register.

Darting to the cooler stacks, Rafi retrieves a bottle of soda water. The clerk, an older Ethiopian man, rings up the purchase. Handing over two bucks, Rafi sees three closed-circuit surveillance camera monitors on a shelf behind the Ethiopian. The center monitor displays the street outside, angled up the block so that the two bodies lying scattered on the opposite sidewalk are plainly visible.

The clerk makes change and offers it to his customer.

Rafi doesn't make a move to collect the coins but simply stares at the old Ethiopian. Only now does he clock the old man's terror. Yazat squirms in his master's arm.

"Your change, sir," the clerk says, with eyes that plead for mercy. The old man recalls the faces of his children. He hears their laughter around the dinner table. And remembers the violence of his country during his childhood. Every day a cycle of waking, death, and hunger. His lips move with a muttered prayer.

At my lowest, God is my Hope. At my darkest, God is my Light.

———————————

TUESDAY, 11:17 A.M. They were heading back to the station house, having handled a van fire on Sixteenth Street, when a call came over the radio of multiple injuries at O Street and Wisconsin Avenue. Sam's unit, Engine Company 5, might get a dozen calls like this in a shift. Consequently, he was relaxed enough to let his thoughts drift to Hayley again. Yes, Sam told her he would wait for her to reach out. But since their conversation during her walk home from work the evening before, he hasn't stopped thinking about the White House staffer. Crazy, right? Though Sam had done his share of dating, he can't remember another woman with whom he so easily and so quickly connected.

Well, no woman since Mara Paladino.

Sam McGovern grew up in Falls Church, Virginia, and the oldest of four children. To the surprise of none of his friends, he made no efforts to apply for college following graduation from high school. His dad, a bartender at a local tavern, couldn't have cared less about the decision. But his mother, who worked for the school district as a librarian, was quietly devastated. Sam knew he wanted to be a fireman since middle school and for all the dopey reasons a kid might be so inclined. When he was ten years old, Sam saw a photograph in a magazine of a fireman—face covered in soot and self-contained breathing apparatus—carrying a baby out of a burning row house. The image stuck to him like gum on the bottom of his shoe. Sam wanted to be a hero. He worked toward paramedic certification through high school and won it when he was eighteen, the earliest possible age. Earning admission to the DC Fire Department training academy on his nineteenth birthday was a foregone conclusion.

He lived at home for a time, when he wasn't staying over at the DCFD Engine 5 firehouse on Dent Place. After months of commuting between Falls Church and the "Nickel" in Georgetown, Sam moved into a condo with some guys from the department. The place was essentially a frat house and could be pretty disgusting at times, but Sam enjoyed the camaraderie. These were his college years, in a way, with all the drinking and carousing associated with that traditionally carefree existence. Life was good. During this time, he wasn't looking for anything serious in his relationships with women. How he met Mara was nuts, actually, like out of some dumb television show. But rescuing her from her burning loft studio, where she painted her huge canvases, was exactly how it happened. No, he didn't carry her out in his arms. But his face was indeed covered with soot and, sure, maybe he did take her by the arm passing through the front door.

Those eighteen months were like holding a tiger by the tail. Sam had never met a woman like Mara, every minute with her an exercise in exhilaration tempered by exhaustion. For every high he experienced with his lover, a new low was certain to follow. He can't recall how many times they "broke up" in that year and a half. A dozen times, maybe? For Sam, the firehouse was a welcome reprieve from an all-consuming romantic relationship. Mara, however, complained bitterly that their difficulties interfered with her artistic endeavors. The romance finally died in the way these things always do, when Mara met some writer dude in the waiting room of the local veterinarian where she had brought her sick dog. The end was blessed relief for both of them.

After Mara, he cooled to the notion of a regular relationship with a woman. Sam is still young, with a seemingly unlimited future ahead. No need to jump back into the ring. Though the Mara debacle left minimal psychological and emotional scarring, Sam nevertheless has put faint effort into dating since that tumultuous period of his life. Now, this new thing has happened. Hayley Chill has happened, appearing from out of nowhere at Darlington House. As if a referee decided that the fireman has had enough time in the penalty box. And Sam is okay with it, willing to take a run at real romance. That decision made, he doesn't want to blow his chances by seeming too eager or needy. So, as Engine 5 brakes to a hard stop on O Street and Sam jumps off the truck with his fellow firefighters, he decides he won't call Hayley. He'll leave it up to her to make the next move.

His unit is the first on the location, alerted by a bystander's 911 call. Sam can't remember the last time the cops have beaten their truck to a 10-53 (man down) and takes pride in the team's efficiency and speed. He sees the two bodies on the sidewalk and, crouching down beside them, knows immediately that both victims are as dead as dead can be. One victim—black male, twenties—is throat cut, his blood pooling to a three-foot radius on the sidewalk. The other victim— black male, late teens—has what looks like a single puncture to the throat. A cheap revolver lies on the sidewalk less than a foot from the second man's hand. There is nothing for Sam or his fellow firefighters to do but keep bystanders from trampling on the crime scene and wait for the cops to arrive.

But, as he is just sitting back on his heels, he hears

screaming. Sam looks to his left, up the block toward Wisconsin, and sees a woman in a 7-Eleven parking lot waving frantically in their direction. He stands and takes off running, EMT kit in hand, accompanied by one of his firefighter housemates.

The woman in the parking lot gyrates in circles, sobbing hysterically, as the two firefighters arrive. She gestures toward the store, gasping and unable to formulate the words. But her intent is clear. Sam and Rick, his housemate, run toward the convenience store entrance. Pushing through the glass doors, they find another woman standing opposite the register. She is pale white and wide-eyed, staring down at the floor behind the counter. Rick goes to the woman and starts to ask if she's okay. Sam hears nothing of what his partner says or how the other woman responds because he has gone to the counter and looks over the other side. He sees an adult male lying in a pool of blood, his throat gashed. Sam knows there is no saving anyone here, either.

Tuesday, 12:31 P.M. Hayley takes a bag lunch to the Mall, a habit that she developed as a White House intern. The midday meal is the same as always: peanut butter and jelly sandwich, apple, and bottle of water. She takes comfort in the routine and simplicity of this lunch tradition, one that she can indulge only on slow days when the weather allows. The crush of work hasn't abated, but she leaves the White House complex anyway, needing time and some distance from the West Wing to think.

She is, by custom, decisive. Since her earliest childhood, Hayley has possessed an almost unnatural ability to take the appropriate action at the appropriate time. Her gut instincts are uncannily accurate. Given those attributes, then, how to explain her current vacillation? The imprecise nature of Wilde's orders to assist April Wu is one reason for Hayley's uncertainty. Assist her, how exactly? How much? Hayley's gnawing anxiety is aggravated by the deeper state's apparent lack of confidence in her. What has she done to incur their distrust? Her performance has been letter-perfect since the first days of the mission.

Running Richard Monroe as a double agent for Publius is her primary responsibility. With the growing crisis surrounding Cyber Jihad's repeated attacks on the United States, however, Hayley's office in the West Wing is beginning to feel more like a gilded cage. How can she possibly be of any service in the pursuit of America's cyber tormentors? What good is she to the deeper state if not a valued participant in this most immediate emergency?

Hayley is just finishing her food when her phone buzzes. Hayley doesn't recognize the number but answers anyway.

"Hello?"

"What are you doing out of the office, slacker?" April's voice booms from the handset. "Where are you?"

"Sitting on the Mall, eating lunch. What can you tell me over an open line?"

"Nothing you don't already know. The trail goes cold after Estonia. I think those little weasels in the upstairs are holding out on us."

"The NSA analysts?"

"Correct."

Internecine battles between federal agencies is a fact of life in Washington, as welcome as the tourists that flood the city every spring and summer. The players like to complain about the turf wars and budget battles, but, in reality, it's the bureaucrat's version of close-quarter combat that makes the drudgery of governance halfway fun. And information is the Saturday night special of these DC gang wars. Gossip and innuendo is a poison, weaponized and used at an antagonist's discretion. Secrets never die. They don't fade away. Confidences are forever.

Hayley can think of someone in her immediate history for whom veiled confidences were the foundation of his lengthy career. A man with a map of where the bodies have been buried.

"What's your plan?" asks Hayley.

"Slap the weasels around. You?"

"Didn't have a clue until this phone call."

April asks, "Have any weasels in mind?"

"I do. Talk later."

Hayley disconnects. In the shadow of the Washington Monument, she pauses to look down the Mall to the Lincoln Memorial. Hayley has always loved this

particular monument, more than any other. Abraham
Lincoln is her favorite president, both in character and
political bent. The sixteenth president's national memorial stirs pride in her heart, for her country and its best
moments.

In the dark hours before the assassination attempt
on Richard Monroe, Hayley took refuge in Lincoln's
memorial shortly after midnight. The would-be assas-
sins had uncovered her identity and were in hot pursuit,
but she was able to snatch a few hours of much-needed
sleep. She prevailed in that struggle against a secret,
government cabal and its mercenaries, intent on an
overthrow of the executive branch. Those few hours of
refuge in the famous landmark played no small part.
Hayley never misses the chance to express gratitude to
Mr. Lincoln. She has a distinct feeling that his laconic
inspiration will be a necessity in the days ahead.

———————————————

TUESDAY, 3:11 P.M. Federal Correctional Institution,
Cumberland, is a little over 130 miles from Washington, on Maryland's side of the border with Pennsylvania. Classified as a medium-security federal prison for
male inmates, it is no country club. The single coil wire
reinforced concertinas are *real*. Current inmates include
Masoud Khan, leader of the Virginia jihad network; Jeffrey MacDonald, former US Army doctor who murdered his wife and two children at Fort Bragg; and Ed
Brown, Sovereign Citizen movement member convicted
of conspiracy for stockpiling bombs and firearms during

an eight-month standoff with the FBI. Parking in the visitor's lot after the two-hour drive from Washington, Hayley shudders as she walks briskly toward the prison's entrance. The thought of being consigned here for the rest of her natural life is simply too awful to contemplate. What if her covert work for the deeper state somehow landed her in this place? She studies the facility and its surroundings for possible security weaknesses.

She is directed to the visiting room after a brief interview by the front lobby officer and takes a seat at the table indicated to her by FCI personnel. No other visitors are present. Though supervision exists in the form of the four guards positioned at various places around the room (augmenting a dozen closed-circuit surveillance cameras), there is no Plexiglas or direct-connect phones. She will be within arm's reach of the subject of her interview. His breathing will be audible to her. Their scents will comingle. It will be remarkable, indeed, to see him again.

He enters through a far door and approaches Hayley, seated at a table underneath the high windows that line one wall of the room. She can see James Odom has shaved off the beard he wore as the CIA deputy director in charge of the Office of Intelligence Integration. His integral role in Operation Damocles, so-called by its conspirators, earned him what is essentially a life sentence and incarceration here at FCI Cumberland. The stated goal of Damocles was to counter Richard Monroe's political agenda, and the first step was the assassination of the president's chief of staff, Peter Hall. It was Hall's murder, staged to look like a fatal heart attack, that Hayley inadvertently discovered. Undercover as a White House intern, she unraveled a conspiracy that culminated in the attempt on Monroe's life. For much of that ordeal, she was entirely on her own in countering the cabal's efforts. James Odom, the primary conspirator and true architect of Operation Damocles, came close to exposing Hayley and eliminating her as a threat. Seeing her again, a little more than one year of incarceration, brings a surprising smile to his face . . . surprising because the White House intern put him in this prison. The former CIA deputy director, a true connoisseur of tradecraft, continues to wish he recruited Hayley Chill. Then and now, Odom has no clear idea of her employers. Despite a lifetime spent in intelligence, there are some things even he couldn't imagine to be true.

Shoulders squared and walking tall, Odom shows none of the common fatigue induced by long-term incarceration on older inmates. He takes a seat at the table, directly opposite Hayley. "You've lost weight, my girl."

"And you've shaved off your beard, sir."

"Without it, I believe I look younger. Turned seventy last month. What do you think?"

"For your age, sir, you look very good."

He appears pleased by her comment.

"I have a job in the license plate manufacturing center. Isn't that something? The trope is one hundred percent accurate."

Hayley nods appreciatively. "Government vehicle plates. I see them countless times a day, sir."

Odom grins, seemingly delighted to be present in Washington in this insignificant way. "The food here is surprisingly good. I've been getting regular exercise. And I see my wife once a week and the kids and grandkids every other month or so. It's not so bad, really. I've even made a friend or two. Ugo Annovazzi. Have you heard of him? He's been here since ninety-two, serving a life sentence for racketeering and murder. Ugo is boss of the Lucchese family, eighty-eight and still giving orders from federal prison. Have to admire that kind of stamina, don't you?"

"I wouldn't know, sir." She allows Odom this time to air out whatever is on his mind, hoping to win his cooperation.

"And you, my girl? Whither Richard Monroe's good luck charm?"

"I'm still at the White House, sir, paid now, thankfully."

"Worth every penny." He pauses, sizing her up. You may take the old spy out of the CIA, but you never really take the CIA out of the old spy. "Why are you here? Not for a victory lap or out of morbid curiosity. I know you at least as well as that."

"Cyber Jihad."

"Yes? What of it?" Odom seems alarmingly uninterested.

"Do you know them, sir? Who might they be?"

He shrugs.

"Please, sir. Whatever you can offer would be helpful. The president is under tremendous pressure to respond."

"Well, that's his job, isn't it? He was elected because the voters thought him best to perform *under pressure*." Odom says the last two words as if describing a sex act.

"Deputy Director Odom, sir—"

Odom interrupts her, smiling. "Dear girl, I haven't been called by that title for some time. Very kind of you."

"But what are your thoughts, sir? The attacks on the newspapers and Metro Blue Line."

"Cyber Jihad. You said so yourself."

"That could be anybody."

"Or it could be real, live Islamic terrorists."

Hayley nods and says, "Or real, live Islamic terrorists, yes."

The former CIA man says nothing, just curiously watching Hayley. He's waiting for her to make the next move.

"Somehow, I have the feeling you know more than what you're letting on, sir."

"You think this business might be the handiwork of one or more of my old pals?"

"I haven't a clue, which is why I've come to you."

" 'Who' isn't so important as 'why.' Someone with your acumen should know that much."

Hayley frowns, uninterested in his cryptic games.

"Why *is* who," Odom says.

"Sir, innocent lives could be at stake. Any actionable intelligence you can offer to help us. "

"Actionable intelligence?" he asks mockingly. He casts his gaze around the visitation room. "Who wants to know?"

He turns his gaze to meet hers. She understands. *The authorities are listening.*

Hayley's hands folded on the tabletop pick up the slightest vibration. Dropping her gaze to Odom's hands, she sees the index finger of his right hand is ever so delicately tapping out a code. She recognizes the pattern immediately.

Based on a Polybius square using a five-by-five grid of letters, the tap code is most commonly used by prisoners of war to communicate silently, from cell to cell. Like any intelligence trainee, Hayley received instructions on utilizing the tap code while at the Publius facility in Oregon. Odom's desire for their conversation to proceed clandestinely is unmistakable. Hayley's prodigious gift for memorization facilitates that process. The system involves up to five taps of the finger for each letter, pausing between each one. It's a laborious methodology, but for short messages, it serves the purpose.

With his subtle finger taps, Odom asks her, *Who do you work for?*

Hayley taps out, *usa.*

Odom grins. *work for me.*

After Hayley has computed the meaning of Odom's finger taps in her head, she reacts to his request with consternation.

Odom repeats the message. *work for me.*

Hayley taps her response. *i work for rm.*

The CIA man's next message requires a dizzying number of finger taps. Hayley watches, decrypting in her head the message's content.

He repeats the final message to ensure she understands.

i help you help me.

i help you help me.

Before Hayley can respond, one of the correctional officers approaches.

"You two just going to stare at each other for another ten minutes?" he asks, checking the wall-mounted clock. "Time's up. C'mon, miss."

She stands up from the table. Odom remains seated, offering her a small wave and smiling eyes as Hayley follows the guard toward the exit.

———————

GETTING BEHIND THE wheel of her car in the parking lot outside the prison's administrative building, Hayley broods on what her former nemesis said—and hadn't said—in their meeting.

Why is who.

I help you help me.

The setting sun's rays slant through the open driver's window. A glorious spring sunset is in the offing, a pleasant contrast to the morning's dreary weather.

You help me.

Fearing an erosion of power accumulated after decades of government service, James Odom led a nearly successful effort to kill a US president. He tried to kill *her*. Is the current cyber crisis so severe that she should offer her assistance to a man capable of cold-blooded murder?

Hayley reaches for the ignition and starts the car. She'll do her job without that old weasel's help.

HAYLEY HAS FOUGHT with her fists for much of her life. Those pugilistic skills, refined in the military, were evident when she was young. Growing up in rural West Virginia meant fighting tooth and nail, or risk losing everything. She was the Sixth Army's female welterweight champ and the pride of ARSOUTH. But since coming to Washington, the West Wing staffer hasn't spent a single minute in a boxing ring. Missing the challenge and camaraderie of personal combat, Hayley intends to get back into the ring one day, when she's not pulled in a million different directions at once. Nevertheless, the deeper state operative still trains like the amateur boxing champion she once was.

Morning jogs followed by military calisthenics in her apartment is her typical regimen, every day if her work schedule allows it. Running, especially, clears her head of extraneous and distracting thoughts. She can focus. So, after the two-hour drive back from Cumberland, Hayley changes into her army T-shirt and shorts. She laces up her running shoes. With an uncluttered mind, she hopes to recall every detail of the Metro incident and examine the entire sequence in its most complete recollection. She can be her own best eyewitness.

She begins to run after dusk, the sky glooming. People hurrying home after work crowd the sidewalks. Hayley weaves through the pedestrians without effort or slackening her fast pace, as if by echolocation. She chooses a different route than usual, heading north on Fourteenth Street. Through Cardozo and Columbia Heights. Her mind wanders, flipping through a catalog of images from the derailment and its aftermath. She hears the shriek of metal on metal as the carriages ahead jump the track. Sees the woman's pale face, unaware of the blood that gushes from the femoral artery in her thigh. Flashlights dart against the cement tunnel walls. A rat scurries between her legs. Hayley does not attempt to filter or organize these impressions and memories as they flit past her mind's eye. With steady and robust running cadence, she passes through Crestwood and runs farther north. Into the Heights. Then Brightwood. No detail of the incident she recalls raises her suspicions or strikes her as out of place. She keeps running. Holds a strong pace. Into the leafy suburbs of Takoma and the terminus of Fourteenth Street. Veering left, at Aspen Street. Entering expansive Rock Creek Park.

Shadows deepen. The running path plunges into dark woods. Traffic on Beach Drive, through the park, is sporadic. Hayley registers none of it, her feet "seeing" for her. Memories of the derailment continue to cascade. The smell of electrical fire. Her helper's cowardly eyes. EMT trucks at the Rosslyn station entrance. The throng of onlookers. Shocked expressions. Sirens rending the morning air.

Then she *sees* him.

He is a young guy, in his twenties. Dark complexion. Black hair poking out of black ball cap and wearing a soccer jersey. Why is he smirking? His grin reminds her of the booking photo of the young man who shot the US congresswoman in Arizona, deranged and ecstatic. Why is he enjoying the spectacle of injured and stunned Metro passengers emerging from the Rosslyn station? Of all the onlookers, only the soccer jersey guy is smiling. Only him.

Hayley stops running and studies the image from her memory as if it is a three-dimensional object in the palm of her hand. Red soccer jersey with a gold Chevrolet logo splashed across the chest. What's the writing on his cap? Iron Pony Tap Room? She's heard of the place. The guy stands out, independent of the crowd. No reason for that smile. Unless he has something to do with the derailment? No one else could enjoy the terror and suffering the crash caused. No one.

Hayley has found what she wanted. She can turn around now and run home, about six miles, at a slower pace on her return. Immersed again in the world.

———————

TUESDAY, 7:54 P.M. Empire Apartments at 2000 F Street, in Washington's Foggy Bottom neighborhood, is an eight-story brick building with vague art deco pretensions. Comprising 150 studio apartments, none more than five hundred square feet in size, the Empire is the housing choice of the budget-minded renter who most likely has grander ambitions. It is a beachhead, from which the young and driven will launch their conquest of the nation's capital, within easy walking distance of more fashionable Georgetown.

Rafi's studio apartment, on the eighth floor, is furnished in total from Ikea and with complete disregard for visual pleasure. Utility is the underlying motif. There is no memorabilia or decoration. Pizza boxes and the detritus of other takeout meals litter a woefully unequipped kitchen. When not playing with dog toys strewn throughout the apartment or sleeping, Yazat is in the habit of grazing on the congealed leftovers in week-old food containers.

Rafi's laptop is open on a sixty-nine-dollar "Melltorp" table. He waits to hear from the Boss. A particularly enticing network exploit, discovered months earlier, remains viable. Rafi accessed it only an hour ago. The malware inserted in the natural gas pipeline's control system is a version of the Stuxnet computer worm. Rafi found the bug in the utility's network purely by chance. Malware like it infests networks across the country and around the globe, left by unnamed bad actors and then just as often forgotten. The revised Stuxnet worm, in this case, a one-shot weapon, is just waiting for someone like Rafi to stumble on, pick it up, and pull the trigger.

Rafi passes the time playing with Yazat. He especially enjoys hearing the dog's toenails clicking across the wood floor, in hot pursuit of a ball. Earlier, he watched some porn and masturbated. And before that, he danced around the room while listening to electronic music on his earbuds. He imagines how weird all of this would seem to the casual observer. But since no one is watching, who cares? With a few keystrokes on his laptop, he denied the United States its precious newspapers for a day. With only fractional more effort, he derailed a Metro train under the Potomac River. And now he is on the cusp of his most audacious hack yet. Rafi experiences a rush of adrenaline just thinking about it.

The warm, spring weather, while perfect for motorcycle riding, will undoubtedly undercut the impact of the attack. Still, taking out the control system that delivers natural gas to one-third of the US is pretty rad. Standing at the window and staring down at the street, he imagines the people walking past his building without hot water and gas for their cookstoves. The fools have no idea how anything in their world works. Do they appreciate the technical marvel in moving cubic tons of natural gas pulled from the earth in Texas thousands of miles across the country? Imagining their dumb, disappointed faces when they turn the knob on their stoves to make dinner makes Rafi hard. Even though it couldn't be more than an hour since he jerked off, he masturbates again.

Afterward, he retrieves the phone in his pocket and opens the Signal app. There is no message from the Boss. Impatient, he decides to break protocol and send a message himself.

I'm ready

Rafi sits at the Ikea table and taps a key on his laptop to bring it out of sleep mode. Keeping the secure messaging app on his phone open, he waits for a texted response.

Minutes pass. Finally receives a response.

Stand down. Assessing the situation.

Rafi shakes his head, frowning. What the fuck is this? Who knows if Transco system engineers won't stumble on the trapdoor themselves and close off the exploit?

He angrily responds to the Boss's text. *Before it goes away!!!!*

The Boss responds immediately. *Negative. Repeat, stand down.*

Rafi slams the phone on the table so hard that his laptop bounces. He can't stand it when people fail to follow through with a promise. He hates any display of weakness or failure of nerve. Full commitment is the only way to get anything done. Rafi stands and starts to pace back and forth across the small room, in high agitation.

Fuck it! The Boss instructed him earlier in the day to tee up the pipeline exploit. He only did as he was told. Time to finish the job.

He pulls the laptop toward him.

THE STAFFORD COMPRESSOR Station #2 in Stafford County, Virginia, southwest of Washington DC, is one of three stations for the Mid-Atlantic Coast Pipeline. Natural gas, extracted from deposits deep underground the Gulf Coast states and then pressurized, is moved to consumers on the East Coast through transmission pipes. Those pipelines are anywhere from six to forty-eight inches in diameter. Every hundred miles or so along its journey east, the natural gas must be repressurized with turbine-operated centrifugal compressors, then pumped forward again through the pipeline. For obvious reasons, compressor stations are located in semirural areas. Explosions of natural gas pipelines occur every year, but accidents that involve an entire compressor station are mercifully rare.

Five employees—one facility operator, an assistant engineer, and three pipeline technicians—are responsible for the operation of the station at any given time. From the Stafford location, two unmanned compressor stations downline are operated remotely. The job isn't exciting, but it does require meticulous attention to detail. Mistakes can have severe consequences. Bob Katz, on the job for more than three decades, initially wasn't too fired up with the idea of women in the control room. But, the truth is, Annie Hopkins has been a great addition to the team. The young college grad never needs to be told twice when given an order—unlike most guys on staff—and she's more interesting, too. Though he'd never admit it to anyone, the Stafford Compression Station nightshift facility operator manipulates the schedule so that his and Annie's shifts overlap.

The blue light of the control system computer screens casts Annie in an alien glow. Bob would swoon if he wasn't pushing sixty and recuperating from a mild heart attack four months earlier. Maybe he swoons just a little bit anyway.

"Tell me again about this knucklehead."

Annie says, "He's not a knucklehead, Bob. Ted is a shaman."

He likes to think of himself as a surrogate father to the young woman, who lost her dad to cancer while she was in college. "Uh-huh. And how do shamans make a buck again?"

"Ted helps people organize their living space so that the energies are beneficial."

The nightshift operator scoffs. "The only energy that matters is the stuff flowing through these pipes, Annie. That's energy!"

She smiles, ever tolerant of her supervisor's old-school crotchetiness. "Oh, don't be such a Bob, Bob."

He frowns comically, secretly loving this dynamic between them. He wonders, from time to time, if he shouldn't write down some of their banter and send it to a nephew he has in LA. Bob thinks this relationship with Annie would be a great TV show. He would call it *Compressor Station*. Judd Hirsch could play him. Is Judd Hirsch still alive? To be honest, he hasn't written more than a postcard since college, and his nephew is a tennis instructor with zero connection to the television business. Maybe in another life.

"Hey," Annie says, looking at one of her monitors. She points for Bob's benefit. "Look at these spin rate numbers."

Bob leans over and sees what Annie sees, elevated readings on every turbine in the joint, and rising. "1750 psi and rising!"

Annie starts tapping on her keyboard and reacts with alarm. "I'm locked out!"

Hunching over his keyboard, Bob squints at his monitor. "Got nothing here, too!"

He grabs a phone on his console. While he's waiting for headquarters to pick up, Annie keeps her eyes glued on the array of system monitors. Loud enough for the guys out in the truck bay to hear, she says, "2100 psi! Bob, we gotta get the hell out of here!"

"Wait . . ." Bob listens as the phone at the other end rings and rings.

"No, Bob, we've got to go *now*!"

Annie is out the door first but holds it open for Bob to exit. Red warning lights flash up and down the station and a loud siren wails, Annie having hit the alarm before fleeing the control room. One of the pipeline technicians jumps in his truck and tears ass for the gate while another dashes for the perimeter fence and woods beyond. There's no sign of the third technician. Stafford Compression Station emits an otherworldly whirring sound that rises in pitch and then deepens into a low, brutish growl.

Annie hightails it across the long grass, with a head start on the conflagration that is sure to follow. Looking over her shoulder, she expects to see the facility operator on her heels, but he's not there. Slowing her gait, Annie twists all the way around and observes her supervisor running back *toward* the control building.

"Bob!" Her scream cuts through the pipeline's guttural roar. The facility operator stops, turns, and faces Annie, a look of disbelief and confusion on his face. She runs back and firmly takes him by the arm. "C'mon, friend. We gotta go."

"Maybe I can fix it."

"Nobody can fix it, Bob. Not even you."

Annie pulls him along, the old man going willingly now. They arrive at the fence. She waits for him to clamber over first before she works her way up and drops down to the ground. Behind them, the turbine wail builds to a freakish intensity. Hand in hand, Bob and Annie run for the woods, where the others have taken refuge. They don't have to wait long. As they gawk in stupefied disbelief, Stafford Compression Station erupts in a crackling, thunderous fireball that expands and expands, enveloping everything in its path with smoke and powdery flame.

County fire officials the next day discover the body of the third pipeline technician in a flattened equipment shed. He represents Cyber Jihad's first kill. A fire engine racing to the incident fifteen minutes after the explosion hit an SUV that had failed to yield to the emergency vehicle. The driver, adult passenger, and three children inside the Toyota bring the total dead to six.

TUESDAY, 8:45 P.M. Due to pick up April at her place in fifteen minutes, Hayley is grabbing a quick shower when the hot water goes out. Not many years removed from army life, she guts out a rinse with cold water. Her television is tuned to cable news. Before she has finished dressing, Hayley sees the first reports of a tremendous explosion at a natural gas compression station thirty miles away in Virginia. The loss of hot water in her shower begins to make some sense. Turning the knobs on her gas stove to no effect, Hayley experiences the disconcerting buzz of being part of an evolving news event. She moves to turn off the television just as the cable news anchor reports a natural gas outage from Norfolk to New York City, the largest disruption of service in US history.

Hayley finds April waiting at the curb outside her place. The disgruntled expression on April's face is hard to miss as she settles into the passenger seat.

"What?"

"A *Volkswagen*?"

"I love my Golf," Hayley says defensively. "What kind of car do you have?"

Ignoring the question, April gestures forward. "Next time, I'll drive."

The Iron Pony Tap Room is a nine-minute drive away. Hungry for honest friendship, Hayley wants to connect with April in a more emotional and meaningful way than the clandestine work that binds them together. She wonders if the army lieutenant is lonely, too. Despite her many talents, Hayley cannot muster the necessary audacity to broach the topic. Instead, she drives in silence while April checks her phone for late-breaking news.

"Compressor station just south of here, in Stafford County. Turbines started to spin out of control, operators on-site couldn't do shit about it."

"Hacked."

April nods. "Sounds like a variant of Stuxnet, a malicious computer worm that alters the programmable logic controllers of industrial machinery like centrifuges and turbines. The malware was developed by US and Israeli intelligence agencies, in partnership to destroy Iranian uranium enrichment facilities at Natanz."

"Thanks for the seminar, April, but I know what Stuxnet is. I also know it took a dozen of your closest friends at the NSA two years to develop. That suggests the Cyber Jihad is no lone wolf."

"Not necessarily. After Iran, some moron inadvertently released the malware into the wild. Bad actors at every level of the cyberterrorism game have repurposed countless versions of it."

Parking down the block from the tavern, they exit the car and walk toward the entrance.

"You really think you'll be able to recognize this guy from memory?" April asks.

"Has Cyber Command or the NSA cracked the case?"

"Can't speak for the NSA, but we're getting nowhere close to full attribution."

They stop outside the entrance into the Iron Pony Tap Room. Hayley says, "Then I guess we should work with what I can remember."

Shaking her head, April follows Hayley through the doors. The motorcycle theme is self-evident, with vintage bikes and accessories in the display window, lined up along a balcony, and tucked into elevated nooks and crannies throughout the room. Music thunders from a stadium-grade sound system. The vibe is roadhouse casual and so is the young, boisterous crowd.

Hayley stands on the second step of stairs leading

up to a mezzanine and scans the throng, looking for the smirking, dark-complexioned man from her memory. The bright red Manchester United jersey would be a helpful beacon, but Hayley finds no one in the crowd who matches the image in her head.

"Anything?" April asks from one step below, shouting over the music.

Hayley ignores the question and pushes her way through the crowd toward the bar. She gestures to one of the bartenders. Making herself heard over the din isn't easy.

"I'm looking for someone. Dark complexion. Maybe Persian?"

"You got a name?"

Hayley shakes her head. "Wears a red Manchester United jersey."

The female bartender, thin as a stick and festooned with tattoos everywhere but on her face, shakes her head. "Sorry. You want something to drink?"

Hayley waves off the offer. "Maybe someone else behind the bar might know?"

"Believe me, I know every regular in the joint."

Hayley gestures her thanks and turns away from the bar. She rejoins April closer at the stairs.

"Waste of time," April says loudly over the music. Hayley doesn't argue.

———

RAFI EMERGES FROM the men's room where management, reluctant to close their doors due to the lack of hot water, has deposited industrial-size containers of hand sanitizer. Checking his phone, he sees he has received a third angry text from the Boss. He ignores it, the same as he disregarded the others. The messages express extreme displeasure with the premature attack on the compressor station. In Rafi's estimation, however, the action was a huge success. With only a few keystrokes on his laptop, he impacted the lives of almost sixty million people, ruining dinner plans, depriving everyone of hot water, and idling dozens of manufacturing plants. Though he has heard early reports of casualties, the big numbers are what excite Rafi the most. Sixty fucking million people impacted by him! How cool is that?!

Leading with the arrogant thrust of his chin, the computer hacker threads his way across the crowded floor to the bar and flags down the same tattooed bartender. "Burkey's," says Rafi, ordering his favorite house lager.

He's pretty sure the bartender is a lesbian and, therefore, another in the vast army of women who wouldn't fuck him if their last, dying breath depended on it. As she turns to fill his order, Rafi imagines shooting her in the back of the head with a Sig Sauer he keeps under his bed mattress. With his mind's eye, he imagines the exit wound in her forehead the size of a fried egg. Just thinking about it brings a smile to his face.

The bartender pulls him a pint. Placing it on the bar, she debates whether to say anything. Rafi is a frequent topic of conversation among the tavern's staff members. She remembers too well the night he accused a female patron of riding the "cock carousel" and got a drink tossed in his face. Several staff members lobbied management to permanently ban Rafi from the premises. But the freak is a riding buddy of Aaron, the manager, and so has staved off banishment for now. It doesn't hurt his cause that Rafi tips decently, for this crowd. Despite her hesitation, the bartender leans over to shout into his ear. "Some chick was just asking after you. Straight, like a cop."

Rafi stiffens visibly. "Who?"

She gestures toward Hayley and April exiting through the front doors. "The blond one. Didn't know your name, which is weird."

Rafi's expression goes flat as he watches the two young women leave. He immediately turns away from the bar, abandoning his untouched pint, and makes a beeline for the doors. The bartender shrugs, only too glad to be rid of him.

———————

HE EXITS THE bar moments after the two women and follows from behind. Fixing his gaze on his prey, Rafi pulls a wave knife from his right-hand pants pocket. With a hook on the spine of the blade that catches the pocket when retrieved, it releases automatically. The computer hacker used the same knife—an Emerson CQC-8—to kill the two muggers and Ethiopian convenience store cashier.

His hand tightens, loosens, and tightens again around the knife's handle as he listens to the two women in conversation.

"You seem distracted. I guess that means you've come up with a plan by now," the dark-haired one tells her blond friend.

"Not quite."

"No more memory slideshow featuring Cyber Jihad?"

"Give me time."

About fifteen feet separate Rafi from the two women. Oxygen moves in and out of his nostrils, massaging nasal mucosa and stimulating respiratory reflexes. Saliva secretes at an increased volume from submandibular and parotid glands inside his mouth in anticipation of slaughtering them both, responding to nerve signals from other centers of his central nervous system. Now that he has popped his cherry with the two muggers and Ethiopian dude, Rafi cannot wait to kill again. Years of martial arts and close combat training have paid off. The time to strike is now.

As he starts to lunge forward, the two young women abruptly veer to the right. More problematically, their paths diverge. The dark-haired female stops at the passenger door of a parked VW. The other one steps into the street and walks around the front of the vehicle, to the driver's side. Before he can be spotted, Rafi darts to his left and disappears into the shadows of a building doorway. He watches from his hiding place as the two young women climb inside the Volkswagen from either side of the car.

Cunts! Who are they? What agency would send them, driving a piece-of-shit car like the Golf? And, more alarming, how the hell did they know to come after *him*? As the VW pulls out from its parking space and surges into the lanes of traffic Rafi emerges from the shadows and is careful to note the Volkswagen's license plate number.

4

★ ★ ★ ★

CYBER JIHAD

*T*uesday, 10:35 p.m. April's place is well-ordered and fiercely decorated, as if still being staged for prospective buyers. Hayley stands in the foyer and takes in the exposed beamed ceilings, pocket doors, open shelving, and mammoth-size, stainless steel kitchen appliances with a muted expression.

"Bitcoin," April explains. "I got out when the dummies got in."

"Sounds legit," Hayley says, her voice dry as burnt toast.

"Don't look now, Chill, but your West Virginia is showing." April gestures toward a rusty pulley bracket still embedded in the exposed brick wall. "Helicopters used to be made in this building."

Hayley shrugs, more interested in the personal computer and large monitor attached to it. "Can you do any real analysis of the Stafford hack on that thing?"

"That 'thing' is an Overclockers UK 8Pack OrionX, two computer systems in one case. Thirty big ones, not counting the Samsung forty-nine-inch Ultra-Wide curved monitor." She sits down at the workstation and taps a track pad, bringing the entire system to life. "Acquisition, documentation, and recovery of data within twenty-four hours of an incident is critical because hackers abandon cyber infrastructure within hours of its discovery. More crucially, advanced malware dissipates in computer memory."

"You can access the affected networks from here?"

"Not *all* of them," April says, adding with a smile, "but a lot."

———

RAFI ZAMANI RIPS down K Street on the Ducati Monster 1200, reaching ninety miles per hour when the traffic lights are in his favor. Valves adjusted over the winter, the bike feels exhilarating between his legs, thrumming with powerful efficiency. Pedestrians scurry out of his way well in advance of his passing through an intersection, alerted by the Testastretta engine's twin-cylinder yowl. An occasional participant in illegal street race gatherings, Rafi revels in the bike's speed. The pure exhilaration and feeling of ecstatic freedom it delivers. He imagines this is what human flight would be like, the sheer exposure and propulsion of a human body through space.

He has gone down once. Riding requires total focus, the computation of numerous real-time factors every second the motorcycle is in motion. Anything less than absolute attention, however brief, invites a catastrophic mishap. Working out a particularly stubborn programming problem in his head while riding resulted in his one accident. Distracted, he had remained for too long a duration—five seconds at most—in a car's blind spot and was unable to evade the driver's sudden merge into Rafi's lane. Full-face helmet, riding boots, armored jacket, and Kevlar-lined pants provided adequate protection. Unharmed, Rafi walked away from the accident. His bike, a Triumph Street Twin, was a total loss. He bought the Ducati that afternoon and has since refrained from programming while riding.

K Street is clear of traffic at this late hour and unfolds under the front wheel of his bike without incident. The two women who came to the Iron Pony looking for him are evidence of a problem he must address. Rafi's sure he heard the dark-haired one say something about Cyber Jihad. Is it possible the attacks have been traced back to him? By any assessment, that would seem extremely improbable. To cover his movements, he initially tunneled into a mobile phone in Uruguay, then a server in Estonia, and finally into the SSH port of a smartwatch in Zimbabwe, which was the actual launchpad of the cyberattacks. There isn't a chance in hell anyone tracked his digital footprints. So how did these two females find him? What was the connection they made between him and Cyber Jihad?

As he parks his bike in a secure garage and heads

around the corner to the apartment on F Street, the thought hits him: one or both of the women were on the Blue Line train. Going to the Rosslyn station after the derailment to gape at the survivors while wearing his Iron Pony hat is the *only* physical connection between him and the Metro attack. Why else wouldn't they know his name? Rafi is astonished they identified him in the crowd of onlookers. No doubt, it was the idiot smile on his face that gave him away. Fuck. Rafi takes pride in his intellectual superiority. He has no tolerance for stupid mistakes, including his own. As punishment, he pauses at the entrance of his apartment building. He contemplates closing the heavy steel door on his fingers but decides the injury might impede his programming. Instead, he decides he will deny himself online porn for seven days. In many ways, Rafi would prefer smashing his hand in the doorjamb instead.

He lets himself into the apartment on the eighth floor. Yazat is dependably excited about his owner's return. The dog is Rafi's best friend and near-constant companion, second in importance only to his computer. Soon enough, with the keyboard under his fingertips, Rafi will again feel powerful and godlike. The females who came looking for him don't know his name or where to find him. He is invincible, beyond the reach of any who defy him.

With the license plate number of the Volkswagen Golf, Rafi will learn much about at least one of the women who dared find him. He has all that he needs to begin to formulate his counterpunch. Those bitches will pay. This is going to be fun! But first, he's got to walk the dog.

———————

WEDNESDAY, 4:11 A.M. Wrenched from sleep, Hayley is unsure where she is and what's happening. Shadowy figures attached to the tracking beams of flashlights flood into her line of sight. Shouting reverberates. Startled, she realizes this is not a dream.

"On your knees! Hands in the air! Now! Lemme see your hands!"

Hayley establishes she is in the compact living room area of her apartment, not in the bedroom. In that split second, she realizes she must have fallen asleep on her couch after getting home late from April's condo. Now there are ten gun barrels pointing at her head and chest. *I am dead*, she thinks. Her instinct is to fight her attackers, to take up the closest weapon, and fend off their assault.

They got me.

Unless I do something. Unless I fight back.

Hayley crouches lower to spring forward and throw herself on her attackers.

"DC Police! Let me see those hands!"

The words slowly permeate her consciousness. They're cops. She heard right, did she not? These are the police.

Fully awake now, Hayley raises her hands.

———————

THE DCP PATROL chief arrives just after sunrise, joining a captain, inspector, and lieutenant. The previous night's incident isn't the city's first case of "swatting"—the harassing tactic in which bad actors deceive emergency services into sending a police response team to another person's address—but it is the closest an innocent victim has come to being killed. The original tip about an individual brandishing a gun from the apartment's window was made via the MPD's online reporting tool. The assumption is that the suspect is a spurned lover or jealous ex-boyfriend. Hayley says nothing to disabuse them of the notion. The patrol chief assures Hayley that department experts will trace the tip back to a specific IP address, but the White House staffer knows better. She is all but sure the "tip" directing the police to her apartment was sent from a computer utilizing a VPN, and therefore untraceable.

Was this another of Andrew Wilde's exercises in mind-fuckery? Another ploy to "keep her on her toes?" Hayley is pissed. Knowing who targeted her will go a long way to improving her mood. She has a hunch that whoever swatted her would want firsthand confirmation their action was successful. After the authorities have departed, Hayley fires up her laptop. The minicam on her bookshelf, which she replaced after April had destroyed the original one, isn't the only surveillance precaution she has taken. The deeper state operative also placed a wide-angle mini-camera in the upper window frame, pointed down at the entrance to her building. The cops stormed into her apartment shortly after four; whoever swatted her desired to achieve the maximum disruption. The wee hours are the best time for operational mix-ups to cause unintended casualties, too. But four a.m. also ensures anyone on the street almost certainly has something to do with the attack.

Accessing the camera web-based server, Hayley rewinds the footage, to when the time stamp reads 04:10.00. She presses play. The video recording shows a dark street devoid of traffic and a deserted entryway leading into the apartment building. Two DCP armored SWAT vehicles and two regular patrol cars, lights flashing, come to a hard stop out front. Personnel exit from all four vehicles. The officers gather briefly at the entry door, until it is popped open with a breaching bar. They immediately pour into the building, disappearing from view.

Hayley continues to watch the footage, which depicts a static image of the stopped police vehicles in the street. At this hour, not even the customary lookie-loos happen upon the scene to gawk at the police action. Three more minutes pass without incident or any movement whatsoever in the street. After six minutes, she sees shifting shadows in the darkness of an alley across the street. A motorcyclist astride his bike, with the headlight switched off, slowly rolls out from a hiding place. The rider, wearing a full-face helmet with a mirrored visor, cannot be identified. But everything about his brief appearance in the footage—running lights off, stealth-like speed leaving the scene, and only

after the authorities head into the apartment building—
leads Hayley to connect the individual on the motorcycle with the swatting incident.

April arrives at seven, entering past a shattered entry
door the cops propped against the foyer wall. After
watching the surveillance footage, she agrees with
Hayley.

"At least we know we're moving in the right direction."

They were up for much of the night before, until
after three. Hayley mostly looked over April's shoulder
as the army lieutenant probed the gas utility's servers as
well as searched the dark web for anyone bragging about
pulling off the attack. Hackers are not known for their
modesty. Part of the thrill is recognition by their peers.
More than a dozen hackers claimed to be Cyber Jihad
on three different forums, but April dismissed them
as obvious wannabes. With only a few hours remaining before the start of another workday, Hayley politely
declined April's offer to spend the night. Ironically, she
assumed she would sleep better at home.

"The guy likes to watch. Seeing the havoc he can
create with his keyboard gives him a sense of power."

April surveys the ruination of the apartment's entryway. "Point taken." She gestures at the surveillance
video on the laptop's screen. "Is there any question this
is Cyber Jihad?"

"Nothing is certain until it is." Hayley freezes the
video on an image of the motorcyclist. "But I think it's
a strong possibility."

"Well, if that's our guy, I don't think he's going to be getting his buzz on at the Iron Pony anymore."

"Probably not."

April recites what they know. "Red soccer jersey. Snapback hat. Dark complexion."

"That's right."

"Age?"

"Midtwenties," Hayley says.

"My mind keeps circling back to the dark complexion part."

"Yeah. Me too."

"My mind keeps circling back to an Arab dude."

"He could be Arab. He could not be. Iran is a non-Arab country."

"This Mideastern fuck almost got your head blown off. Is that the correct usage?"

Hayley checks her watch. "I'm late for work."

"He knows who we are."

The White House staffer grins, just on this side of arrogant. "He knows who *I* am. My plates. Where I live and work."

"And so?"

"I can handle him." Not bragging. Just saying.

April smiles now, too. Fucking Hayley Chill.

WEDNESDAY, 6:45 A.M. Aleksandr Belyavskiy walks quickly up Fourteenth Street, anxious about setting the dead drop signal before seven a.m. That is the time when the GRU agent inside the White House residence will be checking it, as per the standard operating procedure. The weather has turned warmer, with air temperature and humidity that feels more like a typical Washington summer day. Had the city enjoyed the shortest spring on record? With sweat dripping from his brow, despite the early-morning hour, the Russian mutters quietly. It doesn't seem fair.

Of course, Belyavskiy knows he is under surveillance by agents with the CIA or FBI. And by his overseers in the GRU, too. He has no doubt they're all watching him now, though Belyavskiy cannot discern the enemy agents among the few pedestrians out this early in the morning. Are they watching him from the Spectrum TV van across the street? Or is it the transient sitting at a bus stop on the corner of K Street? What difference does it make? The dead drop isn't operated in the conventional sense of the term. Belyavskiy designed the communication link between himself and his asset in the White House. In his humble opinion, the system is ingenious. He takes pride in the fact that the Americans, despite their excellent intelligence services, don't have an inkling of the GRU's massive infiltration of their executive branch.

Konstantin Tabakov demanded a meeting with Belyavskiy late last night at the Ultrabar nightclub where a 106 dB noise level ensured the privacy of their conversation. The news Tabakov reported was a shock. Moscow's interpretation of the signal that Polkan delivered with his most recent message is that the president believes he is under suspicion from US intelligence ser-

vices. For all the GRU knows, the Americans are monitoring communications between Belyavskiy and his
asset. Only a face-to-face interview with the president
will reveal the full extent of damage to the operation.

Dubious of his superiors' suspicions, Belyavskiy
follows the protocol as he approaches the southwest
corner of the park at Franklin Square and casually sits
down on a bench. An FBI team of surveillance agents
is indeed watching the Russian operative. Their subsequent report will suggest Belyavskiy had arrived
at the dead drop but, finding no signal, left without
further activity. But, after the TASS journalist leaves
the bench, he strolls to the intersection at I and Fourteenth Streets. He may still be under surveillance,
but the true extent of his actions go unobserved. With
the tug on a cord inside his pocket, he deposits a few
grams of blue chalk powder at the base of the traffic
signal stanchion from a pouch inside the bottom of his
right pant leg.

The brief stop at the bench was a misdirect. Within
an hour, the patch of powdery chalk will be gone, erased
by the wind, but not before a passing, dark-skinned,
middle-aged man wearing the black uniform of a White
House usher takes note of the signal.

KYLE RODGERS LOOKS up from his reading when Hayley
blows into the office, a quarter after eight and forty-five
minutes later than her usual start time. Repairs to her
apartment door took time she hated to lose.

"Nice of you to join us."

Hayley sees no gain in telling her boss about the swatting incident. Her deeper state supervisor is another matter. She will have to find some time in the morning to make a full report to Andrew Wilde.

"Sorry, sir. Feeling just a little under the weather today."

Rodgers exaggerates rearing away from Hayley, who is standing just inside the doorway. "Infect me and I'll banish you to the EEOB," he says, referring to the Eisenhower Executive Office Building next door and home to most staffers of Hayley's rank. Her unique skills and abilities, not to mention almost single-handedly preventing Monroe's assassination, won her the coveted blue badge that granted her access into the West Wing.

Hayley settles in behind her desk. The stack of paperwork that accumulated in her absence yesterday is almost a foot high. "What's the latest?"

"Have you been in a coma? We're getting killed is the latest. Our friends on Capitol Hill are crawling up the president's ass. The usual criticism. Moscow is behind the cyberattacks, and Monroe refuses to respond because he's in bed with them, blah blah blah."

"POTUS has weathered these storms before," Hayley says evenly. "Holding off our response until attribution is confirmed is the correct course."

"Well, thank you, Madam President. I'll pass along your decision to the Joint Chiefs."

Hayley doesn't fully register her boss's snarky comeback, preoccupied with weightier concerns. Has Monroe heard back from his Russian handler? Hayley is determined to connect with the president at some point in the morning.

"Sir, do you mind if I get to some of this?" She gestures to the paperwork on her desk.

WEDNESDAY, 8:48 A.M. US president Richard Monroe sits on the edge of his bed, wearing only his slacks, socks, and undershirt. He feels a decade older than his sixty-seven years. As if the rigors of being president weren't enough, acting as a double agent with two masters to placate has taken a toll on both his physical and emotional health. So much for all that talk about the most powerful man on earth. He decided weeks earlier that the situation was no longer sustainable. His mission must end. But how? The path forward is treacherous. If the Americans decide he has become uncooperative, they will expose his true identity and throw him in jail for the rest of his life. If Moscow suspects he has been compromised or is cooperating with US authorities, they will surely have him assassinated. Monroe has no doubt the Kremlin has that capability. Look what they did to Jack Kennedy in response to his humiliation of Russia in the Cuban Missile Crisis.

In his latest message to Moscow, he crafted a signal subtle enough to fly over the heads of any American operatives who might be monitoring his communications with Belyavskiy. The worry for Monroe, of course, is he was *too* subtle. What if his masters in the Kremlin failed to interpret his distress call?

Among his many concerns, large and small, Richard Monroe's most pressing worry is for his wife, Cindy. He cannot bear the possibility of inflicting emotional pain on the woman. Nor can he imagine life without her. Is there any way forward that avoids either possibility? Monroe thinks not. Cindy will learn the truth about who he is and the country of his birth. That outcome is unavoidable. The most important thing, then, is keeping the two of them together. No matter what, the president must preserve his marriage to a woman he has loved since first laying eyes on her more than four decades ago.

They met when Monroe was a twenty-three-year-old second lieutenant stationed at Fort Campbell in Kentucky. She was a local girl, just eighteen, and the most beautiful woman he had ever seen in his life. They were married within a year of meeting, and though childless, their marital union has been one of enormous security and contentment. Up until the last two years, Monroe was successful in compartmentalizing his dual identities and shielding his wife from any evidence of his treachery. The integrity of the marriage held fast. All of that changed with Hayley Chill's bold and entirely true accusation that he was a Russian mole. Her hold over him has imperiled the strong, emotional bonds between Monroe and his wife. More than anything—even a bullet in the back of his head—Richard Monroe fears losing Cindy.

A gentle knock on his bedroom door lifts the president from his brooding. He raises his gaze to meet his wife's eyes as she enters.

Cindy Monroe is still the beauty who knocked Second Lieutenant Richard Monroe off his feet. Put together and styled with sensibly good taste, the First Lady is a tribute to that often awkward and unelected office. Seeing him, sitting on his bed, Cindy is shocked by the transformation of her husband. The responsibilities and stresses of his office have most certainly taken a toll on his physical appearance. With every new day, it seems, Cindy believes he has lost one more pound of weight or gained an additional line in his face. She involuntarily recalls the famous before and after pictures of Abraham Lincoln. The ravages of the sixteenth president's countenance are only one measure of the monumental difficulties of holding the country together.

"Darling."

"My love." Monroe stands and warmly embraces his wife.

"You look so tired. I'm worried about you."

"I'm okay. Just a little trouble sleeping, same as any man my age."

She nods with a sad, hopeful smile. "We'll survive this, too, together." The words are a struggle for her. This man beside her, capable of commanding armies and of passionate love, has been an indestructible force of nature for what seems like forever. Will the presidency prove to be his undoing? So many in Washington are out to undermine him. Cindy detests her husband's enemies. She is too familiar with the truly great and moral man that he is.

"Has anyone alive given more of himself for the United States of America than Richard Monroe?" she wonders aloud.

The president lowers his gaze to the lushly carpeted floor and broods. She has no idea. How could she possibly know just how truly stuck he is?

"My love," is all he can think to say. "Thank you. You are such great comfort."

The president again contemplates losing her and nearly buckles at the thought of it. He loves her so very much. Monroe considers the notion of telling Cindy— then and there, every shred of truth—if only to relieve the awful loneliness. As quickly as that idea occurs to him, the president dismisses it again. He'd rather die than tell her of his lies. Another time, under different circumstances.

Cindy sees these fears play across his face. "Darling, what is it?"

Monroe shakes his head and musters a brave smile. "I'm fine." He gives her a quick kiss on the lips. "I best finish dressing and get downstairs."

As she turns to exit the room, Cindy makes a mental note to speak to her husband's physician.

———————————

THE PRESIDENT HAS finished dressing and sits to put on his shoes. Sensing someone in the doorway, he thinks

Cindy may have returned but sees it is Alberto, one of his valets.

Monroe gestures to the staff person—dark complexioned and in his forties—dismissing him in no uncertain terms. "I'm fine. Thank you."

Alberto Barrios, originally from Cuba, arrived in Florida by boat in 2005, under the "wet foot, dry foot" immigration policy. Six feet tall, broad shouldered, with the hooded eyes of a lounge singer and a cleft chin, Barrios seems a collection of disparate human features rather than of one man. With three years of employment in the White House residence, he has compiled a sterling job report. Though the president hasn't exchanged more than a dozen words with the man—one of six valets—Richard Monroe instinctively likes him.

The valet fails to withdraw as ordered. Instead, he boldly steps into the bedroom and locks the door behind him. When he stopped at the corner of Fourteenth and I Street, Barrios observed the chalky signal Belyavskiy had left for him. Immediately retrieving a standard, civilian-grade smartphone from his pants pocket, the Cuban agent checked for a coded message from Moscow on an Internet chat board for amateur breeders of pugs. Among topics ranging from pug nutrition and corneal ulcers, he located a thread on the issue of dog training. Posts by a purported breeder with the Internet handle of "The Pug Whisperer" were coded messages left expressly for the White House valet. A graduate of Cuba's Intelligence Directorate training program on permanent loan to Russia's GRU, the whip-smart Barrios was able to decipher the message in his head. His orders were clear.

Richard Monroe, unaware of Barrios's covert status, is annoyed by the valet's intrusion into his bedroom. "I don't need you right now," he says sharply. "Please, go."

Barrios crosses the room. "*Stand up, Mr. President,*" he says in fluent Russian.

Stunned to hear his native language coming out of the mouth of his Cuban-born valet, Monroe is speechless.

"*Please stand, sir.*"

Barrios's tone compels Monroe to stand.

"What . . . what is this all about?"

"*My real name is Julio Carrera. I am an agent of Cuba's Intelligence Directorate, working in partnership with the GRU.*"

Not yet having regained his bearings, the president looks to the bookshelf holding his Sangamon edition of Carl Sandburg's biography of Lincoln. "You . . . ?" he asks.

Barrios switches to his accented English. In addition to Russian and his native Spanish, he speaks French and Chinese. "Yes. I am the agent responsible for facilitating your communication with Aleksandr Belyavskiy."

"But . . . why am I meeting you now? Like this?" Monroe is worried, fear creeping from the edges of his face. Will this man kill him in his bedroom?

"Spetssvyaz? Your signal in the last communication was intentional, was it not?"

"Yes . . ." His ploy worked!

"Moscow suspects the Americans discovered your operation here. Was that the meaning of your alert? Have you been compromised?"

"Compromised?" Monroe is convincing in his shocked disbelief. "No!"

The Cuban agent, thoroughly trained in interrogation techniques, observes his subject with an eye for psychological tics. No aspect of Monroe's bearing, facial expression, or the tonal quality of his voice escapes Barrios's analysis. The president feels as if he's an insect under a microscope. Monroe only now notices that the valet's hand rests casually on his shoulder, near the carotid artery, where it is undoubtedly registering his heart rate.

"I want to ask you again, Yuri Sergeev. Think carefully before you answer. Review in your mind every conversation and meeting you've had since your election to the presidency. Every one! Have agents from the CIA or FBI contacted you in regard to Operation Polkan?"

"Absolutely not," he responds, more firmly this second time.

Alberto Barrios says nothing and stares deep into Monroe's eyes. The president meets his gaze, unflinching, as his breathing becomes so shallow as to be nearly nonexistent.

"What was the intention of your signal?"

"I received a briefing from the CIA director that they confirmed intelligence of a Russian mole in the West Wing. A high-level asset. They are actively pursuing that intelligence and have reasonable confidence in identifying the individual."

Monroe anticipated the need for an imminent threat to Operation Polkan and gambled the GRU would have no way of confirming it. Though the president is sure Moscow has one or two spies inside the Central Intelligence Agency at any given time—Aldrich Ames being the most infamous example—he can count on the compartmentalized nature of that organization to lend credence to his fabrication.

"Did the CIA director mention any suspects? Not in their wildest paranoia would the Americans believe the US president is our spy."

"They know the asset is someone at the highest reaches, which means they're working extremely hard to expose him. To expose me!"

Again, the Cuban betrays no reaction to Monroe's alarming claims. Barrios was the best student among his peers at G2's training facility outside Havana. No other candidates even came close when Moscow requested a Cuban agent for special assignment to the GRU. Another decade of fieldwork and expectations are that he will return to his native Cuba. There are whispers back in Havana that an elevation to the minister of the *Dirección de Inteligencia* is within his reach.

"I will communicate your report to Moscow. Is there anything else?"

Monroe checks the time on his wristwatch, already late for his first meeting of the day downstairs. Within the hour, he is slated to travel via Marine One to

Andrews AFB for a flight to Cincinnati for the first rally of his reelection effort. "They need to get me out. And my wife. Moscow must exfiltrate both of us, together."

The Cuban doesn't react in the slightest, inscrutable behind his bland expression. With a curt nod, he turns toward the door.

"*I am a patriot!*" Monroe hisses after the valet, using his native Russian. "*Tell them I have always been a patriot!*"

Barrios unlocks the door and exits without comment.

HE CAME TO the United States aboard the *Coral II*, a rickety, barnacle-encrusted thirty-foot fishing boat crammed with twenty-one other illegal immigrants intent on a better life. They had left Matanzas, Cuba, at eight in the morning the day before, making the crossing overnight and approaching Islamorada after a seventeen-hour trip. Winds were light and seas mostly calm. The refugees were silent, rendered mute by anxiety and anticipation. Julio Carrera, not yet employing his "Barrios" alias, was twenty-nine and had been in the Cuban intelligence service for five years. He blended in easily with the other immigrants, sharing with them a rough appearance and haunted countenance. Of West African heritage, Julio Carrera suffered his share of racial bias despite living in Cuba's socialist utopia.

Another male refugee—redheaded, white as Castro,

and in his midfifties—gave him an insolent look in the chaotic boarding process. Julio bumped the man, perhaps not completely by accident. The redhead's hat, a Panama, was ridiculous. So were his leather shoes. The hard stares between them began with embarkation and continued for most of the voyage. The other immigrants kept their gazes down, but not the insolent redhead. Carrera's nemesis never stopped shooting dark glances in his direction. Despite the obvious dangers in crossing *Estrecho de Florida*, the man could focus on little else but his contempt for dark-skinned Carrera, the great-great-grandson of slaves brought to the Caribbean by their Spanish owners to cut sugarcane and toil in the plantation houses. Would the generations-old hate and cruelty of their ancestors spark to life again in a single and inadvertent collision of elbows?

The boat made landfall without incident. Federal authorities processed Julio Carrera and the other twenty *balseros* without delay. All were free to go by five p.m., only twelve hours after they had first set foot on US soil. The man with flagrant red hair emerged from the Customs and Border Protection facility in Miami. By taxi, he headed straight to El Mago de las Fritas, home of the best spicy Cuban "hamburger" in town. So intent was the insolent man on sampling El Mago's frita that he failed to notice Carrera exiting the CBP facility directly after him and following in a second taxi.

After his lunch, the redheaded man exited the small restaurant in West Miami wonderfully sated. He needed to relieve himself but avoided the busy men's room in

the café. Eighth Street, with four lanes of heavy traffic, offered no privacy. A narrow alley one storefront to
the west—running south, all the way to Ninth Street—
seemed more promising. The redheaded man ventured
there. He walked halfway down the alley, stopped at
the side of a trash dumpster, and unzipped, unaware
his nemesis from the *Coral II* was fast approaching.
Carrera held in his right hand a four-foot-long two-by-
four piece of discarded lumber. Hearing footsteps at
the last possible moment, midway through his piss, the
redheaded man turned to regard who would walk up
on someone so indisposed and saw only the big slab of
wood coming at his head.

———————————

STANDING WITH OTHER staffers on the South Lawn,
where Marine One awaits boarding by the president,
Hayley is concerned she has missed her chance to speak
with her double agent. She hoped there would have
been a moment alone with Monroe sometime after he
came down from the residence and before boarding
the Marine helicopter for his short trip to Andrews. But
the president was uncharacteristically tardy arriving
in the Oval Office and was unusually distracted when he
did. Typically, Hayley would find an occasion to speak
with Monroe in his private study, where there was no
possibility of inadvertent eavesdropping or a recording
device. But, with the compressed schedule due to his
departure, the president didn't set foot in the small suite
adjacent to the Oval Office.

Kyle Rodgers will be traveling with the president and moves to board the chopper. He turns to Hayley for last-minute instructions. "I have the agricultural bill briefing?"

Hayley indicates her boss's big, leather Buccio Tuscany barrister briefcase, one of his few affectations. "You have it, sir." She holds a stack of file folders in her arms. "Anything else? I'll be out of the office at lunch-time."

Seeing the president exit the residence and pause to answer questions from the corral of journalists gathered on the circular drive, Rodgers dismisses the other folders in Hayley's arms. "I'm good." He joins other high-level aides who will accompany Monroe on his five-hour trip. As per protocol, the president will be the last to board Marine One.

Finished with the reporters, Monroe strides across the lawn. He waves to invited guests who remain behind a nylon rope far to one side.

Hayley has a contingency plan. She must act now, regardless of protocol. Leaving the small crowd of staffers gathered on the lawn, she walks quickly across the South Lawn, in a direction that puts her on a path to meet Monroe as he nears the helicopter. Four Secret Service agents immediately move toward Hayley to intercept her.

"Mr. President!" she shouts, waving one of the folders.

Monroe sees Hayley. He gestures at his security detail, waving them off. "That's okay, guys."

The Secret Service agents retreat, forming a fifteen-yard-square perimeter around their president. Hayley and the president converge at the Marine helicopter's stairs, out of earshot of the protective unit.

She makes a big show of handing Monroe one of the folders from the stack in her arms. "This is the very important folder I neglected to give Kyle," she says expressionlessly.

Monroe takes the folder from her. "I asked." His tone of voice is sharp. Almost petulant. "Cyber Jihad is *not* a GRU operation." Tucking the folder under his arm, he climbs the stairs without allowing Hayley to speak any further.

She watches the president salute the Marine standing guard at the stairs and quickly board. The reliability of the president's intelligence is anyone's guess.

Minutes later, as Marine One lifts off and turns toward the east, it occurs to Hayley that Monroe was unusually eager to deliver this new information. He could have as easily allowed the Secret Service agents to thwart her efforts to connect. The president usually is so hostile to being "handled." Why cooperate now?

———————

WEDNESDAY, 1:15 P.M. Hayley walks through the doors of a Corner Bakery franchise two blocks east of the White House complex, escaping what is becoming an uncomfortably muggy day. One of the more affordable places to grab lunch in the area, the air-conditioned restaurant is crowded with Washington's support staff like herself. She sees April, in uniform, sitting in a booth with a window view of the street. Sitting down opposite her fellow deeper state operative, Hayley realizes she ate nothing all day except for an apple. There's only a glass of iced tea in front of April, whose appetite also seems to have vanished. Between them is the army lieutenant's open laptop.

"Let me see it."

April spins the laptop around so Hayley can view a video clip, surveillance footage of Rafi Zamani approaching down a sidewalk. He wears his customary Manchester United soccer jersey. The clip is barely six seconds in duration but provides a clear image of the hacker's face and features. Without his motorcycle helmet, he is fully recognizable.

Hayley cannot tear her eyes off the screen. "Where did you get this?"

"Restaurant next door to the Iron Pony had cameras on the sidewalk."

"They just *gave* this to you?"

"Hell no. From Meade, we can even access the baby monitor in your sister's house."

"I'd rather you not." Hayley plays the short video again. "That's him. That's the guy I saw at the Rosslyn station after the derailment."

"Not really Slavic looking, is he?"

"No, not really."

"Iranian more like."

"Retaliation for taking out Suleimani?"

"Maybe. Tehran has sleeper agents in the US. Most came over on student visas and never left."

"Good place to look."

"Iranian foreign exchange students with computer science majors is going to be a really big database."

Hayley receives a text and checks her KryptAll phone. "He's here."

A black Yukon SUV with darkly tinted windows idles at the curb. Walking briskly from the restaurant entrance to the vehicle, Hayley opens the front passenger door and gets in. April climbs in back, carrying her computer tote.

Andrew Wilde is behind the wheel, anxious to be moving again. He steps on the accelerator even before April has closed the door behind her and merges into traffic on Seventh Street, heading north. "Talk to me."

"Sir, we have video of the cyberattacker, or at least one of them," says Hayley.

"This is the individual you saw outside the Metro station?"

"Yes, sir."

Wilde gestures impatiently.

April pops open her computer and holds it up, over the front seat, so that Wilde can view the video. Hayley pretends not to notice him driving without watching the road ahead.

"Mideastern ethnicity, sir. Without a doubt," April says.

Wilde puts his eyes back on the road. "That covers a lot of countries."

"We're thinking Iran's Cyber Defense Command, given the sophistication of the Metro attack."

Wilde looks to Hayley for a second opinion. "What else makes you think this guy is involved?"

"He swatted me hours after we looked him up at the bar he frequents," says Hayley.

"How do you know he was the one who swatted you?"

"You mean, how do I know it wasn't you?"

Andrew Wilde maintains a stony expression, waiting for Hayley to get to the point.

"I have a camera on the street and building entry, sir. This guy likes to watch. He was at both the train and swatting locations."

Wilde doesn't respond to Hayley's statement but instead pulls over to the curb. "Keep pushing, Lieutenant Wu. We'll communicate through normal channels tonight. Tomorrow morning at the latest. Put a name on this guy."

April realizes her superior is ordering her out of the vehicle.

"Are you kidding? I'm blocks from where I parked."

Wilde says nothing but only stares out the windshield, waiting for her to leave.

April pushes open her door, exiting. "And I thought Uber sucked."

Wilde pulls away from the curb the moment April has shut her door. "You have to do what you can to influence the president. The intelligence community is going full tilt at this Russian theory. We need to know why. And we don't want him to do something stupid."

"Like going to war with Russia?"

"That would be one thing."

"Secretary Ryan has essentially asked me to perform the same function."

"Is this your way of asking me if the secretary of Homeland Security is with Publius?"

"No, sir."

"Clare Ryan is *not* one of us." Off her dubious expression, Wilde says, "Our superiors are no longer in government service, remember? That's what makes it work."

"But agendas still might overlap. There are good guys out there, sir."

"Your primary objective remains the same: running Richard Monroe as a double agent. Assist Wu only in that capacity, from inside the West Wing. In other words, stop running around the city chasing after bad guys."

His manner is brusque even by Wilde's standards. Though they have been in almost daily contact for more than two years, it occurs to Hayley that she knows nothing about her superior's personal life. Is Andrew Wilde married? Does he have children? What had he been before he became involved with Publius? He is a specter. Unknowable. Her association with this man is inherently insecure.

"Have I done something to disappoint you, sir? Why am I suddenly not to be trusted?"

"We're not in the trust business." He clearly has no patience for such chatter. "Did the president make contact with his Russian handler?"

"I was able to speak briefly with Monroe. Moscow denied responsibility for the cyberattacks."

"Do you believe him?"

"I have no reason to believe him or not."

"Precisely." Wilde reaches into his pocket and withdraws what looks every bit like a presentation box of a wedding ring. He offers it to Hayley.

"What is this?"

"See for yourself."

Hayley accepts the box and opens it, revealing a gleaming white dental crown.

Wilde says, "Fauchard bug, in recognition of the French physician credited with being the father of modern dentistry."

"A listening device? I thought those were an urban myth, like Bigfoot."

"What makes you think Bigfoot doesn't actually exist?"

Hayley says nothing, wary of the "absence of evidence is not evidence of absence" quagmire.

"DARPA is working on something like it, still in the trial stages, but our people have refined the technology," says Wilde, referring to the Defense Advance Research Projects Agency. "Ingenious, really. Records to an encrypted server. Every fart, every belch. The subject's skull acts as an organic transducer, converting sound that enters the tympanic cavities and drawing from the body's temperature for power. It's good kit."

"For the president . . . or for me?"

Wilde ignores that gibe, too. "We've accessed and

reviewed his dental records. The bug fits directly over his second molar, upper-right side. Completely undetectable."

Hayley pockets the device. "Monroe isn't going to like it."

"Who would?" Wilde checks his watch. He has someplace to be.

———————

WORKING FROM HIS laptop in the Foggy Bottom apartment, Rafi accesses the Pentagon's servers by utilizing exploits he'd discovered months earlier. Blowing through every security measure he encounters, the hacker marvels at the idiocy of his adversaries. Those faceless information technologists have constructed their flimsy firewalls and porous safeguards with the digital equivalent of rice paper. Swatting Hayley Chill and watching it all go down was super cool. But Rafi won't feel completely secure until he has her in his cyber grip. Strolling through the DoD directories and subdirectories, with his pursuer's unique surname as a search term, Rafi prowls for additional nuggets. Now the real fun can begin.

———————

WEDNESDAY, 4:41 P.M. April's team has been on the case since Monday, the day of the Metro derailment. The results of their analysis are similar to those of other units at both Cyber Command and the NSA. Instructions in all of the cyberattacks were sent via different, seemingly random mobile devices, and from every corner of the globe. The server in Estonia was the second link of the chain in each attack, unmistakably linking them. Analysts believe the signature is intentional, Cyber Jihad's way of saying, "Yeah, this is us again." Given the sheer volume of traffic through the Estonian server, however, it is virtually impossible to trace the attack instructions back to a primary source. Cyber Command's soldiers are talented systems engineers. Despite access to some of the most powerful computers in existence, however, they have so far failed to achieve full attribution with an acceptable level of confidence.

The unit's workspace resembles NASA's mission control room. Soldiers wearing army combat OCP uniforms sit before a bank of video monitors stacked in a double row. Larger flat-screen monitors line three walls of the room. Corporal Oscar Nathans, born and raised on the east side of Wilmington, Delaware, occupies a prime position at one end of the rear tier of consoles. With a mind and math skills that might have withered in the public schools available to him, Nathans was fortunate to have a mother who refused to accept a subpar education for her only son. Through a combination of scholarships and his mom's two full-time jobs, Nathans was able to attend All Saints Catholic School, where a dedicated staff emphasized instruction in science and engineering. He excelled in that nurturing educational environment, flourishing in a manner even his mother could not have anticipated. Intending to take advantage of the US military's education benefits, Nathans enlisted in the army the day after high school graduation.

Tireless, good-natured, and uncomplaining, he was a natural for Cyber Command. Corporal Nathans is first to arrive for his shift and often the last to leave. Last summer, the unit got together at a local bar to drink some beer, eat crabs, and watch the Nationals pound the Mets. Some drunken doofus made the terrible decision to make a too hard play on April. With her training, both at basic and the secret Publius camp in Oregon, the army lieutenant didn't need anybody's protection. Regardless, Nathans threw all of his 165 pounds at the drunk *and* his inebriated buddies. By the time the fight was settled, and the combatants separated, the soldiers from Cyber Command bestowed on skinny Corporal Nathans the nickname "Nails." He will separate from the army in four years, lured away by a job in San Jose, California. The software he will develop for the distribution of cryptocurrency will revolutionize blockchain technology, catapulting him to the ranks of the one hundred wealthiest people in America. Not even his closest associates or family members will know the origin story of his company's name, Nails Tech, but Oscar Nathans likes it that way. Who would understand the subtleties of his secret, unrequited affections for the army lieutenant in charge of his old unit at USCYBERCOM?

Though April directed the unit's energies into the analysis of Cyber Jihad's attacks, Corporal Nathans has endeavored to maintain routine monitoring of Defense

Department networks. His genius is an uncanny sensitivity to systemic anomalies, subtle blips in observable data that scroll across the computer screens in real time. Nathans had been working the Cyber Jihad trace when something unusual on one of his monitors caught his attention. Focusing more closely on the DoD net display, Nathans observes what he's sure is an unauthorized intrusion. Though attempts at getting inside government networks occur on the order of thousands of times on any given day, a successful breach is extraordinarily unusual. Nathans sits up straight in his seat.

"Lieutenant?"

April, seated at the first tier of consoles, glances in Corporal Nathans's direction. The look on his face tells her it's important. She immediately stands and goes to his station, looking over Nathans's shoulders at the screen he indicates.

"You see, Lieutenant? DoA records servers."

April says, "Jump on it, Corporal Nathans. Let's see where this bandit's coming from."

Nathan's fingers fly over his keyboard, his face cast in the green glow of the monitor bank arrayed before him.

———————————

YAZAT IS BARKING his fucking head off like an idiot, which means he needs to be taken out for a crap, but Rafi doesn't have three minutes to spare. He got what he wanted. But the hacker is looking for just a little bit more candy in the DoA servers when he sees a digital alarm he placed on his network exploit exactly for this reason. His fingerprints are still fresh on the army servers. There's no time to start erasing them. The Boss didn't approve an attack on the Pentagon—Rafi hasn't received any communication from his honcho in more than a day—but there is no other option. He must zero out the DoA servers.

He knows precisely where to find the logic bomb in the Pentagon system because he placed it there months earlier. Rafi can't suppress a grin. He always wanted to do a number on the US Department of Defense.

———————————

NATHANS WATCHES THE Pentagon servers—specifically Department of Army nets—blow up on the monitors in real time, his face registering his dismay.

"Holy crap!" Nathans's fingers freeze over his keyboard.

About two seconds later, every screen in the unit's command room blossoms with digital gibberish. Three seconds after that, the screens go entirely dark. Cyber Command itself has been taken out.

"Army nets dropped and took out the rest of the DoD!"

April is the unit's commanding officer. She doesn't have the luxury of disbelief. The Pentagon has been attacked in a manner that is as real as terrorists commandeering American Airlines Flight 77 and flying it into the side of the building on 9/11. She stands and directs her voice to the entire room.

"Repair and rebuild, people! Now!" She looks to Nathans. "This could be the same group we've been after. We caught him with his hand in the cookie jar."

"On it, Lieutenant!"

As Corporal Nathans and the rest of the unit swings into action, April reaches for her phone.

5

★ ★ ★ ★

THE TRUTH IS AN ACT OF LOVE

*W*ednesday, 5:10 *p.m.* The takedown of Pentagon servers raises the level of frenzy inside the West Wing to the degree that would alarm the most casual of observers. America is under attack. No one can say with absolute certainty by whom. Seated at her desk in Kyle Rodgers's office, Hayley Chill juggles tasks both complex and mundane. She hasn't been able to communicate with the president since he lifted off from the South Lawn in Marine One that morning. Her orders are clear: exert her influence in the West Wing, as artfully as she can, to prevent the intelligence community from bullying the president into an unnecessary conflict. But that task was made much more difficult by the attack on the DoD servers. An unknown actor is in play. Events threaten to spiral out of control. Hayley hasn't heard from April Wu since their brief meeting at lunchtime. No doubt, the scene at Cyber Command is even more chaotic than at the White House.

Hayley doesn't look forward to informing Monroe of his need to affix the Fauchard bug in his mouth. She plans to assess the president's emotional state at the National Security Council meeting. Hayley is scheduled to attend with Kyle Rodgers. Her primary concern is the attack on the Pentagon's servers will force the president's hand. The deeper state operative can count on Clare Ryan to lobby for a cautious approach. But Monroe has seemed increasingly antagonistic toward his Homeland Security secretary. Does he have a problem with powerful women? Seated at her desk, Hayley watches Rodgers prep for the NSC meeting. His influence with Richard Monroe cannot be overestimated.

"Will it be war, sir?" she asks Rodgers, interrupting his review of the briefing book.

The presidential advisor shrugs. "Define 'war.'"

"Missiles launched. A radioactive Richmond, Virginia. Projected losses in the millions."

"We're several levels lower than that, war-game-wise, don't you think?"

"Not if you're on the chat boards that I monitor."

"Nothing good ever came of a chat board."

"Sir, the president might call on you for your opinion in the NSC meeting."

"Thanks for reminding me what my job entails, Hayley." He is vague for a good reason; they are entering uncharted strategic territory. At Pearl Harbor, the US knew who the bad guys were. The situation wasn't a subtle one. Though Hayley has always struck him as entirely loyal, Rodgers realizes with a start that he might have gravely misjudged his chief of staff. "What are you driving at?"

Hayley says, "I'm just curious what you think, sir."

"I think we're under attack."

Aware she is pushing too hard but compelled to do so by the circumstances, Hayley asks, "And the president?"

"Your guess is most likely better than mine," Rodgers says, more pointedly than he wants. He checks his watch. "It's time."

His caginess does nothing to alleviate Hayley's concerns. Has she lost his trust? Even more than before, she is relieved to have made an ally in Clare Ryan. Friends in the West Wing are in short supply.

———————————————

PARTICIPANTS JAM THE Situation Room in the basement of the West Wing for an emergency meeting of the National Security Council. Every seat at the expansive conference table is occupied. Aides stand two-deep along two walls. Richard Monroe enters the room, looking unusually haggard. Only Hayley Chill, among all assembled in the room, comprehends the true extent of the president's inner conflict. Despite the mercenary nature of their connection, she cannot help but have compassion for the man. Up to this point, his deception has been flawless. No one in the room has the slightest shred of doubt regarding his nationality and allegiance. But assessing the president's distracted expression, Hayley Chill worries the president's usually fierce resolve has begun to bend under the weight of his impossible situation.

Everyone in the room stands with Monroe's arrival and waits while he makes his way to his chair at the center of the table. Without a clear reason, the world's most powerful man pauses where Kyle Rodgers and Hayley stand along the back wall.

"Ms. Chill," the president says, cryptically, fixing his gaze on her.

"Mr. President." Her return of his greeting is both neutral and respectful. But Hayley's mind races. What is Monroe trying to say to her?

He holds her gaze for another awkward moment and then takes his seat. He gestures in Hayley's direction.

"That young lady saved my life, in case any of you didn't know."

Of course, everyone in the room knows the full details of the assassination attempt and respond with throttled silence.

Monroe continues his awkward digression, saying, "Saved my life when *they* tried to kill me."

The assembled council members don't know how to respond. Their anxiety is palpable. Clare Ryan steps into the void of the collective muteness. With a carefully modulated tone, she says, "Perhaps we should hear from General Hernandez first, Mr. President? His best people are on this."

Hernandez, seated at the far end of the table, clears

his throat to speak. But Monroe interrupts the general with an impatient gesture.

"I already know what he's going to say, goddammit. The Russians! The Russians have done all of it!"

The officials gathered around the table exchange more looks of deep concern. Vice President Landers clears his throat more loudly than he intends.

Kyle Rodgers steps forward and bends down to speak discreetly, into Monroe's ear. "Mr. President . . ."

"Anyone want to know what I think? Those Chinese sons of bitches are behind this business. Or the North Koreans, for Christ's sake. They can't afford to hit us with anything *real*. Cyber is one helluva bargain compared to an intercontinental missile."

Once again, stunned silence follows the president's outburst. Hayley aches to do something to help, but inserting herself in the situation would be wildly inappropriate. Prone to act decisively, it pains her to do nothing.

Clare Ryan isn't similarly restrained by protocol. She thumps the table with her closed fist, hoping to take everyone's eyes off the president. "Mr. President, that is *exactly* the point. If we can't go on the offensive because of our inability to determine the identity of our attacker, isn't the most prudent course one that protects us? Sir, with an executive order from you, DHS can begin building defenses into the civilian sector that would mirror those already in place for government networks. This is our sworn duty as public officials. We must protect the people first."

Ryan's proposal is a direct challenge to Hernandez's ownership of all things regarding cyber warfare, whether offensive or defensive. Not a sitting member of the National Security Council, however, he speaks only at the behest of the president or NSC member. For the time being, at least, he must remain silent.

Richard Monroe says, "Maybe we should ask Hayley Chill what she thinks?"

Audible gasps greet this latest aberration of presidential behavior. The president seems oblivious and swivels around in his chair, looking to Kyle Rodgers's twenty-seven-year-old chief of staff. "Ms. Chill? Want to jump into this?"

The focus is on Hayley now. She must exercise extreme caution and not panic. With cool deference, she says, "Sir, with the assistance of the members of this council, I'm sure you'll make the proper assessment and undertake the appropriate course of action."

For a long moment after Hayley's statement, the room wallows in shocked disbelief. Kyle Rodgers, sensitive to the gravity of the situation, positions himself directly behind Monroe's chair. "Unfortunately, the president will have to cut this short. We're due upstairs for a briefing of the Gang of Eight," he says, referring to the eight members within the US Congress that possess a highest-level security clearance. "Mr. Vice President?"

Landers looks startled to be called upon by the president's senior advisor and seems woefully ill-prepared to take over the meeting. What comes out of his mouth aren't so much words as guttural posturing.

Monroe appears confused by his sudden departure from the meeting. More aides enter the room. A scrum of officials gets the president to his feet and out the door. With the vice president's failure to take up the mantle, everyone in the room stands up from the table. The meeting is presumed concluded.

Clare Ryan pauses to have a word with Hayley on her way out the door.

"You handled that well, though I shouldn't be surprised."

"Ma'am, the pressures could get to anybody. The president isn't Superman."

"The other cabinet members will have to be apprised of the situation." Clare isn't above some gallows humor. "Look on the bright side. We're not bombing Moscow."

"No, ma'am." Hayley debates whether to say what's on her mind. "Madam Secretary, I have reason to believe that Cyber Jihad might be a cutout operation for the Iranian intelligence service. More repercussions from the hit on Major General Suleimani."

The cabinet secretary is astonished by Hayley's news. "What's your evidence?"

"I can't really divulge more right now, ma'am. But in regard to our earlier conversations, I can't agree with you more. The president must not order a cyber response on Russia."

Clare says, "I'm not sure the president is in the position to order lunch. But the NSA director's confidence that the Russians are responsible, backed by the full weight of that agency, is going to be difficult to

dislodge, to say the least." With a curt nod, the cabinet
secretary continues out of the room.

HE LEARNED BY phone his son was dead. At the time,
in 2014, Carlos Hernandez was serving as director
of intelligence for the military's Pacific Command,
at Camp Smith in Hawaii. He and his wife had trav-
eled to the mainland for a well-earned vacation on the
Oregon coast. Having just teed off with his group—
good friends he'd known for the entirety of his three
decades in the military—Hernandez was sizing up his
approach shot when one of the young guys from the
pro shop at Bandon Dunes arrived on a golf cart with
an urgent message. Hernandez and his pals had long
maintained a tradition of no cell phones when golf-
ing. He privately cursed the inconvenience as he rode
back up the first fairway toward the clubhouse with the
assistant pro.

A contact in the White House was on the line.
Hernandez received news of the crash of Malaysia Airlines Flight 17 before the wire services had it. A Buk
ground-to-air missile brought down the plane, believed
to have been fired by pro-Russian separatists. His only
son, twenty-six-year-old Diego, was a passenger on the
doomed jetliner, traveling to Kuala Lumpur on business. Now he was dead. The reality of it was almost too
much to bear. His son's body parts were strewn across
the village of Hrabove in eastern Ukraine's Donetsk
Oblast, comingled with the remains of other passen-

gers and the debris left by the crashed Boeing 777. The general hung up the phone. His first thought was for his wife and how the news of Diego's violent death would utterly devastate her. His second thought was of revenge, the beginning of a decade-long obsession that has never abated.

The Russians, of course, denied all connection to the "accident." Despite a meticulous international investigation, officials in Moscow relentlessly deflected blame. Rumors and conspiracy theories arose in the absence of admitted responsibility. The propaganda surrounding the incident was grotesque. Some Russian commentators suggested the bodies recovered from the crash site were already dead when they fell to the ground. As years of investigation and conjecture dragged on, almost all observers understood that the individuals responsible for the atrocity would never be held accountable. No matter how many details were uncovered and then dutifully conveyed to the family members of victims, the truth seemed increasingly difficult to frame.

After a voluminous investigation, even the most casually interested parties learned the Buk missile was capable of traveling at three times the speed of sound and hitting a target as high as ninety thousand feet. A cursory examination of documents revealed that the missile carried a 9N314M-model warhead, with an explosive core containing preformed iron fragments. Guided by radar to its target, the missile passed above and to the right of the cockpit and exploded by means of a proximity fuse. In an instant, that side of the jetliner's airframe was utterly destroyed. But few of the victims' civilian loved ones could fully comprehend the destructive power when the missile's core exploded. Eight hundred preformed iron fragments perforated the fuselage skin of the business class section, where Diego was seated. Carlos Hernandez has experienced combat in many different forms. He's all too familiar with modern weaponry's effect on a human body. That agonizing awareness is a burden the general must bear. He can *see* with his mind's eye all too well the carnage inflicted on his son.

Unit F6 occupies a corner suite on the top floor of the NSA headquarters at 9800 Savage Road. It is a far different working environment than April Wu's windowless bunker in the basement of the same building. Looking more like the offices of a hedge fund than one of the nation's signals intelligence laboratories, the unit is staffed by twenty-four civilians. Mostly men in their twenties and thirties, they represent the all-star team of the NSA's cyber offensive effort. The unit leader, Alfred Updike, dressed in blue jeans, leather sandals, and a Massive Attack T-shirt, hits a button on the wall next to the door. A secure locking mechanism disengages, granting entry to the agency director, Carlos Hernandez.

"Thanks for swinging by, General. Follow me?"

Updike's scruffy beard and slacker attire suggest aging surfer more than math PhD and systems engineering wiz. In his forties and father to six kids with the run of a rambling farmhouse in Spotsylvania County, Virginia, the F6 team leader is an unabashed financial

donor to progressive causes and the antithesis of the
NSA analyst stereotype. Hernandez accommodates
these and other quirks because Updike is the best in
the business. Among many skills in computer network
operations and information systems security, the F6
unit leader is valued most for his ability to marshal
the talents of the younger analysts under his direction.
No mean task, managing the prodigious intellects and
eccentric personalities of the young people in this room
requires an equally intelligent and unconventional
mind. Updike makes it all look easy. He has habitually
delivered results.

The two men stride across the room toward Updike's
work area.

Hernandez is all business. "CYBERCOM rebuilt
DoD nets and got us back online within forty minutes
of the attack, but data loss is widespread. It'll be months
before the Pentagon can restore less critical directories
from off-line archives." Following closely on Updike's
heels, the general nearly trips over a sleeping mouse-
gray Weimaraner.

"For Christ's sake!"

Updike grins good-naturedly. "The kids love bringing
their beasts. Whatever keeps 'em at their desk, right?"
He crouches down to administer a vigorous caressing
to the dog.

Hernandez glances at the wall clock and sees it's
nearly nine p.m. "You mind, Alf?"

"Of course. Sorry, boss."

They take a seat at a cluttered workstation. Updike

indicates computer code on his huge monitor. Written in C++ programming language, it might as well be Sanskrit for all Hernandez knows.

Updike says, "One of my guys found the worm in DoA network stacks thirty minutes ago. We pulled the very same program off a server belonging to one of the Kremlin's proxy hackers-for-hire in Saint Petersburg just a month ago." The unit leader pauses to grin mischievously. "Of course, they didn't know we were ever there."

Hernandez's eyes shimmer with excitement. "Where would you strike, Alf? Game the scenario for me."

Updike doesn't have to ponder it longer than two seconds. "Turn off the lights at the Kremlin. Moscow TV goes dark. Combo of the two, maybe."

The Weimaraner comes over for a pat, which he fails to receive from the general. "Prep the exploit packets. National TV assets. We'll lay off the Kremlin for now." Hernandez stands, always on the go. "And they say I have a hard-on for Russia."

WEDNESDAY, 10:05 P.M. Hayley leaves the White House complex through the Seventeenth Street gate. She looks forward to a slow, meditative walk home after an impossibly long day. But the stroll proves to be anything but leisurely. Cable news and other media outlets cover no other story except Cyber Jihad. With each successive cyberattack, the country experiences a ratcheting up of fear and anxiety. Panic buying swamps gas stations and grocery stores. Lines at ATMs stretch for blocks. The unusually warm, muggy weather is doing nothing to settle nerves. In the ten-minute walk home, Hayley sees numerous manifestations of the fear gripping the city. Though the damage inflicted on the infrastructure in Cyber Jihad's first attacks has been almost immediately repaired in each instance, citizens in the nation's capital are thoroughly terrified. Seven dead from the Stafford explosion and an additional fatality—the heart attack of a civilian employee at the Pentagon's Microsoft-run server farm in Maryland—has only added to the growing terror. How much greater would the nation's apprehension be if the president's erratic behavior in the Situation Room is made public?

She knows the president well enough to understand his impulse to call her out during the NSC meeting. Brooding on the incident as she walks, Hayley considers whether or not she should inform Andrew Wilde and decides against it. Despite the president's worsening agitation, Hayley is now convinced the threat posed by Cyber Jihad is the graver one. The attacks are clearly escalating in severity. The pattern is unmistakable. If Hayley informs her deeper state superior about the president's conduct in the Situation Room, she fears the organization will pull her off of April Wu's mission to concentrate exclusively on Monroe. Aware this obfuscation is potentially dangerous, Hayley is nonetheless confident in her assessment. This isn't the first time she has prioritized the greater of two evils.

While stationed at Fort Hood, before her recruit-

ment by Publius, she enrolled in classes at Central
Texas College. Back home in Lincoln County, higher
education wasn't much of a consideration. The scruffy
kids that comprised Hayley's set viewed with suspicion
so lofty an idea as college. Self-worth wasn't part of the
social fabric. Many of the enlisted soldiers in Hayley's
unit shared that same attitude. An unrecognized caste
system prevented young people of similar socioeconomic backgrounds—whether raised in urban or rural
areas of the country—to seek higher education.

Soldier by day and college student by night, she had
almost no free time. The majority of her classmates had
never been out of the state and were overwhelmingly
the product of overcrowded, low-quality public high
schools. College-level calculus proved to be a challenge
for almost every student in class except Hayley, who
breezed through the course. Perhaps it was because
of that proficiency the ringleaders of a cheating conspiracy didn't approach her. As final exams approached,
two male students broke into the professor's ten-year-
old Jeep Cherokee, rifled through his briefcase, and
obtained a copy of the test. The plan was to steal something else of value to mask the true objective of the
break-in. The thieves, however, discovered something
inside the vehicle they could not have anticipated.

In the professor's briefcase, they found Polaroid-
style snapshots of nude children. Recovered from that
jolt of discovery, the thieves pressed forward with their
original plan. Using a smartphone, they took photos of
the final calculus exam and—leaving the discovered

child pornography undisturbed—locked up the car again without any sign of a break-in. The two thieves told other students involved in the cheating scheme about the child pornography they had found. A furious debate ensued. Many of them thought the best course of action was to file an anonymous tip with the police. Others argued that doing so would endanger their prospects. The administration would surely remove their professor from his duties. A different teacher would replace him, potentially with a new test. Or, worse, exposure of the child porn would also reveal the existence of the cheating scheme.

One of the young women involved in the plot was Latetia Wilson, from a broken home and subject to her mother's frequent rages. Throughout the year, she was particularly dependent on Hayley for friendship and emotional support. Now suffering from pangs of conscience, Latetia confessed all to her older friend and begged for guidance. Hayley pondered her fellow students' predicament. Clearly, something had to be done to stop an obvious sex abuser. But, in alerting the authorities, she would potentially destroy the lives of more than a dozen of the young people in the class. Hayley needed only a few minutes of deliberation before reaching her decision.

The administration offices were just closing for the day when Hayley strode in and demanded a meeting with the dean. A department secretary explained that an appointment was required. Hayley refused to be turned away. Marching past the secretary, she barged into the dean's office and told her about the stash of child pornography in the professor's car. The dean, naturally, wanted to know how Hayley had found the photographs. Without hesitation, the Fort Hood soldier took sole responsibility for the vehicle break-in. Though skeptical, the dean alerted campus security, who located the offensive materials in the professor's car. Local police detectives searched his home that same night. They discovered a much larger cache of pornography there, along with the camera that captured many of the images. The authorities immediately placed the man under arrest.

Though her actions had led to a child abuser's apprehension, Hayley was charged with a Class A misdemeanor—burglary of a vehicle—and expelled from the college for cheating. Local authorities informed her military superiors, who initiated her dishonorable discharge from the army. Throughout the controversy, Hayley remained silent. Only after three days of agonizing guilt did Latetia Wilson come forward and reveal the truth to the dean. Other students in the cheating plot followed that noble example. After much discussion, the punishment meted out to the students involved was a mandatory do-over of the coursework. Absolved of all wrongdoing, Hayley never spoke of the matter again.

When confronted with two evils of unequal severity, Hayley is hardwired to run at the greater calamity. The chaotic street scenes she passes on her walk home convince her of the dire need for uncovering the true identity of Cyber Jihad. Monroe's worsening emotional condition is a concern. But the episode can be written off as an aberration, a momentary falter. Adopting a wait-and-see attitude is warranted. If the situation worsens, Hayley is confident a fail-safe she has in place will prevent outright operational failure.

As she enters her building Hayley resolves to contact April as soon as she's upstairs. Unlocking the door to her apartment, she hears her work phone chime, notifying her of the receipt of an email. Checking her phone, Hayley does not recognize the sender of the message. Who the hell is the.truth.is.an.act.of.love@gmail.com?

She opens the email and reads the simple message: *Thought you would be interested in this*, followed by a smiley face emoji. There are four attachments to the email. Given the risk of malware, Hayley decides to scan them first with more robust threat-detection programs on her laptop.

Sitting down at her dining table, with an accelerating heart rate, she peruses the classified documents from the Pentagon revolving around the death of her father. Within seconds, Hayley comes to understand a few alarming facts. The military knows much more about the details of Tommy Chill's death than previously admitted. A cursory review of the official incident report reveals that her father's death was caused by friendly fire, in this case, the explosion of a missile fired by a Marine Hornet jet. And because the email is signed "CJ," Hayley can confidently assume the sender of these Pentagon documents to be Cyber Jihad.

HAYLEY WAS EIGHT when her father died, returning from the Iraq war in a sealed, metal coffin. Her reaction to the finality of his death was primal rage. In her emotional outburst, she destroyed most of the interior of a modest funeral home and all of its furnishings. The only sizable item in the building she didn't demolish was Tommy's casket.

After reading twice through the classified documents sent to her by Rafi Zamani, Hayley sits very still. For more than an hour, she barely moves a muscle. She has given the country everything, including her father. The Pentagon has repaid that sacrifice with a despicable and cowardly lie. The fury grows. It sinks a taproot, sprouting branches that grow outward and extend to every part of her being. The emotions within her continue to spread from its core and to every fiber of her being, becoming sturdy and unyielding rage.

The hour of stillness is over. It's just past midnight. Most of the city's residents are preoccupied with the identity of Cyber Jihad, and who he/she/they might strike next. Hayley Chill has other thoughts. Like the inconsolable eight-year-old version of herself, unable to close yawning grief over losing a beloved parent, Hayley craves destruction.

6

★ ★ ★ ★

LOSING IT

*T*hursday, 7:42 *a.m.* Where the *fuck* is Hayley Chill? Driving to Fort Meade from her place in northwest Washington—morning commute traffic snarled as usual—April Wu rechecks her phone. Nothing. She's received no message from Hayley, who has been MIA for the last twelve hours. Why hasn't the White House aide responded to multiple calls and texts? Not for the first time, April worries the mysterious, dark-complexioned man they pursue has emerged from his virtual stronghold and physically harmed her friend. Resisting an urge to contact Andrew Wilde, the army lieutenant joins a long line of vehicles waiting at Gate 1 off Savage Road. In the two years she has been at Cyber Command, she has never seen such a long queue in the morning. April assumes the backup is due to the cyberattack of Pentagon servers the previous day.

At a dead stop behind more than three dozen vehicles waiting to pass through security, she shifts her BMW M5 into neutral. And what is up with the weather? The forecasters predict temperatures and humidity readings in the nineties.

After twenty minutes of delay, April is finally able to show her credentials to one of the armed guards at Gate 1, who checks her name against a paper employee roster. Identification established, the army lieutenant enters the vast lot, parks, and makes the long trek to the building that is the headquarters to both NSA and Cyber Command. Her irritation rockets when she finds a sizable crowd of people waiting to enter. Nearly all of the individuals standing around are in military uniform.

April stops and gapes at the bizarre scene.

"What's going on, sir?" she asks a US Army colonel, saluting him.

"Security issue. They can't let us into the building until more of the DoD personnel servers are back online."

"That's bullshit, sir, excuse my language."

"Apologies unnecessary, Lieutenant." He gestures at the civilian employees of the National Security Agency entering the building after the customary security check. Because of the corruption of Pentagon servers, security guards delay the admittance of Cyber Command's military personnel. "Beyond all recognition," says the colonel.

April folds her arms across her chest and waits, anxious to get inside and continue the hunt for Cyber

Jihad. A hot sun beats down on her as the precious minutes tick past.

———————————

SHE STARTED AT Darlington House. Why not? One basement bar with exposed brick walls is as good as any other. If pressed to examine more subconscious motivations, Hayley would have to confess the hope of encountering the fireman. Could Sam McGovern have saved her from an impulse to demolish everything in sight? Perhaps. But Hayley wasn't in the self-examination mode. She walked from her apartment to the joint off Dupont Circle—sitting at the bar without comment or small talk—and ordered one tequila shot after another. Such is her modus operandi. No matter how much she drinks, Hayley doesn't get drunk in the conventional, stumbling manner. Her inebriation is like an improvised shelter. She takes cover there, hunkering down, emerging only to do battle. In this case, war comes soon enough.

The brawl was by the book. One ass-grabbing mook was rendered unconscious, his arm broken in two places. That guy had two friends who tried to intervene on his behalf. The ensuing altercation upended several tables. A classic Fender guitar was ripped down from its place of honor over the bar, but witnesses can't recall by whom. Only after these highlights did Hayley stalk out of Darlington House, shortly after midnight. Despite the bar fight, she had failed to quench her thirst for destruction. Billy Esposito, the bartender, refrained from calling the cops. Had the police arrested her in the altercation's aftermath, Hayley would've lost both her White House job and her covert position with the deeper state.

Long carrying the torch for the White House aide, Billy Esposito spared Hayley from that ignominy. The guy whose arm Hayley broke deserved getting his ass kicked. Threat of a sexual battery charge sent him and his friends packing. Hayley barreled out of the joint not long after, refusing Billy's pleas to stay, her rage unabated. The Darlington House bartender recalled, of course, seeing her with another regular only a few nights earlier. A voice mail was left on Sam's cell phone. The fireman, home from several days on duty, was fast asleep. There was no one, then, to stop Hayley from doing what Hayley does in this worst-case mode. She would never set foot again in the bar. Never know how the bartender protected her from arrest. Billy Esposito's affections for Hayley Chill will go stubbornly unrequited. His consolation prize, three months later, will be matching all six Powerball numbers and sharing the $43 million prize with four other players.

———————————

AND AFTER ALL that, while April is cooling her heels outside the Big Four at Fort Meade the next morning, Hayley finds herself sitting on a curb in front of a mid-century classic brick, two-story home on Fifth Street in Arlington, Virginia. The deeper state operative isn't entirely sure how she came to be at this place. Had she grabbed a ride share? Or did she take the Metro and walk? By now, the consciousness-annihilating effects of the alcohol Hayley consumed have mostly worn off. The memory of all that transpired the night before is patchy, covered in a sheen of muted shame. Some homeless dudes harassed her on the street, not long after she had left Darlington House. Those fellows didn't fare so well. Hayley can remember a run-in with two district cops but, with her training, their pursuit didn't last more than a few minutes. She also seems to remember an incident on the steps of the Capitol Building involving two similarly inebriated leathernecks fresh off Parris Island. With their combined forces, the drunks put four official government cars in the parking lot on their roofs. But Hayley can't remember how or when she separated herself from the boot Marines.

How did she come to Arlington? She can't remember. And why is it so hot and muggy out? With the thin clarity of a morning's sobriety and a few more moments of reflection, Hayley recalls the purpose of her visit. The awfulness of what she learned in the leaked documents adheres to her like the stink of death. That sensation jogs her memory. Knowing her father was blown to bits by a US jet fighter is almost too much to bear, despite the night's futile exercise in alcohol abuse. She still wants to break things. She remains insane with anger.

Hayley stands. She turns and faces the home. Charlie Hicks lives here. Having determined his current address in her early vetting of her father's war buddy, Hayley has come to the house like a homing pigeon returning to roost. How could he have not known the truth when she first interviewed him? The veteran's post-traumatic stress disorder notwithstanding, Hayley is hell-bent on confrontation with Hicks. No one needs to tell her the idea is probably cruel and definitely wrongheaded. She's sober enough now to know that much.

Hayley heads up the walkway toward the front door. She's sure she sees a curtain move, suggesting the occupant has been observing her all this time and steps back away from the window at her approach. She fist knocks on the wood door. Three times, like rifle shots.

She is in no mood for waiting.

"Mr. Hicks! Sir, I know you're in there!"

Hayley listens for a response and hears none.

"Charlie Hicks? I need to talk to you!"

Nothing comes from the other side of the door. But his presence is strong as if the man is standing there on the porch next to her.

"Why didn't you tell me?" she asks. "Why didn't you tell me my father died by friendly fire?"

She hears a shuffling of feet from the other side of the door. His morose, disembodied voice seems as if from beyond the grave.

"I'm sorry, Hayley. Truly, I . . . am . . . so sorry."

"Did you know?" Her question comes with the edge of a rusty fishing knife, ugly and sharp.

"Me? We never knew anything! Sure, we heard rumors and such. But with ten different things just like what happened to your daddy happening every day of that engagement, no one had time to get the facts straight about anything. We were told it was an IED. Then we were told it was an RPG. Then it was a truck bomb. Now you're telling me it was one of our birds? Who knows? What's ever true in a hellhole like Fallujah?" The voice falters, then gains a measure of strength. "I . . . I can't tell you how sorry I am. I just didn't think I should've burdened you with something I didn't know for a fact."

"Do I strike you like someone who can't deal with a little uncertainty?" Hayley asks. "All I want is the truth!"

With shaky voice, he says, "I have nothing for you. I have nothing . . ."

Not for the first time, Hayley has the sense that she's way out of line. God, what is she doing here? The man is obviously suffering. Coming here was a mistake.

She loiters on the porch for another moment, unsure how to end this travesty. Hayley cannot think of another time she felt so bad about her conduct.

"I'm going to go now," she says to the door.

"Okay," comes the relieved voice on the other side.

"I'm sorry, Mr. Hicks. I promise I won't bother you again."

"Okay."

The man's voice is small, vulnerable, and terribly sad.

Hayley turns, steps down off the porch, and heads for the sidewalk. Her mind works furiously to process every moment of what just transpired. Perhaps ten seconds elapsed since the conclusion of her strained conversation with Hicks through a closed door. She stops, rooted in place at the end of the walkway, paralyzed by the belated realization that Charlie Hicks knew it was a US fighter jet that blew her dad to bits. In her brief conversation with him, Hayley can't remember saying anything more than the incident being "friendly fire."

THURSDAY, 9:10 A.M. Rafi Zamini figures he doesn't have to worry about Hayley Chill for a while. The documents he dropped on her, by his calculation, have cut her heart out. Knives and guns are for dunces. Information is the weapon of the twenty-first century. Truth can be split, like the atom, and weaponized. He finally heard from the Boss, of course, whose agitation over the unanticipated attack on the DoD servers was even higher than for his unauthorized compressor station exploit. Rafi doesn't care. Unable to confirm attribution for the escalating cyberattacks, the US government is completely paralyzed. The entire country is a quivering mess, pissing itself with fear and anxiety. And all because of him.

But who *is* Hayley Chill? Despite his best efforts and unlimited access to classified government networks and databases, Rafi was able to discover only superficial information about the White House aide. Not that it makes much difference. With the need for his services nearing an end, Rafi doesn't plan on hanging around town for long. He packed and shipped off all but the most essential of his belongings. An airline ticket was purchased. Only a few more days now and then he's gone.

Rafi hurries the dog through its morning routine. Late last night, he received word from his *real* employer to come in for work, which is unusual. He relishes his freedom as a contractor, spending more time working at home or in coffee shops than on-site. But the late-night summons is proof of his tremendous success. Long lines at ATMs, gas stations, and grocery stores suggest the same thing: he has single-handedly hacked the entire country. Freaking hilarious! As he walks his dog around the block, every pathetic loser he sees wrapped up in his or her little moment of inconvenience is just more confirmation of Rafi's triumph. Sucks that he can't tell anybody about it!

A little under an hour later, he has ridden his Ducati over the river and parked in one of the big lots at work. It's a five-minute walk to the building. With the freakishly hot weather, Rafi feels himself becoming uncomfortably sweaty under his motorcycle jacket. Shedding the heavy, armored jacket and throwing it over his shoulder, he reveals his standard uniform: Manchester United jersey, black Adidas trainers, and TCX Street Ace motorcycle boots. Like one of his biggest heroes, Steve Jobs, he embraces the concept of a signature "look."

Approaching the building entrance, he sees a mob of people waiting to enter through security, most in one military uniform or another. Rafi figured blowing up the DoD servers would delay personnel from US Cyber

Command entering the building today. It amuses him to see the enlisted oafs waiting under the increasingly hot sun, glaring with resentment at the civilian NSA employees strolling into the Big Four unhindered. Rafi fails to clock the Asian American army lieutenant facing in another direction as he walks past.

And, for that same reason, April Wu happens not to see the darkly complexioned young man in the distinctively red soccer jersey, either. They have been on each other's minds, so much so the near miss strikes a psychic spark and the hairs on April's arm rise. Responding to that telepathic itch, she turns to glance toward the building entrance, a fraction of a second after Rafi disappears inside.

HAYLEY DIDN'T CALL ahead, even though she is over an hour late arriving for work. She fails to greet the friendly US Park Police officer at the security gate, as is her custom, and doesn't acknowledge the other staffers in the corridors of the West Wing, either. Her expression discourages interaction. Taking the hint, no one attempts to initiate a conversation with her. Approaching the door to Kyle Rodgers's office, Hayley feels her phone vibrate. Checking it, she sees April is phoning for what must be the tenth time. The call goes unanswered, just like all the previous ones. Hayley doesn't want to talk to her fellow deeper state operative about Cyber Jihad. Texts from Andrew Wilde have gone unanswered also. She's done with all of it.

Rodgers isn't in the office when Hayley enters, wearing the same clothes she'd worn the day before. She knows she looks like hell but doesn't care. Her boss is meeting with the congressional leaders and will be out of the office most of the day. As usual, a small mountain of paperwork is piled on her desk. Needing a break from the hard stuff, Hayley savors the idea of burying herself in this humdrum labor.

But no sooner has she made peace with ignoring her covert responsibilities, Hayley begins to feel a nagging and irksome self-loathing. Plowing through the stupid office work of logging intern hours, assigning research projects to freelancers, and managing her boss's travel schedule, she can almost *feel* her significance deflating. Turning her back on these most critical duties required of her by Publius, Hayley experiences an uncomfortable sensation of becoming like everybody else.

––––––––––––

ALFRED UPDIKE, THE F6 unit leader, greets Rafi with a light fist bump—as much physical contact as the NSA contractor is willing to tolerate—as he enters the office suite on the top floor of the Big Four.

"Rafi Zamani, in the flesh!" says Alfred Updike. Behind him, the unit is buzzing with activity. Every workstation is occupied, many by more than one NSA computer or network engineer.

Rafi drops his motorcycle gear on the floor. His expression remains sullen. "Good to be here, I guess."

"Cyber Jihad is going to keep us employed for a very

long time, brother. I'm thinking you can chip in with Anthony and Namhee running simulations. VGTRK exploits," says Updike, referring to the All-Russia State Television and Radio Broadcasting Company. He turns and starts to walk off.

"Wait, what? We're hitting Moscow TV? For real?"

"Once Monroe gives the okay." Updike holds two fingers a half inch apart. "He's *this* close."

Rafi can't suppress an incredulous grin. "Holy fucking shit." He almost hates that he'll be leaving town and will miss all of the fun.

Updike is anxious to get back to his desk. "That's why we're here, RZ." He continues on his way, saying over his shoulder, "Keep up the great work, slugger!"

THURSDAY, 3:30 P.M. Clare Ryan pokes her head through the open door of Kyle Rodgers's office in the West Wing and sees Hayley on a call. The secretary of Homeland Security appears agitated.

Into the phone, Hayley says, "I have to call you back." She disconnects and looks to Clare. "Ma'am?"

"What the hell happened? Hernandez confirmed attribution. Congressional leaders have been briefed. The president is ordering a cyberattack on Moscow TV." Clare makes an exaggerated display of her disappointment. "You were supposed to keep me apprised of any changes, Hayley. I thought we had an agreement."

Clare knows Hernandez intentionally kept DHS out of the loop to build unstoppable momentum for a strike against Russia. Blaming a low-level White House aide is convenient and an utter waste of time.

"I'm sorry, ma'am. This is the first I'm hearing about it."

This is not the answer Clare wanted to hear. "Jesus!" The older woman turns and disappears from the doorway.

Hayley stands and goes to the door. Stepping into the corridor, she watches Clare Ryan striding in the direction of the Oval Office. How could the NSA have confirmed attribution? Could the young man she saw outside the Rosslyn subway station be a Russian agent? Hayley's growing confusion infuriates her. Fuck!

A few minutes later, the president's secretary shows Clare Ryan into the Oval Office. The DHS director finds Monroe behind the *Resolute* desk. Seated in one of the armchairs on the other side of the iconic desk is Carlos Hernandez. Instantly clocking the president's expression of unmitigated resignation, Clare suspects an argument for continued caution is futile. What will follow here is only the pantomime of policy discussion.

Hernandez stands as she takes a seat. The president remains in his chair, looking wan and defeated. His chief of staff and Vice President Landers hover nervously in the background. Other aides occasionally appear and then disappear again, lending a chaotic air to the proceedings. The White House truly is under siege.

Clare says, "Mr. President, thank you for waiting to hear my thoughts before making your final decision."

Monroe waves off the need for such sentiments. "Glad you could sit in, Clare."

The secretary of Homeland Security refuses to glance in Hernandez's direction, keeping her gaze locked on the president. "Sir, as much as I understand the pressure you're under to do something about these attacks—"

The NSA director interjects. "On the *Pentagon!*"

Clare ignores the interruption. "It's nevertheless vital we don't act too soon. Not only do we risk retaliating against someone who had nothing to do with it, we also gamble on the possibility of igniting an actual conventional war."

"Mr. President, there is no question who did this. Attribution is confirmed."

Clare refuses to cede the argument to her nemesis. "But where is the proof? Where is it, General? In cyber warfare, can attribution ever be made with absolute confidence? Who wrote the malware isn't as important as who *sent it*." Clare then turns to the president. "Sir, some entirely different bad actor might have hacked the Russians to attack us!"

Hernandez does not attempt to hide his disgust and exasperation. "My God! That's preposterous!"

The cabinet secretary locks her eyes on Monroe, pressing her case. "The NSA director knows as well as I do this stuff is littered throughout all networks. Sir, there are malicious implants in our financial networks, in our electrical grids, in the infrastructure that provides water to cities across the country, and in our transportation systems. Throw a rock and you'll hit some malware that China, Russia, Iran, or North Korea has placed in the nation's networks in the event of cyber war. We know it's here because we've put the same implants in *their* networks. All this stuff is just lying around, waiting for some yahoo to it set off!"

A long moment passes as both Clare Ryan and Carlos Hernandez watch the president brooding on the decision only he can make.

Looking past the two of them, Richard Monroe sees Hayley Chill standing in the doorway leading into the Outer Oval Office with an armful of briefing notebooks. The president's secretary stands next to Hayley. It is as if everyone in the building has stopped what they're doing until the president renders judgment.

He is in this impossible situation because of her. Monroe yearns to speak with Aleksandr Belyavskiy, his GRU handler. Or his wife, Cindy. He wishes he could talk to anyone. *Really* talk. Richard Monroe has come to comprehend something that all in his office inevitably realize as fact: being the president of the United States is the loneliest job in the world. But no president has ever been quite so isolated or so alone as him. Who could possibly appreciate the inexorable crush of his dilemma? He can't afford *not* to act any longer. Refusing to retaliate only risks blowing his cover.

But how will the Kremlin react to his ordering an attack on Mother Russia? They could have him assassinated with one encrypted text! Will they understand he had to attack or risk exposure of Operation Polkan?

There is no time to seek approval via the dead drop. The time has come. Monroe looks to the NSA director and says, "A shot across their bow. No military targets or critical infrastructure."

Disgusted, Clare Ryan looks down at her feet. Carlos Hernandez merely nods, jaw clenched, and eyes bright.

Across the expansive room, Hayley takes in the momentous scene and feels nothing.

FRIDAY, 6:45 A.M. (GMT +3) Svetlana Svanidze is running late for her job as a floor nurse at City Hospital No. 40 in Kurortniy District, Saint Petersburg, Russia. She is behind schedule because her husband, Oleg, a computer technician for Russia-1, the state-owned television channel, was up half the night dealing with an emergency at work. Along with the two other major television stations in the country, Channel One and NTV, Russia-1 earlier in the day suffered a devastating, computer-oriented shutdown. All three channels—television stations that capture 74 percent of Russia's viewers—were dark for more than seven hours, a service interruption due to malware that wiped out data on their computer servers. Working feverishly to restore company hard drives from off-site backups, Oleg Svanidze and other technicians got Russia-1 back on-air before its two competitors. Oleg's manager incentivized his team with the reward of a one-week, all-expenses-paid trip to the Kempinski Grand Hotel in Gelendzhik on the Black Sea.

Svetlana is exceedingly pleased with her husband. Because he and his colleagues in the computer-engineering department at Russia-1 are so skilled, she and Oleg will be able to enjoy a much-needed vacation with their two children. More than two years since her last promotion and she has yet to take any time off! She works hard supervising the nursing staff in the intensive-care unit at City Hospital No. 40, with long shifts under suboptimal conditions. Founded in 1748 as a fifty-bed infirmary at Sestroretsky armory and serving more than twenty thousand patients annually, City Hospital No. 40 is understaffed and underfunded. With a rapid turnover of employees, Svetlana must accommodate newer nurses insufficiently trained in the use of high-tech devices and continuously evolving diagnostic modalities. Every work shift, it seems, is a case of narrowly avoided disaster. She quickly gathers the things she needs for a long, twelve-hour shift. Svetlana laughs. *A vacation is just what the doctor ordered.*

Russia's stations went dark at the start of prime-time television viewing. Though Svetlana doesn't watch any shows on the channel where Oleg works, she was looking forward to two of her favorite programs on Channel One, *Adjutants of Love* and *Brief Guide to a Happy Life*. Her disappointment as the outage dragged on into the late hours of the night was profound. Instead of watching her shows, Svetlana spent the night thumbing through fashion magazines, caring for her two young children, and trading a few texts with Oleg. Usually, her husband arrives home by eight in the evening. Restoring the broadcaster's servers a few minutes after two in the morning, Svetlana's husband didn't get back to their apartment until three thirty, long after she had fallen asleep.

He is still awake when she is preparing to leave for the day. After seeing he has enough food to eat for breakfast and a quick kiss, Svetlana heads for the door, grateful the kids departed a few minutes earlier. It was nice having a few moments alone with Oleg. Such a sweet man, her husband! She is already in the hallway and about to close the door when she remembers she made a music mix for a work friend, Olga Lugin. Svetlana considers herself to be something of an amateur DJ, with great taste in popular music and a subtle touch at arranging songs in a satisfying sequence. She dashes back inside the apartment, where Oleg is seated at the kitchen table, and grabs a USB drive from a desk in the living room. Dropping the thumb drive in her purse, Svetlana is unaware that it doesn't contain the latest hits from Elena Temnikova or Max Barskih. The device is actually Oleg's, which he brought back home with him from work.

———————————

THURSDAY, 10:55 P.M. Hayley was home only a few minutes when she is buzzed from downstairs. April's voice, filtered over the intercom, has an edge. Her demand to talk is expressed in no uncertain terms. The White House aide, weary from a long day at work and not entirely recovered from the long night that preceded it, had cranked up the air-conditioning and collapsed on the couch. She reluctantly gets to her feet again and punches the button by the door that lets in her friend.

"What in fuck the fuck?" April asks as she enters the apartment like a mini-cyclone, pent-up frustration carrying her past Hayley and into the center of the living room.

Hayley shrugs. "What?"

Her single-word response, so patently disingenuous, only amplifies April's irritation.

"I've been trying to reach you all day!"

"Really?" Hayley asks with obvious attitude.

April decides obsessing on her fellow operative's failures of the last twelve hours is a waste of time. It's the future that demands their immediate attention.

"We need to come up with a plan. Andrew Wilde has been crawling up my ass all day."

"The NSA has attributed Cyber Jihad to the Russians."

"No." April is so frustrated with Hayley she could slap her. Fear of being slapped back, twice as hard, stays her hand. "No attribution is ever one hundred percent confirmed via normal forensics and analysis. You need the hacker and his computer to be absolutely certain. Essentially, you need a confession."

Hayley shrugs and says nothing.

April is shocked. "What the hell is wrong with you?"

"He emailed me."

"Who emailed you?"

"Cyber Jihad."

"And you're only telling me this now?"

"I remember telling you all it was kind of a busy day."

"What did he email you? Let me see it!"

"I'll forward it to you. But it has nothing to do with the cyberattacks."

"What was it, then? Jesus, just tell me!"

"A one-line message: 'Thought you would be interested in this.' And a classified report concerning my dad's death in Fallujah."

"I can't believe you sat on this all fucking day!"

"They killed him, April. My dad was killed by friendly fire."

For a moment, the army lieutenant says nothing. No combat death is good, but some are worse than others. Put in a box by your own guys is a supremely wrong KIA. The anger floods out of April Wu.

"Shit, Hayley. I'm sorry."

Condolences accomplish nothing. Hayley is mute.

April looks away, shaking her head. "So fucked-up." She turns her gaze on Hayley again. "You know he pulled this info from DoD servers with the intent of throwing you off his trail, then blew them up to cover his tracks. We saw the intrusion at USCC in real time. Obviously, Cyber Jihad perceives you as a threat."

"Maybe. What difference does it make?"

"He's fucking with your head, Hayley."

"Doing a pretty decent job of it, too."

April can see prodding her friend to action is a lost cause. There's no time for convincing her. "Forward the email. *I'm* not ready to give up."

"Untraceable. ProtonMail."

"Forward it anyway. My team can take a run at it." She turns to leave. One hand on the doorknob, she turns to face Hayley again.

"It's fucked-up what happened to your dad. No question. But I never thought I'd live to see the day when Hayley Chill takes a knee, not without a fucking gun to her head." A mirthless laugh escapes April's mouth. "Hell, I didn't think you would take a knee *with* a gun to your head!"

The army lieutenant turns and exits the apartment, disappearing down the hallway.

Hayley shuts the door and returns to the kitchen table, unsure what to do. She feels as if she's buried under a mountain of sand. Revelations regarding her father's death have extinguished her spirit. The mental image of her dad's remains in the plastic collection bags—scattered in his casket like so many items in the clearance bin of a department store—blocks her path forward. She wants to get drunk all over again. Inebriation is some form of self-direction, right? Blown to bits by a Marine jet? Oo-fucking-rah.

She hears the buzz of the door downstairs again. April Wu doesn't give up easily. Hayley stands and goes to the intercom by her apartment door. Pressing the talk button, she says, "Leave me alone, you freak."

"You're not even going to give me five minutes?" The voice, filtered through the intercom system, is male.

"Who is this?" Hayley asks.

"Wow. That burns. It's Sam McGovern. I thought

maybe we could talk?" His voice, distorted by rudimentary electronic transmission, is a relief nonetheless.

_____

THEY SIT AT the kitchen table. She serves coffee instead of booze. He looks magnificent to her. That is a fact. But those emotional pathways remain impeded by the fresh awareness of her father's senseless, stupid death in Fallujah. She tells him everything. He is quiet the entire time, offering no comment, suggestions, or advice. He simply listens. If there is nothing else between them, merely his quiet presence is of great help. Hayley is grateful to the ends of the universe.

When she has finished speaking, Sam McGovern must ask a single, essentially Sam McGovern question.

"How can I help?"

Hayley looks into Sam's eyes, open to reveal her vulnerabilities.

"I want to get up, but I can't."

"It was a good punch you took. Maybe a knockout punch."

"I'm down, not out."

"I know."

"How can I get back up, Sam? I hate it all. I hate everything."

"Nothing I say can help. You know that."

"I know that, yes."

"Time helps."

"Yes."

He waits for a beat, then asks, "Do you want me to stay?"

There is a long moment here, in which she retreats to a place devoid of sensation. The external world seems far away. Nothing in it can do her harm. This is the place inside herself where she can make these potentially momentous decisions.

"Yes."

Afterward, in the blue light of night, they lay across the bed. Sleep is impossible. Staring at the blank-faced buildings outside her bedroom window—this mostly unfamiliar man in her bed lying next to her—a few words slip from Hayley's mouth. "The lives we save."

"What?"

She didn't think she spoke the words out loud. Covering, she says, "I'm not good at this."

"Nobody is good at this. At least, beware those that are."

"You'll stay? All night?" Hayley asks him.

"If that's an invitation, yes."

"It is an invitation. But I'm not sleepy. Don't want to sleep."

"What, then?" he asks.

Sex is slower this second time. More measured. There are spaces between the epic physical clashes of their lovemaking. And then both are seemingly sated.

But still, she cannot sleep.

Covered with a sheen of sweat that is rapidly evaporating in the air-conditioned bedroom, Hayley says, "I want to talk."

"About anything in particular?"

"Actually, I want *you* to talk. I'm sick to death of the sound of my voice."

"Okay . . ." He's unsure, naturally, what to tell her.

"Tell me about your earliest memory. Or how your parents met. Did you ever see them kiss, with any passion I mean? How about the book that changed your life? Who's your best friend? Dogs or cats? Or tell me what you like to eat for breakfast on Sundays. Who would you rather be, Picasso or Margaret Mead? Most of all, Sam, I just want to hear your voice. Maybe if I just listen to you talk, I'll be able to sleep. Do you mind? You can say no. Like I said, I'm not much good at this."

Sam doesn't have a problem with her request, but it's not in him to gab or gossip. He has a natural reticence that recalls another era of the American male. Never glib or frivolous. What he recognizes, however, is that his feelings for this woman are neither a burning building nor a threatening storm. What he believes with all his heart is that, in Hayley Chill, he has found a resting place. Talking won't be a problem—not with her— despite the late hour.

––––––––––

AT VERY NEARLY this same moment, halfway around the world, Svetlana Svanidze arrives at Saint Petersburg's City Hospital No. 40. Having taken the train in from the Kupchino station on the Moskovsko–Petrogradskaya Line of the Saint Petersburg Metro—a ninety-minute commute she endures with the help of favorite authors

like Victor Pelevin and Lyudmila Ulitskaya—the ICU
nurse greets her fellow hospital staffers with a warm
smile. She is popular with staffers and doctors alike, a
welcome presence in an otherwise grim medical environment. Her coworker and good friend, Olga Lugin,
is excited to see Svetlana enter the cramped nursing
station at one end of the cluttered intensive care unit.

"Did you remember?" Olga asks.

"Of course!" Svetlana tolerates her friend's pester-
ing with good humor. Aware that the younger woman's
home life is no picnic, Svetlana endeavors to brighten
Olga's day. She fishes through her handbag for the
thumb drive from home and hands it to the other
nurse.

Olga thanks Svetlana and returns to her work at the
computer. She considers waiting until she gets home
to listen to her friend's mix. But music helps Olga plow
through the drudgery of hospital paperwork. Simply too
eager to wait, she inserts the USB drive into the networked workstation and, initiating the iTunes program,
locates the drive. But instead of the anticipated music
files, the nurse only sees a long series of unrecognized
files. Her disappointment is keen. Clearly, Svetlana
Svanidze has made a mistake and given her the wrong
thumb drive.

The damage is done at the speed that electrons move
across transistors, on the order of trillionths of a second.
The NSA-created worm, uploaded into Russia-1's network by Updike's F6 unit and infecting Oleg Svanidze's
thumb drive, bursts into the hospital network with a

rampaging speed and efficiency not found in the non-digital world. The malware scans the City Hospital No. 40's computer system for root directories. Once it finds those network foundations, the worm makes quick work of destroying them all, effectively wiping all data and applications from hospital servers.

Within a few seconds of Olga Lugin inserting Oleg Svanidze's USB drive into her work computer and infecting the hospital's network with the NSA malware, the software running every single connected device in the hospital turns to digital goo. Administrative workstations, like the one in which Olga inserted the infected thumb drive, refuse to respond to user input, of course. But, in addition to computers, hundreds of networked medical devices throughout the hospital also fail, including those that monitor vital signs and administer medications. The rapidly escalating crisis impacts every part of the hospital. Frenzied personnel act to compensate for widespread computer failure. Administrators immediately cancel or postpone surgeries and procedures. The hospital's information technologists work to restore the network's servers.

Following the system-wide computer meltdown, medical staff remove patients from malfunctioning ventilators and work vigorously to keep them alive with bag valve masks. These heroic measures seem to be sufficient, but as the minutes of the outage lengthen to more than an hour, one of the five ventilated patients goes into cardiac arrest. Had the cardiac monitors been working, nurses in the room would have been alerted to the patient's faulty heart rhythm. Doctors work valiantly to resuscitate the patient but fail. Alexi Morozov, sixty-four years of age and a former metalworker, is pronounced dead fifteen minutes before information technologists restore the hospital network. He thereby becomes the first fatality in a cyber war that threatens to go kinetic between the US and Russian superpowers.

RUSSIAN HACKERS COMPROMISED the Geostationary Operational Environmental Satellite system—operated by the National Oceanic and Atmospheric Administration and responsible for that agency's weather forecasting and meteorology research—in 2012. At that time, they buried malware implants in the programming code responsible for the meticulous calculations that keep the four satellites in proper position above Earth. In response to the NSA attack on Russian television and the inadvertent infection of City Hospital No. 40's computer system, authorities at the highest levels in the Kremlin issue an order to activate GOES's illicit programming and destroy the US satellites. Less than thirty minutes have passed since the death of the former metalworker, Alexi Morozov, in Saint Petersburg.

GOES-17 experiences on-board computer malfunctions that instantly swing it out of its geosynchronous equatorial orbit within forty-five seconds of Russian cyber warriors in Saint Petersburg sending the appropriate commands. Programmed to return to precisely the same position in the sky twenty-two thousand miles above Earth, GOES-17 falls into a degrading, non-geosynchronous orbit around the planet that will result in its disintegration above Mongolia. In the next twenty minutes, GOES-16, GOES-T, and GOES-U also fall out of their geosynchronous orbits and will suffer the same fate. With the destruction of these satellites—orbiters that cost hundreds of millions of dollars to design, build, and launch—the US will be effectively deprived of the ability to track and forecast major storms, including hurricanes, for a decade.

7

★ ★ ★ ★

THE TWENTY-FIFTH

*F*riday, 5:00 *a.m.* Hayley learns the US is at war with Russia before she gets out of bed. Waking up before dawn, without the benefit of an alarm, she opens her eyes and sees Sam's sleeping form beside her in the half-light. She dozed off soon after Sam had started talking, but remembers him speaking of his growing up in suburban Virginia and family life. With the full realization of the previous night's events, Hayley feels a swelling inside her chest all over again. Only this time, she directs her fury at herself. What did she hope to accomplish by inviting this man into her bed? Into her life? Did she expect he'd "fix" her problems? As best she can tell, Sam McGovern is a decent man. But that's really beside the point. Assessing her behavior since learning the details of her father's death, Hayley concludes she has been utterly self-indulgent.

Reaching for her bag on the floor next to the bed, Hayley retrieves her KryptAll phone and checks for messages from Andrew Wilde. He texted three hours earlier, about the US cyberattack on Russia, an inadvertent malware infection at the Saint Petersburg hospital, and Moscow's retaliatory strike against US weather satellites. April and Hayley are expected at a meeting later in the morning.

Hayley leans down to replace the phone in her bag. Sitting up again, she sees Sam is awake, too.

"That's a funny-looking phone."

Needing to leave Sam out of it, she says, "Who asked you?"

He thinks she's making a joke and smiles good-naturedly. Her failure to respond in kind is a signal that the ground has shifted underneath them. "What?" he asks, his grin fading.

With a flat expression, Hayley says, "I've got to go."

And that's enough for Sam. He's been through the dating wars. When it hits the wall, the sound you hear is exactly the tone of Hayley's voice. He won't lash out or insist on an explanation. Sam is merely going to go, too.

Within two minutes, he's dressed and heading for the door. They don't exchange another word. Hayley wants to say something, but the collision of emotions robs her of the power of speech. Far higher stakes are now in play. Her personal life and issues will have zero priority in the hours and days ahead. Only silence follows the fireman out the door.

HAYLEY TAPS ON the passenger-side window of April's BMW as the army lieutenant is about to exit the subterranean garage of her condominium complex.

"This freaking Bitcoin thing," Hayley says, gesturing at the car once April has lowered the window.

"No. Uh-uh. We're not pretending you weren't a complete punk bitch the last twenty-four hours."

"What?"

"What? Oh, fuck no. Not *what!*"

"Nuclear Armageddon is about to break loose. 'What' really is beside the point." She pops the door open and settles into the passenger seat. "I've never been inside a BMW before."

"Relax. A little indulgence isn't going to kill you."

"I'm only a simple girl from West Virginia."

"Some may believe that hillbilly bullshit, but I sure as hell don't. People underestimate you at their peril. Now *talk.*"

"The White House is about three minutes away. Is that enough time for you to brief me on your progress?"

"Wait. Where's your car? How did you get here?"

"I ran. Needed to clear my head. Look, there's not much time . . ." April interrupts the comment with an eye roll. Hayley presses on, undeterred. "You've heard from Andy Wilde, too, I assume. Let's arrange to meet him at the Mills Building parking garage."

"Okay, Deep Throat. But exactly how do you plan

to prevent World War III from your little West Wing office?"

Hayley must remind herself that April has no inkling of Richard Monroe's role as a double agent. Or that a lowly West Wing staffer has the president of the United States at the end of a very short leash. She wishes she could tell her friend the truth. Doing so would make both of their jobs much more manageable. Until Andrew Wilde tells her otherwise, however, Hayley's orders are to withhold this explosive information from her fellow deeper state operative.

"No idea. That's why we're all counting on you."

April smiles. Not every day that Hayley Chill offers this sort of concession. "I've got four of my people reviewing immigration files of Iranians who have come to the US over the last five years to study computer engineering. VAJA has run a bunch of its agents into the country under student visas, and I'm convinced this fucker is one of them," she says, referring to the Ministry of Intelligence of the Islamic Republic of Iran.

"Is it advantageous to have hackers in-country as opposed to working remotely? Could we be wrong in our assumptions about Cyber Jihad's masters? Maybe this guy is VAJA but on loan to Moscow?"

"We won't know for certain until we nab him. But proximity to a target is definitely a positive. Counterintuitively, it's even harder to trace the hack. Attribution is always always *always* an absolute bitch. Which is why we're stupid lucky to have a general idea what one of these guys—"

Hayley interjects. "*If* it's a group. We don't know it isn't a sole actor?"

"Possible lone wolf, but not likely. The sophistication of these attacks, coding, and exploits is nation-state caliber. If this dude is Iranian intelligence, like I suspect, then he could just be the tip of the spear." April ponders on it. "New US sanctions have been putting a big-time hurt on Tehran. Relations between Iran and Russia have never been better. I suppose this fucker could be on Kremlin's payroll."

Hayley feels back on track again. Her emotional detour seems like eons ago. "We need to put hands on this guy."

"We *will* put hands on this guy."

April pulls the BMW over to the curb at Seventeenth and G Street. A second day of the late-spring heat wave discourages loitering in the morning sun. Passersby hurry along, finding shade wherever it exists.

Hayley gestures at the Mill Building, across the street from the Eisenhower Executive Office Building. "Noon, bottom level."

"Woodward and Bernstein got nothing on you, Hayley Chill."

The White House aide climbs out of the car and pauses before slamming the door shut. "You could buy twenty acres of good land in West Virginia with what this vehicle cost."

"You can keep Appalachia. Sixty in two point eight seconds is more my style."

FRIDAY, 8:24 A.M. The president eats his breakfast in the private dining room on the second floor of the executive mansion, across the west sitting hall from his bedroom. Though kitchen staff is visible through the open doorway to his right, Richard Monroe feels painfully alone. He craves the companionship of his wife, but she left yesterday for their home in Hawaii. What could he tell Cindy of his struggles, anyway? She knows nothing and *must* know nothing. Even in his loving marriage, he feels isolated.

Monroe left a message at the dead drop but doesn't believe it was picked up. The Cuban valet hasn't been anywhere in evidence since revealing his covert identity on Wednesday morning. Monroe worries that Moscow holds him responsible for the cyber counterattack on Russia's television stations. The GRU didn't install a mole in the Oval Office just so the US president would turn around and attack Матушка Россия . . . Mother Russia. What is he supposed to do if hostilities between the two superpowers escalate further? Forgetting for now the demands of his taskmasters in the deeper state, Monroe is desperate for instructions from the Kremlin. How did he ever find himself in this hideous bind? His senior White House staff awaits his arrival in the Oval Office. The affairs of the greatest democracy on the planet require his attention. But Richard Monroe only longs for escape.

Through the doorway leading into the west sitting hall, the president sees Alberto Barrios walk past. Despite the presence of kitchen staff nearby, Monroe cannot resist the impulse to connect with the GRU operative.

"Alberto!"

The valet stops and returns to the doorway leading into the dining room. His expression is placid. The president is slightly unnerved by the Cuban agent's calm demeanor. He missed the days when he dealt solely with the more genial Aleksandr Belyavskiy. Though they had never met face-to-face, Monroe and Belyavskiy had developed something of a kinship, sharing stories of Mirnyy and other familiarities. The president meets the valet's dead-eyed gaze. He realizes that if Moscow discovers the Americans have turned him, it will be Barrios who will kill him.

"I left my room a mess, I'm afraid. If you could see to it . . . ?"

Monroe looks over his right shoulder, into the kitchen. He sees the staff hard at work. No one is paying the slightest bit of attention to his exchange with one of his valets.

"Absolutely, sir." Barrios doesn't betray the slightest recognition of the president's veiled request that he retrieve a message from the Sangamon edition of Sandburg's biography of Lincoln. "Is there anything else?"

Mindful of the kitchen staff only feet away, Monroe pushes his chair back and walks to where Barrios is standing in the doorway. He glances to the left and sees Kyle Rodgers arriving at the top of the stairs forty feet away. The president's advisor has come to fetch him.

But Monroe must have an immediate answer to his most pressing question. He leans closer to the Cuban agent, turning his back to the approaching Rodgers.

"Did you pass along my request for exfiltration?"

Barrios is expressionless, his respectfulness as practiced as a mortician's. "Yes, Mr. President. I did as you requested."

"And?" Monroe can barely breathe, his heart pounding. He can *feel* Rodgers's approach. "You must tell them, Alberto, the situation here is untenable. You must tell Moscow the Americans are suspicious."

"Have US intelligence agencies made contact with you?"

"No, for Christ's sake!" Monroe knows his opportunity to get answers from Barrios has all but expired. "Dammit!"

Kyle Rodgers stops at Monroe's side, respectful but firm. "Sir?"

"Yes, what is it?" he asks, more frustrated than impatient.

"Mr. President, you're needed in the Situation Room."

FRIDAY, 10:47 A.M. Running some files needed downstairs, Hayley sees Clare Ryan in the corridor of the West Wing's basement level. The secretary for Homeland Security is exiting the Situation Room to make a call on her cell phone and beckons to her. Hayley follows Clare to a quieter alcove off the main corridor.

"What did I tell you?" Clare asks Hayley, her face flushed. She gestures in the direction of the Situation Room, where the president and his security advisors struggle to manage the growing crisis. "The Russians are moving troops and hardware along its borders with Latvia and Estonia. The defense secretary predicts the war will go kinetic if we respond in any way to the GOES takedown, whether conventionally or cyberattack, gray zone or not."

Hayley remains composed in the face of the cabinet secretary's agitation and chooses her words wisely.

"I don't believe the Russians are behind Cyber Jihad, ma'am."

The cabinet secretary's aggravation seems to get the better of her. "Yes, yes, you told me that two days ago! Where is the proof, Hayley? I need proof!"

Hayley says nothing, a silence that reflects poorly on her bold assertion.

Clare gains control of her temper, however. The White House aide remains a valuable ally. "Look, Hayley, I certainly appreciate your eagerness to play secret agent and uncover the truth about these cyberattacks. But I do think that sort of work is best left to experts . . . in the field. What I need from you is to be that better angel whispering in Richard Monroe's ear. I need the obvious influence you have over the president. The country is depending on you."

"Madam Secretary—"

Clare Ryan silences Hayley with a gesture. She needs to make her call and then get back inside the Situation Room with the president.

As the cabinet secretary turns to head in that direction, she says over her shoulder, "The good news is POTUS is close to broadening Homeland Security's mandate." The cabinet secretary's smile is born from her sensing victory after a long fight. "We'll finally be able to protect our citizens!"

Hayley acknowledges Clare's statement with a respectful nod, anxious to get going. The meeting with Andrew Wilde is in slightly less than an hour. As Hayley starts for the closest stairwell to head upstairs to her office, she retrieves her KryptAll phone.

———————————

APRIL STANDS UP from her workstation at USCC and heads for the door. She had been pushing the personnel in her unit all morning for results. The arduous task of reviewing the thousands of most recent student visas from Iran is almost complete. Sadly, these efforts have produced no positive results. Either available photographs of the students fail to match, or the geographical location is off. Maybe the young man captured in the surveillance video entered the US illegally through Canada or Mexico? Maybe he legally obtained a student visa but more than six years ago? With over sixteen thousand Iranian students currently in the US, it will take days to follow up on these additional possibilities, with a slim chance of success. For all she knows, the hacker is an American citizen and they've been wasting what precious time they have on a wild goose chase.

April Wu has begun to resent Hayley for failing to provide her with adequate backup. Her fellow deeper state operative seems needlessly focused on her cover as White House aide. Hayley's original mission after leaving the Publius training camp in Oregon two years ago, whatever it may have been, undoubtedly must be completed by now. Instead of hunkering down in the West Wing, Hayley could be helping review the students' visa applications. Scouring the streets of Georgetown or Foggy Bottom for any sign of the hacker would be a help. April is sure their suspect is close. She just *knows* it.

The army lieutenant climbs the stairs up from the basement, anticipating a cup of coffee in the main cafeteria. Often enough, the best way to solve a seemingly intractable problem is to step away from it. As she exits the stairwell, onto the wide ground-floor corridor, April feels her phone vibrate and connects after checking the caller's identification.

"I got nothing for you," she tells Hayley, walking up the long hallway toward the cafeteria entrance. Just a few minutes after ten, some civilian NSA staffers are only now arriving to work. *Slackers*, thinks April.

Hayley, standing in Kyle Rodgers's office at the White House, says, "We have Andy Wilde in fifty minutes. Moscow is threatening to 'liberate' ethnic Russians in Estonia. We're on the brink of all-out war, April. We need something tangible, man. We need Red Jersey."

In her zeal, Hayley reveals a trace more of her West

Virginia accent than she usually lets on. April feels that old resentment is creeping up again. Fucking Hayley Chill, superstar.

"I'm trying," she says, recalling their physical alter-cation while at the Publius training camp. Before the West Virginian's arrival, April had been queen bee of the camp. No other candidate came close to her evalu-ation numbers. Then Hayley happened. Despite April's best efforts to intimidate and out-hustle her rival, the result was never really in doubt. Their superiors tapped Hayley for the first operation. All April got was a broken finger as a consolation prize.

Phone pressed to her ear, April hears Hayley saying something about Secretary Ryan. But the army lieuten-ant is distracted by the sight of a person approaching from the other end of the ground-floor corridor. Dark complexion. Black snapback hat. Manchester United football jersey, with the gleaming yellow and gold Chev-rolet "bow tie" splayed across the front.

April freezes where she stands.

Rafi Zamani sees the Asian American female in an army combat uniform staring at him. He recognizes her as the other young woman who had come looking for him at the Iron Pony with Hayley Chill. At the same moment, April recognizes him.

"Hey," April says quietly. Then, louder, she says again, "Hey!"

Standing in the West Wing office, Hayley uncon-sciously grips her phone harder. "What is it? April?"

At the NSA headquarters on Savage Road, Rafi's

brain is finally able to communicate with the muscles in his legs. Pivoting about-face, he flees in the direction he had just come.

April Wu starts forward again, not one to shy away from a fight. Not ever. She charges down the gleaming hallway as Rafi dashes for the exit. "Somebody! Stop that guy!"

As she runs in pursuit of Rafi Zamani, April shouts into her phone, never taking her eyes off her quarry's retreating figure. "It's him, Hayley! It's fucking Cyber Jihad, in the headquarters of the NSA!"

HIS PARENTS HAD noticed the odd behavior before Rafi was three. Significant developmental concerns included communication and sensory challenges, problems in socializing with his peers, and repetitive behaviors. Rafi's mother was a successful real estate broker and his father a trial lawyer, emigrating from Iran in 1979 as a couple in their early twenties. Ormazd and Donya Zamani adapted effortlessly to their new lives in the United States and thrived. Assimilation was a priority, more so than with many of the other émigrés from Iran. While not inclined to turn their backs completely on the traditions and heritage of their country of birth, Ormazd and Donya believed in the power and saving grace of the American Dream. The United States was their new homeland of their future.

Donya assumed the responsibility for raising Rafi and

his younger brother, Hamid, while Ormazd attended Yale Law School. After obtaining his degree, Ormazd was recruited by Arnold & Porter in Washington and subsequently moved his young family to suburban Maryland. From the outside, the Zamanis appeared to be the picture of success. With the purchase of a new, five-thousand-square-foot home in a desirable neighborhood and a marriage that seemed strong, any recent immigrant to the United States would have been suitably envious of what the Zamanis had achieved. But a more intimate perspective would have revealed that a deep problem existed within the home. Ormazd and Donya's eldest son, Rafi, was a behavioral time bomb.

Rafi's parents searched for a clear diagnosis after administrators sidelined the boy for special education services in preschool. Rafi Zamani was a keenly intelligent child, but his cognitive abilities only aggravated his social problems. His conduct became increasingly erratic and, in some instances, physically violent. Sadistic tendencies manifested themselves in the torture of small animals and insects. Most parents in the neighborhood forbade their children from playing with Rafi. Even his younger brother, Hamid, avoided him. No amount of therapy seemed to help. Ormazd and Donya's marriage suffered under the strain of their oldest son's disruptive presence in the home. Ormazd, having established himself as one of Washington's most elite corporate lawyers, found escape in his extremely demanding work. Donya, Rafi's staunchest defender, wasn't so lucky. After her son had cycled through four different schools by the seventh grade, Donya elected to homeschool him. When he was thirteen, Rafi's parents divorced. Tellingly, eleven-year-old Hamid chose to live with his father.

Isolated and friendless from the earliest age, Rafi found companionship in computers and expression with their mathematically based languages. He blazed through computer science courses offered by local community colleges. Diagnosed with multiple syndromes and psychological maladies, conventional enrollment in a university was out of the question. Rafi remained, for the most part, holed up in a bedroom of the only home he had ever known, a prisoner of his anxieties. He even avoided Donya's physical presence, preferring to communicate with her via email. Despite her devotion and dedication to him, Rafi blamed his mother for Ormazd's leaving the marriage. He distrusted all women and considered them selfish beyond redemption. Eventually, this extreme misogyny led Rafi to embrace the *incel* community of similarly "involuntary celibate" young men. Never having so much as held a female's hand, smoldering resentment, rage, and self-pity dominated his everyday thoughts.

Donya had enough by the time Rafi was twenty-one. After several years of being single, Donya Zamani met a nice, middle-aged widower in line at the Yekta Kabobi Restaurant & Market. Within three months, they became engaged. Two weeks after that startling announcement, Donya informed her eldest son that she was selling the house and moving in with her fiancé. The young man had many dark thoughts in these furious weeks after his mother's engagement. Chief among them was to murder Donya in her sleep. But Rafi loved computers too much to get himself sent to jail for the rest of his life, where his love affair with those beloved machines would certainly be curtailed. Instead of killing his mother, Rafi called the National Security Agency.

The human resources office failed to return his multiple phone messages. Inspired perhaps by the British teenager from the East Midlands who infamously broke into the email inbox of CIA director John Brennan in 2015, Rafi hacked the NSA account of Carlos Hernandez. In a taunting email exchange with the chagrined NSA director, the young computer wiz offered to reveal exactly how he had managed the feat for the price of a lunch at the local Cheeburger Cheeburger. Deemed unfit for a salaried position with the clandestine US agency, Rafi was hired as a part-time contractor one week shy of his twenty-first birthday. He moved out of his mother's house on a rainy Sunday morning without telling her he was leaving. Since that date, Rafi Zamani hasn't had a single word of communication with any member of his family. Even though he lives and works only a dozen miles from his family home, Rafi may as well be dead as far as Ormazd and Donya know.

Getting his place in Foggy Bottom and a job he worked mostly from home marginally improved Rafi's social skills. His immediate supervisor at the NSA's

F6 unit, Alfred Updike, valued the young man's programming talents enough to give him huge leeway. Consequently, Rafi reported to work at Savage Road only a few times a week. On the occasions he did make an appearance at the Big Four, however, Rafi entered a work environment crammed with math geniuses, PhDs, and computer engineering prodigies. In other words, he had found a world in which his behavioral maladjustments weren't entirely unusual.

Compared to the world outside Savage Road, Rafi got along reasonably well with his NSA colleagues. It was through his acquaintance with another programmer there that he discovered the world of motorcycling. Second only to his computer, Rafi Zamani loves his Ducati Monster 1200. Never having a girlfriend, or much in the way of male friends, either, Rafi expresses himself in only three ways: computer programming, *incel* chat rooms, and his motorcycle riding.

Rafi remade himself after his mother's abrupt engagement in one additional aspect. Less than a year after he had rented his first apartment, he was mugged on the street just down the block from his building. Three guys about his age had cornered him on the sidewalk and demanded money. Under the threat of violence, Rafi had silently handed over his wallet. One of the young men demanded the backpack containing his work computer. Rafi hesitated. The thug punched Rafi in the face and stripped him of the bag. Rafi always secured his devices with powerful password protection, so he had zero concerns the thieves would be able to

access the laptop. He emerged from the ordeal determined never to allow something like it to happen again.
Rafi immediately enrolled in classes specializing in
the Krav Maga form of military self-defense. Derived
from the street-fighting experience of Hungarian-
Israeli martial artist Imi Lichtenfeld and perfected by
the Israel Defense Force, contact combat provided
the young NSA contractor with the tools he needed to
defend himself.

Or kill people, should the opportunity, er, need
arise.

No doubt, being recognized on the ground floor of
the Big Four was bad luck. Despite having to lug his helmet, gloves, and motorcycle jacket, Rafi loses the army
lieutenant in the vast parking lots of the campus. When
he returns to the bike and throws his leg over the saddle
a couple of minutes later, he is dripping wet with sweat
from his exertions in the morning heat. As he hauls ass
through the main gate and up Savage Road, the rush
of wind blow-drying the sweat from his neck and face,
he realizes the game has changed. Rafi Zamani, NSA
contractor, will be invariably linked to Cyber Jihad. In
an hour or less, he will be a wanted man. But an intellect like his doesn't fail to plan for contingencies. Rafi
Zamani won't be your average fugitive, armed with a
knife and a sport bike. He has an additional skill set
with which to evade capture. The game has changed,
but it is far from over.

Rafi Zamani is confident he will prevail. The Ducati
gives him tremendous speed and agility. With a com-

puter and a link to the Internet, he projects the strength of nations. His mind and technical skills are unmatched by anyone at the NSA. Nothing can stop him. The motorcycle thrums between his legs, its engine in a high shrill and hurtling him through space. No one can catch him. He is free!

———————

INVESTIGATORS FROM THE FBI and military intelligence swarm the office suite of Unit F6 at the NSA headquarters. They begin the long process of rigorously interviewing Alfred Updike and every member of his team. Within the hour, April identifies the young man wearing the Manchester United jersey as Rafi Zamani. For the time being, her allegations regarding the contractor are only that: allegations. Sitting on a bench in a corridor on the top floor, April waits with two officers from military intelligence whose only job, it seems, is to babysit her. Finally, a grim-faced official emerges from a conference room across the corridor. They are ready for her.

She enters the brightly lit room and stands at attention, eyes locked forward. General Hernandez, seated at the head of the long conference table and wearing his green service uniform, is reserved in his emotions. He says, "Have a seat, Lieutenant."

"Thank you, sir."

April sits, back ramrod straight and hands folded neatly before her on the tabletop.

"Lieutenant, please can you tell us how you came to know Mr. Zamani and why, precisely, you believe he has anything to do with the hacker group known as Cyber Jihad?"

"Sir, I am socially acquainted with a White House aide, Hayley Chill, who was on the Metro train that derailed. When she emerged from the station at Rosslyn after the incident, Ms. Chill observed Zamani at the scene, enjoying the spectacle of wounded and displaced commuters. My friend is a highly observant individual, with a near-photographic memory, and she recalled Zamani. Subsequent investigation led me to believe he was involved with Cyber Jihad."

"I've read your report, Lieutenant. It didn't mention how *you* recognized Zamani this morning."

"Sir, I accessed surveillance footage from a local restaurant. I had good reason to believe that Zamani frequented the location."

"You 'accessed' the surveillance footage?"

April is surprised by the general's hostile tone. "Extralegal access, sir."

"You're a computer engineer, Lieutenant. What are you doing out in the field, acting like a cowboy and chasing after *bad guys*?"

She continues to be taken aback by Hernandez's blatant antagonism. "Sir, while I'm aware my duty assignment is here, at my desk, with USCC, I perceived a unique opportunity to identify a hostile actor and confirm attribution for an ongoing cyberattack. I regret if any of my actions have been contradictory to our mission."

Hernandez frowns and turns toward the deputy

commander seated at the table to his right. "Loop in the FBI, with discretion." He gestures in April's direction without looking at her. "No interviews with Lieutenant Wu. She's on lockdown until we've finished our investigation."

The deputy commander nods. April understands she's been dismissed and immediately stands. That's it? Hernandez is done with her? It's as if they don't *want* her to reveal the results of her admittedly unsanctioned investigation.

A colonel shows her out the door. In the corridor, he pauses to have a word. "You have a weapon at home?"

"Yes, sir. Licensed for concealed carry."

She doesn't mention that, as an operative for the deeper state, she undoubtedly has received more extensive weapons training than a Marine officer assigned to the Cyberspace Operations Group.

"Good. Go home, Lieutenant, and stay there. Don't talk to *anybody*." He returns inside the conference room, leaving April Wu alone in the deserted corridor.

FRIDAY, 1:15 P.M. Hayley sits at her desk in Kyle Rodgers's West Wing office feeling trapped and useless. As best she can ascertain, the president hasn't come down from the residence after his relatively brief appearance in the Situation Room earlier in the day. Absent a firm hand on the helm, the nation seems adrift. Her clandestine rendezvous with Andrew Wilde—a meeting April had missed because of the chaos at Fort Meade—was discouraging. Despite a massive break in identifying the true identity of Cyber Jihad, Wilde seemed more focused on the president's comportment. The primary mission of the deeper state remains running a counter-espionage operation against the Russians from inside the White House.

In Hayley's opinion, the rogue NSA contractor, Rafi Zamani, is the more significant and wholly unpredictable threat. Within the hour, she is on the phone with the one person she believes can provide some answers.

"I commend your talent for persuasion, Ms. Chill. I'm normally limited to phone calls only on weekends," James Odom tells her from the recreation room at FCI Cumberland.

"It helps when the call comes from the White House, sir."

"I imagine it's a rather hectic day over there. I'm flattered you'd steal a few moments to phone an old friend."

Hayley is aware prison authorities are most likely monitoring the call, with perhaps the intelligence agencies listening as well. "I'd still like to count on your help, sir. Your love of country has never been in doubt."

Odom has to grin to himself. "Home of the free."

Hayley chooses to ignore his sarcastic aside. "Sir, if I came out to Cumberland—"

"A waste of time, dear girl. You might recall our last *quiet* conversation."

Of course she remembers. Odom will help her if she helps him. Hayley rejected out of hand his offer of a quid pro quo. Assisting the disgraced deputy director in any manner was stooping too low. That was then; this is now.

"I do recall, sir." She pauses, then says, "How can I be of assistance?"

"Wonderful. Perhaps then you can check on an old family friend for me. Nice woman who runs a florist shop in the District. Little Shop of Flowers, quaintly enough, on Eighteenth Street. My friend is getting on in years. I worry about her."

"I'll see what I can do, sir."

Hayley ends the conversation not long after Odom relays his request. She feels the weight of another yoke thrown around her neck. How many masters must she serve to accomplish the things she knows are right?

———————————

SITTING ASTRIDE A Honda CB1000R—a backup ride he keeps garaged at a second location rented under an assumed name—Rafi watches the FBI agents and military intelligence officers exiting his apartment building on F Street. Sweating profusely under a visored helmet, he has no reason to fear the authorities will recognize him as their person of interest. No doubt, the cops have turned his apartment upside down by now and located his Sig Sauer under the mattress. In his rush to grab his stuff and go, he had forgotten the handgun. Rafi had prepared for this day in more ways than a backup motorcycle with an untraceable plate. Adverse to the concept of prison with every molecule of his being, he readied not just a bug-out bag but also a bug-out life.

Creating an alias, supported with all the necessary official documents, was a trivial matter given Rafi's hacking skills and obsession for detail. Under that false identity, he rented an extra studio apartment and purchased an extra motorbike. Given the thoroughness of his arrangements, Rafi's self-exfiltration was only a matter of grabbing Yazat and his computer, ditching the Ducati, and stepping into his assumed identity. Too bad about the fucking gun, though.

Imagining the cops traipsing through his apartment, however, truly pisses him off. He had expected his role as a rogue cyber warrior to last longer and blames Hayley Chill for its premature demise. His days in the nation's capital are numbered. Not that he minds leaving. Rafi has never been out of the country and relishes the prospect of new horizons. What was the George Carlin quote he had seen on Twitter? "Think about how stupid the average American is, and then realize half of them are stupider than that."

If he had *real* balls, he'd flip the switch on the entire country. He and his colleagues in Unit F6 had located exploits in the networks of every major utility. The backdoor exploit in the Stafford Compressor Station network was one such gem. Uploading the entire library of these vulnerabilities onto a hard drive the size and thickness of a credit card was no trouble at all. With this arsenal, Rafi could drop the United States back into the pre-Industrial Age.

The longer he watches the cops in their stupid uniforms and their seriously stupid expressions go in and out of his building, the angrier Rafi becomes. Do they think they've got problems finding him right now? Watch what happens when he turns off the lights.

———————

HAYLEY ENTERS THE florist shop in the Adams Morgan neighborhood a little after three p.m. The proprietor, a small, gray-haired woman of slim build and bright manner, is taking care of another customer as the White House aide comes through the door.

The older woman says, "Be with you in just a moment, dear."

Hayley stands patiently to the side until the other customer departs. The elderly proprietor approaches, wearing a pinafore-style apron over an Eileen Fisher linen blouse and sensible jeans.

"What can I do for you, dear?"

"James Odom asked me to stop in, ma'am."

"You're Hayley Chill."

"Yes, ma'am."

"Jim thinks very highly of you."

Hayley couldn't care less what Odom thinks about her. "You have my instructions?" she asks.

"Yes, of course. A few days ago, Jim's attorney had a meeting with him at Cumberland. Word was passed along to me."

"Word about what, ma'am?"

"That you would be the one who would take care of something for us."

Hayley realizes Odom had never doubted she would circle back to him. "Continue, please," she says.

"You see, I was with the agency and served with Jim Odom. You could say we came up together. A good friend of ours, another agent with whom we had undergone training at Camp Peary and joined in early operations was assigned the hazardous mission of going undercover in Cuba. Juan Martin was his name. Juan was quite successful in developing numerous assets in Havana. But, suspecting that his cover has been blown, Langley ordered him out of the country. Poor man, he had made it home safely, only to be murdered in a Miami alley the day he had stepped off a boat from Cuba."

"What does any of this have to do with me, ma'am?" asks Hayley.

"Jim and several others of us, since retired from the intelligence services, never forgot what the other side did to our friend. We've received new information from a developing source in Moscow. The man who murdered Juan Martin is still in the US, operating under an alias, Alberto Barrios, and working as a valet in the White House residence." The older woman pauses artfully. "You work at the White House, don't you, dear?"

Hayley hears these revelations without change of expression. She can deduce what Odom wants of her.

"I understand."

"Of course, you do. Otherwise, Jim wouldn't have chosen you." The older woman's demeanor shifts. She no longer seems like the gentle florist of Adams Mor-

gan but a former intelligence officer for the Central
Intelligence Agency, remorseless and cold-blooded.
"Verify our intelligence, won't you, Hayley? Take the
appropriate action. Perhaps then Jim Odom can be of
some service to *you*."

HAYLEY EMERGES FROM the florist's shop feeling over-
whelmed, an emotion mirrored by the city's pervading
mood. With the threat of a kinetic war breaking out
in Europe and the expectation of more cyberattacks,
Washington seems on the verge of a nervous breakdown.
Standing at the intersection of Eighteenth Street and
Kalorama Road, Hayley studies the faces of passersby
and sees collective anxiety on all of them. Despite these
well-founded fears, however, people in the nation's
capital persist, going about their business. She draws
strength in this observation. The bus driver continues
to drive his bus. The lobbyists continue to lobby. Even
the panhandlers do as they always do, despite a pervading sense of doom. If these ordinary people can cope
with uncertainty, then she can continue to perform her
duties as well.

But Hayley must question her decision to do the
bidding of the disgraced CIA deputy director with blind
obedience. She knows what's being asked of her. James
Odom doesn't only want Barrios exposed; he wants the
Cuban operative dead. Hayley has killed once in her
life. When a hit team was moments from assassinating
Richard Monroe at Camp David, Hayley intervened,

taking out the unit leader. She felt little in the immediate aftermath of the event and only later suffered moderate emotional distress over causing the man's death. A lifelong psychological detachment, she learned not long after her recruitment, was the primary factor in Publius seeking her out. If the White House valet is a Cuban agent, then Hayley will have no problem killing Barrios. What gives Hayley pause is not the act of killing this man but rather a desire to understand James Odom's true intention fully. That old weasel, Hayley muses, is capable of masterful deceit.

She decides against contacting Andrew Wilde. Does Publius know about Alberto Barrios? Why wouldn't they have trusted her with that information? Or maybe James Odom is playing her, setting Hayley up for an act of revenge on a personal enemy. She has almost no evidence on which to base an evaluation of Barrios's guilt. But what keeps emerging from the static inside her head is the image of Rafi Zamani's smiling face outside the Rosslyn train station. Whether he is a rogue agent, a traitor working at the behest of Russia, or carrying out the demands of some other hostile actor, the self-professed cyber jihadist must be stopped. And, at the present moment, her instinct is that James Odom is her best ally in that operation. Handling Richard Monroe will have to take a second position in her priority list.

That she has made the correct decision is underscored about fifteen seconds later, when Hayley sees the traffic light at Columbia Road and Eighteenth

Street go dark. Perplexed, the deeper state operative looks to a Starbucks coffee shop at the same intersection and sees that the electricity is off there as well. In every direction she looks, Hayley sees darkened storefronts. She makes the likeliest deduction: Rafi Zamani, aka Cyber Jihad, has struck again.

———————

FRIDAY, 4:45 P.M. "I'm beginning to develop a strong dislike for this prick," April Wu says to Hayley as she joins her on a bench at the northern end of Meridian Hill Park. Walking to the impromptu meetup was far easier than dealing with local traffic brought to a standstill by a cyberattack on the entire Eastern Seaboard's electrical grid and subsequent six-state blackout. This midpoint between the florist shop and April's condo is a short, five-minute walk. There is no respite, however, from the constant blare of car horns as commuters vent their frustration with immovable traffic on every street and lane in the city.

Hayley says, "Chances are the feelings are mutual. Zamani's a fugitive because of you."

"Finally, something to feel good about."

"Why? What else happened?"

"Oh, nothing, except being grilled by the director. Like he was pissed that I identified Cyber Jihad. He only wanted to debrief me enough to know to shut me down."

"What're you saying?" Hayley asks.

"I'm saying that flipping the switch on the Eastern

Seaboard and laying it off on Moscow is a pretty good way to get the president to sign off on a heavy-duty cyber counterattack."

Hayley shakes her head, not buying it. "No matter what anyone might think about the NSA, its leadership isn't in the habit of attacking the country they've sworn to protect."

"Apparently, the same can't be said for Rafi Zamani, a contractor for the *National Security Agency*."

"Underscore 'contractor,'" says Hayley.

April throws up her hands, exasperated with her fellow deeper state operative. "What the fuck do I know? I just work there."

"I'm not saying you're wrong, April. But some hard evidence, for instance, would be a nice thing to have."

The army lieutenant laughs gloomily. "Great. The country is circling the drain and you want to make this about us."

Hayley is stone-faced. She learned long ago the strategic value of remaining silent. People, in general, tend to talk themselves into the correct course of action. It just takes time. Hayley is rewarded once again for her disconcerting silence.

"Fuck it. We'll do it your way," says April. "Your president-assassinating jailbird is going to tell us what I already know."

Given what Hayley must do next, she needs April for cover. On the walk over from the florist shop, she had decided to tell her fellow deeper state operative about the phone call with James Odom and subsequent visit to the florist. "James Odom was one of the architects of the CIA's reorganization after 9/11 and the Reform and Terrorism Prevention Act. If someone inside the IC has Zamani on secret retainer, a deputy director of Intelligence Integration is the most likely person to know it."

"And you're willing to put this Cuban dude in the ground? Seriously?"

Hayley doesn't want to freak out her friend. "Of course not. But if I can get the goods on Barrios and spoon-feed it to the FBI? That ought to be enough to gain Odom's cooperation."

She would prefer this business with the Cuban to be bloodless. But there isn't much time for formalities. If the White House valet proves to be a GRU agent, Hayley is all too willing to deliver his head on a silver platter to her "jailbird."

April hasn't given up on the idea of tracking down the NSA contractor herself. "Think I'll head back over to the Iron Pony."

"Zamani is too smart to go back there."

"I'm not expecting to find him sitting on a stool and drinking an IPA, wiseass. Just want to ask around about him. Maybe get a better sense of what kind of guy he is. His habits."

Hayley nods, getting to her feet. "Better hurry. I don't imagine that place will be open very long with this power outage." She turns and starts jogging south through the park.

April stands erect, grumbling. *This isn't my first blackout, okay?* she muses, and starts jogging south, too.

HER MOTHER DIED from breast cancer when April was ten. Raised by her father and four older brothers, she grew up in a home environment saturated with testosterone. Everything was a competition. Whether on the local ball field or in their modest three-bedroom Long Island rancher, where they endured a perpetual contest for the use of the only bathroom, the survival of the fittest was the Wu family's operating principle. The five kids numbered enough to make up a team for any sandlot sport. Their fierce competitive zeal was near legendary for miles around. With their father often in the city running his import business, the Wu kids were left to fend for themselves. No one dared mess with little April; her brothers would protect her with their lives. But that didn't mean the four boys refrained from mercilessly teasing their kid sister and pushing her to excel. If any Wu received so much as a B in school, the mockery and abuse heaped on the shameful dunce by the other siblings would ensure it wouldn't happen again. Despite these challenges in her childhood, April wouldn't trade it for another. Family is her bedrock.

If any upbringing might have prepared her for the rigors of West Point, it was hers. Nominated for admission by her congressional district's representative, April had long held the dream to follow her older brother Owen to USMA. The traditions and rigor of the institution appealed to her. Free tuition to one of the nation's most distinguished colleges wasn't such a bad deal, either.

But from the earliest days at West Point, April understood she was in a hard place. With Owen having gradu-
ated two years before, there was no one to protect the
ambitious and obsessively directed eighteen-year-old.

After excelling at basic training the summer before
her freshman year, April arrived at West Point full of her
typical piss and vinegar. As was the case of her entire
childhood, she was determined to keep up with the
young men that comprised 80 percent of the student
body. Her athleticism, competitiveness, and bravado
stood out even in a hyperaggressive environment like
West Point's, drawing the attention of other athletes on
campus. She became friends with members of the football team, including its captain and starting quarterback
Joseph Stackhouse. Thoroughly acclimated to the West
Point culture within the first few weeks of her freshman
year, thriving in classes and thrilled to be learning the
arcane customs of this iconic institution on the Hudson
River, April Wu was a happy plebe as any.

Everything changed one afternoon during the last
week in October when April returned to her room from
taking a shower. She found Stackhouse waiting for her.
Wrapped only in a towel and anticipating nothing but
a friendly chat, April asked the college quarterback to
leave for a moment so she could get dressed. The boy
made awkward jokes that suggested he was hoping
for more than conversation. April disabused her male
friend of that hope in clear terms but remained smiling and cheerful. Stackhouse continued with his stilted
idea of flirtatious banter, moving closer to April and

crowding her into the corner of the room. He wedged two fingers between the towel and her chest, trying to push the fabric down off her. No longer smiling, April demanded that he leave. But Stackhouse persisted. When April started to raise her voice, the young man leaned his 225-pound frame against hers, clamped his hand over her mouth, and shoved two of his fingers into her vagina.

She fought him off. Within seconds of the sexual assault's start, Stackhouse retreated out the dorm room door. April filed a written complaint with school authorities that night, and the school dutifully launched an inquiry. After a cursory investigation, the school determined that the sexual contact between April and Joe Stackhouse had been consensual. Both students were charged with violating Article 1 of the Cadet Disciplinary Code for improper use of government facilities. Local police accepted the college's findings and refused April's demand for further scrutiny. Because of the subsequent disciplinary action, Stackhouse was unable to participate in the traditional Army-Navy football game. Instead, he joined April "walking the area," with sabers shouldered, for hours one cold December weekend in the school's vast plaza, a traditional form of punishment at USMA.

That same weekend, Army lost to Navy in that all-important game. Few cadets didn't blame April for the loss. From that day forward, the entire West Point student body ostracized her. April never wavered in her dedication to the academy. She never complained about being shunned, not once. Throughout her four years, April ranked near the top of her class. Ten days before graduation, two other female cadets came forward and accused Joseph Stackhouse of sexually assaulting them, too. They had witnessed April's fate for speaking out and chose to remain silent until just before graduation. For the courage and dignity with which she had conducted herself while a cadet, April Wu was nominated by her fellow students and awarded the Distinguished Graduate Award. Duty, Honor, Country, indeed.

FRIDAY, 5:11 P.M. Washington, DC, without electrical power and in the grip of an unseasonal heat wave, is deranged. As April Wu jogs south through traffic-clogged streets, she witnesses the escalating effects of a widespread blackout on an American urban center. A nine-story apartment building on Sixteenth Street is engulfed in flames, trapping tenants inside. A liquor store on Massachusetts Avenue spews looters, one of whom is shot dead by responding police. Emergency vehicles, sirens blaring, struggle to respond to calls in snarled traffic congestion. With surface streets almost impassable and trains not operating, people have no choice but to take to the sidewalks. Like turning over a rock and exposing thousands of ants that scatter in all directions, the thin veneer of civilization has been ripped away, revealing the terrified soul of its people.

As she jogs, sweating heavily now, April begins to doubt the likelihood of the Iron Pony Tap Room being open. She has indeed experienced the disorder that results from a blackout in the past, but nothing like this one. Given the rapidly deteriorating situation in the city, April wouldn't be surprised if the bar is burnt to the ground or overrun by plunderers. It's awe inspiring, really, the destructive power a networked world invests in a single person.

A lone hacker is responsible for all of this mayhem, she muses. If the NSA's Unit F6 employs Zamani, then he must be unusually talented. A computer engineer from Alfred Updike's team would know about the country's most potent exploits, whether offshore or domestic. That was their job. Left unchecked, Rafi Zamani has the capability of inflicting horrific pain and suffering on the country. One man! As North Korea had already realized, cyber warfare is the great equalizer.

Picking up her pace as she jogs through the congested streets, April speculates the FBI and military intelligence would be all over Zamani's residence, NSA work space, his family, and any known friends, acquaintances, or likely accomplices. But she and Hayley have an inside track on the hacker's habits: his affinity for motorcycles and the Iron Pony. That avenue of investigation has been thwarted by the electrical outage, at least temporarily. April curses as she runs. Hitting the electrical grid was a smart play on Zamani's part; no doubt, the authorities on the hacker's trail are experiencing similar complications amid a widespread blackout.

Turning right at Seventh Street and within blocks

of the Iron Pony, April increases her pace. She recalls marching in the rain as punishment at West Point and being shunned from that day forward by her fellow cadets. With Hayley Chill, she shares an ironclad determination and relentlessness in the face of a fight. If the tavern is dark and shuttered, there are other avenues of investigation to pursue. After the Iron Pony, she will return to Savage Road, despite the director's ordering her home. Hell, she'll ride her bicycle to Fort Meade if the traffic is still gridlocked. Her team at Cyber Command needs direction. Now that the authorities have identified Cyber Jihad as an actual contractor for the NSA, the vast catalog of network vulnerabilities that had been at Zamani's disposal must be shut down. Certainly, Updike and other units of the NSA are working that massive project but can't be relied upon for completeness. Shutting down exploits to Rafi Zamani means denying those same tools to US intelligence agencies. As she jogs south on the sidewalk, being careful to look out for traffic at the intersection with K Street, April makes a mental note to call the soldiers under her supervision at Cyber Command once she's done at the Iron Pony.

On K Street, a lawyer behind the wheel of a 2017 Audi Q7 breaks free of the gridlock west of Seventh Street and guns the engine. With cell phones on the entire Eastern Seaboard rendered useless by the blackout, he has no idea how his wife and kids are faring. He's frantic to get home in Silver Spring. At the same time, a young mother driving a Honda Fit south on Seventh Street and traumatized from looters banging on her vehicle when it was caught in traffic in Columbia Heights, stands stiff-legged on her accelerator out of pure fear. When the drivers of the two speeding vehicles appear in each other's field of vision at the intersection of Seventh and K Street, it's too late to prevent the inevitable collision. Hit broadside by the much larger SUV, the Honda goes airborne and careens into a jogging April Wu, who barely has time to flinch on hearing the tire squeal and crunch of steel.

8

★ ★ ★ ★

THE BOSS

Friday, 5:15 p.m. Hayley Chill, only slightly winded from her two-mile run from Meridian Hill, enters the White House complex and can't recall an atmosphere there as bizarre as the one she encounters on this confused and anxious evening. National Guard vehicles jam the driveways, including two IAV Strykers, eight-wheeled armored fighting personnel carriers equipped with either .50-cal M2 machine gun or Mk 19 grenade launcher. Three times as many Secret Service personnel swarm the property as is customary, augmented by M4-toting US Marines from Marine Barracks Washington. Walking past one of the combat vehicles on her way to the West Wing, Hayley questions the need for a grenade launcher on Pennsylvania Avenue but dismisses that idle speculation. Some brass hat with the Maryland Army National

Guard felt it necessary to deploy a Protector Remote Weapon Station on the front lawn of the "people's house," and given everything on her plate at the moment, that's good enough for Hayley. She has yet to figure out how she will confront Alberto Barrios.

Inside the West Wing, cast in semidarkness and stifling warm despite emergency-generated electrical power, she senses a feeling of impending doom. Even the Secret Service agents, usually so calm and contained, betray their anxiety with haunted expressions and frantic movements. Everyone seems to be running, no matter if the journey is only ten feet down the corridor to the office next door. Hayley, having perfected the art of hunkering down, remains poised as she threads her way through the shifting crowd of staffers, aides, military personnel, and government officials coursing through the West Wing. Climbing the stairwell to the main floor, Hayley finds a semi-panicky Kyle Rodgers in his office.

"Where the fuck have you been?"

There is no better indication that the country is in serious trouble than Hayley's boss's use of profanity. The standard levers of government seem all of a sudden inadequate to the task. Hayley wonders how April is faring at the Iron Pony. Judging by the sights she witnessed on her journey from their meeting at the Meridian Hill to the White House, Hayley wouldn't be surprised if the ersatz biker bar were a burnt ruin. The city is going to hell in the proverbial handbasket. And Sam McGovern? Emergency services, typically stretched thin in the perennially underfunded city, must be utterly swamped. Hayley can't imagine what kind of day the fireman might be having and regrets her cold treatment of him when they woke up together.

"I got caught in the blackout, sir. I'm sorry."

Rodgers immediately regrets the obscenity and regains his usual composure. "Same with me, a half hour ago. Absolutely mental out there."

"How is the president, sir?" She's almost afraid to ask.

"I'm told he hasn't been seen since leaving the Security Council meeting this morning. Another meeting is planned in an hour. Have no idea if he'll even show up." Rodgers broods, staring at his shoes and shaking his head. "I've worked with the man for more than two years, seven days a week, and even I don't understand what's happened to him. His critics might complain about his friendliness for all things Russian, but this latest crisis seems to have completely undone him."

"But after the Russian television stations and Leningrad hospital, how can they still accuse him of having a blind spot?"

"Yes. POTUS responded, after being presented with strong attribution by the NSA. And now the president seems to have completely fallen apart over it. Like he was hitting his brother or something."

Hayley reserves comment. This is all bad news.

"The cabinet, sir?"

"In near rebellion, thinking the Twenty-Fifth Amendment is a valid option to get us out of this mess," Rodgers says, referring to the constitutional provision that allows for the cabinet members to adjudge a president's fitness for the office and the apparatus with which to remove him from that position.

"They need to stand behind the president, sir."

An involuntary laugh escapes from Rodgers's mouth. Hayley's earnestness can surprise him at times. "I'll tell them you said so. Clare Ryan is fit to be tied, threatening to haul him down from the residence with her bare hands if necessary."

The secretary's distress is understandable. Dealing with the country's internal turmoil rests on her shoulders. Hayley's assessment of Clare is that she is an exceedingly capable administrator and cool under pressure, unlike several of the male cabinet officials. Clare Ryan would make an excellent president, Hayley muses. Is that the Homeland Security secretary's ultimate ambition? When things calm down, it would be interesting to become better acquainted with the woman.

Rodgers heads for the door. "I'm going up there."

The second floor of the executive residence is precisely where *she* wants to be right now. Is Alberto Barrios working this evening? Who on staff even possesses information regarding residence personnel? Given the present crisis, however, it would be far too abnormal for Hayley to ask to accompany her boss up to the residence.

"Good luck, sir."

He acknowledges her comment with a diffident wave of his hand before disappearing out the door. After

Rodgers departs, Hayley retrieves her KryptAll phone. Perhaps April has news.

———————————

FRIDAY, 5:20 P.M. Sam McGovern's Engine 5 is responding to a building fire in the northwest when the report comes over the radio of a vehicular injury accident on Seventh Street. Aware that other engine companies are already on scene at the fire and the car masher is only two blocks from their present location, the crew captain elects to detour to the accident. The fire engine pulls to a stop in the middle of the street where a Honda Fit lies on its roof on the west sidewalk, propped against the wall of a building, and just short of an Audi Q7 with a smashed-up front end. The crash had occurred approximately four minutes before the firemen's arrival. Given the nature of the three victims' injuries—one of them, in particular—every second counts.

As paramedic on the five-person engine crew, Sam quickly assesses the scene. The fire engine and disabled Audi SUV block traffic in either direction. Both drivers have exited their vehicles and sit on the ground. A female pedestrian, however, lies supine on the sidewalk. Sam quickly surmises that she requires the most immediate attention.

"Request EMS assistance," he says to his partner, Ankit Dhirasaria.

Sam checks April Wu for responsiveness.

Bleeding profusely from a head wound and her eyes closed, April doesn't respond to Sam's verbal question,

"Ma'am, can you hear me?" Receiving no response, the fireman performs a trap squeeze, gripping and twisting a portion of the trapezius muscle in April's shoulder. Again she fails to react in any fashion whatsoever.

"Unresponsive," Ankit notes.

The head injury is visible. Sam must quickly assess April for additional, possibly even more life-threatening injuries. Cutting away most of her clothing reveals multiple compound fractures but nothing as severe as the head wound. Sam retrieves a gauze dressing from his paramedic go bag and applies it to the injury, immediately stopping the flow of blood.

Ankit checks April's airway. "Going to need to OPA."

Sam retrieves an airway adjunct, a plastic medical device used to maintain or open a patient's airway. After inserting the device into April's mouth, Sam observes her chest rise for respiratory rate. After a moment's assessment, he says, "Five and shallow. Going to ventilate."

Ankit has the bag valve mask device ready and sets the oxygen tank to fifteen liters per minute. Sam places the BVM over April's face and begins to ventilate her. He next checks her carotid artery for a pulse. "One forty-eight and rapid."

"She's going into shock."

They place a blanket over April, pulling it up to under her chin. "High-priority transport."

"Already called in," says a third fireman in the crew, coming over to help out.

While Sam holds April's head steady, Ankit fits a cervical collar around her neck. Then he and the other two firemen lift April's body to one side and fit a backboard under her and strap her down.

An EMS truck pulls to a stop behind the fire engine. It is exactly seven minutes and eleven seconds since the Honda Fit nearly crushed the life from April Wu. Two blocks farther south on Seventh Street, the manager of the Iron Pony Tap Room is putting the heavy-duty padlock on the tavern's front doors. With no end in sight to the current blackout and looting breaking out all over the city, the owner doesn't pay him enough to suffer the possible consequences of protecting the place from marauders.

The manager, Aaron Beckett, from England's Peak District—a Ducati enthusiast and supporter of Manchester United—is probably the only person outside of work that Rafi Zamani can call a friend, sharing mutual enthusiasms in motorbikes and English football. In the next several harrowing hours, the authorities will fail to discover the bikers' casual association.

———————————

FRIDAY, 5:32 P.M. What better way to witness the city's incapacitation than by motorcycle? Wearing a full-face helmet with mirrored visor, Rafi tours a Washington that has been transformed by the blackout. Every building fire, car accident, and looted supermarket and liquor store is another bucket of endorphins dumped over his cerebral cortex. More than anything, the rogue NSA contractor relishes the idea that with just a few keystrokes on his laptop, he has inconvenienced every bitch who ever refused to fuck him. Astride the Honda, Rafi threads his way through blackout-induced traffic jams with vastly satisfying ease. Fucking beautiful. He owns this town! And the police and FBI investigators on his trail? Like so many blind mice.

Passing a Chick-fil-A engulfed in flames as he heads north on Fourteenth Street, Rafi reluctantly steers the Honda in the direction of his safe house. The hacker could probably revel for hours more in the destruction he has wrought but must acknowledge that he's pushing his luck staying out in the open. His safe house is a foul studio apartment in Columbia Heights. More than one or two days hiding out there will be quite enough for his taste. Poor Yazat doesn't even want to go for a walk in that shithole neighborhood. He's done his part. Time to get paid and get the fuck out of town.

FRIDAY, 8:31 P.M. The Russian intelligence operatives do little to hide their meeting from prying eyes, given the widespread disruption caused by the blackout. Certainly, the Americans are otherwise busy keeping their society from disintegrating completely. The utility company restores power as night falls, sparing Washington (and hundreds of other municipalities up and down the Eastern Seaboard) the dreaded prospect of a hot, muggy night without electricity. The blackout lasted approximately four hours. Konstantin Tabakov, as senior GRU officer, chose the location for their meeting, in this case, the Washington National Cathedral. Occupying folding chairs just outside the Bethlehem Chapel, where Woodrow Wilson is buried, Tabakov sits with Aleksandr Belyavskiy and Alberto Barrios.

Besides the three conspirators, who arrived separately, there are no other visitors in the entire sanctuary. Despite the trying times, few of Washington's distressed citizens have sought the solace of God. The light is dim, the air smelling seductively of myrrh and frankincense. The senior GRU agent speaks first, as is his prerogative.

In his native Russian, Tabakov asks Barrios, *"Your assessment?"*

The White House valet says, in accented Russian that is otherwise fluent, *"Sir, my evaluation is that if he hasn't been compromised already, then Polkan is extremely vulnerable to enemy influence and manipulation."*

Belyavskiy, the president's handler, retains a paternalistic affection for his asset. That he believes the darker complexioned Barrios is less qualified to have an opinion by nature of his ethnicity is an attitude the Russian does little to hide.

"No disrespect to our Cuban friend, but Polkan has been a loyal and diligent servant of Russia since he was barely out of his teens. Whether with infiltration of America's military or its presidency, this man has funneled thousands upon thousands of classified documents to the GRU and its predecessors. While installed in the Oval Office, Polkan helped mute the customary criticism of Russia by the US government and has given us freer rein in pursuit of our geopolitical agenda in the Balkans, the Mideast,

*and elsewhere. And, if that wasn't enough, he has desta-
bilized American domestic politics and its alliances overseas. Let's not forget all of these important contributions
the man has made. No less than President Malkin is on
the record, congratulating Polkan for his achievements!"*
says Belyavskiy, referring to Fedor Malkin, the Russian
president currently in the twentieth year of his term.

Tabakov seems less than convinced by his Russian
colleague's recitation of Monroe's accomplishments.

"That was then. This is now." He gestures toward Barrios, his fingers stained black by the sunflower seeds he
obsessively consumes. *"Our Cuban 'friend' has observed
him with his own eyes. Polkan himself admits he is under
suspicion!"*

Uncharacteristically bold, Belyavskiy presses his
case. *"If the American intelligence agencies can appre-
hend the cyber terrorists attacking their country, perhaps
the search for a mole in the White House will be lessened."*

Tabakov snarls as he says, *"What makes you so sure
Moscow isn't responsible for the cyberattacks on its enemy,
Aleksandr Belyavskiy? Perhaps a pretext was needed to
rearrange our borders in the Balkans. Who knows?"*

The "journalist" falters as he speaks, *"I . . . I . . . I
simply assumed—"*

Tabakov switches menacingly to English, his accent
thick and phlegmatic, and says, "Perhaps Polkan isn't
the only one to have become a dangerous liability."

Belyavskiy backpedals furiously. *"In truth, I've never
even met the man, not in person. What do I know of his
reliability?"*

Tabakov nods, satisfied to have his way. He shrugs, grimacing, and says, "Если он бьет тебя, он любит тебя."

Alberto Barrios looks to Belyavskiy for clarification.

"An old Russian proverb. 'If he hits you, it means he loves you.'"

While Barrios ponders the implications of the proverb, Konstantin Tabakov stands with a weary sigh. "There is another saying, more popular here in the West." He pauses to retrieve the bag of sunflower seeds from his jacket pocket. In English, he says, "All good things must come to an end."

Popping the sunflower seed into his mouth, the gruff GRU officer turns his back on the other two men and heads back up the cathedral aisle, toward the exit.

HAYLEY CHILL HAS no way of knowing Alberto Barrios isn't in the White House residence but rather a little over three miles away, at the Washington National Cathedral. The way forward remains murky. With electricity restored everywhere but a few rural counties in Pennsylvania and Maryland, the siege mentality that had gripped the West Wing has abated. Air-conditioning has brought the temperature inside the building to a comfortable level again. Hayley nurtures the hope that the worst is in the past. Kyle Rodgers dashes that brief optimism when he returns from the residence empty-handed forty minutes later.

"Not good," he says to Hayley when she asks after Monroe.

"The Security Council just convened, sir."

"I'll tell them he has the flu."

"They won't believe you."

Her boss can't mask his annoyance. "You're treating me like a slow ten-year-old because why exactly?"

"I'm sorry, sir." Hayley pauses, thinking frantically of a way to get into the residence. "Does the president need anything? What can I do to help?"

Rodgers is gathering his papers to go downstairs to the Situation Room. "Oh, I don't know. Maybe *you* can tell the folks down in the Situation Room that the president has the flu."

Hayley stares at her boss, stone-faced. He hates it when she does that.

"Forget it. Go home. Or, better yet, figure out who the hell Cyber Jihad is and punch that sonuvabitch in the face." Rodgers immediately regrets the mild obscenity. "I'm sorry, Hayley."

"That's all right, sir. I've heard much worse."

"Yes, I imagine you have," Rodgers says. "We'll get through this."

Behind her boss's back, Hayley smiles grimly to herself. *If he only knew the half of it.*

"Thank you, sir. I'm sure we will."

Rodgers has his briefcase packed and walks out the door, heading to the meeting of the Security Council.

Once he's gone, Hayley retrieves her KryptAll phone. She had missed a call from Andrew Wilde five minutes earlier. She dials his number.

Wilde's stuck in a jam on Interstate 95, the traffic situation having not wholly recovered from the blackout.

"I wanted you to know there's a situation regarding our mutual friend from Oregon."

Hayley reacts, the muscles in her face constricting. She knows Wilde won't go into specifics over the telephone, KryptAll or not.

Taking a stab in the dark, she says, "Can I visit her in the hospital?"

"Tomorrow. Or the day after. Stay focused. You have two jobs now. Understand? Your country needs you."

Wilde disconnects the call. Hayley sits in her chair, motionless. She understands why she hasn't heard from April since their meeting at Meridian Hill Park. That her friend is injured or incapacitated in some way is clear. She contemplates calling area hospitals for more information but decides against it. Wilde had been explicit in his directive. In addition to her duties running Monroe as a double agent, Hayley has inherited April's operation to chase down Cyber Jihad as well. Now more than ever, she must gain James Odom's cooperation. Alberto Barrios is the key.

At this very minute, the Security Council is meeting in the basement of the White House to determine the next move by the US. Regardless of Rafi Zamani's motivations for launching Cyber Jihad on America, the nation is now engaged in an evolving cyber war with Russia. April Wu's accusations against Rafi Zamani won't be thoroughly investigated in time to prevent further retaliation against Moscow. The two superpowers haven't been closer to all-out war since the thirteen-day confrontation in October 1962, during the Cuban Missile Crisis.

ALMOST TWO HOURS later, Kyle Rodgers walks back into the office. "You're still here?" he asks on seeing Hayley at her desk.

"Just finishing up. How'd it go, sir? Are we at war?"

"In a weird way, it was good the president wasn't downstairs. Without POTUS, the more lunatic fringe on the Council couldn't hold sway over him. The vice president tried to hold sway, but he was easily rebuffed."

Hayley nods. More time is a good thing.

Rodgers checks his watch and quickly gathers up his personal items from his desk. "I've got late drinks."

Hayley checks her watch. It's almost eleven p.m.

Rodgers hurries for the door. "Go home!" he says over his shoulder.

After her boss has left, she considers her options. With April's apparent incapacitation, by whatever cause, stopping Rafi Zamani has become Hayley's responsibility. How fitting, then, that the one person who can help is her asset, President Richard Monroe. As a double agent for the deeper state, he has performed well, providing a voluminous amount of faked documents and intelligence to his GRU handler that undoubtedly has the Russians chasing their tails. A falsely annotated briefing paper on the Air Force's latest stealth bomber technology, fabricated diplomatic cables from a NATO ally . . . Hayley and her cohorts at Publius have flooded the Kremlin, through their mole in the Oval Office, with a bewildering trove of misinformation. If only the CIA or NSA were so successful in their counterespionage activities.

But now Hayley needs Monroe for equally important reasons, if not more so. The new challenge is a more prosaic one, for sure. She simply needs the president to put her in front of his valet, Alberto Barrios. Despite the president's apparent emotional collapse, and his hostility toward her, Hayley is convinced she can compel him to help.

Picking up the phone on her desk, Hayley dials the number for the office of the Secret Service detail on-site.

———

FRIDAY, 11:03 P.M. Hayley climbs the elegant staircase to the second floor of the White House's main building and is met by an usher who wordlessly leads her toward the president's bedroom at the western end of the central hall. Secret Service agents stand at the top of the stairs, in the central hall, and at the doorway leading into the west sitting hall. The pretext for her seeing the president was easily established, given his absence from the Oval Office for the last twenty-four hours. With most of the West Wing staff having departed for the day, Hayley must deliver briefing materials for Monroe to "review." The senior agent on detail obtained the president's approval. Despite his antagonism toward her, Hayley guesses Monroe is feeling terribly isolated. She knows the whole story. By that right, she is better company than most. He can speak freely with her.

Hayley doesn't expect to run into Alberto Barrios by simply passing him here in the central hall of the White House residence. Confirming that belief, she observes no indication of the Cuban being on the premises. A valet shows Hayley into the president's private sitting room, just off his bedroom. Monroe, wearing pajamas and a silk robe, sits in an easy chair by the fireplace. A small fire crackles in the hearth, despite the warm spring weather outside. He seems mesmerized by the comforting flames, not looking toward Hayley as she enters the room. The usher retreats into the corridor but leaves the door open.

Hayley, clutching a briefing book to her chest, stops short of the circle of couches and comfortable chairs oriented to the fireplace.

"Mr. President?"

He finally looks toward her, his eyes expressing a bottomless sorrow. Richard Monroe is a defeated man. Iconic facial features that were at least partially responsible for his election to the presidency are collapsed and gray.

When the president gestures in a vague direction of the couch, Hayley clocks the tremor in his hand. "Sit, please."

Hayley takes a seat. She racks her brain for the words that will bring solace to a ruined man collapsing under the weight of dueling superpower masters. If the bromide of being caught between a rock and a hard place was ever more apt, Hayley can't imagine one. And the deeper state wants Richard Monroe to run for reelection and potentially serve an additional four

years? Looking at him, Hayley can't fathom it. She only hopes the president can survive the night.

"Difficult times, sir. For the entire country."

"They want me to attack Russia again. Take out their telephones and Internet. Can you imagine? Malkin and his gang will kill me, just like their predecessors killed Kennedy."

"It's true. You're in a terrible fix, sir."

"I never wanted this," he says, gesturing vaguely to the ornate, august room they occupy. "I could have retired from the army, lived a quiet life until the day I died. It was that damn book." Monroe is referring to the best-selling memoir that catapulted him to the White House. The best-selling memoir had truly started it all.

"Have you been contacted recently by your GRU handler, sir?"

"The usual dead drop messages." Monroe gestures toward the Sangamon edition of Sandburg's biography of Lincoln.

Hayley keeps her gaze locked on the president. "What about your valet, Alberto Barrios?" she asks. The question is like a tossed grenade, with no cover from its blast radius.

Richard Monroe has seen and done many things in his life as a warrior, horrific spectacles not witnessed by the average man. He has spent a life in the military and excelled there. In command of an M1 Abrams tank at the Battle of Medina Ridge, outside Basra, during Operation Desert Storm or leading the Third Infantry Division in its seizing Baghdad in the Iraq War, he has inflicted great

violence on cities and their citizens. He has been trained
all his life not to flinch in the face of adversity. Sitting
across from twenty-seven-year-old Hayley Chill, he manages not to recoil despite his fragile emotional state.

"What about my valet? I have six of them."

Hayley watches the president carefully, intrigued by
his bold defiance.

"Barrios, sir. He's the man I'm interested in."

"Alberto? I didn't know his last name. Cuban fellow.
Works the day shift. What of him?"

Hayley wants to hit Monroe square in the eye with
it. "He's an agent for the GRU. You know that, don't
you?"

"I did not. Moscow deliberately withheld the identity of their operative inside the White House. That's
how dead drops work."

Hayley refuses to be sidelined. "Is he on staff tonight,
sir? I'd like to speak to him."

"Haven't a clue. There's been a few things on my
mind other than the whereabouts of one of my valets."

"I require the absolute truth from you, sir. Failure to
tell me everything may result in your imprisonment in
a federal penitentiary for the rest of your life." Hayley
lets a moment pass so that what she has threatened can
sink in. "Is Alberto Barrios an agent for the GRU?"

Monroe's distress increases with Hayley's persistence, pushing the limits of his ability to control it. "I
told you. I have zero ideas if he is or isn't." With sagging
shoulders and etched-in-stone frown, he looks again
into the fire. His life is finished.

Hayley stands. The president doesn't move a muscle, as if he's forgotten she's even there.

"Sir?"

He turns his gaze toward her, reluctantly.

"Yes? What is it?"

"Instruct Alberto Barrios to meet me downstairs, tomorrow morning at nine. In the Palm Room. Tell him I'm bringing a message from the First Lady. Tell him anything to get him there. Do you understand? Downstairs at nine."

"Yes. I understand." His voice sounds remote. Robotic.

A FEW MINUTES past eleven p.m., Rafi Zamani waits under a marble arch of the World War II Memorial. The Mall beyond is deserted. After a tumultuous day in the nation's capital, no one ventures outside for a midnight stroll along the Reflecting Pool simmering in the moonlight. The oval-shaped fountain at the center of the memorial splashes agreeably, encircled by fifty-six pillars standing sentry over the scene. A little bit like Las Vegas, Rafi surmises. War memorial? The United States is a country only pretending to be respectful of sacrifice.

But where is the Boss? Rafi experiences creeping anxiety he's been set up. He has several contingencies in place in the event of a trap. If Rafi isn't around to stop the transmission scheduled in ninety minutes, he'll send a data dump implicating his boss to the *New York*

Times, the *Guardian*, WikiLeaks, the *Washington Post*, and, for good measure, the Federal Bureau of Investigation. The superficial normalcy that has returned to the city—only a handful of hours removed from the chaos of the blackout that he had caused—depresses Rafi slightly. It occurs to him that he is becoming addicted to inflicting damage on a world he despises. With each consecutive cyberattack, Rafi feels a need for a bigger and more traumatic impact to achieve the same gratifying thrill. His psychiatrist, if he still saw one, would no doubt have a field day with this shit.

He sees a figure approach. Fucking bitch, it's about time.

Clare Ryan walks across the marble-lined plaza and joins Rafi under the arch. A low mist swirls at their feet like a pale feral cat. In the Baltics, the Russian army mobilizes along its border, threatening the Baltic States. The president hasn't moved from his chair in the sitting room on the second floor of the White House. A ventricular catheter inserted through a twist-drill craniostomy at April Wu's bedside monitors her brain for swelling due to her traumatic injury. These disparate incidents stem from two unlikely associates—a cabinet secretary and a misogynistic NSA contractor—meeting clandestinely at Washington's newest memorial.

"Have you gone mad?" Clare asks. Laying eyes on the young man instantly triggers her fury.

Jeffrey Williamson, an executive protection agent assigned to the Homeland Security secretary during her former life as a Boeing executive, had brokered Zamani's

hiring. Formerly with Hillard Heintze, a Chicago-based security consultancy that counts several Fortune 500 companies among its clients, Williamson left that firm after Clare departed from Boeing. He's been employed by her, on a contract basis, ever since. With more than a dozen years in the US Secret Service and combat experience in Afghanistan as a Marine Corps officer, Williamson exudes dispassionate competence. His loyalty to his only client is absolute. But with so much at stake, Clare insisted on a personal involvement with the operation. That arrogance has cost her dearly. Her biggest mistake was assuming she could manipulate Rafi Zamani.

The NSA contractor giggles. "Some might be of the opinion that I'm not well," he says in answer to her rhetorical question.

"I told you to *stop* days ago!"

He shrugs. "Events transpired."

"People died today. Dozens more injured!"

And now a smirk.

More than any sympathy she may or may not feel for the innocent victims of Rafi's cyberattacks, Clare is most concerned with her welfare. The NSA contractor's antics have put her in tremendous jeopardy. But what's done is done. Survival instincts kick in. Endurance is her heroin. Reasoning with the young man, however, is futile.

"You're done. It's over." There is a threatening subtext to her statement.

"As long as I'm paid for my labors, I think I could be finished here."

"And then you're gone. Forever. I don't care where."

"They won't find me," Rafi says with complete confidence. "A new me in a new place."

"Good."

"It's not like the old me or the old place was all that hot," he says, giggling awkwardly again.

Clare retrieves her phone from her bag and checks it for messages, overtly repulsed by the young man. "Whatever."

"My money?"

"You'll have it tomorrow."

The Homeland Security secretary turns and starts walking away.

Rafi mutters to himself, "*Cunt.*"

She spins on the balls of her feet. "Excuse me?" Clare had heard the vile obscenity.

More than a little scared of her—all females, for that matter—Rafi smiles nervously. "Did you get everything you desired, Madam Secretary?"

Was it worth all of this? Was an expanded and more powerful Department of Homeland Security worth her association with this . . . *creature*? These questions bang around in her head as she stares at the young man in a motorcycle jacket. "You'll get your goddamn money tomorrow."

Clare Ryan turns again and strides off. Like a spurned lover, Rafi imagines.

───────────────

THIRTY-SEVEN-YEAR-OLD BOEING EXECUTIVE Clare Ryan was kidnapped from the underground parking garage of

her condo in downtown Chicago. Bound, gagged, and
crammed into the 32 x 18 x 16 inch "footlocker," she was
driven hours north in the cargo hold of a battered white
panel van to an isolated farmhouse. Clare spent the first
ten days locked in the trunk. In those earliest days of her
kidnapping, the gang let her out for only two bathroom
breaks a day. The Boeing executive correctly guessed the
farmhouse's location on the Upper Peninsula. Something
about the light up there. Mercifully, her kidnappers had
chosen early June to initiate their plot. Temperatures in
the winter often remained below zero for days on end.
The farmhouse seemed ill-equipped for the cold.

Only after Clare was allowed more time out of the
trunk did she gain more than a superficial awareness
of her kidnappers and their characteristics. Though
she had counted seven individuals in the gang—three
women and four men, all in their twenties or early
thirties—only four members of the kidnapping crew
spent a considerable amount of time at the Upper
Peninsula farmhouse. The two male and female *Yoopers*, as these caretaker kidnappers called themselves—a
takeoff on the area nickname derived from "U.P.-ers"—
were hard-core members of the War Resistance League.
In the judgment of the WRL, Clare Ryan's work for the
Boeing Corporation made her nothing less than a war
criminal. Accordingly, she was released from the trunk
on the tenth day for her "trial." In the mostly bare living
room of the ramshackle farmhouse, musty with the smell
of mouse droppings and aspergillus mold, Clare Ryan
was convicted of multiple crimes against humanity—

specifically, the murder of civilians in Yemen—and sentenced to death.

Fortunately for her, the kidnappers' need for money was greater than for justice. After her guilty conviction, life assumed something approximating a normal routine of any farmhouse in Gogebic County. The Yoopers, all committed paleo-vegans, subsisted on a diet of almonds, cooked lentils, and baked yams. Every other day, the kidnappers added blueberries to the otherwise drab diet as a special treat. Clare shed pounds from her frame and suffered from terrible fatigue exacerbated by extreme stress. Ironically, her treatment by the kidnappers improved following her death sentence. Freed from the cramped confines of the trunk, Clare began to get a better sense of her kidnappers as people.

Susan, the daughter of college professors in California, had quit her PhD program at Madison and joined the cause after falling in love with Tony, a perennially angry ex-con who signed on with the WRL because being a career criminal was too dangerous. Louise was a minor poet who cried while watching the evening news and was responsible for cooking and cleaning. William, a former college football star, was simply insane. "Wild Bill," as the others called their presumed leader, was quiet, brooding, and a rapid blinker, suffering from acute headaches that seemed to short-circuit his entire nervous system. Clare once witnessed Wild Bill force Louise's hand over the open flame of an oven burner when she criticized him for his filthy bathroom habits. Everyone in the farmhouse feared Wild Bill, but no one more than Clare.

will suspect these hours of deep slumber were due to her subconscious awareness that the worst was yet to come. Recuperation, however brief, was of vital necessity. Her dreams had revolved around home, in Lincoln County, West Virginia, and of her father, Tommy Chill. In the kitchen. Dancing to music coming over the cheap radio on the counter. Younger brothers and sisters underfoot. Smiles and laughter. It had been a good dream. She awakes to the reality of seemingly intractable problems of epic scale.

Hayley reaches for her smartphone and checks Twitter for the latest news, finding only the usual posts reflecting the general chaos of a world gone berserk. There is nothing about the White House or the president other than the everyday jeremiad. And so she is relieved.

But what of April?

Hayley is determined to discover what had happened to her friend and fellow Publius operative, regardless of her awareness that doing so will piss off Andrew Wilde. Time is in short supply. She will allocate ten minutes to tracking down April. Following that, she must get to the White House. Low-level staff may receive some weekends off but, amid an escalating crisis, this will not be one of them.

With her third call, Hayley determines April is at George Washington University Hospital. Twelve minutes after springing from her bed, she is out the door and jumping in an Uber for Twenty-Third Street.

The enormous medical facility is still reeling from the aftershocks of the previous day's blackout. Anxiety warps the faces of hospital staffers and visitors alike. Taking the stairs instead of slow elevators, Hayley locates April in the ICU, where doctors have put her in a medically induced coma. The ventricular catheter continues to monitor pressure on her brain, diverting potentially dangerous excess cerebrospinal fluid into a drainage bag. None of the doctors on duty are willing to discuss her condition with Hayley, but, with some persistent cajoling, one of the intensive care nurses is more forthcoming.

The harried nurse, stealing a few moments to answer Hayley's questions, says, "Vehicle versus pedestrian. Your friend was the pedestrian, unfortunately."

"Is she going to be okay?" Hayley asks.

"She's in critical condition. The worry is for more intracranial hemorrhaging. They've induced a coma until the swelling can go down. Infection from the ventriculostomy is a risk, of course."

"Can I see her?"

The nurse shakes her head. "What about family? Does April have anyone close by?"

"There's just me."

Retrieving her phone, the nurse says, "Give me your number. If there're any developments, I'll call you."

Exiting the intensive care unit, Hayley is vastly relieved to have established a line of communication with her friend's caregivers. Nearly walking into Sam McGovern as he enters through the same doors upends that satisfaction.

"Hello?" he says with an awkward grin on his face, slightly confused by the serendipitous encounter.

"What are you doing here?" Hayley asks. Sam wears his navy-blue fire department uniform.

"Just dropped off a patient downstairs at the ER. Thought I'd get information on a female car accident victim we helped last night."

"April Wu?" Hayley can scarcely believe it.

"Yes! You know her?"

Hayley is guarded, as they are veering into that part of her that she must wall off from her personal life. Normal life. "I do know April, yes," she says warily, warding off further inquiry.

Sam notes her reticence. And he is also aware by this point that the young woman whose life he saved the previous night is stationed at Fort Meade, with Cyber Command. "Okay. How is she? When we got there, your friend was in pretty bad shape. I just wanted to know she'd pulled through," he says with exaggerated circumspection, keeping the conversation well inside the white lines.

"She's in critical condition. The doctors will know more in a few hours, but I think she's going to make it."

Sam nods. He'll leave it at that. "And how are you?" he asks.

"Busy," Hayley says evenly. The emotions she experiences seeing Sam again defy articulation or even her basic understanding.

Sam wishes there was more he could do to help her. Why she had abruptly turned him out the day before is a question that weighs heavily on his mind. Too much self-doubt is in the space between them. He remains mute.

She intuits his silent desires and is surprised by the feeling she is experiencing, a need to make *him* feel better. But no time for that. Never enough time.

Hayley says, "I'll be okay. Call you in a day or two, okay? Soon."

Sam knows she is more than capable of taking care of herself. "Yeah. Talk soon."

Hayley exits the hospital. She contemplates walking. The White House is just under a mile away. The hot, muggy weather has mercifully abated. Spring has resumed. But there isn't enough time for such luxury. She is inside another Uber within two minutes.

HAYLEY WALKS INTO Kyle Rodgers's office in the West Wing at half past seven. As usual, she finds paperwork and files that need attention. How did it appear on her desk overnight? Bureaucracy elves? Only one task looms in her mind: confronting Alberto Barrios. She assumes Monroe has done what she had requested and ordered the valet to meet her in the Palm Room, a staging room for West Wing visitors, at nine. Everything hinges on her hunch that James Odom knows the identity of Zamani's secret client. As the former head of the CIA's Office of Intelligence Integration, the disgraced deputy director formulated the cooperation of analysts, technical and human intelligence collectors across a spectrum of the US intelligence community. Odom's offer of a quid pro quo to Hayley—his assistance in exchange for Alberto Barrios's head—is, in her estimation, a significant indication the bet is a good one.

Kyle Rodgers strolls into the office an hour after Hayley. Reflective of a more casual, weekend vibe, he wears Carhartt khakis and an untucked button-down shirt open at the neck. He seems in better spirits than the day before.

"I think the worst is behind us," he says without Hayley prompting. His apparent relief is manifest in his irrepressible grin.

"What makes you think so?"

"Just a gut feeling. Did you hear about this business over at Savage Road?"

"Sir?" she asks, playing dumb.

"Something about one of their contractors going rogue? I'm not sure. Bunch of crazies over there anyway, led by the biggest nut of all."

"General Hernandez." Hayley pauses as she registers what her boss is saying. "The consensus is that Cyber Jihad is this NSA contractor? Russia is off the hook?"

Rodgers nods. "Thank God, yes. We'll walk back the war talk. The president is obviously with me there." Monroe's senior advisor holds his thumb and forefinger an inch apart. "We were this close to blowing up the world!"

"When is POTUS due downstairs, sir?"

The president's senior advisor is positively giddy. "He's already in the Oval!" He gathers a few papers off his desk and heads for the door. "C'mon. I'm prepping him for a cabinet meeting at ten."

Hayley drops what she's doing on her desk and follows her boss out the door.

A few moments later, they're waiting inside the Outer Oval. The president's secretary is on the phone. Rodgers leans against the door frame leading inside the executive office.

"When all of this is over, I'm taking three days."

Hayley stands next to him. "Where?" she asks absently. Her mind is still wrapped up with Alberto Barrios.

"Barbados. Three days lying on the beach. I'm doing it."

Hayley nods. "Excellent, sir."

"I can't think of anyone who deserves it more than me," the senior advisor says, moments before the crack of a gunshot thunders from the other side of the door.

Hayley pushes past a stunned Kyle Rodgers and opens the door leading into the Oval Office. She sees the president of the United States seated behind the *Resolute* desk, where he has clearly shot himself.

9

★ ★ ★ ★

DEAD-ENDING

*S*aturday, 7:48 *a.m.* The next seconds implode, events collapsing into one another. Hayley enters the room and sees the president slumped down in his chair. Blood splatter covers the drapery behind him. She moves forward, propelled by instincts that command her to give assistance. Before she reaches Monroe, however, Hayley is shoved aside by a phalanx of Secret Service agents who have entered the office only a few seconds after her. One of the agents forces Hayley to the floor and plants his knee on the center of her back. Immobilized, the deeper state operative cranes her neck to watch other agents swarming the president, only to have her head forced down, too. Her line of sight is now limited to the carpeted floor under the couch. Later she will register the half-empty bottle of vodka stashed there. But, in the moment, Hayley experiences the unfolding pandemo-

nium inside the Oval Office exclusively with her ears. The
barked commands of senior Secret Service, Kyle Rodgers's
anguished shouting, and the sobs of the president's secretary all blend into a horror show cacophony.

Approximately three minutes after the crack of gunshot, she hears what she guesses is the US Secret Service's Rapid Intervention Safety and Command team
rushing into the room with a wheeled stretcher. What
Hayley can't know, given her inability to see the newly
arrived team, is that the first responding medical team
is from DC Fire and Emergency. Fortunately for the
president, the EMS unit had been passing the White
House at precisely the same time the Secret Service
put out the call and, with more experience in precisely
this type of emergency, was prioritized over the on-site
RISC unit by the senior agent on detail.

Assessing what appears to be a single shot to the
head, the EMS technicians apply a gauze bandage
around the president's skull to staunch the loss of blood.
With the assistance of Secret Service agents, they get
Monroe on the MOBI Pro X-Frame stretcher and wheel
him out of the Oval Office, west down a corridor that
has been cleared by other agents, out of the West Wing,
and into an EMS vehicle waiting on West Executive
Avenue. Two Secret Service agents climb into the back
of the coach to accompany the gravely wounded president. Only after he hears the emergency vehicle on its
way—presumably to George Washington University
Hospital, the nearest medical facility—does the agent
kneeling on Hayley allow her to get up from the floor.

She bears witness to an Oval Office in the grip of panic. In time, a more orderly process of review and investigation will commence. For now, Hayley Chill is completely ignored by the flood of officials and authorities surging into the room. Retreating from the Oval Office, she heads up the corridor to Kyle Rodgers's deserted office and closes the door behind her. Her thoughts threaten to overload her ability to process them all. Her potential culpability in driving the president to suicide is too awful to calculate. Right now, in these early minutes after the disaster, Hayley recognizes the absolute importance of speaking with Andrew Wilde. Texting news of this magnitude is unthinkable. She connects with Wilde on the third ring.

"I don't like talking on phones!" he snaps at her in greeting.

"Sir, Monroe has shot himself."

"What?"

"Just now. Seated at the *Resolute* desk."

"Is he dead?"

"I'm not sure. There was a lot of blood. I only had a momentary glimpse of the president before being forced to the floor by Secret Service agents."

"Christ . . ."

Hayley can almost hear Wilde crunching the contingencies over the phone.

"Sir, what should I do?"

"Sit tight. I'll be in touch."

"Rafi Zamani—"

"Not now, damn it!"

But she persists. "Sir, there could be more attacks planned. Russia—"

Wilde interrupts her a second time. "Your mission was to keep Monroe in a box, not put him in a coffin!" His last word is a slap across her face.

Andrew Wilde disconnects the call. Hayley sits at her desk for a moment, motionless. She feels all-too-familiar anger welling up within her. No time for it. Never enough time.

THE EMS TRUCK carrying the injured president races up Pennsylvania Avenue, bracketed by a frenzied scrum of DC Police patrol cars and Secret Service SUVs. Without street closures that typically precede a presidential motorcade, city traffic soon impedes the progress of the speeding caravan. No amount of wailing sirens and flashing emergency lights can dislodge the gridlocked vehicles. Frantic radio calls from the police patrol cars determine a serious accident at Twentieth Street is the cause of the jam. The driver of the EMS truck abruptly bails left, cutting across lanes to travel west on H Street. Surprised by the maneuver, accompanying Secret Service vehicles attempt to follow the EMS truck but are held up by snarled traffic in the intersection.

Agents jump out of the lead SUV to open a path for the Secret Service vehicles to pass through the intersection. Racing west on H Street, the agents in the lead SUV can't see the EMS truck ahead. With the assumption that the paramedics turned right on Twenty-Third

Street, which leads directly to GWU Hospital only a few blocks north, the Secret Service agents take that route. After making the turn, however, they still don't spot the emergency vehicle containing the injured president.

"Where the fuck is it?" asks the agent behind the wheel of the lead SUV.

Could the emergency vehicle have covered so much ground—a whole city block—while cross traffic had momentarily stopped the Secret Service SUVs? It doesn't seem possible. The EMS truck had had no more than a twenty-second head start. The agent in the front passenger seat of the lead SUV gestures toward the hospital up the road.

"They must be at GWU! Go, go, go!" His partner is already relaying the information over his radio.

Within the next minute, Secret Service vehicles and DC Police patrol cars behind them screech to a stop at the emergency room entrance. The EMS truck is nowhere in sight. A senior Secret Service agent gets on his phone. But whom, exactly, should he call? Standing outside their vehicles and unsure what to do next, the dozen Secret Service agents experience a collective sickening feeling that they have just lost the president of the United States.

SATURDAY, 8:25 A.M. Clare Ryan only has moments to spare, but the call she must make cannot wait. Blowing through red lights with car horn blaring, her driver races toward the White House complex. The secretary of Homeland Security has heard only the earliest reports of

a medical emergency involving the president. Astound-
ingly, this news is of secondary importance to the radioactive potential of an unhinged Rafi Zamani in her life. The
NSA hacker has gone far beyond the operational param-
eters Clare had explicitly laid out for him. Her strategy
seemed sound at the time of conception, the most efficient way possible to expand her mandate at the Department of Homeland Security. The awful truth Clare
discovered upon her appointment as head of DHS was
that her abilities to accomplish anything meaningful—
in terms of cyber defense, as well as other national security needs—were severely limited. Without funding and
the full support of the president, a secretary of Homeland
Security plays a never-ending game of catch-up. Alarmed
by the severity of America's vulnerability to cyberattack,
Clare Ryan was determined to armor civilian defenses by
any means necessary.

Created in 1978 as a joint program of the CIA and NSA
with the mission to infiltrate computers around the world,
the F6 unit was a piece of intelligence real estate that
Clare Ryan had long coveted. Her efforts to integrate the
unit's programs with Homeland Security were thwarted
effectively by NSA director Hernandez, with or without an
executive order from the president. Clare resorted instead
to poaching one of the unit's best and brightest rising stars.
Through his work for the NSA, Rafi Zamani had acquired
the skills and a working knowledge of the highly classified
exploits needed to mount a sustained and carefully modulated attack on the US. Psychological profiling performed
by Clare's private security agent had highlighted Rafi as

disaffected and a loner, making him highly susceptible to recruitment. Jeffrey Williamson made initial contact with the young man. After a negligible amount of courtship, he negotiated a fee for Rafi's services.

Clare Ryan had calculated the cyberattacks on the Metro line and compressor station at Stafford would have been sufficient for her purposes of convincing the president—and the public at large—that civilian cyber defenses required immediate attention. She was confident the NSA director, Carlos Hernandez, could be sufficiently contained, avoiding a confrontation with Russia, her scheme's patsy. But Zamani blew up those well-laid plans. His attacks on the Pentagon servers and, for Christ's sake, the country's electrical grid, have scrambled the "action and response" plan beyond Clare's legendary skills to manage it. Those incidents led to a regrettable attack on Russia and very nearly war. But the secretary of Homeland Security believes her ultimate goal is still within reach. She has kept Hernandez on a leash. The threat of full-scale conflict has abated, replaced by demands by the media and in Congress for expanded protection of civilian targets. From any perspective she analyzes the Rafi Zamani situation, however, Clare concludes that she cannot allow the NSA contractor to live. One life for the lives of many is not a difficult ethical hurdle to clear by her reasoning.

As the car speeds toward the White House, she picks up her phone. Williamson answers before the first ring.

"What's up, Boss?"

Clare privately thrills when called this and does nothing to discourage it.

"Not sure. Something crazy at sixteen hundred. Going over there now."

"Anything I can do to help?"

"I'm fine there. It's the other issue, the one we discussed yesterday."

"Yes?"

"I think it's time we deal with the problem. Can you see to it?"

"Absolutely."

"Soon, Jeffrey."

"Yes, ma'am. Today."

She disconnects the call and almost simultaneously receives a text from the director of US Secret Service, an agency under the Department of Homeland Security, informing her that Richard Monroe shot himself. Her first thought upon reading this astounding news, once the initial shock has passed, is to wonder if the president's apparent suicide helps or hurts her chances of increasing her mandate at DHS.

———————————

SATURDAY, 1:55 P.M. Hayley is forbidden from leaving the White House complex, even though she has already been interviewed multiple times by investigators from a smorgasbord of government entities. Four hours have passed since the president had fired a bullet into his head. The Secret Service cannot confirm the true extent of his injuries because of the simple fact that they cannot find Richard Monroe. At a few minutes before ten a.m., authorities located the DC Fire Department EMS truck that had transported the president from the White House in the underground parking garage of a GW University building on H Street. Found inside the abandoned emergency vehicle were bloody sheets, discarded EMS uniforms, and two dead US Secret Service agents. Both agents—male and female—were shot in the back of their heads at point-blank range. For the time being, utter confusion holds sway over the West Wing. Indeed, the shock waves are felt throughout the entire federal government and around the world.

No one knows where the president is or whether he is even alive. As for Hayley, she can't abide sitting around until someone tells her what to do. Despite Andrew Wilde's orders for her to "stand down," Hayley is determined to bring Rafi Zamani to heel. She is sure the rogue NSA contractor, left unchecked, will strike again. To win James Odom's cooperation, Hayley knows what she must do: take the disgraced CIA deputy director's revenge on Alberto Barrios. But how long will she be trapped here in the West Wing? All personnel and staff on-site—whether the president's chief of staff or a gardener—are sequestered until investigators have the opportunity to interview them multiple times. No one is going anywhere anytime soon.

One question asked repeatedly by investigators: How did the president get his hands on a gun, inside the White House of all places? Hayley came up with the best answer within the first minutes of medical technicians wheeling the president out of the building. Who better to arm Monroe than his valet? If Alberto Barrios is, as James Odom alleges, an operative for the Russian intelligence service, then suspicion must be centered on him. And here, Hayley realizes, her needs dovetail with those of every authority frantically in search of the missing president. The White House valet is almost certainly linked to the president's disappearance.

She goes to the door and enters the corridor, looking for the FBI agents who questioned her an hour earlier. Venturing down the hallway in the direction of the Oval Office, Hayley encounters a tall, balding agent. She must take great care in what she says to him or risk blowing her cover. But time is of the essence. Convinced Barrios was involved in Monroe's disappearance, Hayley can only assume the Cuban will flee the country once released from the White House complex.

"Sir?"

"Not now," the agent says, continuing down the corridor.

Hayley chases after him. "I thought of someone you need to look at more closely."

The FBI agent stops but, with his body language, makes it clear he won't be stopping for long. "Who?"

"One of the valets, sir. Alberto Barrios? He should—"

The agent cuts her off. "We've questioned the domestic staff and cleared them all. Stay put. We'll circle back to you." He moves on, leaving Hayley just outside her office door.

She knows for sure now that Alberto Barrios has left the White House complex. Hayley must get off the property and intercept him. Nothing is more important. Looking out her window, she can see staff members from the residence—housekeepers, kitchen help, ushers—leaving the complex one or two at a time.

Hayley hears a commotion in the corridor and goes back to the open office door. Stepping in the hallway, she nearly gets knocked over by three FBI agents running past. Investigators congregate outside the Oval Office. She follows the phalanx of law enforcement agents, encountering Kyle Rodgers just outside the Cabinet Room. Disbelief and disorientation slacken his facial features.

"What's happening, sir?" she asks her boss.

"He's . . . he's gone . . ."

"President Monroe? He's dead?"

Rodgers shakes his head, numb. "The Russians took him. Monroe *defected*."

SATURDAY, 7:29 P.M. (GMT) Richard Monroe—born Yuri Sergeev—feels he can relax only as the Gulfstream G650ER makes its approach to Reykjavik, Iceland, for a refueling stop. The operation to exfiltrate him from the White House was a terrifying experience, but he is safe now and blessedly free. When the GRU operative posing as his valet, Alberto Barrios, proposed the escape plan, Monroe agreed on the spot. It was a bold and complex operation, with success contingent on several independent actions. His role was quite simple. Barrios gave him the gun and a bladder filled with blood. Monroe experienced enough warfare in his military career to know what a gunshot can do to a human head. He knew how to properly dress the scene and play the part of a suicide victim. It was absurdly easy, with shock value providing the vital suspension of disbelief.

The automobile accident that had been staged by GRU agents on Pennsylvania Avenue was the pretext needed for the Russian crew manning the EMS truck to deviate onto H Street. Once the medical technicians in the front seat had left behind the escorting Secret Service vehicles, they executed the two agents riding in back with the president. Less than fifteen seconds after making its detour, the emergency vehicle darted inside a parking garage. Monroe was loaded into a waiting Mercedes with dark tinted windows and driven to the Potomac Airfield, where a Gulfstream GIV was fueled and waiting with jet engines thrumming. Forty-five minutes after "shooting himself in the head," the president—along with the entire exfiltration team—lifted off from the private aviation airfield in Friendly, Maryland, destined never to set foot in the United States again.

Only one individual of the sixteen passengers on board has spoken with Monroe since takeoff. Konstantin Tabakov introduced himself after the US president had settled into a seat near the front of the plane and then mostly ignored him. None among the passengers or crew seemed the slightest bit interested in speaking with Russia's greatest spy operative since Ramón Mercader, Trotsky's assassin, who spent twenty years in a Mexican prison before returning to a hero's warm welcome in Moscow. What compelled their unanimous avoidance of him, he could not say. Monroe had hoped to meet Aleksandr Belyavskiy in person finally. He was told his longtime GRU handler was staying behind in the United States, his cover as a working journalist intact. So Monroe spent the hours en route to Iceland in contemplative silence.

The world must know the truth by now: the US president is a Russian mole. He has discerned from the conversations of his fellow passengers that the decision to trumpet their astonishing success was a difficult one to make. Monroe is surprised the GRU didn't work out these details in advance of his escape. Then again, the operation came about so suddenly. Who had time to consider the finer points? He is relieved that Moscow determined that his outlandish exfiltration was of greater propaganda value than simply killing him. Despite the mission's demise, the Kremlin can declare victory with real justification. Given ironclad assurances that Cindy would be allowed to join him in Russia—should she *want* to, an outcome that Monroe must admit is not guaranteed—he agreed to the exfiltration plan. But should he tell his countrymen about Hayley Chill and her deeper state masters?

Richard Monroe knows there are only two possible futures for him when they land in Moscow: A long and comfortable retirement on an estate far from the capital, kept almost entirely out of public view except for heavily orchestrated showings by the Kremlin. Alternatively, he will receive a bullet in the back of his head. The ex-president—and surely he must have been succeeded by that nitwit of a vice president by now—fully appreciates the Russian mentality that will forever hold him in suspicion. Having been raised nearly from birth in the United States, Yuri Sergeev's corruption by the West is a given. His trustworthiness will never be presumed. Betraying the existence of the deeper state and its hold over him is a certain death sentence.

In these earliest hours of his flight from American justice, Richard Monroe makes the sensible choice. He won't breathe one word of the deeper state's existence to his fellow Russians, not for as long as he lives.

As the ex-president ruminates on these thoughts, Konstantin Tabakov rises from his finely upholstered seat farther aft and heads toward where Monroe sits. The Russian intelligence officer is a dour fellow, and thoroughly representative of the Slavic ethnicity. Monroe finds himself vaguely repulsed by the man. Is he ready to be Russian again? Does he have any choice?

Tabakov locks his gaze on Monroe and says in their native language, *"Home then for you, finally."*

"Yes! Thank you, Konstantin Tabakov! Back to the warm embrace of Mother Russia!"

The GRU spymaster laughs, his eyes watery and gray. He knows more of what lies ahead than the fugitive US president.

"Warm or cold, it's still a mother's embrace all the same, Yuri Sergeev."

Both men laugh, but Monroe's chuckle has a slight tremor.

WHILE KYLE RODGERS's declaration would stun just
about anyone else, Hayley Chill is unsurprised by the
news. So Moscow successfully exfiltrated their agent
rather than kill him. She has to admire the tradecraft.
Smuggling a president out of the country from under the
noses of his Secret Service protection detail is no mean
feat. Richard Monroe's worsening mental state could
only have made the operation that much more challeng-
ing. The Russian intelligence services must be in full
self-congratulatory mode.

She stands with her boss in the carpeted corridor
outside the Cabinet Room, filled with government officials whose world has been turned upside down.

"We know about all of this how, sir?" Hayley asks
Rodgers.

"Private jet, approaching Russian airspace." He fits
the pieces together in his mind, the full and terrifying
realization forming as he speaks. "No. He didn't defect!
My God, Monroe was a *mole*!"

Hayley says nothing, looking past Kyle Rodgers, into
the Cabinet Room, where she sees Vincent Landers
surrounded by a scrum of government officials, FBI
agents, and administration aides. A supreme court
judge is being ushered into the room, holding a large,
leather-bound Bible. The United States of America is
currently without a president. Saner heads have seen fit
to swear in a replacement.

An agitated Secret Service agent suddenly appears
in front of Kyle Rodgers and his young chief of staff.

"You both need to return to your offices . . . *now*."

The agent's tone leaves no room for negotiation. Without a word, Rodgers turns and heads back up the corridor. Hayley follows on his heels, with the realization that now is her last chance to escape the building. Given this latest turn of events, the authorities will be questioning West Wing staffers for hours to come. Richard Monroe is gone. Her primary mission went with him. No doubt, from her superiors in the deeper state, Hayley will incur much of the blame for losing him. She will come under even greater scrutiny from regular law enforcement entities. None of that makes any difference right now. She must get out of the West Wing.

As she passes the doorway leading into the Outer Oval Office, Hayley sees that the reception area is deserted. With all of the chaos of the morning, nobody is manning the gate into the nation's chief executive office. Hayley peels away from Kyle Rodgers and darts inside the reception area. Walking quickly to the partially open door leading into the Oval Office, she sees it is also uninhabited. She enters, going straight to the door that leads into the portico and Rose Garden.

Hayley pauses to look back over her shoulder. She knows this very well may be the last time she sets foot in this historic, hallowed room. The moment is only a few seconds in duration but feels saturated with memories and significance. That she ever came to this place astonishes her. Having been raised in near poverty, with the barest of college education and a stint in the army, she has come farther in her relatively young life than she ever would have imagined. But there is no time for further reflection. Events hurtle forward. She must hold on for the ride or risk falling by the wayside.

She pushes the door open and exits. The spring day promises to be a hot one.

———————————

WHEN KYLE RODGERS returns to his office, he is surprised not to find Hayley right behind him. He admires his staffer's bold decision to bug out, correctly guessing she exited through the unoccupied Oval Office. As she also must have intuited, no one is going to be authorized to leave the West Wing anytime soon. Rodgers, as Richard Monroe's closest advisor, is kept longer than most, finally exiting the building after ten p.m. He will never see his chief of staff again, not since encountering her in the corridor outside the Cabinet Room on the afternoon of the president's defection. It will be as if Hayley Chill had vanished into thin air. Her abrupt disappearance is only one of many mysteries on that extraordinary day in American history. At the time, Rodgers has much greater concerns. FBI agents not only question him for hours on end but also grill his wife. Small wonder that the investigators don't similarly interrogate his four-year-old twins. The experience is not a happy one.

He had no inkling the man for whom he had worked so diligently was, in fact, an agent of Russia. Love of country was always one of the prime motivations for Kyle Rodgers's dedication to public service. Money wasn't an incentive. Unlike his college pals from UVA pulling down high six figures in the private sector, Rod-

gers has had to rely on his wife's salary from a midlevel
DC law firm to maintain a decent standard of living.
The professional repercussions that will arise from his
association with Richard Monroe will leave a bitter
taste. His work in the public sector is at an end.

Increasing federal oversight of Big Tech firms cre-
ates a lucrative demand for guys with Rodgers's résumé.
Facebook will hire him at a starting salary of more than
a million dollars, including signing bonuses. A little
brother will join the twins almost nine months to the
night of Rodgers's dismissal from his West Wing interrogation. With a growing family, his wife will quit her
law firm and develop a passion for watercolor painting.
The *Washington Post* will profile the couple, a family to
be envied and emulated. His life transformed by a president's faked suicide, Rodgers will enjoy a long career in
the private sector before retiring. Seven years later, he
will find himself sitting in a comfortable leather chair
one muggy Sunday afternoon, a reasonably content
old man. Kyle Rodgers will be reading the galleys of a
new book on the history of America's most catastrophic
presidency, an administration with which he enjoyed
particular intimacy. Failing to find mention of his astonishing chief of staff, Hayley Chill, he will make a mental
note to call the author. Five seconds after that thought, a
massive stroke will bring a conclusion to a life well lived.

SATURDAY, 2:46 P.M. Alberto Barrios notices the young
woman when he is halfway down the block on G Street,

just after leaving the White House complex and crossing Seventeenth Street. The weather is achingly beautiful, but he couldn't care less. Barrios must get to Union Station in time to catch the 3:25 train for New York. At Penn Station, he expects to be met by a GRU agent and driven to the Port Newark–Elizabeth Marine Terminal. There he will board a Panamanian-registered container ship bound for the Port of Oslo, in Norway. His work, in the United States at least, is finished. Yuri Sergeev is safely aboard a private jet bound for Moscow. America is on the cusp of suffering the kind of national humiliation heretofore unknown in human history. If not for the female operative in pursuit of him, Barrios would be feeling nothing but complete satisfaction with his mission performance.

Seeing the young woman's reflection in large display windows, he crosses midblock, walking briskly in the direction of the GW Delicatessen on the north side of G Street. Barrios knows the deli well, having patronized the establishment throughout his tenure at the White House residence. He is familiar with the store's layout. He plans to exit out a rear entrance and take the back alley to Twenty-Second Street. But observing his pursuer pause to make a phone call as he heads inside the deli convinces Barrios that she has alerted compatriots of an American intelligence service. He must make his stand here, in the narrow confines of this dreary grocery.

He has only seconds to decide on the best course of action and where to stage his attack. Barrios briefly considers the possibility of taking a hostage. Armed with only a knife, however, he rejects the plan as having low odds of success. If the female operative has a gun, which is entirely likely, she will shoot him dead without pause. His best hope, then, is in taking refuge in the bathroom at the back of the deli. Perhaps his pursuer will believe he's fled out the back door, as was his original strategy. The woman's dogged pursuit infuriates him. Barrios craves ending her life. But a clean getaway, without further conflict, is the absolute best result of his predicament. He has survived this long in the espionage game, in no small part, by possessing an ironclad discipline.

The clerk at the register doesn't acknowledge his presence as he enters. Barrios continues to the back of the store, checking the three aisles for other customers as he goes. He is alone. The deli counter is currently not staffed. Ducking inside the tiny bathroom, the Cuban considers locking the door behind him. Doing so, he realizes, would accomplish nothing but betray his presence inside. A second door opens to the even smaller room, equipped only with a toilet. He enters that cramped space and pulls the door closed. Then he waits.

Barrios hears nothing until approximately a minute later when the bathroom door squeaks open. Footsteps scuff the floor just on the other side of the toilet room door. After a pause, the door is pulled open, revealing his pursuer. Relieved that the young woman is unarmed, Barrios grips the female operative by the arm and yanks her inside the narrow space. Simultaneously, he thrusts his knife at her throat. She deflects the knife strike. Only then does Barrios realize the young woman has spiked her keys between her fingers. He is shocked by the speed with which she launches her counterattack, repeatedly striking him in the face with her fist. Rending his skin with the keys. The female agent is smaller than him and, by that feature, much more agile in the cramped space. Blinded in one eye and fighting for his life, the Cuban slams the knife handle into the side of the young woman's head. Stunned, her legs buckle. Barrios kicks her hard in the shin with his steel-tipped boot. He has her. The fight is now tilted decidedly to his advantage. The Cuban flips the knife around in his hand and thrusts the blade at her throat again. But his adversary has collected her wits in those few seconds. She ducks out of the knife's path.

Barrios struggles to withdraw the knife's tip from where it is buried deeply in the hollow-core door. The young woman comes at him again with her fists, keys turning his face to a bloody hash. The Cuban attempts to use his superior strength and size to overwhelm his nemesis, but the combination of tight quarters and her ferocity continue to defeat those efforts. Barrios loses a grip on his knife when the young woman drives her right elbow into the side of his head. In a fog of near unconsciousness, the Cuban imagines she has gone and fled. He no longer can see through the flesh and blood that clog his eyes. Alberto Barrios wants to believe his adversary has given up, that she was, like him, desperate for relief. *Dios mío, no en este lugar*. The Cuban doesn't want to die in this dingy bathroom. He doesn't want—

AT ALMOST THE same moment Hayley kills the Cuban GRU agent, Rafi Zamani stands over the corpse of the hit man sent by Clare Ryan. Earlier in the morning, Rafi received instructions to go to Prospect Hill Cemetery at one p.m. Meeting in person seemed unnecessary, of course. Clare possessed all the information she needed to transmit his fee. But the Homeland Security secretary said she couldn't figure out how to make the "whole cryptocurrency thing" work, insisting they meet so that he could help her with the transfer. Of course, Rafi smelled a setup from the start. Consequently, he was ready for this sorry-ass motherfucker lying on the grass between alabaster headstones. After gutting the nameless hit man, Rafi found a Glock 19 equipped with Osprey suppressor jammed in his waistband. Fuck him.

Rafi heads down the small cemetery knoll to the parking lot and tosses the hit man's F-150. He finds nothing of significance inside. No money. Nothing.

———————————

CLARE RYAN HASN'T left the Cabinet Room for so much as a bathroom break since arriving hours ago. But her hard work and sacrifice have paid off, in spades. Minutes earlier, the new president signed an executive order dramatically expanding the mandate of the Department of Homeland Security. Clare has succeeded. The journey was long and arduous. But, in the end, those exertions were worth a safer homeland. More than anything, Clare craves to return to her office at DHS and commence the Herculean task of armoring the country's civilian cyber defenses. Banks, the electrical grid, transportation systems, oil and gas transmission— all of these networks require her attention if they are to be safe from cyberattack. The work will require years of effort and countless millions of dollars to complete. Time to get started.

She feels her phone vibrate while the president addresses the cabinet regarding the sweeping powers he has assigned to the Department of Homeland Security. Clare basks in the envious glances of the other cabinet members. But her phone won't stop buzzing with an incoming call. Finally, she has to look.

Glancing at the phone's display, she sees the caller's identity is "Odious," her nickname for the NSA contractor, Rafi Zamani. Clare feels her stomach grip. Could that psychopath still be alive? She considers the more likely possibility that the hit man contracted by Williamson is using Zamani's phone to call her. Clare decides to ignore the call. Her momentary panic ebbs. She is okay. All unpleasant and morally questionable acts are behind her. Then a text comes through from the same number.

I'm not dead. Enjoy the consequences, bitch.

The twist in her gut tightens. The room spins. Clare Ryan cannot hear the words being spoken by the new president, only a few hours into his administration. The mantra inside her head changes, the voice in monotone and ominous. No one is safe. No one can ever be safe.

SATURDAY, 6:21 P.M. Hayley sits with James Odom at a picnic table in the prison's recreational yard. The former CIA deputy director stares at the photo on her phone of an absolutely dead Alberto Barrios. He seems satisfied.

"Great."

Hayley says nothing. Waiting.

"Did he suffer? I would like to think so."

"I stabbed him in the heart, sir."

He sits back and takes a deep breath, the fresh air filling his lungs. Cumberland's rec yard may not be scenic, but the sunset sky is magnificent.

"You must have friends in high places," he says to her, regarding their environs. "Regulations, you know."

"I have friends."

Odom nods. He returns the phone to Hayley.

"The score is evened. One of theirs for one of ours."

"The score is never even. They will calculate it differently than you." Hayley pauses, and says, "Someone will answer for the Cuban's death. Maybe you."

Odom shrugs. "You're correct, of course. The game goes on."

Hayley is finished talking about Barrios. She has done as he asked and must be repaid in kind. "The man responsible for the cyberattacks is Rafi Zamani, a contractor at the NSA, sir. General Hernandez's animosity to Russia is well-known."

His grin is sly and unnerving. "There you have it then. Case solved."

"You know I need more than that. I need evidence of Hernandez's complicity." Her impatience grows incrementally by the second. "That's why I left a man lying on a bathroom floor. In a pool of his own blood. You know these people. You've operated in this world for decades. Tie it together for me, sir. Give me a document. A dossier. An eyewitness to the conspiracy. I need a smoking gun that will absolutely compel the FBI to arrest the NSA director and stop these attacks."

The demoralizing smile has not left Odom's face for the entirety of her speech. It stays there even after she has finished. Suffering its insolence and lacerating judgment, Hayley can feel the surge of emotional upheaval that has undone her throughout her life. The weasel is toying with her, and she can do nothing about it.

He says, "You scarcely believe your own words. How do you expect to convince someone else? I can smell your uncertainty and self-doubt from here."

She is helpless before him, a sensation foreign to her. "Mr. Odom, sir . . ."

Something approximating sympathy fills his heart. Barrios's death represents finality. It signals the true end of his long career as spymaster. "I want to help you, dear girl, *despite* our history."

"Then help me, sir. Please."

"Forget about Hernandez. I've known the NSA director for more than three decades. He'd no sooner attack his own country than stroll down Pennsylvania Avenue stark naked with a parasol over his shoulder."

"Who, then? Is it the Russians after all? Is Zamani another Edward Snowden?"

"Is he?" Odom smiles again. He *is* toying with her.

"I don't know! Sir, there's no time for games, either!"

Odom is unperturbed by her rising temper. "Your instincts have failed you, Hayley Chill. Just because you haven't a hunch, it doesn't mean nothing is there." The prisoner pauses, leaning imperceptibly closer to her. "Even superheroes stumble from time to time, yes?"

Hayley's anxious expression betrays recognition that Odom speaks some version of the truth. Precious minutes are ticking past. When, where, and how will Rafi Zamani strike next?

"Sir, I need your help. The next cyberattack will take more American lives, perhaps many more." She pauses, her voice low and emphatic. "I truly believe you love your country. Redemption is possible."

For several seconds, Odom says nothing. His gaze settles on the concrete-and-steel building that will be his home for the remainder of his life. Oddly, he has finally found peace in this place. Incarceration has been good for him, revealing his more contemplative side.

"Money isn't so much. We print it on paper. It's made by selling soap. In Washington, at least, power is the real currency. If you want to find Cyber Jihad, dear girl, ask yourself who has gotten richest off his clandestine labors."

That is enough for now. Done. Their transaction completed.

James Odom sniffs the air like a hunting dog and grins. "Salisbury steak. You won't have me missing my dinner now, will you?"

SATURDAY, 9:22 P.M. Hayley sits at the back table in Clyde's, too distracted to properly appreciate the classic saloon decor. There have been other secretive meetings in this Georgetown bar, from what seems like a lifetime ago. That history, like the venue's upscale design scheme, fails to register. Hayley can only focus on her confrontation to come with Clare Ryan.

She heard the news of Landers's executive order on the radio, driving back to DC from Cumberland. With her new responsibilities, the secretary for Homeland Security has become one of the most powerful people in the entire government, second only to the president himself. The DHS budget, currently at $52 billion, is expected to rise to levels north of four hundred billion, more than the Chinese, Russian, and British militaries *combined*. It is a historic moment in national defense. The United States of America is determined to be the first country on the planet to harden civilian network infrastructures. And Clare Ryan, as cabinet secretary in charge of the Department of Homeland Security, will be at the helm of that massive effort.

Having delivered the murderous Cuban's head, Hayley's reward from James Odom was a thinly veiled insinuation. Whether or not the crafty former CIA director knew the truth all along or deduced it with her mention of Rafi Zamani makes no difference. The implication is clear. Only the all-important proof is lacking. If Hayley's suspicions are correct, then revealing them to Clare Ryan will, at bare minimum, serve the purpose of scaring the DHS secretary straight. Or she may have Hayley quietly killed. Without any other cards to play—or the time for her deeper state superiors to formulate a plan—she is willing to take the risk.

Convincing the cabinet secretary to meet wasn't an easy task. Clare has a late dinner planned with her fixer, Jeffrey Williamson. With everything that's already on her plate, only a few minutes allocated to a lowly White House staffer seems excessive. The alliance with Hayley Chill served its purpose; Clare doesn't need her anymore. But the younger woman was persistent, reaching Clare with her second call and important news regarding Rafi Zamani's probable client. The cabinet secretary agreed to meet for a quick drink.

Hayley watches the older woman approach from her booth at the rear of the bar. The smile on her face seems brittle and false.

"Do they make days any crazier than this? Thank God, we somehow survived!" Clare says, sitting.

"Ma'am, did you hire Rafi Zamani to attack the US, taking advantage of his expertise and access to NSA cyber weapons?" Hayley decided that hitting hard and fast was the best strategy, hoping to catch the cabinet secretary off guard.

For a few seconds, Clare Ryan remains motionless. Only her eyelids move, lowering and rising in a painfully labored blinking action that suggests the short-circuiting of an android's programming. Then, in a hostile monotone, she says, "I have no idea what you're talking about."

"Rafi Zamani, ma'am. The cyber hack of the national

newspapers. The Metro Blue Line. Stafford compres-
sor station. The DoD servers and electrical grid. Rafi
Zamani is Cyber Jihad. You hired him to attack the
US to expand your mandate at the Department of
Homeland Security."

"How dare you . . . ?" Clare draws herself upright,
at peak indignation, guffawing at the sheer absurdity of
Hayley's accusation. "You can kiss your job in the West
Wing goodbye."

Clare starts to stand up out of her seat.

"You won't get away with it, ma'am. Zamani won't
escape. And when he's caught, who do you think he's
going to throw to the wolves to save his skin?"

These words land with Clare, giving her pause. Everything hinged on erasing the NSA contractor from the
face of the Earth. What if the FBI manages to catch
Zamani before she can have him eliminated? She was
hoping Jeffrey would have some ideas at their dinner.
A contingency plan is needed. Now Clare has to worry
about the Chill girl and how much she knows? The cabinet secretary begins to get an inkling of what it feels like
for those clichéd "walls" to be closing in. The phrase is an
apt one. Clare Ryan finds it difficult to breathe.

Hayley says, "Help us catch him, ma'am. Your cooperation now will only benefit your cause after this is
over."

The cabinet secretary doesn't speak in response for
several seconds. Hayley's plan of attack was sound. Her
accusations have temporarily floored Clare. Caught her
off guard. How or why the White House staffer dis-

covered the truth could be determined in the future. Hayley Chill's fate is also in question. If the younger woman cannot be manipulated, then she will need to be silenced, too.

"I wonder how Richard Monroe got his hands on that gun? Who supplied him with the blanks? Who's been unusually close to a man now revealed as a Russian intelligence agent?" Clare asks, with a flair for the rhetorical. She leans closer to Hayley, eyes narrowed and mouth drawn tightly across her face. "I'm going to flatten you, Ms. Chill. You're roadkill."

Hayley watches the Homeland Security secretary stand and stride out of the bar at a measured pace, seemingly confident she has her young adversary's number.

SATURDAY, 10:13 P.M. The mostly bare studio apartment in Columbia Heights smells of dog piss and mildew. He didn't dare take Yazat out for a walk, not in broad daylight. With nightfall, Rafi Zamani figures it'll be safe to venture outside. The dog badly wants release, bored out of his little dog mind. Too bad. Yazat will just have to wait. With the help of the single, greatest technical achievement of mankind—the Internet—Rafi has been following the progress of the FBI's pursuit of the notorious Cyber Jihad. Laying the groundwork for his revenge against Clare Ryan is of equal importance.

The FBI is no longer a credible threat. According to the emails and text messages he intercepted in real time, the nation's best investigative agents believe Rafi has fled the region. Besides prepping a safe house, he took the precaution of leaving a paper trail for a faked exit strategy. At this minute, the FBI believes their suspect is driving north to Canada. The NSA contractor purchased an airline ticket from Montreal to Ecuador to throw off investigators. Hell, judging by the latest communications he's intercepted, the bureau isn't even entirely certain Rafi Zamani *is* Cyber Jihad. Some authorities credit his disappearance to illicit activity unrelated to the cyberattacks. Without additional evidence that Rafi was involved, federal agents currently explore a theory that the cyberattacks were a Russian diversion to aid Monroe's exfiltration.

Clare Ryan, of course, is a soft target. Rafi took the trouble to initiate full-spectrum cyber surveillance of the DHS head at the outset of their contact. Naturally, he wanted to vet the cabinet secretary's precise intentions thoroughly. Once he had determined she was not part of an NSA-sponsored sting operation, Rafi continued surveillance of her emails and cellular SMS. To be on the safe side. And who should reappear in those phone texts but Hayley Chill? He believed the threat posed by the White House aide was sufficiently inoculated by his information dump a few days ago. Hayley's messages two hours earlier, essentially demanding a meeting with Clare Ryan, signals that she has resumed her vigorous pursuit of him. Rafi needs a deterrent that will buy him a few more precious hours. Fortunately, he kept ammunition in reserve exactly for this purpose.

Without a doubt, he has to do something about the West Wing staffer. But Clare Ryan is Rafi's reason for remaining in town just a few hours longer. He is hell-bent and determined to do a number on that two-faced, duplicitous bitch. Leaking incriminating evidence of her involvement with his illegal activities—documents that would undoubtedly lead to her arrest and imprisonment—would be too pedestrian for a computer jockey of his skills and proclivities. No, Clare Ryan deserves a more fitting send-off. Her scheduled departure on a United Airlines flight to Mexico City later that night was the perfect opportunity to give her one.

———————————

SATURDAY, 10:16 P.M. April is awake. Encouraged by the reduction of swelling in her brain, doctors brought her out of a coma two hours earlier. Having been moved out of the ICU and into a regular hospital room, the patient is even allowed visitors.

Hayley stands next to the bed, relieved by her friend's partial recovery. "Pays to have a hard head I guess." Obscuring her true feelings with mild mockery is less than courageous, but these two have insurmountable walls between them.

"You're going to look a lot worse after I get out of here." April is tired and half-blitzed with medication. Nevertheless, riposte was mandatory.

Hayley nods. Her friend is going to be okay after all.

"I'm still getting after him. Only a matter of time," says Hayley.

"Did I miss anything?"

Hayley's smile could go for miles. "Not much."

"Fine. Don't tell me. Finding out on my own gives me a reason to live."

"You're going to live either way."

With half-open eyes, April says with a grin, "God, I hate you."

Hayley squeezes the patient's hand. "Gotta go."

"About time."

"One more thing." Hayley never really stops. The mission is never far from her mind, not even while seeing her grievously injured friend in the hospital. "Did you ever get the chance to ask the manager at the Iron Pony if he knew anything about Zamani?"

"You didn't give two shits about how I was doing. Just wanted the goods."

"Is it that obvious?"

"I never got there. That Honda kinda landed on me first, remember?"

Hayley turns to go.

"Hey . . ."

She stops and turns to face April again.

"Don't forget to duck."

This second time Hayley can only smile with her eyes.

———————————

As SHE EXITS the hospital, Hayley checks her phone for messages. Three more irate messages from Andrew Wilde will have to wait. Glancing at her work phone, she comes to a dead stop on seeing a new email from Rafi Zamani. Her heart begins pounding. Hayley feels the rush of blood in her head as she opens the email. The message is brief: *The Truth Will Set You Free*. A single-page PDF is attached to the email. It's a report from an unidentified investigating officer with the Marine Corps Criminal Investigation Division, drafted in a nearly indecipherable blend of legal jargon and military acronyms. But Hayley can glean from it a single, shattering allegation: Corporal Charles Hicks is suspected of having fed coordinates "with malicious intent" to coalition officers in an operations center far from the front lines, leading to a Marine jet fighter executing a bombing run that killed Lance Corporal Thomas Chill.

Hayley remains rooted in place, where she stopped on the sidewalk outside of the hospital's entrance. Devouring the contents of the classified document again and again, she feels light-headed. The world seems to spin at her feet. Fury rises, threatening gale force. She craves destruction. Nothing else matters anymore. The mission be damned. The pain will subside only when everything around her is in shambles.

10

★ ★ ★ ★

ZERO DAY

*C*harles Hicks murdered my father.

Standing on the sidewalk outside of George Washington University Hospital, Hayley finishes reading the CID document for a fifth and final time. The reality of the shocking truth is just sinking in. A best friend and brother-in-arms—a fellow Marine!—intentionally killed Tommy Chill. That fact goes a long way toward explaining Hicks's reluctance to meet with her face-to-face. The most obvious questions demand answers. Why did Hicks do it? And how can he be sitting behind a desk at the Pentagon if the allegations remain unresolved? What malevolent forces must be at work behind the scenes to have the ability to bury the investigative report? Hayley shudders at the thought of a rogue element within the US military, of the danger such a group might pose to the nation's democratic spirit.

But what will be her more immediate reaction to this shocking revelation regarding her father's death? When eight-year-old Hayley pried open Tommy Chill's military casket and bore witness to his obliterated body, destruction ensued. She had utterly lost her shit, the first of many rage-fueled episodes that have occurred throughout her life. Indeed, Rafi Zamani's first data dump had the intended effect. Hayley's loss of control effectively shut down her pursuit of the rogue NSA contractor. The pattern is usually the same. After the fury burns off, she regroups and gets back on track.

Today must be different.

Pausing outside the GWU Hospital, the memory of her father and words he once had said to her clear the angry fog clouding Hayley's thoughts. *Smart beats angry any day of the week.*

She will respond to Charlie Hicks's hateful act, but not today.

Hayley returns the phone to her pocket. Can she spook Clare Ryan into forcing Rafi Zamani to stand down? Assuming as much might be overly optimistic. Something about Zamani's Joker smile convinces her he will never stop.

The Iron Pony Tap Room is a twelve-minute Lyft ride away. Hayley walks through the doors a few minutes after eleven. In the blackout's aftermath, Washington nightlife hasn't yet fully regained its footing. She finds less than thirty patrons inside the bar, despite it being a Saturday night. The mood is subdued. The same skinny, tattooed bartender pours drinks.

"I'm looking for the manager," says Hayley, wishing she'd lucked into someone more cooperative.

The bartender regards her with suspicion. Reluctantly, she points out a man sitting at a table in the back.

Aaron Beckett, in his early thirties and dressed with hipster flair, is categorizing receipts when Hayley approaches. There's a cup of black coffee in front of him. A longtime veteran of restaurant and bar work in the city, he had stopped drinking alcohol years ago. The alternative is death before the age of forty.

"Excuse me?" Hayley asks, interrupting his work.

The bar manager looks up. He regards her with the expression of someone who expects a problem and is confident he can solve it. "What can I do for you?"

"I'm looking for Rafi Zamani. He's a regular, I think."

Beckett's chin dips. His shoulders curve in like he's preparing for a fight. "Okay."

"I need to pay him some money back. Do you know where I can find him?"

The bar manager grins, skeptical. "Need to pay him back, huh?" He gestures toward the chair opposite him. "Have a seat."

She sits. Her gut instinct regarding Beckett is positive. Without a radar for bullshit and bad actors, life can be a misery of serial failure. Hayley Chill, up to this point, has been a fairly decent judge of character. With a couple of significant exceptions.

Aaron Beckett doesn't have such a lousy instinct for people, either, and intuits all of that. "You don't have to lie to me. I told you, I know Rafi."

"Great. Talk to me."

"Look, I don't think the guy's been laid once in his life. That does weird things to a dude in his late twenties." He gestures toward the bar. "Stephanie, my bartender, absolutely detests him."

Hayley nods, musing on the bartender's inexplicable hostility. *She thinks I'm a friend of Zamani!*

"He's stalking you or something?" Beckett asks.

"Not exactly," she says. "I just need to find him."

"You check his apartment?"

"On F Street?"

"Yeah."

Hayley shakes her head. "No good."

"What about the other one?"

"What . . . other one?"

"I think he has another place. In Columbia Heights."

Hayley tempers her growing excitement. She recalls something else her father once said to her. *A little luck doesn't hurt.* A little luck, indeed!

"Another apartment? What are you talking about?"

"I was out riding with him two weeks ago. After midnight. We were going to a street race, out in Forestville. Quarter-mile straightaway sprints. On a good night, you can pick up a grand or two in those races. Rafi got a flat heading out. There was no place or time to get it fixed at that hour. He jumped on the back of my bike and we rode over to some dump on Fourteenth Street, where he grabbed a backup bike from the garage there."

Her excitement becomes a storm. Zamani has a safe house!

"Can I have the address?"

Beckett is dubious. "Sure you wanna do this?"

"Don't worry. I can handle him."

"Yeah. I bet you can." The bar manager racks his brain. "Euclid at Fourteenth Street. Building just west of the BP gas station on the corner. Justice Park Apartments, I think."

Hayley stands.

"Let it go, huh? He's not worth the hassle."

She appreciates the bar manager's concern. It would be easy for him not to give a shit. Over her shoulder, Hayley says, "You can tell your bartender Rafi Zamani won't be coming around here anymore."

2310 TRACY PLACE, in Washington's exclusive Kalorama neighborhood, was the consulate of Portugal in its former life. The seven-thousand-square-foot four-bedroom Georgian Revival home comes with high-profile neighbors, a well-tended, postage-stamp-size front lawn, and a property tax bill of just slightly under $55,000 a year. Clare Ryan and her husband had purchased the place when their son, Otto Jr., was one year old. Currently, however, a whole week can go by without the three of them being under its roof at the same time. More often than not, Clare's handsome surgeon husband is "in hospital." Or "at a conference." Otto's philandering doesn't bother the Homeland Security secretary all that much. It feels like another lifetime ago she could say the two of them enjoyed each other's company. The daughter of divorced parents, Clare isn't concerned about what effect the marriage's inevitable dissolution will have on her son. He'll thrive, just as she has thrived. No point in equivocating. Time to leave.

After receiving Rafi Zamani's threatening texts, Clare's initial reaction was to continue fighting. Persistence is her default mode. She could dispatch another assassin to eliminate Zamani before he did more damage. But Clare realizes now this was only so much magical thinking. The gnawing despair that began with Zamani's texts became a raging terror when the White House aide made her allegations. How Hayley Chill arrived at her suspicions makes no difference. The accusations were an unmistakable jolt of truth that Clare cannot afford to ignore. Her dream of protecting the country is hopelessly and irrevocably at an end.

Heading to the magazine-perfect house on Tracy Place, Clare intends to pack bags for her and Otto Jr. and go straight to the airport. Her flight bound for Mexico City departs from National at 11:55 p.m. As she hurries home in her chauffeured car, Clare reflects on the series of events of the last two weeks and feels a profound, nearly debilitating sadness. She never meant for things to get so out of hand.

The chauffeured SUV glides to a stop on Tracy Place. Clare can't precisely remember her husband's schedule—it changes with the day—but doesn't expect to find Otto Sr. home. His absence would be preferable, because she has no intention of including him in her getaway plans. Climbing the front steps and unlocking the door, Clare enters the house. She locates her eight-year-old son in the kitchen with the nanny, Sophia. The man of the house is indeed out. Clare can safely presume her husband is holed up somewhere with his young girlfriend. Will he miss his son? Perhaps. Once the dust has settled, Otto Sr. can always come to visit them in Mexico or wherever she finds extradition-free refuge.

With only a few words to her son and nanny, Clare heads upstairs and retrieves three suitcases from a hallway closet. Otto Jr.'s things barely fill a single bag halfway. Packing it takes only a few minutes. Selecting her personal effects and clothing for a new life requires more time and attention. As Clare sets to work—laying out items and then carefully stowing them in Mark Cross leather trunks—the soon-to-be-former head of DHS feels her prior depression lifting, replaced by a whisper of exhilaration. Recent events prove the United States is finished, a faltering democracy on a downward spiral. How else to explain the election of a Russian mole to the nation's highest office? Lesson learned. Now is the time to focus her remarkable abilities on the safety and well-being of her son. Her detractors might argue that her flight from justice is self-serving, but Clare doesn't see it that way. An eight-year-old boy needs his mother more than anything else in the world. With self-imposed exile, she is protecting Otto Jr., not herself.

Clare brings the bags down one at a time. Arriving

downstairs with the third bag, she finds Otto Jr. and his nanny waiting at the front door where she had left the first two suitcases.

"What's going on?" Sophia asks. The twenty-two-year-old daughter of French immigrants, the nanny is self-possessed and intelligent, and she has a natural affection for her eight-year-old charge. The young woman's opinion of Otto Jr.'s distracted parents is less favorable. Sophia has long worried about the emotional health of the boy.

"Unexpected trip!" Clare announces too brightly.

"What? Where?"

The Homeland Security secretary doesn't bother answering the nanny. She opens the front door and gestures to her driver waiting inside the vehicle parked at the curb. The portly middle-aged man in the dark suit exits the SUV and heads up the walkway to retrieve the luggage.

Sophia presses. "I'm confused. Are you going to be away for long? I was scheduled all this week."

Clare offers a bank check she'd already prepared. "Everything we owe and an additional three months' severance."

Stunned, Sophia accepts the check. She doesn't know what to say.

Clare takes Otto Jr. by the hand. "Come on, darling. Time to go!"

The boy resists his mother leading him out the front door. "I'm tired."

"You can sleep in the car, dear."

"I don't wanna," says Otto Jr.

His mother begins pulling him out the door. She says to Sophia, "Tell my husband I'll be in touch."

The nanny is still processing what's happening. "Your husband . . . ?"

"Does *not* need to know until I'm gone, Sophia." In Clare's tone, there is an implied threat.

Clare hustles her sleepy, mewling child down the porch steps and into the waiting SUV. The driver has just finished loading the suitcases. Within a few moments, all are safely stowed inside. The vehicle lunges from the curb and speeds off, heading east on Tracy Place.

Sophia stands in the open doorway of the handsome Georgian Revival brick house, backlit by the foyer's glowing lights. She considers calling the police. It's impossible to view what has just transpired as anything but unethical, if not illegal. The nanny disapproves of Clare Ryan only slightly less than she does Otto Sr. But does that make it okay for the man's son to be stolen from him? Despite these qualms, Sophia resists the temptation to call 911. Clare Ryan is a powerful woman. What form of retaliation against the young woman might she take? Sophia's mother isn't in the country 100 percent legally. Does the nanny want to get her and her family mixed up in the dispute?

With a long sigh, Sophia closes the door and turns to gather her belongings inside the home. God knows she doesn't want to be here when Otto Sr. finally shows up.

SATURDAY, *11:40 P.M.* Military snipers think they're such hot shit. Sure, nailing some rug-hugging Islamic fanatic from two miles out is pretty fucking rad. One shot. He gets it. But how about knocking two jetliners filled with passengers out of the sky with a few keystrokes on a laptop from twenty miles away? Or two thousand miles? Hell, he could be sitting on a beach in Cancun and put two 737s on a collision course. That's pretty sick, too, right? The CIA isn't a stranger to aviation-centric, cyber covert action. The death of Poland's president Lech Kaczyński in the "accidental" crash of a Polish Air Force jet during a landing attempt at Smolensk North Airport in Russia is only one example. The talented folks at Savage Road are thoroughly acquainted with the vulnerabilities of air traffic control systems. Hackers at the NSA—and presumably other cyber warriors around the world—had long ago stolen the unencrypted passwords needed to gain access to the FAA's networks. Blame it on that agency's continued use of hardware long beyond manufacturer "end-of-life" recommendations. Without upgrades, FAA networks are extremely susceptible to hacking. Which is how Rafi Zamani penetrated the air traffic control system at the Dulles International Airport's ATC tower. Knowing his way around the exceedingly complex interface happens to be one of Rafi's specialties. Without the full awareness of his supervisors at the National Security Agency, he had amassed a sizable library of exploits for airports around the world.

In the Columbia Heights safe house, Rafi sits on

a ladder back chair—the single piece of furniture in the entire apartment—with his laptop perched on his knees. He's hacked both the cabinet secretary's email account and the Dulles air control system. All is ready. Rafi checks the status of the DHS secretary's plane at its gate while simultaneously monitoring passenger jetliners as they approach the airport. Putting the cabinet secretary's plane into an unavoidable collision course with another jetliner will be the karmic culmination of his work for the past two weeks.

CLARE RYAN SIGHS with relief as the plane prepares to push back from the gate. Sitting in first class with Otto Jr. beside her, the head of DHS believes the worst might be over. She estimates it will be hours, if not days before Hayley Chill can sound an alarm loud enough for the FBI to launch an actionable investigation. Getting out while the getting was good, Clare has to admit, was a wise choice. Her phone has been exploding with messages. She has received frantic messages from her husband, of course. But Jeffrey Williamson, her security guru, has also been trying to reach her. The texts from Otto were easy to ignore. Screw him and his latest pretty thing. He'd better brush up on his Spanish if he wants to see his son anytime soon. But the terse messages from the former corporate security contractor command Clare's attention as the plane joins the lineup of aircraft taxiing past airport terminals.

Whoever Jeffrey sent to take out Zamani did not come back. Clare's suspicion the NSA contractor killed his assassin is all but confirmed. She imagines her security expert's consternation when she hadn't shown up for dinner. With her seemingly successful escape, Clare has decided to leave the whole mess for Jeffrey Williamson to handle. They had a brief romance years before when she was in Chicago. She never intended the affair to be anything more than a casual fling. But when Jeffrey dumped her for a young celebrity chef, Clare felt the sting of rejection. In such instances, it's imperative to mask hurt feelings. Their professional relationship survived the breakup intact. But leaving Jeffrey Williamson in the lurch tonight is just a teeny, tiny bit easier because of that ancient rebuff. With a shrug, Clare Ryan powers off her phone and helps Otto Jr. shut down his Amazon Fire HD 10. They will be taking off soon, winging their way into a new life. It will be good, Clare decides. She will *make* it good.

————————————————

As HAYLEY EMERGES from the Iron Pony, she is already on the phone with the FBI. The agent who eventually takes her call seems disinclined to take the White House aide's tip seriously. Infuriated, Hayley leaves both her phone number and the location of Zamani's safe house. A call to DC Police draws similar skepticism. Hayley slips the phone back into a pocket. So be it. This will be on her. At her feet, she catches sight of a small fragment of jagged concrete on the sidewalk. Hayley bends down and palms the serrated shard. And starts running.

She jogs at a hard, steady pace up Seventh Street. The cool, night air feels good on her face and arms. Thoughts drift to Rafi Zamani and his possible plans. Undoubtedly, dumping the CID report on her was a diversionary tactic. Was it a bid to buy time to make his escape? Hayley doesn't think so. Now that Zamani has developed a taste for destruction, she doubts he will stop. Killing people is a logical progression of his mania. That realization quickens Hayley's pace. On Georgia Avenue, she veers slightly west, straight into Columbia Heights. Feet seem to fly across the pavement, the dark city unfolding before her. Cyber Jihad's burlesque grin has been haunting her for days. She is determined to punch it off his face.

Hayley covers the two miles between the Iron Pony and Columbia Heights neighborhood in less than fourteen minutes. Turning left off Georgia Avenue, she runs west on Euclid Street. When she crosses Fourteenth Street, Zamani's building comes into view. As the Iron Pony manager had vividly described, the Justice Park apartment building adjoins a brightly lit BP gas station. A check of the intercom directory reveals one missing entry: unit eleven. With luck, she will find Rafi Zamani in his apartment and detain him until the authorities finally arrive. She's counting on the rogue NSA contractor having the incriminating laptop computer in his possession.

Pausing on the sidewalk outside Zamani's building, Hayley glances down at her clenched right fist. Opening it reveals the jagged concrete she picked up outside the Iron Pony. She drops the fragment and briefly studies the small, bloody cuts in her skin. These self-inflicted, ritualistic wounds are a process that has been a feature of her life since early childhood.

There is nothing to fear. Blood has been drawn. Now she can fight.

"Hayley Chill?" asks a male voice.

She looks to her left and sees a man and a woman, blatantly FBI, exiting their parked car.

The male agent produces credentials for Hayley to review. "Steve Woodward, FBI."

Hayley's relief is visible. "Great. Zamani's upstairs . . ."

The female FBI agent places her grip lightly around Hayley's forearm. "Mind coming with us, Ms. Chill?"

Hayley's face reflects her disbelief. "Go with you? Where?" More emphatically, she says, "Rafi Zamani is Cyber Jihad! He's upstairs, in this building!"

"We need to talk to you about your work at the White House, Ms. Chill. Why you exited the complex without authorization," the male agent says. He seizes her by her other arm.

————————————————

SUNDAY, *12:04 A.M.* As the Airbus A320 jetliner begins to accelerate from a dead stop at the eastern terminus of Runway 19C, Clare Ryan experiences the satisfying effects of g-force thrusting her back into her leather-

cushioned, first-class seat. Otto Jr. has fallen asleep
beside her, looking small and sweetly vulnerable. With
158 passengers and nine crew members on board,
the narrow-body, twin-engine jet airliner—designated
UA1826—is scheduled to arrive in Mexico City at nine
a.m., after a short layover in Houston. The plane's liftoff
is the start of welcome deliverance from the mess of her
life and ruined aspirations.

In hindsight, Clare can now identify several errors
of judgment on her part. With the investigatory powers
available to her at DHS, she should have better vetted the psychological makeup of Rafi Zamani. More
second-guessing nags at her. Should she have laid off
attribution on the North Koreans rather than Russia? Doing so would have removed the rabid passions
of NSA director Hernandez from the equation. But
her gravest mistake was attempting to manipulate
Hayley Chill. Who could have imagined the White
House staffer would prove to be such a clever rival.
Clare can only shrug. There's no use in trying to figure out the identity of Hayley's *real* boss. Those days
are over. High time for the next generation to enter the
arena.

Clare decides to close her eyes and sleep. The last
seventy-two hours have been an absolute beast. With
luck, her slumber will be dream-free. To not think
or problem-solve or worry for a few hours would be
the ultimate luxury. With eyes shut, she reaches out
with her right hand and places it on Otto Jr.'s arm,
making that crucial physical connection. Admittedly,

she has been a somewhat distracted parent up until this point. Clare is determined to change. Her son is what's important now. Otto Jr. will learn to appreciate his mother's care and attention more than the country ever did.

While the cabinet secretary strives in vain for mindless sleep, eight miles away, American Airlines 5095 makes its approach to Dulles from a westerly direction. The Bombardier CRJ900's manifest shows seventy-four passengers and five crew members onboard. ATC instructs the pilot to land on Runway 12. United Airlines 1826, meanwhile, has just lifted off from Runway 19C. Air traffic control has ordered its pilot to climb to ten thousand feet and execute a big, arching turn for a southwest heading.

In the Dulles tower, windows on four sides of the control room offer an unobstructed view of all runways and air lane approaches. Highly trained personnel inside the room are responsible for aircraft approaching and taking off from the airport, as well as those taxiing on the ground. Their displays, computers, flight, and data plans are networked together. Every device is linked. All are vulnerable. Without the assistance and data provided by the ATC, every plane in the air would be flying blind. Timing is critical. Data integrity is most important of all. The assumption of aircraft crew and passengers alike is that the ATC network is secure. What's on the screen represents what's in reality. At least, that's always been the belief.

Steve Woodward lies across the sidewalk, gripping his right leg. Hayley had kicked the FBI agent's knee, violently compressing the shinbone inward and stretching the outer-side ligament. A total rupture of the exterior collateral ligament was the result. Woodward played college football. He knows exactly what sort of injury he has suffered. Players never walked off the field without assistance after a collateral ligament injury. Woodward considers giving chase after the White House aide—and he wonders how and where a White House staffer learned to fight so efficiently—but his partner, Linda Steele, needs his immediate attention. The female FBI agent is flat on her back. After the White House aide staved in Woodward's knee, she elbowed Steele in the left temple.

Give me a motherfuckin' break. Woodward watches their suspect gently ease his unconscious partner down to the ground lest she fracture her skull on the sidewalk. He reaches for his gun and fails to find it in his holster. Damn! Who the hell *is* Hayley Chill? After the White House aide flees—into the apartment building, he thinks—Woodward pulls himself across the sidewalk to Linda Steele's side. He checks her pulse. While no doctor, the injured FBI agent is fairly certain his partner has been merely knocked unconscious.

"Rafi Zamani," says Hayley, having kicked in the door.

She stands framed in the shattered entryway. The

NSA contractor is across the 480-square-foot room, sitting on the wooden ladder back chair next to one of two windows. His fingers hover over the keyboard. Yazat, naturally, is going thermonuclear.

"I'd advise you not to take another step," he says.

Hayley gestures at the yappy French bulldog. "Because of *that*?"

"Cunt."

Rafi says the word like a toxin spit from his mouth, vile and cringing and full of crippled self-esteem. His fingers begin dancing again across the laptop's keys. Hayley propels herself forward, having discarded the FBI agent's service weapon in the hallway. Properly launched, she impacts roughly shoulder-high with Zamani. The laptop skitters out of his grip and smashes into the wall as Rafi and Hayley collide. They fight. He scraps like a cornered animal, lacking economy of energy and focused strength. Taken by surprise and only studio-trained, the NSA contractor forgets the lessons he learned in his Krav Maga classes. In contrast to Rafi's frenzied resistance, Hayley's physical movements are measured. Having tuned up with the two FBI agents downstairs, she peppers her adversary with a series of concentrated jabs to the left eye socket. Without knowing it, she's fortunate Rafi was armed with a laptop and not his fighting knife. The dog is more of a nuisance. So Hayley kicks him, too, though reluctantly.

Knocked to the ground and thoroughly beaten, Rafi lies on his back, arms and legs extended like da Vinci's

Vitruvian Man. Blood flows copiously from a broken nose and cuts above his left eye. He offers no further resistance. Hayley sits back on her heels, barely winded. She gestures toward the busted laptop.

"What have you done?"

Rafi smiles his Joker's smile. "Well, let's put it this way . . . I wasn't on Facebook."

Hayley deflates just a little bit. She was too late. "Why?"

"The truth is an act of love." Failing to get a rise out of her, he asks, "Say hello to Charlie Hicks for me?"

Hayley's face is a mask behind a mask. She'll be damned if this emotional cripple will get her goat.

Footsteps thunder up the stairwell, an oncoming storm. The cavalry has arrived.

Hayley says to him, "It's over."

"I sincerely doubt that."

The FBI agents make a tactical entrance into the room, storming in with a bouquet of guns. Their target is a female who matches Hayley's physical description. As they swarm to subdue her, Rafi Zamani rises to his feet. Unmolested by the authorities, he pushes open the window to the fire escape outside.

"Stop him! That's Cyber Jihad!"

The FBI agents, having observed what Hayley had done to their injured colleagues downstairs on the sidewalk, ignore her strenuous protestations. Rafi escapes clean away.

———————————————

THE BLIP THAT flashes across the monitor lasts less than a few seconds. One of the controllers, responsible for ground traffic, gasps. His display for ASDE-3 Surface Movement Radar zeroes out.

"Hey! I'm down!"

The sallow and prematurely gray man begins flipping switches and slamming keys on his console, to no avail. A supervisor comes over to look over his shoulder. He sees the dark screen and whips around to check his controllers working air traffic.

Their screens appear to be unaffected.

"Everybody else okay?" he asks the room, nevertheless, with breath bated.

Thumbs-up and "A-OK"s are the response. Relieved, the ATC supervisor turns his attention back on the SMR display to start troubleshooting the problem there. The shift supervisor tries to coax the network controlling ground traffic on the airport's tarmacs back to life. Sweat begins to bead on his brow. He's never seen a complete system knockdown like this one in twenty-two years on the job.

In the dark skies fifteen thousand feet above them, United Airlines 1826 follows its flight pattern as designated by the Dulles tower. In doing so, the plane arcs a mile wide of American Airlines 5095 making its approach to the airport from the west.

In the weeks and months that follow, forensic computer engineers will determine that Rafi Zamani's efforts to penetrate the ATC network were only partially successful. By every analysis, investigators concluded the NSA contractor was interrupted at a critical juncture. Forced to detonate his logic bomb before he had a chance to place it where he intended, the hacker had paralyzed only *ground* control operations at Dulles. As a result, the worst damage suffered in the incident was a fender bender between an Alaska Airbus 319-100 and a Boeing 737 flying for Sun Country Airlines at the hold block east of Runway 1C.

Strapped in her seat on the United flight bound for Mexico, Clare Ryan has finally found sweet, delicious sleep. She dreams of the ocean. Sand and sun. She dreams of a man. He has no face. His arms are strong. On her face and arms, she feels a cool breeze. She hears the sounds of children playing. She is safe.

SUNDAY, 12:27 A.M. He wears no helmet or armored jacket. He abandoned all of his regular riding gear in his escape from the apartment building. On this ride, it's only him and his naked motorbike. Wind buffets his chest as Rafi maintains blistering speed through traffic and stoplights. Acceleration for acceleration's sake. The pure, kinetic power in his control is intoxicating. This. This is it!

That vicious, little bitch may have ruined the last brushstrokes of his masterpiece. No way to know for sure. Not until he can check the news on Twitter. But what difference does it make? Contrary to what that Title IX hillbilly said, it's not over. Not even close. Rafi is taking a short sabbatical, that's all. A change of venue

is necessary, of course. But he will rise again. To para-
phrase Archimedes, give me an exploit big enough and
network in which to place it, and I shall destroy the
world. Shut it down. Kill them all. His ultimate goal is
to stomp out mankind, if possible, and all of its spawn.
Every last, stinking one of them. So, it's goodbye for
now. Goodbye, corrupt Washington. Goodbye to Yazat,
too. Time to go.

He heads east on Michigan Avenue, to where he's
not entirely sure. Anywhere out of fucking Washington DC. Without his riding jacket, he feels the bracing
cold of a nighttime temperature dipping into the fifties. His right hand cramps around the throttle control, but fuck it feels good to be on the bike. He thrills
at the thrum of the Honda's engine, yowling between
his thighs. Lights and sights flash by in the blur of his
peripheral vision.

Rafi rolls on the throttle and goes faster still. Almost
250 million people over the age of eighteen reside in
the US, which translates into 122 million women who
refuse to sleep with him. So fuck all of those vile, con-
niving cunts who never give him any sex. And fuck all
the brainless nitwits who *do* get laid by the vicious cunts
who won't fuck him. Fuck 'em all. He's bet—

The cab that jumps out from the intersection at
Thirteenth Street clips the Honda motorbike with only
a glancing blow. Just enough to separate the rider from
his machine. The cab's driver had been looking down at
his phone, at a message from his seven-year-old daughter. He is thirty-seven and from South Korea. His name

is Min-jun, in the US for eight years. Colliding with the Honda ridden by the soon-to-be infamous domestic terrorist, Rafi Zamani, is the biggest thing that will ever happen in his entire life.

And Rafi? He is free. Truly free. Unconstrained by earth's ghastly chains, he is a human projectile, hurtling through the air headfirst. Zamani unbound. In these brief, airborne seconds—just before impact into a brick wall—he has attained the very best version of himself. And so, as his spine shatters into a thousand pieces, Rafi Zamani smiles.

———————

SHE SLEPT THE entire way to Houston, waking up only when the flight crew switched on the cabin lights for landing. Otto Jr. remains asleep beside her, even as the aircraft rolls toward its gate. It's after two in the morning. The airport runways are mostly quiet. Has Rafi Zamani been apprehended? Were there any further cyberattacks? Is the US at war with Russia after all? Anxious for news, Clare Ryan powers up her government-issued phone. Even though the plane has been on the ground for almost five minutes, she can't seem to get a signal. The other passengers in the first-class cabin are asleep. Their stop in Houston is scheduled for only forty minutes; passengers continuing to Mexico City need not deplane.

Otto Jr. rouses from his slumber as the plane jerks to a stop at the gate. Clare lays a comforting hand on the boy's back.

"Go back to sleep, darling. We're just stopping here for a few minutes."

She wishes they'd turn the lights off. Surely the passengers can leave the plane without veritable floodlights illuminating their way.

Otto Jr. stares dazedly out the window. "Where are we?" he asks.

"We're in Houston, baby. Just a short layover."

There seems to be some delay in getting the aircraft's door just forward of the first-class section open. The pilot's voice crackles over the aircraft's public address system. "Seat belt sign is still illuminated, folks. If you could remain seated for just a couple more minutes, thanks."

Finally, Clare can hear the plane's door pulled open and low voices from that direction. Next, she sees four federal marshals come aboard and look in her direction. They move in on her. She understands these are her last few moments of real freedom. That she is about to undergo the truly unique degradation of an extremely public arrest.

The federal marshals stop in the aisle beside her seat.

"Clare Ryan?"

"I'm Clare." What else is there for her to say?

"Ma'am, please stand up."

Otto Jr. is understandably confused and alarmed. "Mommy? What's happening?"

Clare looks past the federal marshals and sees a middle-aged woman, an agent with child welfare services. A kind face, the soon-to-be disgraced cabinet secretary decides.

"It's okay, Otto darling. Mommy is going with these nice people for a little chat."

Marshals hoist Clare up from her seat by her arms.

"Mommy!"

The child welfare agent moves forward, anxious to calm the boy.

"Hi, Otto," she says too brightly for Clare's taste. "My name is Susan. Are you hungry? Can I get you something to eat?"

The boy is now hysterical.

"Mommy!"

Clare Ryan is on her feet. The marshals deftly handcuff her, as if by magician's trickery. They hustle their prisoner up the aisle to the door not fifteen feet away.

Over her shoulder, Clare says, "Be a good boy, Otto. Be safe!"

Within a few seconds, the marshals have rushed the cabinet secretary off the aircraft. The only sounds on board are the wails of an eight-year-old child.

11

★ ★ ★ ★

THE KICKER

ONE WEEK LATER

These first few days back home have been disorienting. Having spent all but the first year of his life in the US, Monroe finds the country of his birth to be hopelessly outclassed in manners large and small by its superpower rival. Russia is the second world in every respect but its ability to wage war. The food his handlers put on his table is good enough. The private villa where he has been installed is undoubtedly luxurious. They have even offered him female company of the highest caliber, a ludicrous proposition that he had rejected out of hand. But Yuri Sergeev, aka Richard Monroe, can't shake the nagging feeling that he's playing for the losing team. Moscow seems so dreadfully provincial in comparison to any major metropolis in the West. The Russians aren't even playing a game of catch-up; there will *never* be true parity in standards of living and cultural leadership between the superpowers. Instead of equivalence, Moscow's strategy is one of disruption. Degrading America's ability to thrive is a much less expensive form of competition. His fellow Russians are killjoys, he muses. They are spoilsports. Losers.

Naturally, Yuri Sergeev keeps these thoughts to himself. His best leverage over the Kremlin is his value as an instrument of propaganda. How great can the United States be if it had managed to elect a Russian intelligence agent as its highest leader? Monroe's eventual deterioration while in the Oval Office notwithstanding, Operation Polkan had been a stupendous coup. From just about any perspective, the Russian mole is worth more alive than dead. That is, as long as the truth of the Americans compromising him remains a take-it-to-the-grave secret.

From the first conversation with his handlers at the GRU, and then in the earliest hours home with ministers in the Kremlin, Yuri Sergeev has resisted a plan to exile him to the hinterlands. He actively promoted the notion that he has much more to offer than propaganda value. Raised as an American boy by Russian parents, enjoying a long and lustrous career in the US military, and then elected to the highest office in the land, Yuri Sergeev has experienced the epitome of the American dream. He knows all of the important players. He understands the US political system at its highest levels, inside and out. In a future crisis or with long-term strategic planning, Yuri Sergeev's advice could prove to be a decisive boon to the decision makers in Moscow.

He knows allies in the Kremlin have taken his proposal for a more active role to the highest levels of the government. Waiting for further news has been agony, despite the luxuriousness of his temporary home off the Minsk highway, ten kilometers from Moscow. He couldn't care less for its home theater, indoor swimming pool, billiard room, and wine cellar. Yuri Sergeev is a prisoner in this twenty-room, €27 million monstrosity, built by some forgotten oligarch who got on the wrong side of the Russian president. Having been at the center of action—in one arena or another—all of his life, Richard Monroe/Yuri Sergeev is bored in this opulent, backwater villa.

At long last, on the morning of his seventh day back in Russia, he is told to be ready at noon for a car driving him to the Kremlin. Whether it will be a bullet in the back of his head or a battle plan, Yuri Sergeev, the most successful mole in the history of espionage, is prepared to learn his destiny.

———————————

SATURDAY, 6:57 A.M. He knocks on her apartment door ten minutes after Hayley has returned home from her morning run one week after the president's calamitous "suicide." Hayley can guess it's him. Who else would knock on her door at seven a.m.? No doubt, he had been waiting in his car and saw her return. Spooks can be so predictable. Confirming her hunch through the peephole, Hayley opens the door for Andrew Wilde. Her deeper state supervisor is tanned, as always, and wears his uniform of a blue suit, double monk leather shoes, and a blue oxford shirt.

"Lieutenant Wu is doing better," he announces without ceremony as he crosses the threshold, walks to the dinette set, and sits.

Hayley closes the door and stops halfway to the table. She is wary but customarily composed. "I've seen her every day since she entered the hospital, sir."

"I know," Wilde says, his tone desert dry. "I was only making conversation."

Hayley feels no need to defend her conduct. Her conscience is clear. Consequently, she says nothing.

Wilde stares at her with his best impression of sympathy, one that isn't very convincing. He has always been impressed with her. It would be impossible *not* to be impressed with Hayley Chill. She is a magnificent operative. But he is not in charge. He's not sure who is. His orders come to him from another man whose alias is Garcia. And Garcia's superior in Publius? What difference does it make? Wilde is committed to the organization's cause. The directive is clear. But where will they ever find another like her?

Wilde asks, "You know why I'm here, Ms. Chill?"

"Yes, sir. Of course."

"You were asked to assist Lieutenant Wu. That didn't

mean dereliction of your primary duty. Our enemy has injured us because of your mission failure."

"Mr. Wilde, sir . . . ?"

He won't be interrupted. "Of course, averting the collision of two jetliners and saving the lives of hundreds of people is the very best reason possible to take your eye off the ball. But Richard Monroe was *everything*. It wasn't your decision to prioritize one operation over another."

Hayley's face expresses only transitory impatience. Without saying another word, she retrieves her laptop from her desk and brings it to the dining table where Wilde sits. Taking the chair beside him, Hayley opens the computer and begins tapping keys.

"What?" he asks, gesturing mildly at her computer.

It dawns on Wilde that Hayley's holding all the cards even before she shows them. His familiarity with the young woman allows him to intuit that much. We all have our roles to play, he muses. In the second or two before Hayley responds, Andrew Wilde reflects without judgment on the undeniable fact that his role, in this situation, is to get properly ass-kicked by this twenty-seven-year-old woman from West Virginia.

She says, "I've done many things in my life, sir. Drugs. Sleeping with gorgeous deadbeats. I've stolen from convenience stores and driven fifty miles per hour in a twenty-five-mile-per-hour zone. I've lied to a priest and even ripped tags off a sleeping mattress. But, sir, not once have I been in dereliction of my duty."

Having pulled up the computer application she requires to prove her point, Hayley pauses her finger over the volume button on the keyboard.

"What time is it in Moscow, sir?"

Without checking his watch, he says, "Two o'clock."

"And what happens in Moscow at two p.m. on the first Saturday of every month?"

Wilde sighs. "You tell me."

"Members of the Security Council of the Russian Federation gather in a conference room of the Senate building at the Kremlin. The president. The chairman of the government. Ministers of all the important departments, including their foreign intelligence service and internal affairs. They're all there. At this very minute, sir. The first Saturday of every month at two p.m., local time, is when shit happens."

Here it comes, Wilde thinks. The kicker.

Hayley taps the volume up on the laptop. Over the computer's tiny speakers, the sound of men talking in Russian can be heard. The sound quality is poor, but it's clear enough for the two Russian-speaking agents of the deeper state to understand the conversation.

A baffled Andrew Wilde asks, "Malkin . . . ?" referring to the Russian president.

Hayley nods. "Yes, sir. "

They hear another voice now, speaking in response to whatever Fedor Malkin had said.

"Thank you, Mr. President. I thank the chairman and other ministers as well. Your trust in this humble son of Russia will not go unrewarded. With all my heart, for

love of country, I believe I can be of service! Thank you, gentlemen!"

Wilde looks to Hayley. He still can't quite believe what he's hearing. "That's our guy. That's Richard Monroe."

Hayley simply nods, without a trace of gloat.

Gesturing at the laptop, he asks, "This is in real time?"

"Yes, sir."

"How . . . ?" He simply cannot form the words.

Hayley is unnervingly matter-of-fact. "The president's cover had been blown, sir. The Russians were taking Monroe out, one way or another. Our operation, running him as a double agent in the Oval Office, was over."

"What convinced you Moscow was onto him?"

"Actionable intelligence, sir, with the highest level of confidence in its integrity."

He can see that she doesn't intend to elaborate further on the source of her information. Wilde can undoubtedly appreciate her reticence. A good operative in the field maintains his or her spy network, independent of his or her superiors. More often than not, those sources are religiously protected, lest third-party interventions spook an asset. Wilde imagines this isn't the last time he'll hear Hayley Chill utter these words.

She says, "I couldn't know for sure if they were going to terminate Sergeev or exfiltrate him, but I was prepared if the GRU returned him safely to Moscow. An intelligence asset in the Kremlin's inner sanctum could be useful, yes?"

"Yes. It would be useful in the extreme. His cooperation . . . ?"

"We have file cabinets filled with incriminating evidence that substantiates his betrayal of his Russian masters. If they were to find out that we had compromised Yuri Sergeev, then no more twenty-room villa off the Minsk highway."

"No more Yuri Sergeev."

"No, sir. No more Yuri Sergeev."

Wilde reaches to volume up the feed from the Kremlin Senate building conference room. A different gruff Russian voice crackles from the laptop speakers. He lowers the volume again to barely audible.

"Every fart, every belch," she says, quoting him. "Every meeting and every phone call, if he participates, we will hear it."

"The Fauchard bug?" Wilde asks, already knowing the answer.

IN HIS PRIVATE *sitting room, just off the bedroom, the president sits in an easy chair by the fireplace. A small fire crackles in the hearth, despite the warm spring weather outside. He seems mesmerized by the comforting flames. Pressed, a distracted Richard Monroe agrees to her demand to produce Alberto Barrios for her interrogation.*

"Yes. I understand." The president's voice sounds remote and robotic.

"There's one more thing." Hayley retrieves the jewel case containing the Fauchard bug.

"What is that?"

"Your new crown."

Monroe sits up from his slouch, alarmed. "Crown? I don't need a new crown. My teeth are fine!"

"Don't worry, sir. This one requires no drilling. And no one will ever know it's inside of your mouth." Hayley's expression is placid. "Where you're going, we need to know what's being said. Every word."

"Going? Where am I going?" he asks with commendable disingenuousness.

She stares at the president in a manner that utterly unnerves him, despite his impressive military résumé. He may have conquered dictators in the past, but Hayley Chill won't be bamboozled or bluffed.

"You signaled your GRU masters, sir. You've led them to believe your cover was under threat. You alerted them, sir, because you wanted out."

"That's all preposterous! What's your proof?"

"My proof?" She can't resist a small grin. "Spetssvyaz."

Monroe's head jerks backward, involuntarily. How . . . ? Who? Then it dawns on him. "Belyavskiy!"

Hayley nods, faintly, modest to a fault. "You told me who your handler was, sir. I made you tell me. He resisted recruitment by me for several months, but eventually, I turned him." She pauses, unsure whether or not to elaborate her methods further. "He's extremely fond of you, you know. Your grandparents showed kindness to his family back in Mirnyy. Aleksandr Belyavskiy has repaid that gen-

erosity by informing me of Moscow's intentions regarding your imminent exfiltration. We can still protect you, sir, but you must protect us."

Monroe once again must resign himself to his fate, one that is imposed upon him by this relentless girl and her deeper state superiors. He had attempted to orchestrate an escape from the soul-crushing pressures of his life as a double agent. He had imagined that he could outsmart Hayley Chill. The president realizes now that he was delusional thinking either goal was achievable.

Hayley says, "This listening device will allow us to continue our mutually beneficial collaboration, without risk." She displays the crown for Monroe to see. "Congratulations are in order, Mr. President. For your new life, and new responsibilities, in Russia."

IN HER APARTMENT, Hayley nods in answer to Wilde's question. "And if that one is ever lost or becomes inoperable, Sergeev knows our other assets in Moscow will be able to replace it immediately."

"Publius doesn't have any other assets in Moscow . . . or all of Russia for that matter."

Hayley grins ever so slightly. "Yuri Sergeev doesn't know that."

Andrew Wilde broods a moment. A troubling thought occurs to him.

"How do we know he isn't playing us?"

"How do we know he hasn't always been playing us,

sir?" Her light smile evaporates. "How do I know you won't have my place ransacked again?"

He had hoped she wouldn't bring that up. "We had to make sure. About you."

"And are you? Finally? Are you 'sure' about me?"

Wilde cowers just slightly against the onslaught of her intense gaze, hoping to avoid it. He stands. "As much as we hope we can be."

Hayley also gets to her feet. "When you came here, I was out."

"Yes."

"And now?"

Wilde pulls the door open and steps into the hallway. "We'll be in touch."

She watches him head down the stairs, his footsteps fading with every floor he descends. Until there is silence. She strains to hear the elevator descending to the ground floor. She listens for a faraway police or fire engine siren. But the sounds simply don't exist. Not even wind blows on this impossibly still morning. Silence reigns.

There it is, Hayley thinks. *This is peace.*

———————————

SAM PARKS THE car at the curb. It is Sunday morning, mercifully cool for a summer day in Northern Virginia. Yazat, the French bulldog, sits in the front seat between Sam and Hayley. After Rafi Zamani's escape and subsequent demise, his pet was destined for the city's animal care and control services. Hayley adopted the dog, reluctantly. The French bulldog is her first pet since childhood. She hopes, in a conscientious effort of self-improvement, Yazat will be a friendly antagonist. Something to help get her outside of herself. That's the theory, at least. But, so far, Rafi Zamani's dog has been mostly a pain in the ass.

It's been a little over twenty-four hours since Andrew Wilde came to her apartment to drum her out of Publius. She hasn't heard from him in that time, but she's confident of her status with the deeper state. Hayley Chill will be assigned a new mission. Much will be at stake. Perhaps the fate of nations will hang in the balance. Great leaders will fall, others will rise, and in her intrepid way, the deeper state operative from Green Shoals, West Virginia, will be a vital instrument of the Constitution's preservation.

Hayley's intention until her next operation is to slow down. To see if this "smell the roses" business is all that it's cracked up to be. The man who sits beside her—this kind and stalwart savior of lives—seems willing to start the long journey of becoming friends. The promise of intimate companionship exists. But friendship first, they have decided. Hayley has told Sam McGovern nothing of her work for Publius, of course. But he knows why she nearly lost her mind with rage that awful day a few weeks earlier. And he understands why they are now parked in front of this modest home on Fifth Street in Arlington, Virginia. The brick, two-bedroom bungalow belongs to Charlie Hicks. The man who killed Hayley's father lives in this house.

"You sure about this?" Sam asks her after he shuts off the car's engine.

"If I was going to kill him, do you think I'd let you drive me?"

He takes stock of her calm demeanor and decides the risk of violence is minimal. "I'll wait for you here."

Hayley smiles and leans over to give him a light kiss. She *seems* fine.

The twenty-foot walk to Hicks's front door is an Odyssean journey, populated with the recollected tragedies and struggles she endured just to get to here. She reflects on the small miracle of finding herself at this strange moment of her stubborn existence, in possession of facts no one wanted her to have. Does anyone but herself really care about the death of one Marine in a war most Americans would rather forget? As much as she hopes for some final resolution, Hayley also fears that inside the house is yet another vortex, an abyss she doesn't even know exists. She hasn't decided what she will say to her father's murderer. Or what she will do to him. At a bare minimum, she has decided, Charlie Hicks must live with the awareness that Tommy Chill's unaltered memory is alive within her. The truth resides within Hayley.

She knocks on the door and waits. There is no response. Hayley had chosen a Sunday morning to see Hicks. Better to confront the man here at his home than at work. This time she will not be turned away. She is grateful for Sam's presence out front, the guarantee of a sane process. Some independent, external control on her emotions. But everything depends on Charlie Hicks and his response. He will determine what happens next. Will he confess to his crime? Will he then offer to turn himself in to the authorities? And what about those hidden forces inside the Pentagon who have protected him all these years? Who will stand up against them?

Hayley tries the doorknob and is mildly surprised to find it unlocked. She pushes the door open and puts her head through into the house. "Hello? Mr. Hicks?"

There is still no answer. But the smell is unmistakable. Hayley recognizes the reality of what had happened here even before she called out his name.

But she must see him with her own eyes. It won't be over until she sees him.

Hayley steps inside the house. The small living room just beyond the door is haphazardly furnished, with castoffs from thrift stores and yard sales. A torn and yellowed window shade pulled down to the sill. Stained rug and faded paint on the walls. Houseflies circle the room with uncertain trajectories. So this is the home of Charlie Hicks. The ambiance couldn't be sadder. It suggests a man who has lived a life on the margins, one devoid of human connection.

She is a conflict of emotions. Fear battles pity, but neither trumps rage. Hayley can't imagine the hell the home's inhabitant has experienced inside his head to live in this manner. With this much grief. She can't possibly know what compelled Hicks to commit his despicable act. What can't be understood, therefore, must be discarded from her decision to act. Perhaps if he hadn't taken the cowardly way out, then he might have provided her with some explanation. In the seconds she stops there in the sad, cramped living room, Hayley decides the man's final act is indictment enough of his past motivations. Hicks chose that route because he could not face her. It was murder, plain and simple.

Hayley presses on. To finish it.

Entering the bedroom down the short hallway from the living room, Hayley stops, arrested by a sight she could not have expected. *Even superheroes stumble.*

The body hangs by the neck from the door. He is shirtless, shoeless, and entirely dead. He cannot be Charlie Hicks, however, because the body hanging by the neck from the bedroom door is her father. The dead man is Tommy Chill.

She recognizes his features, of course, as readily as recognizing her face in a mirror. Still, the reality is too outrageous to accept. Her obsessions must be toying with her powers of perceptions. It simply can't be! Drawing nearer to the body, Hayley forces herself to study the body more closely. Take a good, hard look. *It's him.* No avoiding the truth now. If she has any shred of remaining doubt or disbelief that the man hanging from the rope isn't her father, the crossed arrows tattoo on his right side is a thunderclap of absolute confirmation.

Her mind reels, struggling to process the reality before her. Her father didn't die in Iraq. He returned home from the war. But how? Under the assumed identity of another man? That can be the only answer, explaining why he avoided meeting her face-to-face at all costs. Whatever the desperate reason, her father chose to separate himself irrevocably from his old life— from his wife and children—to live *this* alternative life in Arlington. More questions loom. What of the real Charlie Hicks? Did the grieving family bury a stranger's body parts back home in West Virginia? That sort of deviousness would give the conspiracy a logical symmetry, of course. But there's something worse. One more twist of the screw. To her horror, Hayley makes the next leap of logic: her father killed Hicks to steal his identity. But what insane circumstances would drive him to do such a thing?

Knees giving out, she must prop herself up with a hand on the hallway wall. The shock of seeing her father is almost too much. Hayley wishes she could claw her eyes out, that they had never seen such a thing. The senselessness of her father's decision to abandon his family torments her. How can it ever possibly be explained? Who inside the military could have engineered the plot? What was his relationship to that cabal?

Staring at her father's corpse, Hayley feels the push, not the pull of these relentless questions. Steadying herself, she takes a step backward. And another. Hayley experiences an overwhelming desire to be outside again. Away from *this*. She craves to be next to Sam, with the bulldog in the front seat between them. Driving to the

park. To a Nationals game. The beach. For the man
she remembers from her youth—a good father, always
wise, loyal, and true—Hayley will leave the scene here
untouched. With the others in her family, she needs
that memory of him to remain intact. No one else must
know the truth she has learned today. More than anything, however, she wants to be out of this house.

———————————

HAYLEY HASN'T SPOKEN a word about what she had
found in the brick home on Fifth Street. The sun
feels so good on her face, the hot air blowing across
her elbow as Sam's car speeds down the parkway. The
Eastern Shore they had decided. Maybe a little fishing.
There will be a time when she will need more answers,
but it is not today.

　　Dog to her left, she exhales a long breath. Not a sigh,
but release.

　　"You okay?" Sam asks.

　　She's tough. Sucks it up. "I'm fine."

　　"Tough week?"

　　"You don't know the half of it, believe me."

　　He takes her hand in his. "Let's keep it that way."

12

★ ★ ★ ★

TOMMY

NINETEEN YEARS EARLIER

amily organized the get-together on account of her father being home briefly from the war in Iraq. What he was doing over in that cartoon-ish, exotic land, and why he has to go is a mystery to his eldest child. Her dad was forever gone, absences more real than his all-too-rare presence. Tommy Chill's military deployment isn't so different from his previous job as a long-haul trucker. Both pursuits are the natural inclinations of a man who can't sit still for anything lon-ger than a haircut. No one in town is surprised Tommy volunteered for another go at the jihadists. His war bud-dies are the best friends he's ever had. By extension, the Marine Corps is a second and more enticing family than the one he leaves behind. With a stoic grin and the rangy looks of a movie cowboy, Tommy is a snapshot taped to the refrigerator that occasionally comes to life. Eight-year-old Hayley didn't sleep a minute the night before her dad's homecoming.

Her grandmother has come down from Charleston, provisioned with four grocery bags of her famous fried chicken, vegetable oil soaking through the brown paper. Tommy's two brothers journeyed from out of state with their families for the gathering. A few of Tommy's high school buddies stop by, too. Linda Chill, riding her youngest on her hip, is recovering from a mysterious illness that envelops her in impenetrable fatigue. Having rallied somewhat that morning, she generally helps more than she imperils preparations. The picnic site is a clearing next to the Big Ugly Community Center, within earshot of the unlikely rapids in the creek. Torrential downpours in the preceding five days threatened plans to hold the gathering outdoors. But on the morning of the big day, the sun peered through scattered clouds. The organizers decided to go ahead and set up at the center's ancient picnic tables. With the addition of a few folks from church, Hayley's four younger siblings, and her best friend, Jessica Cole, just over twenty people come together to welcome Tommy Chill home. Simultaneously, they gather there to see him off again.

Hayley can barely tear herself away from her father's side for the first two hours of the party. She soaks up his every look and word, storing them away with her prodigious memory. Wearing denim cutoffs, a Shrek T-shirt, and cheap, no-brand sneakers from Walmart, Hayley dresses the part of an unapologetic tomboy. If Tommy needs another beer, Hayley will be at his elbow, offering a cold one with the top already popped. If his jokes seek appreciative laughter, her guffaws will be louder than any other. Wherever the war hero mingled with guests, his adoring daughter is certain to follow. With a lean reserve and quiet competence, Tommy Chill mostly earns this dogged worship. For what he lacks in quantity of time allocated to his young family, he compensates for that deficiency with the mesmerizing quality of his sterling presence.

"Go play with the other kids, girl," her mother scolds, shooing Hayley away from Tommy like a sovereign's loyal courtier. "Your friend looks half-sick with boredom."

Hayley doesn't glance in Jessica's direction. "She just wants to smoke cigarettes down by the creek."

"Don't make jokes," Linda Chill says.

With a clear favorite in this unfolding drama, Tommy puts a hand on Hayley's shoulder. "She isn't bothering anybody," he says to his frustrated wife.

Linda takes a rebuking pull off her beer. "She's bothering me."

The look Tommy exchanges with his wife carries the weight of countless nights apart, of a marriage joined at too early an age. Travels away from home have given twenty-nine-year-old Tommy Chill a perspective on broader possibilities, one that finds his wife lacking in just about every respect. The feeling is mutual. Linda wants something more—she isn't quite sure what—from Tommy. Sincere physical affection? Respect? A bigger, newer house? Whichever it might be, the marriage seems destined to crash. Lacking the sophistication and money necessary to redress the grinding failure of their union, the Chills soldier on with the unspoken agreement to let fate intervene. Hayley, of course, has no awareness of her parents' dysfunction. Their behavior toward one another is no different than most other couples in Lincoln County, West Virginia. Like two wary prizefighters, the Chills mostly dance through these long, middle rounds of the bout. Taking measures of each other. Rarely drawing blood.

"Go on. Git!" Linda says sharply to Hayley. "Go *play*!"

———————————

HAYLEY AND JESSICA have been walking along the creek's steep bank for more than twenty minutes when the older girl draws a flattened Marlboro pack from a pocket. A single cigarette is retrieved and lit up. Jessica, ten years old, inhales a modest amount of smoke and immediately exhales it, all without so much as a whisper of a cough.

She smiles, triumphant. "I love smoking."

"You look dumb."

They resume their exploration of the swollen and churning waterway. For Hayley, the metamorphosis from a benign creek to raging river is a wonder. Captivated by the apparent power of the bucking waves, she momentarily forgets all about the startling novelty of her father's return. But Jessica is unimpressed with the creek's wild abandon. Away from the thrill of social interaction, she feels bored and useless.

"My mom thinks your dad is hot."

Hayley makes a face in response. "Shuddup, freak!"

Standing on the edge of the creek bank, Jessica shrugs and takes another drag on the cigarette. "My mom would screw the mailman if he stopped walking long enough."

The older girl is so pleased with her outrageousness that she fails to notice the clay riverbank has started to collapse beneath her feet. She is saved from the roiling, brown water below only by Hayley's alert intervention. The younger girl hauls her friend backward, away from the shattered precipice.

They tumble atop one another on the grassy embankment. Safe! Their ensuing laughter is spontaneous and a little shrill.

"Holy shit, that was close!" says Jessica.

Hayley remembers her father again, imagining him with one foot up on a bench and one arm akimbo, telling stories that enthralled his rapt audience. God is in that vision, a love too profound for her eight years to comprehend. With every molecule of her being Hayley craves to be at Tommy's side, no matter how much her mother might carp and carry on.

"Let's go back."

Jessica sighs with exasperation. "You used to be fun."

They stand, brushing the muck from their backsides. Hayley turns to head back up the way they had come.

Jessica pauses, her hand repeatedly patting her pants pocket.

"My cigarettes!"

Looking in all directions, both girls clock the distinctive, red-and-white Marlboro pack lying on the ground at the creek bank's edge.

"Jess! Stop!"

The older girl disregards Hayley's command and traverses the distance to the cigarettes in a few seconds. Retrieving her prize, Jessica holds the Marlboro pack aloft in triumph as the clay ridge under her feet disintegrates. An absurd yelp escapes her mouth as she drops into the roiling, flood-choked Big Ugly Creek.

Hayley springs forward, drawing as near as she dares to the water's edge. She spies Jessica's head bobbing in the surging waves as the current carries her friend downstream. Though she is only in the second grade, Hayley already possesses a remarkable ability to formulate decisive action, a trait that will serve her well in future years.

THE CREEK BANK is relatively free of brush and impeding overgrowth, allowing for Hayley's pursuit of her friend. "Hold on, Jess! I'll get you!" she calls out, though it is obvious the older girl could not possibly hear her. In the rare moments Jessica's face emerges from the undulating torrent—eyes blind with panic and ears oozing watery sediment—it is a mask of terror.

Hayley runs in this manner for nearly two minutes,

never failing to keep her friend in sight. But then the topography of the creek transforms. A wall of brush and fallen trees obstructs the way ahead. Without pause, eight-year-old Hayley Chill pivots and leaps with a rescuer swimmer's urgency, jumping into the maelstrom. Arms churning, she begins to swim. Catching up with Jessica seems impossible. But her friend's momentary pause in a providential eddy allows Hayley the opportunity she needs. Reunited in the clattering rapids, the two girls throw their arms around one another and embrace like victors of the big game.

Jessica can barely hear Hayley over the water's roar.

"I got you, Jess. It's gonna be okay!"

Seconds later they are swept into the fast part of the current again. With a narrowing of the creek's width, the rapids increase in size. Unseen beneath the churning mass of waves are countless obstructions—rocks, tree limbs, automobile parts, and other metal debris—that claw at their legs and threaten to pull them beneath the river's surface. Despite her depleting strength, Hayley isn't about to save herself and leave Jessica to drown. But the older girl has all but lost all ability to help her cause. Only Hayley can save them both.

Jessica coughs and sputters. "We're going to die!"

Hayley sees a boulder rising slightly above the raging rapids, the peak of which is miraculously dry. Kicking hard, she steers them in its direction.

"Do you see that rock, Jess? Get ready to grab it!"

Jessica looks downriver. A feeble hope reignites in her eyes. "I see it!"

"Grab it, Jess! Now!"

Within just a few seconds, they are at the upriver side of the rock. Though the current nearly sweeps them past the boulder, both girls can wrap their arms around its rough girth. But that refuge is short-lived. Waves threaten to dislodge the exhausted girls from their precarious perch.

"I can't do it!" says Jessica, panicking again.

Hayley already knows as much, making her decision before Jessica spoke.

"Hold on to the rock, Jess. Hold on until someone comes to get you."

Realization of her friend's intentions hasn't yet quite sunk in. "What?" asks Jessica.

"Just hold on. You can do it. I know you can, Jess."

Hayley lets go of her hold of the rock, releasing herself into the river's folds.

SHE CANNOT REMEMBER when she last drew a breath. In the grip of the river's maw, eight-year-old Hayley Chill cartwheels through a world of roaring and bucking water thickened with dark sediment washed down from the West Virginia hills. The consistency of alluvium that fills her mouth and nostrils reminds her more of the cold, dense cream her grandmother would pour over a bowl of fresh strawberries. The memory of that treat brings an incongruent peace of mind. Transported to her grandmother's gracious kitchen, Hayley is seated at the big, round table with her brothers and sisters.

Everyone is talking at once. "Raising Cain" her grand-mother would call it. Before she can savor the moment, it's gone. Too exhausted to fight against the river's cur-rent, her mind is in free fall and loses focus. With the thud of a boulder lurking beneath the water's surface, however, Hayley gains keen awareness that her predica-ment is probably terminal.

Last school year, a classmate mysteriously disap-peared. Every morning during attendance, eyes would briefly flit to Carl Zaphee's vacant desk. Hayley's teacher refused to discuss the boy's disappearance with the class, saying only that his absence was none of their business. The Zaphees lived in a converted barn off Big Ugly Road, east of the Tucker Fork, a makeshift home that lacked most basic utilities and other in-town comforts. Because of the family's relative isolation, news of them rarely rose above the level of speculation. Carl wouldn't have been the first child in Hayley's class of thirty-three to get knocked around a bit by one or both parents. Was this the cause of his absence? Cases of actual physical abuse would typically be kept secret by strategic, week-long absences from school. But the Zaphee boy was gone for almost a month. Eventually, word filtered down from parents to their children that Carl died, a casualty of inattentive medical care and leukemia.

The seemingly bottomless watery vortex sucks into its depths. Hayley can't help but recall the unsettling weirdness of Carl's nonappearance in the classroom and an awareness of mortality that accompanied it. A sudden and intense rage wells up within her.

Fight it. Don't be Carl Zaphee. Fight the river. Fight death.

Her hip slams into yet another submerged boulder. The frigid cold water mostly mitigates the expected pain. Mostly.

Fuck you, rock!

Hayley sweeps past that obstacle, continuing underwater and, frankly, near death.

Fuck you fuck you fuck you!

She rages. Kicking. Punching. Ecstatically and combatively alive.

But the creek is a bottomless black hole from which there is no escape. The swirling depths of an eddy wall finally stop her progress downstream, pulling her down into its watery pit. Resistance is a cosmic joke. Hayley thinks of her school desk on Monday morning, the ghostliness of her empty chair. She hears the whispers of her classmates. Sees their darted glances in the direction where she ought to be sitting had it not been for her drowning in the Big Ugly Creek. Hayley goes around and around underwater, stuck in the washing machine of the river's turbulence. She thinks of her four siblings, all younger and utterly dependent on her. Gets angry all over again. Angrier than ever before.

She gifted Jessica with a realistic chance of survival, leaving her on a dry boulder while letting the awful flood take herself. A cascade of sensations and regrets had followed that choice. But remorse was flushed out of her and replaced by fury. She fights now with grit and determination. Against the torrent, but to zero effect.

No one is present to witness her scrappiness. Certainly, the river doesn't care. Hayley is only one more bit of the river's debris, mixed in with tons of scrap, branch, and loosened soil.

Hayley has fought past the point of exhaustion. At last, the struggle is over. Facedown and mostly submerged in the creek's watery storm, she is spent. The creek narrows to less than a few dozen feet and drops in elevation by half that distance. The storm's runoff rises up as if in outrage, undulating with manic intensity. She has been whipped by the absolute worst the Big Ugly Creek can muster. The water is at its most cruel. Sucked down into its depths, Hayley has a dim recollection of the passage of time. So this is death. Fuck you, death.

Only then she feels yanked up and above the water's surface. Someone takes a grip of her hand, wrapping his arm around her narrow, drenched frame. He carries Hayley across the tempest. Dimly she knows what has happened without seeing. Conscious of who has saved her. He brings her to the water's edge and up the mud-slick bank. The side of her head rests on his shoulder. With eyes closed and despite the creek's muck, she can smell him. Father.

Once he's confident that his daughter's air passages are clear, Tommy gently lays Hayley down on her back. His close-cropped, chestnut brown hair has caught odd bits of grass and mud. His copper complexion highlights his magnificent blue eyes, traits he has passed on to his daughter. Under his right armpit, a tattoo of crossed arrows is visible through his wet T-shirt. The number of hours the two of them had spent alone together could be collected inside of a single day. But the connection between them is strong, a mutual love more profound than any other in their experience. These feelings have gone unsaid. Neither father nor daughter is prone to revealing their inner selves to others. But that's another story. Here, on this day, habitual inhibitions are broken down by the experience of near death. Of unspeakable grief drawing terrifyingly close.

Opening her eyes fully for the first time and seeing him, Hayley says, "Daddy."

"Baby girl," he says, near tears. Sitting on his knees beside her, Tommy squeezes his daughter's hand.

"You're okay," he says as if to convince himself.

"Jess?"

He nods. "They were pulling her out a few hundred yards upstream as I was comin' after you." The voices of other men can be heard from farther up the way, the brittle shouts of amateur rescuers.

Moments later, she sits up. Tommy stops her from standing. He doesn't want her to rush things. For her part, Hayley only wants to preserve their isolation, this extraordinary time with just the two of them. A moment she will not forget for the rest of her life. That she had nearly died is of far secondary significance.

"Thank you, Daddy. Thanks for comin' to get me."

Tommy squeezes her hand in acknowledgment. "Your mother's probably worried sick. We should get back."

Hayley nods, mute.

"You okay to stand up, baby girl?"

She nods again and accepts his hand getting to her feet. They start walking in the direction of the far-off voices.

"What happened, Hay? How'd you two girls end up in the creek?"

"Jess slipped in and I went in after her."

"To save her?"

"Yes, sir." After a pause, Hayley says, "She would've drowned for sure if I'd only gone lookin' for help."

"Yes, I'm pretty sure you're right," Tommy says with a nod. "You set her up on the rock?"

Hayley nods. No false modesty for her, even at this age. Just the truth, as she experiences it. Leave it to others to judge.

"You were just about gone there, baby girl. I almost lost you."

"I was tired, Daddy." She wants to please him and win his admiration. "I fought that dang creek best I could."

"Uh-huh."

They walk in silence for a moment. People are visible across the glade, folks from the busted-up welcome home/going away party, as well as passersby from town. A near drowning by two school kids is a seismic event in Lincoln County. Gossip will later suggest the Chill girl, known to be a discipline problem at home and school, pushed her friend into the rampaging creek. Small wonder the girls' friendship survived the gossiping. Jessica Cole knew who put her in that creek. And who saved her.

"What, Daddy?" Eight-year-old Hayley knows something is on her father's mind. "I'm sorry."

Tommy clasps his daughter's hand a little tighter. "You didn't do a damn thing wrong, girl. You're a tough little nut that don't crack. I've seen enough of the world to know you're gonna need that kinda spirit."

"I was mad, Daddy. I was mad at the river."

"I know you were, baby. When you're in a fight, make that anger a small thing. Otherwise, you wind up just beatin' yourself."

Hayley nods, for the very first time in the long afternoon almost crying. Almost, but not quite. Tough nut, indeed.

Tommy says, "You've got the spirit of a whole army, Hayley Chill. That kinda strength, it can take on something bigger than itself. Win despite impossible odds. But, if it's winning you gotta have, then you're gonna keep that anger small. Keep cool, baby girl. Smart beats angry any day of the week." With a smile, he adds, "And a little luck don't hurt."

ACKNOWLEDGMENTS

★ ★ ★ ★

No acknowledgments can be made without first mentioning my editor, Emily Bestler. Despite a global pandemic and its horrendous disruptions, Emily shepherded publication of this book with acumen, good cheer, and a fierce editorial eye. I am so grateful for her belief in my work. Whatever the outcome, my friend, we will always have Savannah.

I would also like to acknowledge the enthusiastic support of my publisher, Libby McGuire, and everyone at Atria Publishing Group, including associate editor Lara Jones, production editor Sara Kitchen, art director Jimmy Iacobelli, publicist David Brown, and copyeditor extraordinaire Tricia Callahan. Many thanks to all of you.

Also deserving special mention are the outstanding people at Simon & Schuster UK. Ian Chapman, Suzanne Baboneau, Bethan Jones, Genevieve Barratt, and Polly Osborn have brought the adventures of Hayley Chill to all four corners of the globe. I'm so grateful for their sterling efforts on my behalf.

Huzzah, too, for the singular greatness that is my agent, Dan Conaway. He keeps watch from the dugout with a steely gaze and makes sure everyone on the field is doing their job. This being my analogy and not his, Dan is wearing Dodger blue.

Jordan Bayer has been my film and television agent for nearly thirty years. For every minute of our long association, he has been my greatest advocate and one of my best friends. Thank you, Jordan.

Jack Carr, Matt Betley, Kyle Mills, Jamie Freveletti, Lisa Black, Rogue Women Writers, James Swallow, Simon Gervais, Brian Andrews, Jeff Wilson, Lynne Constantine, and Don Bentley have welcomed me into their community of authors with astonishing generosity. I am so appreciative of their collegial support and friendship.

Mention must be made of all event organizers and booksellers who endeavor tirelessly to put my books—and the books of all authors—into readers' hands. In particular, I'd like to thank Jan Wilcox with Men of Mystery, Julie Slavinsky at Warwick's, Kristin Rasmussen at Pages: A Bookstore, Jen Ramos at Book Soup, the amazing Barbara Peters at Poisoned Pen, Debbie Mitsch at Mystery Ink Bookstore, and Anne Saller at Book Carnival.

I want to thank book bloggers everywhere on the planet, including Ryan Steck, Liz Barnsley, Liz Robinson, Slaven Tomasi, Sean Cameron, Mike Houtz, C. E. Albanese, Eric Bishop, as well as superfans like Sarah Walton, Tracy Green, Kenton Long, Jon Brooks, Julie

Watson, Tom Dooley, and Marc Harrold. Your enthusiasm and support are much appreciated.

Christie Ciraulo was first and last eyes on the book. Thank you.

George and Jackson Hauty have encouraged and supported me in the writing of this book and everything I've written in the last quarter-century. Their father is an extremely fortunate man.

Lauren Ehrenfeld deserves special thanks for being the best of partners, always of good humor, unsparingly kind, and an unshakable pillar of support. She makes the journey not only joyful but effortless. Of a year and then some, darling woman.

Mention must be made of Ann Rittenberg, who ushered me onstage for this miraculous third act. For her astute expertise and support, I am eternally grateful.

Morgan McNenny deserves acknowledgment not only for his ability to beat a California Form FTB 3532 into submission but also for being a good pal. Thank you, Morgan.

I also want to thank Clint and Heidi Smith for their generosity in sharing their home and vast knowledge of firearms. Their dedication to weapons training and education is nothing short of inspiring.

And finally, I would like to thank and acknowledge the late Carolyn Reidy, CEO of Simon & Schuster. It was my misfortune that I never met Carolyn in person. I was the recipient of one of her legendary handwritten notes, however, congratulating me on the publication of my first novel. That simple act of kindness made an enormous impact on this baby author. Her sincere enthusiasm, love of books and their authors, and a zest for life serve as a model for me and, undoubtedly, many others. Thank you, Carolyn.

Turn the page for an exclusive look at
Chris Hauty's new Hayley Chill thriller,
STORM RISING.

1

★ ★ ★ ★

TATER HOLE SAVINGS & LOAN

Hayley Chill's most glaring weakness, Brazilian jiu-jitsu, has been her primary focus for the fourteen weeks she's been in camp. Days start with a ten-mile run at sunrise, followed by a healthy breakfast, rest, and then four hours of skills training. Nights begin at seven after a light dinner. For warm-up, she hits pads for three rounds. Circuit training follows, with double-arm rope slams, dumbbell thrusters, two-hundred-pound sled pulls, and a sixty-yard farmer's walk with eighty-pound barbells. Twice through, before starting a second circuit.

In the last months of her tenure as an aide in the West Wing, Hayley gained fifteen pounds. Many days in that harrowing time passed without any physical exercise whatsoever. Since leaving the White House—twenty-seven years old and unemployed—Hayley Chill is determined to regain the physical fitness of her years in the US Army. Holed up in Princeton, West Virginia, and training six days a week at Elite Martial Arts Academy seems as good a way as any to accomplish that goal.

Today isn't a typical workout day, however. In anticipation of her first amateur MMA bout later that week, Hayley's coach has limited her to stretching and a single sparring session at 50 percent. The problem is her sparring partner. Almost six feet tall, with a murderous arm reach, Jewel Rollins ratchets up the intensity with every round. Flustered and stung by a snapping jab that feels like something more than 50 percent, Hayley retaliates. An amateur boxing champ in the military, she never suffered a loss in the ring. Her strategy when attacked—in the ring and outside of it—is to counterattack. Never relent.

Fuck 50 percent.

With her back foot slightly splayed for increased leverage, Hayley throws a jab, cross, and then hook at her sparring partner's head. She then feints with her left hand, drops low, and shoots a stiff right, hitting the other woman dead center in her sternum. The perfectly timed jab lands with a thud, catching Rollins as she exhales. The punch might have rocked a fighter with less experience; Hayley has put opponents on the canvas with lesser stuff. But Rollins is an NAAFS amateur women's champion. Her mixed martial arts skill set is deep. Hayley doesn't see the wheel kick coming until it's too late. If not for thickly padded headgear, the blow would have knocked her out.

Fredek Kozlov steps between the fighters to stop the session, helping Hayley to her feet. "You plan to lose, yes?"

His cartoonish Russian accent is made less comical by dint of an always-on physical intensity and Olympic gold medal for judo. A back injury short-circuited his transition to professional MMA fighter. Elite Martial Arts is the top training camp for three states around and Kozlov's ticket to prosperity in the United States.

Winded by her exertions, Hayley tucks her chin as if in preparation to throw a jab at her coach. Instead, she shakes her head and fixes her powder blue eyes on Rollins.

Her coach says, "I tell you. Fifty percent. What is wrong with you? Stupid!"

"What about her?" Hayley asks, gesturing toward her sparring partner.

"What about her? Maybe I tell her to go seventy percent. Or one hundred percent. Your directions are to go fifty percent, yes?"

Hayley stares at the mat, recognizing now that she has screwed up. Again.

"You fight your fight!" Kozlov points a sausage-sized index finger at Rollins. "You don't fight her fight. Fight your fight!"

Basic stuff. The earliest lesson. Hayley can scarcely believe her embarrassing lapse.

I was played. What is wrong with me?

Kozlov says, "Angry, you are blind. Emotions, you are stupid!"

"Yes, sir."

She can think of nothing more to say, wanting only

Kozlov to step aside and open a path to her sparring partner. To redeem herself. If that's possible.

But the Russian remains between the fighters. To Hayley, he says, "That's enough. Go home. We fix this tomorrow."

Rollins sneers from behind the Russian. Kozlov plants both feet on the mat and anchors his weight, anticipating Hayley's loss of temper.

"Save it for Friday, *tyolka*. You are going to need it."

HER MOTEL IS two miles east on Oakvale Road. Hayley jogs there at a comfortable pace. Past a sub shop. The local Dairy Queen. A Mitsubishi dealership. Losing fifteen pounds is only one part of the motivation for finding refuge in West Virginia. Transitioning from amateur boxing to mixed martial arts isn't the whole point, either. Hayley left a tumultuous Washington, DC, after a revelation so shattering that escape seemed the only option. What she found inside a modest, brick home across the Potomac River, in Arlington, destroyed all reverence for the one person she loved most in the world. Without a job or apparent purpose—trapped in a city that never felt like home—her emotional anguish was like a third eye. Impossible to disguise. Every waking moment after that fateful Sunday morning in Virginia was filtered through a lens of despair and loathing. Only time and distance would alleviate the pain.

The focus and discipline required by her MMA training help speed the process of mental disassociation. In the meantime, she waits for a call or message from the one man in her life who matters. Not Sam McGovern, the fireman she started seeing before she fled Washington. Not anyone from work, either. Her West Wing colleagues have dispersed, forced into exile after the historical abomination that was the Monroe administration. Future employment in government for any of her White House co-workers would be a miracle. Hayley is different. As a trained operative in a clandestine effort to preserve the nation's constitutional democracy —a kind of "deeper state"—her job as chief of staff for the president's senior advisor was only a cover. The phone call she anticipates is from her direct superior in that secret organization, Andrew Wilde.

The man who recruited her.

He represents a loose affiliation of powerful Washington emeriti—ex-presidents, former Supreme Court justices, retired NSA and CIA directors, senators, and military brass—linked by lifelong government service and unambiguous love of country. There is no official name for this group. Nor is there a definitive leader or hierarchy. All members have left their official offices, thereby guaranteeing that their motivations are pure and shorn of self-serving incentives. Few of the participants have ever met each other, their true identities hidden behind pseudonyms. An ultra-secure, cloud-based intranet run from a server farm in north-central Canada facilitates communication among members. Though the group has no name, Wilde and other members have come to call themselves Publius, a nod to the Federalist Party formed by Alexander Hamilton, James Madison, Jr., and John Jay in support of the still-unratified US Constitution. The essence of their cause, and entire reason for being, is the protection of that hallowed document and its tenets, no matter the origin of the threat to its preservation.

Hayley was recruited from the US Army for inclusion in a corps of similarly capable individuals to act as covert agents of Publius. Her first mission was an unqualified success, protecting the president from harm and turning him against his Russian paymasters. The second operation was more problematic. Had it not been for Hayley's initiative and ingenuity—not to mention her extraordinary gift of eidetic memory—the country might have stumbled into a third world war. The stress of these grave responsibilities has taken its toll and laid her emotions bare, to be subsequently ravaged by family revelations almost too grotesque to imagine.

Retreat to her home state of West Virginia—in equal parts beautiful and tragic—has been a soothing balm. God bless the Mountain State. Almost heaven, indeed.

The motor-court-style Turnpike Motel is low-slung and strenuously well-kept. Older-model cars occupy one in five parking spaces. Newer, franchise hotels can be had in town at double the price, but Hayley prefers these modest, humdrum lodgings.

Hyperventilating slightly as she slows her pace and then stops running entirely, the deeper state operative is surprised by her elevated heart rate.

Hayley bends over at the waist and places her hands on her knees for support. A wave of inexplicable fatigue washes over her. She feels sick to her stomach.

What the hell is wrong with me?

Standing up straight, Hayley Chill waits for her heart

rate to slow. The shortness of breath dissipates. She opens her room door with a key card. Stepping inside the darkened room, Hayley clocks a figure sitting in a chair by the window and drops into a defensive crouch. Only after recognizing the intruder as her fellow Publius operative does she relax.

"Jesus. You startled me."

"I'm a spook. That's the idea, isn't it?"

April Wu's apparent ill health—pale and visibly weak—wins her little compassion from Hayley, who is displeased by the surprise visit.

"Are you comfortable? Put your feet up on the bed, why don't you?"

"Sarcasm doesn't suit you, Chill. Clashes with your unabashed earnestness."

Hayley strips off her trail pack and drops it on the bed. "What are you doing here?"

"I'm worried about you. I've seen you do this before—though usually, you're breaking stuff."

"This?"

"This," says April, gesturing at their surroundings.

Hayley pulls an insubstantial chair out from the sad motel desk. Sits. Her silence concedes the point.

April smiles, pleased with the win. "How was your workout?"

"Light." She considers leaving it at that but adds, "I have my first bout Friday."

"Sam coming down?"

Hayley shakes her head. "Working."

"Uh-huh."

"Will you stop? He's been here three or four times."

"Three 'or' four. Must've been extremely memorable."

Hayley resists an urge to throw a water bottle at her friend. "You look like hell, by the way."

Before her accident, April Wu had been at the mercy of fashion. Pairing ripped jeans with a James Perse T-shirt and Chanel bouclé jacket was as effortless as breathing air. The expense was never an impediment. But today, in this sad, dumpy motel room, April wears tragically banal canvas cargo pants and a black Army pullover hoodie. The dark clothing only heightens her sallowness and the circles under her eyes.

"I *feel* like hell. Wish that car landed somewhere besides on my head."

"Me too."

"Has the pope called you?" April asks, referring to their superior with the deeper state.

Andrew Wilde recruited them both, Hayley out of Fort Hood and April from Cyber Command at Fort Meade.

"Nothing."

"Maybe he can't find you."

Hayley suspects Publius has the resources to find anyone on the planet, but there's no way of knowing for sure. "I'm training, April, not hiding."

"Hard to tell the difference."

This has been their way forever. The best of friends *and* diehard competitors.

April asks, "Wanna talk about what happened?"

"You mean that business with the president faking suicide, his exfiltration to Moscow, and unmasking as a Russian mole?"

"That was fun. But I mean the other thing."

"What other 'thing'?'"

"What you found at Charlie Hicks's place," says April, referring to the house of horrors in Arlington. The world shifted on that Sunday morning. What didn't change no longer matters. Recovering in the hospital following her accident, April remembers Hayley's visit later the same day. The West Virginia native was emotionally shattered.

April Wu discovered something new about her friend that day: Hayley Chill wasn't invincible after all.

"I found Charlie Hicks. Hanging by his neck. From the bedroom door."

"Really? Is that all?"

"What do you want from me?"

"The truth."

How much April already knows or doesn't know isn't clear to Hayley. This is a given now. As an operative for the deeper state, she can trust no one. Not even good friends inside the organization. Not completely.

"Maybe I just don't want to talk about it."

Hayley stands and begins to empty the trail pack of her workout gear.

"I'm not going away, you know," says April.

"I suspected as much."

She walks a damp gym towel toward the bathroom.

"Are you going to win Friday?"

"Can't remember the last time I lost," Hayley says as she disappears into the bathroom.